Her last week at home, Maisie is tender. . . .

She mistakes my mood for sadness that she is leaving. At night, while I sit outside alone by the pool, she even climbs onto my lap, all legs and pointy elbows. "Mom," she whispers, "I'm going to miss you."

I stroke her long dark hair, work out the tangles gently with my fingertips the way I used to when she was a little girl and fit in my lap. . . . I have agreed to let Robert take her to the airport in the morning. Now she tells me that she wants to date other boys at school.

"I mean," she says, "he's never even heard of *Jane Eyre*. My all-time favorite book."

I don't tell her how relieved I am. I just try to memorize how she looks at this very moment.

"You bought me all my favorite books," she says. She reaches across the table and squeezes my hand. "*Jane Eyre* and *Wuthering Heights*. You and your silly yard sales."

I see that her eyes are moist, teary. I make myself look away.

"And you wanted to give me something before I left," Maisie tells me. "You gave me everything."

She squeezes my hand again.

I look back at her. Look, look, I think. I smile. Go. Go.

—from "Maisie" by Ann Hood

MOTHER

*Famous Writers Celebrate Motherhood
with a Treasury of
Short Stories, Essays, and Poems*

EDITED BY
Claudia O'Keefe

POCKET BOOKS
New York   London   Toronto   Sydney   Tokyo   Singapore

An *Original* Publication of POCKET BOOKS

 POCKET BOOKS, a division of Simon & Schuster Inc.
1230 Avenue of the Americas, New York, NY 10020

ISBN: 0-671-52998-6

First Pocket Books trade paperback printing May 1996

10 9 8 7 6 5 4 3 2 1

POCKET and colophon are registered trademarks of Simon & Schuster Inc.

Cover design by Melody Cassen.
Front cover illustration After the Bath. Pastel, ca. 1901, 66 × 100 cm. Mary Cassatt, American, 1845–1926. © The Cleveland Museum of Art, 1995. Gift of J. H. Wade, 20.379

Printed in the U.S.A.

Credits

⤙⤚

To my mom,
who wouldn't let me write
a goopy dedication

Acknowledgments

Many thanks to:

my agent, Kay McCauley,

Linda Marrow, a superb editor, and her assistants, Amy Pierpont and Kate Collins, and to Gina Centrello and Bill Grose at Pocket for the ninth-inning stretch,

Sheryl Parrott, Pamela Pia, Douglas Clegg, and Laurent Bouzereau for their suggestions and lobbying efforts,

Erika Holzer, a real stand-up friend,

and the authors and their agents, as well as the estates of Laurie Colwin and Robert Aickman.

Contents

Introduction
Claudia O'Keefe

When I was finishing my last year of high school, my mother suggested that my family move back east from California. My sister, Lisa, was less than thrilled with this idea, as she was with most ideas, but I was exuberant. Back east meant snow, something I'd only seen once. It meant we'd have four seasons.

We sold the ranch the three of us had built ourselves two years before, and prepared to move, leafing through home magazines from Massachusetts, drooling over tiny, badly printed photos of horse farms with their very own covered bridges.

Then came the shock. Escrow closed on our ranch and the IRS took everything in order to pay one of my stepfather's back tax bills. It didn't matter that my mother had divorced him three years earlier; the money was gone. Adding to the insult, our only car picked that moment to experience an untimely death.

"We're still going," my mother said. "Let's scrape together what we can."

What we could scrape together came from selling two horses, five goats, and a pile of metal stakes for barbed wire fencing. We had sixteen hundred dollars, a quarter of which was allocated to buying a car. Since we also had seven dogs and seven cats from the ranch, our chariot of choice turned out to be a repulsive blue station wagon from the sixties. It wore bubbling retreads and shimmied as we drove down the road.

We packed up the dogs and cats, as well as two tons of books in a U-Haul trailer—my mother refused to give up our library—and started off. We decided on a destination first, of course. Actually, I think my mother yelled back from the front seat, as I madly flipped through *The United Farm Catalog,* "Pick something we can afford!"

Since we couldn't afford anything, I picked the least expensive property in the magazine. I thought I was fairly brilliant. It was a lease option on a kennel in Indiana.

The trip was horrendous. Our car smelled ripe an hour out of town. People goggled at us as we rolled into the K.O.A. campgrounds each night. Loaded down as we were, we couldn't make it over the Rockies. The wagon was like a hot-air balloon trying to lift off with too much weight.

"Throw out the Dickens! Throw out the Dickens!" my mother shouted.

Yet, as she had vowed we would, we reached Indiana.

We intuited, as we drove into the very small town and all eyes stared at us warily—something we should have been used to by then—that we might not belong here. When we saw the kennel, intuition became certainty. The place was disgusting, filthy, scary. It looked like a state mental hospital for dogs. I had visions of shih tzus being hooked up for electroshock therapy.

"Okay, that was fun," my mother said, once we had escaped the real estate agent and expressed a collective shudder. "Now where do we want to go?"

She opened our map of the U.S. "How about Charlottesville?" she asked. "I think I went there once and it was pretty."

Now, this was a true gamble. My mother is notorious for her lack of direction. I sometimes doubt she could find her way to the mall, even if she had a laser-guided missile strapped to the hood of her Jeep Cherokee.

We found Virginia, though, and she was right. It was truly stunning. We spent one of the most memorable years of my life there. But as fondly as I remember the trip from California, it was also a terrifying and uncertain time for us. My mother's blind faith that we would make it was the only thing that kept us going—other than a desperate need to make our final destination and air out the car. Never mind that the cottage we rented turned out to be one in a community where the other tenants were part of a coven and that our animals began to disappear one by one. That wasn't her fault.

My mother's willingness to take a risk started us on a long series of adventures I will always cherish, no matter how harrowing or stressful. What she taught me has kept me from shying away from a few risks of my own. She prepared me to meet the good and bad and not flip out over either.

I've learned from her that it doesn't always take faith to become pregnant, but it does take faith to have a child. I'm not talking about a religious faith, but instead something purely, instinctively human. Sometimes, however, even faith is not enough. I don't know where mothers go then to find that extra quality that will make sure their child not just survives but has what he or she needs. I've tried to put my finger on it. Is it unwavering knowledge? Is it gall? Is it bravery? Some sort of weird Freudian selfishness? Some might simply say it's love. I don't know. Love is a big part of it, sure, but motherhood is a force unto itself. I don't believe anyone has, or ever will, put an adequate name to it.

It is precisely this mysterious attribute that I hope you will discover and enjoy as you read the contributions of these fascinating and exemplary authors. Each has explored a different expression of a mythic figure with a half billion or more unique faces. Is it your face? Or the face of your mother? Your grandmother from the old country? Between them, these writers show us women at turns learning, reveling in, living for, praying for, frustrated by, terrified by, losing, rejecting, finding redemption in, drawing upon, championing, and offering to others what it is to be a mother.

Perhaps, you will even find the name you'd most like to put to that face.

MOTHER

My Wild Irish Mother
Mary Higgins Clark

In 1967, when she was eighty, I tossed a birthday party for Mother. There were over seventy people present; my generation and hers; friends and cousins; our children; cronies from way-back years. The party started at three in the afternoon because I was sure that Mother and the other old girls would get tired early. I should have known better. Twelve hours later, my contemporaries and I sat limply in the den while Mother and her peers stood around the piano lustily singing "Sweet Molly Malone."

That night I marveled at Mother. Wearing her best beige lace dress, her silver hair framing her almost unlined face and bright blue eyes, she was obviously having the time of her life. Before that party finally ended, she had cast her cane aside, locked arms with the remaining "Bungalow Girls"—Rockaway Beach circa 1912—and led a spirited rendition of an Irish polka.

My mother, Nora, the first generation of her family to be American born, was the second child of Bridget Kennedy Durkin and Thomas Durkin, a pair of youngsters newly arrived from County Sligo. All her life she was to personify the best of her Irish heritage—a generous heart, faith in her God, unswerving allegiance to the Democratic party, resiliency in trouble and always, always, an unquenchable sense of humor.

1

By the time she was thirteen, seven more children had arrived to fill the parlor-floor-and-basement apartment on East 79th Street and she went off to work. Her first job at McCreery's department store paid three dollars for a forty-eight-hour week. She walked the two miles back and forth each day to save the nickel carfare and at nights went to high school and later to Hunter College. She worked her way up from messenger girl at McCreery's to buyer at Altman's.

She was determined that when she married she would be able to give her children everything and would have enough money saved for lifelong security. Hers was a typical Irish courtship. She and my father "kept company" for seven years and were nearly forty when they exchanged vows.

She promptly produced three children. The firstborn was Joseph. I, Mary, was next. When my younger brother arrived a few years later, the doctor came into her room, looked at the baby nestled in her arms and the rosary entwined in her fingers and sighed, "I assume this one is Jesus."

All her life, Mother had dreamed of owning a home of her own, and she and my father bought one a few years after they were married. To Mother, Buckingham Palace, the Taj Mahal, and Shangri-la were all wrapped up in that six-room, brick, semidetached dwelling in the Bronx. But then the depression years set in. My father's once-flourishing Irish pub began to lose money. Their stocks were lost; their savings dwindled to nothing. My father let one of the bartenders go and began working twenty-hour days. One morning he didn't wake up, and at age fifty-one Mother was left with the three of us and a mortgaged house.

It was impossible to get a job. So she put her "thinking cap" on and came up with a solution. A sign, "Furnished Rooms, Kitchen Privileges," was tacked over the doorbell. The neighbors demurred. They didn't mind "Furnished Rooms," but "Kitchen Privileges" stuck in their craw. Always agreeable, Mother snipped off the bottom half, thanking the Lord she hadn't wasted money on a metal sign.

And then began the parade of people who were to be woven into the fabric of our lives for the next five years.

There was Miss Mills, the schoolteacher who tried valiantly to teach me the piano. I never got past "Drifting."

There were Mr. and Mrs. Fields, who took the big, front bedroom for five dollars a week with the garage thrown in. They asked Mother if they could bring their dog, Buck. No dog lover, Mother asked doubtfully how big he was. Mrs. Fields made a little cupping move with her hands, suitable to describe a toy poodle, and reluctantly Mother agreed.

Buck was a wild-eyed boxer. He had the instincts of an attack dog, and we huddled behind closed doors in the dining room when Eddy Fields brought him down for his airing. Eddy was a slight man and his feet never seemed to touch the floor as he came hurtling down the stairs behind Buck, who by then was frenzied to relieve himself.

Before any new tenant came in, Mother gave what we called her "palace guard" speech. "Yes," she would say, "we're blessed with excellent police protection. There's Officer Potters to the left and Officer Ahlis on the right. Sergeant Garrigan is across the street and directly opposite him—" here she paused so the full weight of her pièce de résistance could sink in—"directly opposite him we have *Inspector* Whelan."

Mother had been going steady with a moving man when she was in her twenties and had somehow caught the virus that is the sine qua non of his profession. She *loved* to move furniture. We all got to recognize that speculative look in her eyes. "I was thinking if we put the piano at the window and the couch on the stair wall and . . ." No matter how loud and heartfelt our protests, Joe and John and I would find ourselves on the lighter end of the piece to be moved, lifting and hauling as she admonished, "Now don't strain yourself."

Her peccadillo led to the entrapment of her one and only paying-guest failure, who was two weeks behind in his rent and was trying to tiptoe out at dawn. Unfortunately for his scheme, we'd moved the furniture the night before and he tripped over a lamp that had been freshly placed at the bottom of the staircase. Mother rushed out to find him sprawled on the floor, his feet entangled in the lamp cord.

She sighed. "If you didn't have the money to pay, all you had to do was to tell me," she said. "God knows I can understand that." When he left, he had two dollars pressed in his hand. He'd claimed he'd been promised a job in New Jersey. It would be nice to say that our departing roomer never forgot the kindness and returned the gift a thousandfold, but unfortunately that was not the case. He was a deadbeat.

In spite of all our concerted efforts, Mother couldn't keep up the mortgage payments and lost the house. Our next stop was a three-room apartment and into it she moved the full contents of the six rooms, sure that someday our fortunes would change and we'd get the house back. We never did, and whenever she returned from visiting the old neighborhood, her eyes would shine with unshed tears as she remarked how beautifully her roses had grown.

As the only girl, I was guarded with the vigor of a dragon-slaying St. George. She felt it was her duty to my dead father to see that I came unscathed through the dating years. I called her Barbara Frietchie because whenever I came up the block with a date, no matter what the hour, she would be at the window. Shoot if you must this old gray head, I'd groan inwardly and wait for the familiar call, "Is that you, Mary?" I'd want to reply, "No, it's Gunga Din." But her methods were effective. No date ever got "fresh" with that alert sentry dangling twenty feet above his head.

When at twenty-one I began dating Warren Clark, she was delighted. So very good-looking, so bright, half the girls in the parish had set their caps for him. How had he stayed single for twenty-nine years? And a more respected family could not be found. His mother, Alma Claire Clark, was the national head of the Companions of the Forest of America. For the first time Mother withdrew from her window perch and went to bed early because I was safe with Mrs. Clark's son. When I remarked that dating Mrs. Clark's son was not precisely the same as dating Mrs.

Clark, the insinuation sailed completely over her head and she continued to slumber blissfully away, while in between kissing him goodnight, I would hiss, "Warren, you know better than that!"

My mother's occupation and hobby, vocation and avocation was Motherhood. A Jewish mother looks into the cradle and sees a possible Messiah. It's equally true that an Irish mother gazes at her firstborn son and sees the Christ-child. Joseph was a premature baby weighing only four pounds when he was born. She fed him with an eyedropper that first year and never left him for an instant. I found a diary she kept and in it she wrote, "I was so afraid he'd slip away. He was such a beautiful baby. The other two had allergies."

Growing up, Joseph justified her pride in him. He won the General Excellence medal all eight years of grammar school. He won a scholarship to Fordham Prep. He was the captain of every team, the lead in every school play. He had the newspaper route, and every penny he earned he brought home to her, turning his pockets inside out to make sure he didn't forget a dime. Then they shared their own special treat, a half-pint of ice cream.

At thirteen, Joe contracted osteomyelitis. Mother was told that an operation to remove the hipbone was necessary to save his life. Widowed only a few months, she made the stunning decision not to operate. She wouldn't make a cripple of Joseph and she knew God wouldn't take him from her. It was Christmas. He was on the critical list and the doctors held no hope for his recovery. Mother and John and I carried all his presents to the hospital. His main gift was a hockey stick. "You'll use it next year," she promised him. He did.

Joe graduated from high school in 1944. Mother could have claimed him as her sole support and kept him out of service. Instead she let him enlist in the navy with his friends. Six months later she took the only long trip of her life, a plane ride to California to be at Joe's deathbed in the Long Beach Naval Hospital. To the people who fumbled for words of sympathy she said, "It is God's will. I couldn't let Joseph go when he was sick the other time, but now God wants him even more than I do."

That June when I graduated from Villa Maria Academy, Mother threw a party for me that held no hint of sadness. It was my day and nothing was going to spoil it. Johnny graduated from grammar school a few weeks later and he too had all the aunts and uncles and cousins and friends there to celebrate. She bought a black and white print dress to wear to both occasions. She felt her black mourning dress was out of place.

Her pride in all of us was enormous. We were never simply doing well in school. We were "taking all the honors." I never had a job. I had "a big job." When John went to Notre Dame, she must have written a dozen letters to long-forgotten cousins. The letters began, "My, what a busy summer, what with getting John ready for Notre Dame . . ." This kickoff would be followed by an explanation of why Notre Dame was the finest college in the world and therefore eminently qualified to educate her son.

After Warren and I were married, she never quite forgave us for moving to New Jersey. Warren urged her to live with us and avoid the bus trips back and forth, but even given carte blanche to come with all her beloved furniture there was never the faintest chance she'd move. You only had to drive her halfway across the George Washington Bridge to have her start sniffing the air and remarking on the heavenly breezes that originated in the Bronx.

She delighted in being a grandmother. She had a horror of my leaving the children with a baby-sitter and thought nothing of taking the two-hour, three-bus trip to New Jersey to mind them.

From the time they could toddle half a block alone, Mother was whisking them on the Circle Line Tour, to the Central Park Zoo, to the Statue of Liberty, to parades and to beaches. She especially adored amusement parks. In 1939 she took my brothers and me to the World's Fair. It was the summer Daddy died, and I can still see her, the long mourning veil trailing wraithlike behind her as we plunged down on the parachute jump. A quarter of a century later, when she was seventy-six, she was taking my five offspring on the steeplechase at Coney Island.

Long years of making one dollar do the work of ten couldn't be unlearned, and if the kids had any complaint, it was that

Nanny made them share a soda or divide a sandwich in the Automat. She once promised my then five-year-old that she'd take him up to the top of the Empire State Building. Upon realizing that she had to pay for the tickets to the Observation Tower, she whisked him up on the business elevator to the eighty-fifth floor, stood him at a window and said brightly, "Here we are at the top. Isn't this fun?"

Her caring for the children encompassed Warren and me. She adored Warr, and to her "himself" was the grandest husband any girl could have.

She would fuss over him, making his tea just the way he liked it, worrying over his habit of never wearing a hat even in the coldest weather. One night I awoke to find Mother tucking the covers around him. "Mother, in God's name, what are you doing in here?" I groaned. "Mary, he'll catch his death of cold," she sighed. After that, whenever she stayed over, I locked the door of the master bedroom and she darkly murmured about "you two barricading yourselves in there when your children might need you."

We'd been married ten years when Warren began having chest pains and we learned that, incredibly, this handsome, vibrant man, who excelled in every sport, had the arteries of an eighty-year-old. In the next four years he had two heart attacks. He'd just come home from the hospital when a third attack took him from us.

"God's will, but, oh, it is so hard sometimes," Mother said, and I made myself remember that she'd never taken her grief out on us and I wouldn't take mine out on my children. It was because of Mother that I was able to go out to work, but of course she didn't think she was minding only five youngsters. She immediately resumed her role as guardian of a young girl . . . me.

A week after Warren's death, the funeral director came in with some papers for me to sign. Mother herded the boys upstairs. In five minutes my visitor was gone and Marilyn, my high school freshman, turned on her French language records. For the next thirty minutes, a suave masculine voice asked such questions as "Voulez-vous aller à la bibliothèque avec moi?" When the record was finished, Mother rushed down the stairs, indignation in every line of her face. "Mary, what was that fellow doing talking French to you?" she demanded.

Another evening I came home at midnight to find her waiting in the living room. "Mary, what will the neighbors think of a girl your age coming home at this hour of the night?" she demanded. I was then thirty-six.

Mother began having arthritis when she was twenty. It was in keeping with her whole approach to life that she got it dancing barefoot in the snow in Central Park. As she aged it spread into her knees and legs. Her feet were the worst, so swollen and sore she could hardly endure her weight on them. She probably would have been confined to a wheelchair except that her need to do for other people was so great she kept pushing herself, forcing those tired limbs to function.

Paradoxically she may have sped her own end by electing to go into a nursing home for a few weeks' rest. After all, she pointed out, she was spending three dollars a month for Medicare and getting nothing out of it. As soon as she began to take it easy everything in her body slowed up. Her heartbeat became more and more uncertain. I knew it would soon be over when one day she said drowsily, "Mary, I had the children at the beach and Carol wandered off. I couldn't find her. I don't think I can take care of them anymore." She could no longer take care of others and didn't want anyone to have to take care of her.

She had tied together in an old brown envelope a total of seventeen hundred dollars in insurance from nickel-and-dime policies she'd paid on for years. There was a note to Johnny and me with them. It said, "Don't waste more than a thousand dollars on the funeral. Give one hundred dollars to each of my grandchildren." She'd already given us all a priceless legacy, her ceaseless devotion and unfailing love.

And Mother is still part of us. "Remember when Nanny . . . " is heard frequently in my home, and after the story is told, there's bound to be laughter. The year when Patty, my youngest, was getting ready for college, she spent an afternoon in the attic rummaging and came down, wrapped in a pale pink terrycloth robe. "It still smells like Nanny," she said and surely it did. The faint scent of her talcum was there and the robe went off to college with Pat.

I have Mother's old black felt hat with the black veiling in my closet. Over the years, when things weren't going well, when the bills were piling up or one of the children was sick, I'd give it a quick rub and say, "Come on, Nora, do your stuff." I had no doubt that my first novel would be successful because it was dedicated to her. "I can just see Nora," a friend said, laughing, "'Dear Lord, not to bother you . . . the paperback sale on the book was excellent but *how about the movie rights?*'"

Time is slipping by so quickly. Months and seasons become years. My contemporaries and I ruefully discuss the fact that now *we* are the older generation. But when dawns the day that shall be my last, I'll have no fear. I am very sure that the first sound I hear when I enter eternity will be that loved voice anxiously asking, "Is that you, Mary?"

≈

EDITOR'S AFTERNOTE

After reading "My Wild Irish Mother," I called Mary Higgins Clark to talk with her about the piece.

Your mother sounds as if she was incredible, I told her, the archetypal good mother. You must miss her very much.

Yes, she was a great old gal, Clark admitted. But she'd had a difficult time at the end. Clark wished she could have gone sooner.

She then recounted an incident that crystallizes the humor and affection in the relationship they had.

Clark's mother was in her final decline when someone dear to her passed away while drinking a cup of tea and watching *The Ed Sullivan Show.*

Isn't she lucky to have gone like that, watching Sullivan? her mother said, envious of the peaceful way in which her friend had died.

"Mom," Clark said, "lots of people die watching Ed Sullivan."

Clark's fourteen novels, including *Remember Me, The Lottery Winner, Let Me Call You Sweetheart,* and *All Around the Town,* have sold more than twenty-five million copies in the U.S. She is also the author of two collections of short stories and recently signed a three-picture deal with CBS. A mother of five, one of her children, Carol Higgins Clark, has followed in her footsteps onto the best-seller lists. Her other children are just as distinguished, two judges, one producer of syndicated radio programs, and another who works on Wall Street. Clark is a New York City native who now lives in Saddle River, New Jersey, and has a summer house on Cape Cod.

Touring Home
Susan Power

A snake coils in my mother's dresser drawer; it is thick and black, glossy as sequins. My mother cut her hair several years ago, before I was born, but she kept one heavy braid. It is the three-foot snake I lift from its nest and handle as if it were alive.

"Mom, why did you cut your hair?" I ask. I am a little girl lifting a sleek black river into the light that streams through the kitchen window. Mom turns to me.

"It gave me headaches. Now put that away and wash your hands for lunch."

"You won't cut *my* hair, will you?" I'm sure this is a whine.

"No, just a little trim now and then to even the ends."

I return the dark snake to its nest among my mother's slips, arranging it so that its thin tail hides beneath the wide mouth sheared by scissors. My mother keeps her promise and lets my hair grow long, but I am only half of her; my thin brown braids will reach the middle of my back, and in maturity will look like tiny garden snakes.

My mother tells me stories every day: while she cleans, while she cooks, on our way to the library, standing in the checkout line at the supermarket. I like to share her stories with other people and chatter like a monkey when I am able to command adult attention.

"She left the reservation when she was sixteen years old," I tell my audience. Sixteen sounds very old to me, but I always state the number because it seems integral to my recitation. "She had never been on a train before, or used a telephone. She left Standing Rock to take a job in Chicago so she could help out the family during the War. She was so petrified of all the strange people and new surroundings, she stayed in her seat all the way from McLaughlin, South Dakota, to Chicago, Illinois, and didn't move once."

I usually laugh after saying this because I cannot imagine my mother being afraid of anything. She is so tall, a true Dakota woman; she rises against the sun like a skyscraper, and when I draw her picture in my notebook, she takes up the entire page. She talks politics and attends sit-ins, wrestles with the Chicago police and says what's on her mind.

I am her small shadow and witness. I am the timid daughter who can rage only on paper.

We don't have much money, but Mom takes me from one end of the city to the other, on foot, on buses. I will grow up believing that Chicago belongs to me, because it was given to me by my mother. Nearly every week we tour the Historical Society, and Mom makes a point of complaining about the statue that depicts an Indian man about to kill a white woman and her children: "This is the only monument to the history of Indians in this area that you have on exhibit. It's a shame because it is completely one-sided. Children who see this will think this is what Indians are all about."

My mother lectures the guides and their bosses, until eventually that statue disappears.

Some days we haunt the Art Institute, and my mother pauses before a Picasso.

"He did this during his blue period," she tells me.

I squint at the blue man holding a blue guitar. "Was he very sad?" I ask.

"Yes, I think he was." My mother takes my hand and looks

away from the painting. I can see a story developing behind her eyes, and I tug on her arm to release the words. She will tell me why Picasso was blue, what his thoughts were as he painted this canvas. She relates anecdotes I will never find in books, never see footnoted in a biography of the master artist. I don't even bother to check these references because I like my mother's version best.

When Mom is down, we go to see the mummies at the Field Museum of Natural History. The Egyptian dead sleep in the basement, most of them still shrouded in their wrappings.

"These were people like us," my mother whispers. She pulls me into her waist. "They had dreams and intrigues and problems with their teeth. They thought their one particular life was of the utmost significance. And now, just look at them." My mother never fails to brighten. "So what's the use of worrying too hard or too long? Might as well be cheerful."

Before we leave this place, we always visit my great-grandmother's buckskin dress. We mount the stairs and walk through the museum's main hall—past the dinosaur bones all strung together and the stuffed elephants lifting their trunks in a mute trumpet.

The clothed figures are disconcerting because they have no heads. I think of them as dead Indians. We reach the traditional outfits of the Sioux in the Plains Indian section, and there is the dress, as magnificent as I remembered. The yoke is completely beaded—I know the garment must be heavy to wear. My great-grandmother used blue beads as a background for the geometrical design, and I point to the azure expanse.

"Was this her blue period?" I ask my mother. She hushes me unexpectedly; she will not play the game. I come to understand that this is a solemn call, and we stand before the glass case as we would before a grave.

"I don't know how this got out of the family," Mom murmurs. I feel helpless beside her, wishing I could reach through the glass to disrobe the headless mannequin. My mother belongs in a grand buckskin dress such as this, even though her hair is now too short to braid and has been trained to curl at the edges in a saucy flip.

We leave our fingerprints on the glass, two sets of hands at different heights pressing against the barrier. Mom is sad to leave.

"I hope she knows we visit her dress," my mother says.

There is a little buffalo across the hall, stuffed and staring. Mom doesn't always have the heart to greet him. Some days we slip out of the museum without finding his stall.

"You don't belong here," Mom tells him on those rare occasions when she feels she must pay her respects. "We honor you," she continues, "because you are a creature of great endurance and great generosity. You provided us with so many things that helped us to survive. It makes me angry to see you like this."

Few things can make my mother cry; the buffalo is one of them.

"I am just like you," she whispers. "I don't belong here either. We should be in the Dakotas, somewhere a little bit east of the Missouri River. This crazy city is not a fit home for buffalo or Dakotas."

I take my mother's hand to hold her in place. I am a city child, nervous around livestock and lonely on the plains. I am afraid of a sky without light pollution—I never knew there could be so many stars. I lead my mother from the museum so she will forget the sense of loss. From the marble steps we can see Lake Shore Drive spill ahead of us and I sweep my arm to the side as if I were responsible for this view. I introduce my mother to the city she gave me. I call her home.

EDITOR'S AFTERNOTE

"I shared 'Touring Home' with my mother after writing it," Susan Power says, "as I share all of my creative work with her, and she liked it tremendously—but then, she is my mother and likes all of my work. She said, 'Oh, you make me sound so interesting.' 'No,' I quickly responded. 'You are much more interesting than I make you sound.' It's true. I'll never be able to capture her on paper; she has such a spontaneous imagination, and she is a much better storyteller than I am."

Power is winner of the 1995 PEN/Hemingway Award for her first novel, *The Grass Dancer,* and her short fiction has appeared in several prestigious journals; among them, *The Atlantic Monthly, The Paris Review, Story,* and *The Best American Short Stories of 1993.* She is a graduate of Harvard/Radcliffe and Harvard Law School. Born and raised in Chicago, she now makes her home in Cambridge, Massachusetts, where she is working on her second novel, *War Bundles.*

Maisie

Ann Hood

Hemlines are dropping," I tell my daughter, Maisie.

She is drifting in our pool, draped across a dolphin-shaped float. Beside her, on a float shaped like a whale, is Robert, our former pool boy, now Maisie's boyfriend.

My toes grip the edge of the pool. The water kisses at them. In one hand I hold a fashion magazine that promises to tell Maisie everything she will need for college.

"Hemlines are dropping," I say again, louder this time.

Their floats, I realize, are tied together somehow, bobbing and bumping into each other, unable to break completely free. I smell coconut and chlorine, the smells of summer. Maisie and Robert have their fingers laced together, their bodies oiled. Maisie's lips move ever so slightly, and that is when I see the black cord of a Walkman snaking up her neck and into her ears.

For an instant I think of danger, of electrocution. Pools and Walkmans surely don't mix safely. For eighteen years I have kept her safe—out of the bathtub during thunderstorms, seat-belted into cars, knee and elbow pads on during rollerskating. In one month, a mere thirty days, I will send her off, into the world alone, armed with just her clothing, a blue-and-black Amish quilt, and a rented refrigerator.

In a burst of emotion, I bend forward and reach for her, to pull her close. But the raft skims the very tips of my fingers, then drifts just out of my reach.

"Hemlines are dropping," I say. I am practically shouting now.

As slow as a movie star, Maisie lifts her Jackie Onassis sunglasses and stares at me.

They say that newborn babies cannot see, but when Maisie was only a minute old, she looked at me just the way she is now—direct, calm, slightly aloof. Even then she had the ability to fluster me, to leave me completely disarmed.

"Hemlines," I say, feeling foolish, waving the magazine like a surrender flag.

Maisie stares at me an instant more, unblinking, then lowers her sunglasses again. Her fingers tap against the edge of the raft. At first I think she is playing along with the music in her head. But then I realize that no, what she is doing is counting, counting off the days until she goes.

Maisie.

Maize.

That is what I had in mind when I named her. Something important. Something that nourished. I imagined the gold of a crayon I had as a child, the color called maize. I imagined golden fields of maize, swaying in the breeze under a true blue prairie sky in Iowa, Kansas, Nebraska. Places I have never been but thought of as sturdy. Places that seemed to hold the two opposite ends of the country together.

I expected a child with straw blond hair, eyes the color of that prairie sky, a smattering of freckles, an open face. MAISIE. Instead, she is dark haired, dark eyed, olive skinned, mysterious. Instead of maize, she seems to have been named for a maze, a puzzle, full of twists and turns, sharp corners, dead ends.

When Drew and I got divorced, he moved into Manhattan. To be near Wall Street, he explained. His apartment was in a new high-rise in Manhattan at Battery Park City. It made me think of wars—the name, the cold concrete front, the way it seemed shielded from what lay below it.

Maisie and I stayed in the house in Connecticut, half a mile from a pebbly beach that borders Long Island Sound. Every other Saturday, I put her on a train to Penn Station for an overnight with Drew. She called him a "fancy daddy." They ate ice cream out of silver bowls at Rumplemayer's, skated at Rockefeller Center in front of golden angels blowing trumpets in the snow, had expensive dinners at Windows on the World, high above the city.

While Maisie spent those weekends with her father, I haunted yard sales, flea markets, swap meets. I picked through the pieces of other people's lives. Their old photographs and baby furniture, postcards and china. Holding a cobalt blue glass vase to the light, I tried to imagine what the woman selling it was going through, the pain of what kind of separation she was feeling. I always smiled when I paid them; I always gave the price they asked.

When I picked Maisie up on Sunday evening, she'd wrinkle her nose and move away from my hug. In her hand she clutched a pale blue bag from Tiffany. "You smell like mothballs," she'd tell me. "Like someone's attic."

I always bought her something. Once I found an old wooden desk from a schoolhouse. It had an inkwell, strangers' initials carved into it, a scratched lid that lifted to reveal old textbooks. Maisie learned to read from those books. Dick and Jane and Sally, Spot and Puff. The happy, white-aproned mother, the father with his briefcase, waving good-bye.

Look. Look. Her finger touched each letter as she read. See Spot run. Run, Spot, run. Go. Go.

Watching Maisie and Robert float in the pool, I think of all this. Of the straw blond child I'd hoped for, the promise of a place I had never even been. I stand inside the kitchen, behind the sliding glass door, looking out at her, already missing her.

Reluctantly, Maisie agrees to take a walk to the beach with me one night after dinner. She has become a vegetarian this summer, so I grilled fresh zucchini from the garden, fat slices of red onion, and peppers in a trio of surprising colors—yellow, purple, orange.

"Robert is calling at seven," she reminds me when we leave. She seems to hold the door an instant too long when she closes it. She is frowning.

I am surprised to see, as we walk barefooted toward the Sound, that she has painted her toenails a bright shocking pink. Usually, Maisie rejects jewelry, makeup, any ornamentation. She wears faded Levi's and gypsy peasant blouses. She keeps her dark straight hair long. Those hot pink toenails shake me up enough to reach out and grab her arm for balance.

"What?" she says.

We stop walking and look right at each other, eye to eye. She is a few inches taller than me. I remember how it felt to hold her on my hip for this walk to the beach. How she used to wrap her arms around my neck and hold on tight when I stepped into the water. I remember taking her to the circus when she was five years old, right after Drew moved out. She held my hand the whole time, through the elephant act, the high-wire routine, the clowns and acrobats. She did not let go. Not even once.

Now she shakes her head, looks down at the ground. It has been a stormy summer and the air is heavy with the smell of seaweed.

"I want to give you something," I tell her. "For going away to school."

"Like what?" Maisie says.

"I don't know." I studied that fashion magazine. The long woolen skirts in fall colors. The thick sweaters and nubby blazers. "Clothes, maybe," I say, though none of those things are what Maisie likes or even needs. She will pack her jeans, her peasant blouses, her worn sweaters, and the pea coat she bought at a garage sale with me two years ago.

"I have clothes," she says.

"Well, then," I say, watching a seagull hard at work on a crab, "how about a typewriter?"

Maisie sighs. "I have everything," she tells me.

Indeed, she does have everything. Including a fancy word processor from Drew last Christmas.

"There must be something you need." I feel almost desperate.

We reach the beach and climb over the low wooden fence that separates it from the road.

"How do you feel about leaving Robert behind?" I ask her stupidly.

"Awful," she says. "What do you expect?"

Before I can answer she runs off, toward the water. Her hair flies out around her in the wind, a dark jumble.

Maisie always goes out with boys I'd rather she didn't date. The one who used to pump our gas. The one who was known around town for setting the school on fire. And now Robert, our former pool boy, who is taking the summer off to figure out what he wants to do next. I never see her talking to these boys. They just seem to hang on to each other, to touch too intimately, to float beside one another all day.

I sit down on the beach. Maisie is gone. I scan the shore but cannot find her. When Drew first remarried and moved to Long Island, Maisie and I used to pretend we could see him across the Sound at his new house. We would come here each evening so she could wave to him and say good night.

Sitting here now, I play the game alone. I squint my eyes at the horizon and imagine Drew on his deck, barbecuing hamburgers. He is drinking an imported beer, wearing one of those foolish aprons that says something like "World's Greatest Chef." I imagine Samantha, his wife, in her high-heeled sandals and French manicure, makeup in place, hair freshly cut, suntanned and sleek, sipping white zinfandel, leaving a lipstick smear on the rim.

Maisie startles me by appearing at my side with her arms full of beach roses, thorny and pink; she bends down to lay them in my lap. I catch a whiff of her, slightly like chlorine mixed with the musk oil she likes. Before she straightens, she places a quick kiss on my lips.

"I see Daddy," she says, staring out at the water, as if she knew the game I was playing. "He's swimming laps in his pool," she says. "And there's Samantha, watching." Maisie looks at me and winks wickedly. "Yuck!" she says. "Her bathing suit is gold lamé."

It is not until the week before she leaves for college that I decide what Maisie needs. Something to carry all of her belongings away in. The morning I get this idea is a Saturday. The sun is golden in a clear sky. The humidity has broken. It's a perfect yard-sale day.

Maisie and Robert are already in the pool when I leave the house. They are tethered together, floating, bumping into each other, faces turned upward toward the sun.

"Good-bye," I call to them. But of course they don't hear.

I drive along the coastal road, across the state line into Rhode Island. Along the way I stop at a few yard sales, resisting the chipped porcelain, the worn blankets and dusty lamps. I buy fresh peaches and strawberries from a roadside stand. I buy local sugar and butter corn. By the time I reach the final yard sale, the car smells like summer produce, rich and fertile.

The house is a ranch-style one that someone put a lot of time into sprucing up. There is an intricate multitiered deck on the back, a trellis bursting with the last roses of the season, a gazebo that has a sign hanging from its roof: I'M FOR SALE TOO!!!!

There is something sad about the place, and for a moment I consider getting back into the car and driving off with my corn and peaches and strawberries. The afternoon has turned muggy again, and I imagine driving back to Connecticut, setting the corn still in its husks into a pan of cold water to soak, and diving into the pool. But then I remember that in just one week from today, Maisie will leave for college. She chose the University of Wisconsin, and I try to imagine her there, in Madison, but I come up blank every time.

"Wisconsin?" Drew said when she told him. "When there are so many good schools here?"

I was surprised too. I would have thought Maisie would choose a warm place. California or Miami or Atlanta. "It's cold there," I told her. "Mom," she said, "it's cold here."

Sighing, I walk toward the side of the house, where the family's belongings spill into the yard, onto that complex deck.

"Hello," I say, forcing a smile.

After so many years of practice, I can size up a yard sale quickly. This one is all wrong for me, full of baby things—Snuglis and mechanical swings and car seats, those bright plastic toys that fill playpens, the playpen itself, empty and forlorn.

The man and woman who are holding the sale smile at me politely. A divorce, I think. I can size up that easily too. The baby who used all this stuff is a little girl now, six or seven years old, with sad eyes and a dirty face. It is as if she is watching her entire past being sold off here.

I turn to leave. Not only won't I find Maisie's luggage here, but this is making me feel too bad, robbing me of my earlier happiness. Behind me, I hear the sound of a woman's voice, a strong Rhode Island accent making an offer for all the baby items.

"No!" the little girl shrieks. "Those are mine!"

The mother's voice is calm. "Maisie," she says, "you haven't used them in years."

I stop midway back to my car. "I have a daughter named Maisie," I say to no one and everyone.

The little girl's eyes grow wide. "YOU have a little girl?" she says.

I laugh. "She's all grown up," I tell her. But standing there, in the middle of their lives, I realize how this Maisie could be mine, how this man agreeing to sell everything, helping to fold up the playpen, to move it all away could be Drew, how this tall sad woman will be left behind with her roses, her fancy deck, her daughter.

My eyes flit across the objects that cover their lawn. I suddenly feel that I must buy something, anything. And then I see it—three pieces of luggage, old soft American Tourister in a muddy lavender. I pay the price it's marked and carry it back to my car, my spirits beginning to lift again.

"Is that for *your* little girl?" their Maisie asks me.

"Yes," I tell her. "For my little Maisie."

* * *

I plan on surprising Maisie with the luggage when she starts to pack next week. I imagine her stuffing her clothes into her old backpack and duffel bag and, just as she runs out of room, presenting her with the three cleaned-up pieces.

All the way home I replay the surprise. By the time I get there, I have decided to make my special corn chowder for her. And a peach pie for dessert. I will invite Robert to join us. Maybe I can even talk them into a game later, Pictionary or Trivial Pursuit. As I walk in the back door, I hear the *zzzzzt* of the bug zapper catching mosquitoes. When I first got that, the sound used to make Maisie cry.

The house is strangely quiet. I put all the produce down on the kitchen counter.

"Maisie?" I call.

I flick on the light switch in the living room. It illuminates a room full of luggage—brown real leather bags in all sizes and shapes. Each piece, I see as I bend to examine it, is monogrammed with Maisie's initials in gold. I pick a shiny card from on top of the largest piece. The card is all gold and silver with good wishes expressed in raised letters. Inside, it is signed in Samantha's handwriting with lots of love.

I feel suddenly exhausted. Without even turning off the light, I climb over the tote bag, the overnighter, and make my way down the hall toward my room. A shaft of light peeks out from under Maisie's bedroom door.

Her voice is harsh, mocking. "See Spot run," she says. "Run, Spot, run."

I hear Robert laughing along.

"And smell it," she is saying. "Like mothballs. Like someone's attic."

Her last week at home, Maisie is tender. She mistakes my mood for sadness that she is leaving. At night, while I sit outside alone by the pool, she even climbs onto my lap, all legs and pointy elbows. "Mom," she whispers, "I'm going to miss you."

I stroke her long dark hair, work out the tangles gently with my fingertips the way I used to when she was a little girl and fit in my lap.

On her last night, I take her to her favorite Chinese restaurant for dinner, the Houkilau. We order a fancy drink that comes in a fake coconut with tiny paper umbrellas and skewers of cherries and pineapples. I have agreed to let Robert take her to the airport in the morning. Now she tells me that she wants to date other boys at school.

"I mean," she says, chewing on her straw, "he's never even heard of *Jane Eyre*. My all-time favorite book."

I don't tell her how relieved I am. I just try to memorize how she looks at this very moment.

"You bought me all my favorite books," she says. She reaches across the table, past our flaming pupu platter, and squeezes my hand. "*Jane Eyre* and *Wuthering Heights*. You and your silly yard sales."

I see that her eyes are moist, teary. I make myself look away.

"And you wanted to give me something before I left," Maisie tells me. "You gave me everything."

I think again of her name. I think, maze.

"Maisie," I say.

She squeezes my hand again, then releases it suddenly to pop a fried wonton into her mouth.

I look back at her, watch her chew fiercely. Look, look, I think. I smile. Go. Go.

EDITOR'S AFTERNOTE

"Nobody prepares you for the day your children leave you," a friend of Ann Hood's commented to her about his grown children.

"That struck me as an important event and emotion," Hood says, "a time when you would question how good a parent you had been, and what your future relationship with your child was going to be. It seemed too that it would be a time when you thought about old memories. Part of letting go, I suppose, is deciding what you hold on to."

Hood thinks of "Maisie" as "a sad story, in a way. There is great longing in it—longing to keep your child close, to have successfully won your child's love and respect, and then finally a coming together, which, though positive, is the first step in Maisie's own adulthood and independence."

A contributing editor to *Parenting* magazine, where she writes the baby column "That's My Baby!" Hood has authored six novels, her latest being *The Properties of Water*. A frequent writer for publications such as *Cosmopolitan, Glamour, The New York Times,* and *The Washington Post,* Hood lives in Providence, Rhode Island, with her husband and two-year-old, Sam.

Momma Welfare Roll
Maya Angelou

Her arms semaphore fat triangles,
Pudgy hands bunched on layered hips
Where bones idle under years of fatback
And lima beans.
Her jowls shiver in accusation
Of crimes clichéd by
Repetition. Her children, strangers
To childhood's toys, play
Best the games of darkened doorways,
Rooftop tag, and know the slick feel of
Other people's property.

Too fat to whore,
Too mad to work,
Searches her dreams for the
Lucky sign and walks bare-handed
Into a den of bureaucrats for
Her portion.
"They don't give me welfare.
I take it."

EDITOR'S AFTERNOTE

"I have fond, fond memories of Mama," Maya Angelou told audience members during a speech she gave at the University of South Florida a couple of years ago.

She was speaking of her grandmother, one of Angelou's two most significant inspirations in life, the other being her mother. At six feet tall, Mama was a "tree of a woman," the poet said, who drew Angelou out of five and a half years of self-imposed silence when she was a girl. Angelou had been raped at age seven, and the man convicted of the crime found brutally beaten to death two days after his release from prison.

"I stopped talking, because I thought my voice killed people."

Her voice was strong, clear, and resonant, however, when she read her chapbook-length poem "On the Pulse of Morning" to the nation at President Clinton's inauguration. Author of the modern classic, *I Know Why the Caged Bird Sings*, Angelou is often referred to, rightly, as a literary giant. Her accomplishments embody five collections of poetry, including *Shaker, Why Don't You Sing, And Still I Rise,* and *Just Give Me a Cool Drink of Water 'fore I Diiie,* five books of autobiography, plus her poem, *A Brave and Startling Truth,* later published in book form, but first read on June 26, 1995, at the fiftieth anniversary of the founding of the United Nations. She has received numerous awards and honorary degrees. A child of rural Stamps, Arkansas, Angelou now holds an endowed chair at Wake Forest University.

The Four Girls
Julia Alvarez

Carla, Yolanda, Sandra, Sofía

The mother still calls them *the four girls* even though the youngest is twenty-six and the oldest will be thirty-one next month. She has always called them *the four girls* for as long as they can remember, and the oldest remembers all the way back to the day the fourth girl was born. Before that, the mother must have called them *the three girls,* and before that *the two girls,* but not even the oldest, who was once the only girl, remembers the mother calling them anything but *the four girls.*

The mother dressed them all alike in diminishing-sized, different color versions of what she wore, so that the husband sometimes joked, calling them *the five girls.* No one really knew if he was secretly displeased in his heart of hearts that he had never had a son, for the father always bragged, "Good bulls sire cows," and the mother patted his arm, and the four girls tumbled and skipped and giggled and raced by in yellow and baby blue and pastel pink and white, and strangers counted them, "One, two, three, four girls! No sons?"

"No," the mother said, apologetically. "Just the four girls."

Each of the four girls had the same party dress, school clothes, underwear, toothbrush, bedspread, nightgown, plastic cup, towel, brush and comb set as the other three, but the first girl brushed in yellow, the second one boarded the school bus in blue, the third one slept in pink, and the baby did everything she pleased in white. As the baby grew older, she cast an envying look at pink. The mother tried to convince the third daughter that white was the best color, and the little one wanted pink because she was a baby and didn't know any better, but the third girl was clever and would not be persuaded. She had always believed that she had gotten the best deal since pink was the color for girls. "You girls are going to drive me crazy!" the mother said, but the girls had gotten used to the mother's rhetorical threats.

The mother had devised the color code to save time. With four girls so close in age, she couldn't indulge identities and hunt down a red cowboy shirt when the third daughter turned tomboy or a Mexican peasant blouse when the oldest discovered her Hispanic roots. As women, the four girls criticized the mother's efficiency. The little one claimed that the whole color system smacked of an assembly-line mentality. The eldest, a child psychologist, admonished the mother in an autobiographical paper, "I Was There Too," by saying that the color system had weakened the four girls' identity differentiation abilities and made them forever unclear about personality boundaries. The eldest also intimated that the mother was a mild anal-retentive personality.

The mother did not understand all that psychology talk, but she knew when she was being criticized. The next time the four girls were all together, she took the opportunity of crying a little and saying that she had done the best she could by the four girls. All four girls praised the good job the mother had done in raising four girls so close in age, and they poured more wine into the mother's glass and into the father's glass, and the father patted the mother's arm and said thickly, "Good cows breed cows," and the mother told the story she liked to tell about the oldest, Carla.

For although the mother confused their names or called them all by the generic pet name, "Cuquita," and switched their birthdates and their careers, and sometimes forgot which husband or boyfriend went with which daughter, she had a favorite story she liked to tell about each one as a way of celebrating that daughter on special occasions. The last time she told the story she liked to tell about the eldest was when Carla got married. The mother, tipsy on champagne, seized the mike during the band's break and recounted the story of the red sneakers to the wedding guests. After her good cry at the dinner table, the mother repeated the story. Carla, of course, knew the story well, and had analyzed it for unresolved childhood issues with her analyst husband. But she never tired of hearing it because it was her story, and whenever the mother told it, Carla knew she was the favorite of the moment.

"You know, of course, the story of the red sneakers?" the mother asked the table in general.

"Oh no," the second daughter groaned. "Not again."

Carla glared at her. "Listen to that negativity." She nodded at her husband as if to confirm something they had talked about.

"Listen to that jargon," the second one countered, rolling her eyes.

"Listen to my story." The mother sipped from her wine glass and set it down a little too heavily. Wine spilled on her hand. She looked up at the ceiling as if she had moved back in time to when they were living on the Island. Those downpours! Leaks, leaks— no roof could keep them out during rainy season. "You all know that when we were first married, we were really really poor?" The father nodded, he remembered. "And your sister"—the stories were always told as if the daughter in question were not present—"your sister wanted some new sneakers. She drove me crazy, night and day, she wanted sneakers, she wanted sneakers. Anyhow, we couldn't afford to make any ends, no less start in with sneakers! If you girls only knew what we went through in those days. Words can't describe it. Four—no, three of you, back then—three girls, and no money coming in."

"Well," the father interrupted. "I was working."

"Your father was working." The mother frowned. Once she got started on a story, she did not acknowledge interruptions. "But that measly little paycheck barely covered the rent." The father frowned. "And my father," the mother confided, "was helping us out—"

"It was only a loan," the father explained to his son-in-law. "Paid every penny back."

"It was only a loan," the mother continued. "Anyhow—the point is to make the story short—we did not have money for one little frill like sneakers. Well, she drove me crazy, night and day, I want sneakers, I want sneakers." The mother was a good mimic, and everybody laughed and sipped their wine. Carla's husband rubbed the back of her neck in slow, arousing circles.

"But the good Lord always provides." Although she was not particularly religious, the mother liked to make her plots providential. "It just so happened that a very nice lady who lived down the block with a little girl who was a little older than Carla and much bigger—"

"Much bigger." The father blew out his cheeks and made a monkey face to show how much bigger.

"This little girl's grandmother had sent her some sneakers for her birthday from New York, not knowing she had gotten so much bigger, and the little sneakers wouldn't fit her."

The father kept his cheeks puffed out because the third oldest burst into giggles every time she looked over at him. She never held her liquor well.

The mother waited for her to control herself and gave the father a sobering stare. "So the nice lady offers me the sneakers because she knows how much that Carla has been pestering me that she wants some. And you know what?" The table waited for the mother to enjoy answering her own question. "They were just her size. Always provides," the mother said, nodding.

"But Señorita Miss Carla could not be bothered with white sneakers. She wanted red sneakers, she wanted red sneakers." The mother rolled her eyes the same way that the second daughter had rolled her eyes at her older sister. "Can you believe it?"

"Uh-huh," the second daughter said. "I can believe it."

"Hostile, aren't we?" Carla said. Her husband whispered something in her ear. They laughed.

"Let me finish," the mother said, sensing dissension.

The youngest got up and poured everyone some more wine. The third oldest turned her glass, stem up, and giggled without much enthusiasm when the father puffed out his cheeks again for her benefit. Her own cheeks had gone pale; her lids drooped over her eyes; she held her head up in her hand. But the mother was too absorbed in her story to scold the elbow off the table.

"I told your sister, *It's white sneakers or no sneakers!* And she had some temper, that Carla. She threw them across the room and yelled, *Red sneakers, red sneakers.*"

The four girls shifted in their chairs, anxious to get to the end of the story. Carla's husband fondled her shoulder as if it were a breast.

The mother hurried her story. "So your father, who spoiled you all rotten"—the father grinned from his place at the head of the table—"comes and rescues the sneakers and, behind my back, whispers to Carlita that she's going to have red sneakers just like she wants them. I find them, the both of them on the floor in the bathroom with my nail polish painting those sneakers red!"

"To Mami," the father said sheepishly, lifting his glass in a toast. "And to the red sneakers," he added.

The room rang with laughter. The daughters raised their glasses. "To the red sneakers."

"That's classic," the analyst said, winking at his wife.

"Red sneakers at that." Carla shook her head, stressing the word *red*.

"Jesus!" the second oldest groaned.

"Always provides," the mother added.

"Red sneakers," the father said, trying to get one more laugh from the table. But everyone was tired, and the third oldest said she was afraid she was going to throw up.

Yolanda, the third of the four girls, became a schoolteacher but not on purpose. For years after graduate school, she wrote down *poet* under profession in questionnaires and income tax forms, and later amended it to *writer*-slash-*teacher*. Finally, acknowledging that she had not written much of anything in years, she announced to her family that she was not a poet anymore.

Secretly, the mother was disappointed because she had always meant for her Yo to be the famous one. The story she told about her third daughter no longer had the charm of a prophetic ending: "And, of course, she became a poet." But the mother tried to convince her daughter that it was better to be a happy nobody than a sad somebody. Yolanda, who was still as clever as when the mother had tried to persuade her that white was a better color than pink, was not convinced.

The mother used to go to all the poetry readings her daughter gave in town and sit in the front row applauding each poem and giving standing ovations. Yolanda was so embarrassed that she tried to keep her readings a secret from her mother, but somehow the mother always found out about them and appeared, first row, center. Even when she behaved herself, the mother threw her daughter off just by her presence. Yolanda often read poems addressed to lovers, sonnets set in bedrooms, and she knew her mother did not believe in sex for girls. But the mother seemed not to notice the subject of the poems, or if she did, to ascribe the love scenes to her Yoyo's great imagination.

"That one has always had a great imagination," the mother confided to whoever sat next to her. At a recent reading the daughter gave after her long silence, the mother's neighbor was the daughter's lover. The mother did not know that the handsome, graying professor at her side knew her daughter at all; she thought he was just someone interested in her poetry. "Of all the four girls," the mother told the lover, "that Yo has always loved poetry."

"That's her nickname, Yo, Yoyo," the mother explained. "She complains she wants her name, but you have to take shortcuts when there's four of them. Four girls, imagine!"

"Really?" the lover said, although Yolanda had already filled him in on her family and her bastardized name—Yo, Joe, Yoyo. He knew better than to take shortcuts. Jo-laahn-dah, she had drilled him. Supposedly, the parents were heavy-duty Old World, but the four daughters sounded pretty wild for all that. There had been several divorces among them, including Yolanda's. The oldest, a child psychologist, had married the analyst she'd been seeing when her first marriage broke up, something of the sort. The second one was doing a lot of drugs to keep her weight down. The youngest had just gone off with a German man when they discovered she was pregnant.

"But that Yo," the mother continued, pointing to her daughter where she sat with the other readers waiting for the sound system to work properly so the program could begin, "that Yo has always had a great imagination." The buzz of talk was punctuated now and then by a crackling, amplified "testing" spoken too close to the microphone. Yolanda watched the absorbed conversation of her mother and lover with growing uneasiness.

"Yes, Yoyo has always loved poetry. Why, I remember the time we went on a trip to New York. She couldn't have been more than three." The mother was warming to her story. The lover noticed that the mother's eyes were those that looked at him softly at night from the daughter's face.

"Testing," a voice exploded into the room.

The mother looked up, thinking the poetry reading had begun. The lover waved the voice away. He wanted to hear the story.

"We went up to New York, Lolo and I. He had a convention there, and we decided to make a vacation of it. We hadn't had a vacation since the first baby was born. We were very poor." The mother lowered her voice. "Words can't describe how poor we were. But we were starting to see better days."

"Really?" the lover said. He had fixed on that word as one that gave the appropriate amount of encouragement but did not interrupt the flow of the mother's story.

"We left the girls back home, but that one"—the mother pointed again to the daughter, who widened her eyes at her lover—"that one was losing all her hair. We took her with us so she could see a specialist. Turned out to be just nerves."

The lover knew Yolanda would not have wanted him to know about this indelicacy of her body. She did not even like to pluck her eyebrows in his presence. An immediate bathrobe after her bath. Lights out when they made love. Other times, she carried on about the Great Mother and the holiness of the body and sexual energy being eternal delight. Sometimes, he complained he felt caught between the woman's libber and the Catholic señorita. "You sound like my ex," she accused him.

"We got on this crowded bus one afternoon." The mother shook her head remembering how crowded the bus had been. "I couldn't begin to tell you how crowded it was. It was more sardines in a can than you could shake sticks at."

"Really?"

"You don't believe me?" the mother accused him. The lover nodded his head to show he was convinced. "But let me tell you, that bus was so crowded, Lolo and I got our wires totally mixed up. I was sure Lolo had her, and Lolo was sure she was with me. Anyhow, to make it a short story, we got off at our stop, and we looked at each other. *Where's Yo?* we asked at the same time. Meanwhile, that bus was roaring away from us.

"Well, I'll tell you, we broke into a run like two crazy people! It was rush hour. Everyone was turning around to look at us like we were running from the police or something." The mother's voice was breathless remembering that run. The lover waited for her to catch up with the bus in her memory.

"Testing?" a garbled voice asked without much conviction.

"After about two blocks, we flagged the driver down and climbed aboard. And you won't believe what we found?"

The lover knew better than to take a guess.

"We found that one surrounded by a crowd like Jesus and the elders."

"Really?" The lover smiled, admiring the daughter from a distance. Yolanda was one of the more popular instructors at the college where he chaired the Comp Lit Department.

"She hadn't even realized we were gone. She had a circle of people around her, listening to her reciting a poem! As a matter of fact, it was a poem I'd taught her. Maybe you've heard of it? It's by that guy who wrote that poem about the blackbird."

"Stevens?" the lover guessed.

The mother cocked her head. "I'm not sure. Anyhow," she continued, "imagine! Three years old and already drawing crowds. Of course, she became a poet."

"You don't mean Poe, do you? Edgar Allan Poe?"

"Yes, that's him! That's him!" the mother cried out. "The poem was about a princess who lived by the sea or something. Let's see." She began to recite:

> Many many years ago, something . . . something,
> In a . . . something by the sea . . .
> A princess there lived whom you may remember
> By the name of Annabel Lee . . .

The mother looked up and realized that the hushed audience was staring at her. She blushed. The lover chuckled and squeezed her arm. At the podium, the poet had been introduced and was waiting for the white-haired woman in the first row to finish talking. "For Clive," Yolanda said, introducing her first poem, "'Bedroom Sestina.'" Clive smiled sheepishly at the mother, who smiled proudly at her daughter.

The mother does not tell a favorite story about Sandra anymore. She says she would like to forget the past, but it is really only a small part of the recent past she would like to forget. However, the mother knows people listen to absolute statements, so she says in a tired voice, "I want to forget the past."

The last story the mother told about her second oldest was not in celebration but in explanation to Dr. Tandlemann, senior staff psychiatrist at Mount Hope. The mother explained why she and her husband were committing their daughter to a private mental hospital.

"It started with that crazy diet," the mother began. She folded and refolded her Kleenex into smaller and smaller squares. Dr. Tandlemann watched her and took notes. The father sat by the window quietly and followed the movements of a gardener, who was mowing first one, then another, darkening swath across the lawn.

"Can you imagine starving herself to death?" The mother pinched little bits off her Kleenex. "No wonder she went crazy."

"She's had a breakdown." Dr. Tandlemann looked at the father. "Your daughter is not clinically crazy."

"What does that mean, clinically crazy?" The mother scowled. "I don't understand all that psychology talk."

"It means that," Dr. Tandlemann began, looking down at his folder to check the name, "it means that Sandra is not psychotic or schizophrenic, she's just had a small breakdown."

"A small breakdown," the father murmured to himself. In the middle of a row, the gardener stopped, machine roaring. He spat and shrugged his shoulder across his lips, wiping his mouth, then he continued his progress across the lawn. Grass bits spewed into a white sack ballooning behind the motor. The father felt he should say something pleasant. "Nice place you got here, beautiful grounds."

"Ay, Lolo," the mother said sadly. She made a fist of what was left of her Kleenex.

Dr. Tandlemann waited for a moment in case the husband wanted to respond to his wife. Then he asked the mother, "You say it started with that diet she went on?"

"It started with that crazy diet," the mother said again as if she had just found her place in a book she had been reading. "Sandi wanted to look like those twiggy models. She was a looker, that one, and I guess it went to her head. There are four girls, you know."

Dr. Tandlemann wrote down *four girls* although the father had already told him this when he asked, "No sons?" Out loud, he noted, noncommittally, "Four girls."

The mother hesitated, then glanced over at her husband as if unsure how much they should disclose to this stranger. "We've had trouble with all of them—" She rolled her eyes to indicate the kind of trouble she meant.

"You mean other daughters have also had breakdowns?"

"Bad men is what they've had!" The mother scowled at the doctor as if he were one of her ex sons-in-law. "Anyhow, that makes sense, heartbreak, breakdown. This is different, this is crazy." The doctor's hand lifted in protest. But the mother ignored the gesture and went on with her story.

"The others aren't bad looking, don't get me wrong. But Sandi, Sandi got the fine looks, blue eyes, peaches and ice cream skin, everything going for her!" The mother spread her arms in all directions to show how pretty and pale and blue-eyed the girl was. Bits of her Kleenex fell to the floor, and she picked off the specks from the carpet. "My great-grandfather married a Swedish girl, you know? So the family has light-colored blood, and that Sandi got it all. But imagine, spirit of contradiction, she wanted to be darker complected like her sisters."

"That's understandable," Dr. Tandlemann said.

"It's crazy, that's what it is," the mother said angrily. "Anyhow, this diet took over. When her sister got married, Sandi wouldn't even taste the wedding cake, taste!"

"Did they get along?" Dr. Tandlemann glanced up; his hand had a life of its own and kept writing.

"Who?" The mother blinked in disapproval. The man asked too many questions.

"The siblings," Dr. Tandlemann said. "Were they close? Was there a lot of rivalry between them?"

"Siblings?" The mother frowned at all this crazy psychology talk. "They're sisters," she said by way of explanation.

"Sometimes they fought," the father added. Although he was looking out the window, he did not miss a word the doctor and his wife were saying.

"Sometimes they fought," the mother raced on. She wanted to get to the end of this story. "So Sandi kept losing weight. At first, she looked good. She had let herself get a little plump, and with her fine bones Sandi can't carry extra weight. So losing a few pounds was okay. Then, she went away to a graduate program, so we didn't see her for a while. Every time we talked to her over the phone, her voice seemed further and further away. And it wasn't because it was long distance either. I can't explain it," the mother said. "A mother just knows.

"So one day we get this call. The dean. She says she doesn't want to alarm us, but could we come down immediately. Our daughter is in the hospital, too weak to do anything. All she does is read."

The father was timing the gardener's treks across the rolling lawns. When the man did not stop to spit or wipe his forehead, each row took him approximately two minutes.

The mother tried to open the Kleenex in her lap, but it was too ragged to spread out. "We took the next plane, and when we got there, I didn't recognize my own daughter." The mother held up her little finger. "Sandi was a toothpick. And that's not the least of it, she wouldn't put a book down, read, read, read. That's all she did."

At the window the father's view of the lawn was blurring.

The mother looked over at her husband and wondered what he was thinking about. "She had lists and lists of books to read. We found them in her journal. After she finished one, she crossed it off the list. Finally, she told us why she couldn't stop reading. She didn't have much time left. She had to read all the great works of man because soon"—the mother got up her courage to say it—"soon she wouldn't be human."

In the ensuing silence the mother heard the drone of a distant lawnmower.

"She told us that she was being turned out of the human race. She was becoming a monkey." The mother's voice broke. "A monkey, my baby!

"Already the other organs inside her body were a monkey's. Only her brain was left, and she could feel it going."

Dr. Tandlemann stopped writing. He weighed his pen in his hand. "I understood you committed her only because of the weight loss. This is news to me."

"Small breakdown," the father murmured quietly so Dr. Tandlemann wouldn't hear him.

The mother was in control of her voice again. "If she read all the great books, maybe she'd remember something important from having been human. So she read and read. But she was afraid she'd go before she got to some of the big thinkers."

"Freud," the doctor said, listing names on his pad. "Darwin, Nietzsche, Erikson."

"Dante," the father mused. "Homer, Cervantes, Calderón de la Barca."

"I told her to stop reading and start eating. I told her those books were driving her crazy. I made her everything she liked: rice and beans, lasagna, chicken à la king. I made her favorite red snapper with tomato sauce. She said she didn't want to eat animals. In her own time, she said, she would be that chicken. She would be that red snapper. Evolution had reached its peak and was going backwards. Something like that." The mother waved the very idea away. "It was crazy talk, I tell you.

"One morning, I go in her room to wake her up, and I find her lying in bed and looking up at her hands." The mother held up her hands and reenacted the scene. "I call her name, Sandi!, and she keeps turning her hands, this way, that, and staring at them. I scream at her to answer me, and she doesn't even look at me. Nothing. And she's making these awful sounds like she's a zoo." The mother clucked and grunted to show the doctor what the animals had sounded like.

Suddenly, the father leaned forward. He had caught sight of something important.

"And my Sandi holds up her hands to me," the mother continued. She turned her hands towards Dr. Tandlemann and then towards her husband, whose face was pressed up to the window. "And she screams, *Monkey hands, monkey hands.*"

The father shot up from his chair. Outside, a fair, willowy girl and a heavy-set woman in white were walking across the lawn. The woman was pointing out the flowers and the leaves of the bushes in order to cajole the girl forward towards the building. At one end of the lawn, the gardener wiped his forehead, turned the mower around, and began a new row. A dark wake spread behind him. The girl looked up, wildly searching the empty sky for the airplane she was hearing. The nurse followed her distracted movements with alarm. Finally, the girl saw a man coming at her with a roaring animal on a leash, its baglike stomach swelling up as it devoured the grasses between them. The girl screamed and broke into a panicked run towards the building where her father, whom she could not see, stood at the window, waving.

At the hospital, the mother leans on the glass with one hand and taps with the other. She makes a monkey face. The cradle has been turned towards her, but the tiny, wrinkled baby is not looking at the grandmother. Instead the baby's eyes roll about as if she hasn't quite figured out how to work them yet. Her lips pucker and stretch, pucker and stretch. The grandmother is sure the baby is smiling at her.

"Look at that," the grandmother says to the young man at her side, who is looking at the baby in the neighboring cradle.

The young man looks at the stranger's baby.

"She's smiling already," the grandmother brags.

The young man nods and smiles.

"Yours is asleep," the grandmother says in a slightly critical voice.

"Babies sleep a lot," the young man explains.

"Some do," the grandmother says. "I had four girls, and they never slept."

"Four girls, no boys?"

The mother shakes her head. "I guess it's in the blood. This one is a girl too. Aren't you, Cuquita?" the grandmother asks her granddaughter.

The young man smiles at his daughter. "Mine is a girl too."

The grandmother congratulates him. "Good bulls sire cows, you know."

"Huh?"

"It's a saying my husband used to tell me after I had one of the girls. *Good bulls sire cows.* I remember the night Fifi was born." The grandmother looks down at her granddaughter and explains, "Your mother."

The young man studies his baby daughter as he listens to the old woman's story.

"That girl gave me more trouble getting born than any of the others. And the funny thing was she was the last and smallest of the four. Twenty-four hours in labor." The grandmother's eyebrows lift for punctuation.

The young man whistles. "Twenty-four hours is a long labor for a small fourth child. Any complications?"

The mother studies the young man a moment. Is he a doctor, she wonders, to know so much about babies?

"Twenty-four hours . . ." The young man is shaking his head, musing. "Ours lasted only three and a half."

The grandmother stares up at the young man. *Ours?* Men! Now they're going to claim having the babies too.

"But I'll tell you, that Fifi, we didn't name her wrong! Sofía, that's her real name. My daughter, the poet, says Sofía was the goddess in charge of wisdom long ago. We Catholics don't believe in that stuff. But still, she's the smart one, all right. And I don't mean books either! I mean smart." The grandmother taps her temple, and then repeats the gesture on the glass. "Smart, smart," the grandmother tells the baby. She shakes her head, musing to herself. "That Fifi, she might look like she's headed for trouble, but it always turns out to be her luck.

"That night she was finally born, her father came in, and I knew he was a little disappointed, especially after such a long wait. And I said, *I can't help it, Lolo, they come out girls*, and all he said was, *Good bulls sire cows*, like it was a credit to him. He was almost falling over with exhaustion. So I sent him home to bed."

The young man yawns and laughs.

"He was so dead tired, he didn't hear the burglars when they broke in. They stole us blind. They even stole my shoes and my under—" The grandmother remembers it is indelicate to say so. "Every last article of clothing," she adds coyly.

The young man pretends to be alarmed.

"But this is what I mean about luck—they caught the burglars, and we got every last stitch back." The grandmother taps the glass. "Cuquita," she coos at the baby.

"Lucky," she says to the young man. "That Fifi has always been the lucky one. Not to mention her luck with"—the grandmother lowers her voice—"with Otto."

The young man looks over his shoulder. Otto? Who would name a poor kid Otto?

"Imagine," the grandmother continues. "Fifi drops out of college and goes off on a church trip to Perú, chaperoned, of course, otherwise we wouldn't have let her go. We don't believe in all this freedom." The grandmother frowns as she looks out over the nursery. Beyond the glass, between the slender white bars of their cribs, half a dozen babies are fast asleep.

"Anyhow she meets this German man Otto in a Peruvian market, who can't speak a word of Spanish but is trying to buy a poncho. She bargains for him, and he gets his poncho for practically nothing. Well, just like that, they fell for each other, corresponded, and here they are, parents! Tell me that isn't lucky?"

"That's lucky," the young man says.

"And you're going to be a lucky one too, aren't you?" The grandmother clucks at her granddaughter, then confides to the young man, "She's going to look just like an angel, pink and blond."

"You never can tell when they're this young," the father says, smiling at his daughter.

"I can," the grandmother claims. "I had four of them."

"Mami picks up like these really gorgeous men," Sandi laughs. She is sitting cross-legged on Fifi's living room floor. The new mother sits in Otto's recliner, the baby asleep on her shoulder. Carla is sprawled on the sofa. At her feet, Yolanda is knitting furiously at a tiny blanket, pink and baby blue and pastel yellow squares with a white border. It is early morning. The family has gathered at Fifi's house for Christmas, which falls a week after the baby's birth. Husbands and grandparents are still asleep in the bedrooms. The four girls lounge in their nightgowns and tell each other the true story of how their lives are going.

Sandi explains that she and the mother were in the waiting room, and the mother disappeared. "I find her at the nursery window talking to this piece of beefcake—"

"That's offensive," Yolanda says. "Just call him a man."

"Lay off me, will you?" Sandi is close to tears. Since her release from Mount Hope a month ago, she cries so easily she has to carry Kleenex with her anti-depressants in her purse. She looks around the room for her bag. "Miz Poet is so goddamn sensitive to language."

"I don't write poetry anymore," Yolanda says in a wounded voice.

"Goddamn it, you guys," Carla says, refereeing this one. "It's Christmas."

The new mother turns to the second oldest sister and runs her fingers through her hair. This is the first time the family has gathered together in a year, and she wants them all to get along. She changes the subject. "That was really nice of you to come see me at the hospital. I know how you just love hospitals," she adds.

Sandi looks down at the rug and picks at it. "I just want to forget the past, you know?"

"That's understandable," Carla says.

Yolanda lays aside the baby blanket. She has the same scowl on her face her sister wore a moment ago, a family sign of approaching tears. "I'm sorry," she says to Sandi. "It's been the worst week."

Sandi touches her hand. She looks at her other sisters. Clive, they all know, has gone back to his wife again. "He's such a turd. How many times has he done this now, Yo?"

"Yolanda," Carla corrects her. "She wants to be called Yolanda now."

"What do you mean, *wants to be called Yolanda now?* That's my name, you know?"

"Why are you so angry?" Carla's calmness is professional.

Yolanda rolls her eyes. "Spare me the nickel-and-dime therapy, thank you."

Trouble brewing again, Fifi changes the subject. She touches the evolving blanket. "It's really beautiful. And the poem you wrote the baby made me cry."

"So you *are* writing!" Carla says. "I know, I know, you don't want to hear about it." Carla makes a peace offering of compliments. "You're so good, Yolanda, really. I've saved all your poems. Every time I read something in a magazine, I think, God, Yo's so much better than this! Give yourself credit. You're so hard on yourself."

Yolanda keeps her mouth shut. She is working on a thought about her bossy older sister: Carla has a tendency to lace all her compliments with calls to self-improvement. *Give yourself credit, Believe in yourself, Be good to yourself.* Somehow this makes her praise sound like their mother's old "constructive" criticism.

Carla turns to Sandi. "Mami says you're seeing someone." The eldest weighs her words carefully. "Is it true?"

"What of it?" Sandi looks up defensively, and then, realizing her sister means a man, not a therapist, she adds, "He's a nice guy, but, I don't know—" She shrugs. "He was in at the same time I was."

What was *he* in for? hangs in the air—a question that none of her sisters would dare ask.

"So, tell us about this cute guy at the nursery," Fifi pleads. Each time her sisters seem on the verge of loaded talk, the new mother changes the subject to her favorite topic, her newborn daughter. Every little detail of the baby's being—what she eats, what she poops—seems an evolutionary leap. Surely, not all newborns smile at their mothers? "You met this guy at the nursery?"

"Me?" Sandi laughs. "You mean Mami. She picks this guy up and invites him for lunch at the hospital coffee shop."

"Mami is so fresh," Yolanda says. She notices she has made a mistake and begins unraveling a lopsided yellow row.

Fifi pats her baby's back. "And she complains about us!"

"So we all have lunch together," Sandi continues, "and Mami can't shut up about how God brought you and Otto together from opposite ends of the earth in Perú."

"God?" Carla screws up her face.

"Perú?" Fifi's face mirrors her sister's scowl. "I've never been to Perú. We met in Colombia."

"In Mami's version of the story, you met in Perú," Sandi says. "And you fell in love at first sight."

"And made love the first night," Carla teases. The four girls laugh. "Except that part isn't in Mami's version."

"I've heard so many versions of that story," Sandi says, "I don't know which one is true anymore."

"Neither do I," Fifi says, laughing. "Otto says we probably met in a New Jersey Greyhound Station, but we've heard all these exciting stories about how we met in Brazil or Colombia or Perú that we got to believing them."

"So was it the first night?" Yolanda asks, her needles poised midair.

"I heard the first night," Carla says.

Sandi narrows her eyes. "I heard it was a week or so after you guys met."

The baby burps. The four girls look at each other and laugh. "Actually"—Fifi calculates by lifting her fingers one by one from the baby's back, then patting them down—"it was the fourth night. But I knew the minute I saw him."

"That you loved him?" Yolanda asks. Fifi nods. Since Clive left, Yolanda is addicted to love stories with happy endings, as if there were a stitch she missed, a mistake she made way back when she fell in love with her first man, and if only she could find it, maybe she could undo it, unravel John, Brad, Steven, Rudy, and start over.

In the pause before someone picks up the thread of conversation, they all listen to the baby's soft breathing.

"Anyhow, Mami tells this guy about your long correspondence." Sandi helps Yolanda wind the unraveled yarn into a ball, stopping now and then to enjoy her story of the mother. *"For months and months after they met in Perú, they were separated, months and months."* Sandi rolls her eyes like her mother. She is a remarkably good mimic. Her three sisters laugh. *"Otto was doing his research in Germany, but he wrote to her every day."*

"Every day!" Fifi laughs. "I wish it had been every day. Sometimes I had to wait weeks between letters."

"But then," Yolanda says in the ominous voice of a radio melodrama, "then Papi found the letters."

"Mami didn't mention the letters," Sandi says. "The story was short and sweet: *He wrote to her every day. Then she went to see him last Christmas, then he proposed, and they married this spring, and here they are, parents!*"

"One, two, three, four," Carla says, beginning a countdown.

Fifi grins. "Stop it," she says. "The baby was born exactly nine months and ten days after the wedding."

"Thank God for the ten days," Carla says.

"I like Mami's version of the story," Fifi laughs. "So she didn't bring up the letters?"

Sandi shakes her head. "Maybe she forgot. You know how she keeps saying she wants to forget the past."

"Mami remembers everything," Carla disagrees.

"Well, Papi had no business going through my personal mail." Fifi's voice grows testy. The baby stirs on her shoulder. "He claims he was looking for his nailclippers, or something. In my drawers, right?"

Yolanda mimics their father opening an envelope. Her eyes widen in burlesque horror. She clutches her throat. She even puts on a Count Dracula accent to make the moment more dramatic. She is not a good mimic. "*What does this man mean, 'Have you gotten your period yet?'*"

Sandi choruses: "*What business is it of Otto's if you've gotten your period or no?*"

The baby begins to cry. "Oh, honey, it's just a story." Fifi rocks her.

"*We disown you!*" Sandi mimics their father. "*You have disgraced the family name. Out of this house!*"

"*Out of our sight!*" Yolanda points to the door. Sandi ducks the flailing needles. A ball of white yarn rolls across the floor. The two sisters bend over, trying to contain their hilarity.

"You guys are really getting into this." Fifi stands to walk her wailing baby to sleep. "Nothing like a story to take the sting out of things," she adds cooly. "It's not like things are any better between us, you know."

Her three sisters lift their eyebrows at each other. Their father has not uttered a word since he arrived two days ago. He still has not forgiven Fifi for "going behind the palm trees." When they were younger, the sisters used to joke that they would likelier be virgins than find a palm tree in their neck of the woods.

"It's hard, I know." As the therapist in the family, Carla likes to be the one who understands. "But really, give yourself credit. You've won them over, Fifi, you have. Mami's eating out of your hand with this baby, and Papi's going to come around in time, you'll see. Look, he came, didn't he?"

"You mean, Mami dragged him here." Fifi looks down fondly at her baby and recovers her good mood. "Well, the baby is beautiful and well, and that's what counts."

Beautiful and well, Yolanda muses, that's what she had wanted with Clive, all things beautiful and well, instead of their obsessive, consuming passion that left her—each time Clive left her—exhausted and distraught. "I don't understand why he does it," she tells her sisters out loud.

"Old World stuff," Carla says. "You know he got a heavier dose than Mami."

Sandi looks at Yolanda; she understood whom Yolanda meant. She tries to lighten her sister's dark mood. "Look, if beefcake's not your thing, there's a lot of fish out there," she says. "I just wish that cute guy hadn't been married."

"What cute guy?" Carla asks her.

"What guy?" the mother asks. She is standing at the entrance to the living room, buttoning down a multicolored, flowered houserobe. It is a habit of hers from their childhood to buy rainbow clothes for herself so none of the girls can accuse her of playing favorites.

"The guy you picked up at the hospital," Sandi teases.

"What do you mean, *picked up?* He was a nice young man, and it just so happens that he had a baby daughter born the same time as my little Cuquita." The mother puts out her arms. "Come here,

Cuca," she croons, taking the baby from Fifi's hands. She clucks into the blanket.

Sandi shakes her head. "God! You sound like a goddamn zoo."

"Your language," the mother scolds absently, and then, as if the words were an endearment, she coos them at her granddaughter, "your language."

The men trail in slowly for breakfast. First, the father, who nods grimly at all the well-wishing. He is followed by Otto, who wishes everyone a merry Christmas. With his white-gold eyebrows and whiskers and beard, and plump, good-natured, reddish face, Otto looks very much like a young Santa Claus. The analyst shuffles in last. "Look at all those women," he whistles.

The mother is walking her granddaughter up and down the length of the room.

"Just look at them." Otto grins. "A vision! What the three kings saw!"

"Four girls," the father murmurs.

"Five," the analyst corrects, winking at the mother.

"Six," the mother corrects him, nodding towards the bundle in her arms. "Six of us," she says to the baby. "And I was sure of it! Why, a week before you were born, I had the strangest dream. We were all living on a farm, and a bull . . ."

The room is hushed with sleepiness. Everyone listens to the mother.

EDITOR'S AFTERNOTE

Though they aren't sisters, the four Latina writers Julia Alvarez, Sandra Cisneros, Ana Castillo, and Denise Chavez comprise one of literature's newest and most vibrant cliques, Las Girlfriends. The book world has a passion for inner circles. It is in love with the notion of the salon as epitomized by Dorothy Parker in the 1920s, who assembled many publishing wits of the day around the fabled Round Table at the Algonquin Hotel in New York City.

Las Girlfriends are less caustic than Parker and her fellow schmoozers, however; as their profundity tends toward lyric prose rather than the gregariously snide bon mot.

With her second novel, *In the Time of the Butterflies*—nominated for a National Book Critics Circle Award—Julia Alvarez represents the group well. *Butterflies* was aggressively *hand sold,* the term for a book given an extra push by a store's salespeople themselves, largely because, publisher's hype or no, they like what they've read.

Alvarez was born in the Dominican Republic and emigrated to the U.S. in 1960. In addition to her first novel, *How the Garcia Girls Lost Their Accents,* she is also the author of two collections of poetry, *Homecoming* and *The Other Side/El Otro Lado.*

Another Marvelous Thing

Laurie Colwin

On a cold, rainy morning in February, Billy Delielle stood by the window of her hospital room looking over Central Park. She was a week and a half from the time her baby was due to be born, and she had been put into the hospital because her blood pressure had suddenly gone up and her doctor wanted her constantly monitored and on bed rest.

A solitary jogger in bright red foul-weather gear ran slowly down the glistening path. The trees were black and the branches were bare. There was not another soul out. Billy had been in the hospital for five days. The first morning she had woken to the sound of squawking. Since her room was next door to the nursery, she assumed this was a sound some newborns made. The next day she got out of bed at dawn and saw that the meadow was full of seagulls who congregated each morning before the sun came up.

The nursery was an enormous room painted soft yellow. When Billy went to take the one short walk a day allowed her, she found herself averting her eyes from the neat rows of babies in their little plastic bins, but once in a while she found herself hungry for the sight of them. Taped to each crib was a blue (I'M A

51

BOY) or pink (I'M A GIRL) card telling mother's name, the time of birth, and birth weight.

At six in the morning the babies were taken to their mothers to be fed. Billy was impressed by the surprising range of noises they made: mewing, squawking, bleating, piping, and squealing. The fact that she was about to have one of these creatures herself filled her with a combination of bafflement, disbelief, and longing.

For the past two months her chief entertainment had been to lie in bed and observe her unborn child moving under her skin. It had knocked a paperback book off her stomach and caused the saucer of her coffee cup to jiggle and dance.

Billy's husband, Grey, was by temperament and inclination a naturalist. Having a baby was right up his street. Books on neonatology and infant development replaced the astronomy and bird books on his night table. He gave up reading mysteries for texts on childbirth. One of these books had informed him that babies can hear in the womb, so each night he sang "Roll Along Kentucky Moon" directly into Billy's stomach. Another suggested that the educational process could begin before birth. Grey thought he might try to teach the unborn to count.

"Why stop there?" Billy said. "Teach it fractions."

Billy had a horror of the sentimental. In secret, for she would rather have died than showed it, the thought of her own baby brought her to tears. Her dreams were full of infants. Babies appeared everywhere. The buses abounded with pregnant women. The whole process seemed to her one half miraculous and the other half preposterous. She looked around her on a crowded street and said to herself: "Every single one of these people was *born*."

Her oldest friend, Penny Stern, said to her: "We all hope that this pregnancy will force you to wear maternity clothes, because they will be so much nicer than what you usually wear." Billy went shopping for maternity clothes but came home empty-handed.

She said, "I don't wear puffed sleeves and frilly bibs and

ribbons around my neck when I'm not pregnant, so I don't see why I should have to just because I am pregnant." In the end, she wore Grey's sweaters, and she bought two shapeless skirts with elastic waistbands. Penny forced her to buy one nice black dress, which she wore to teach her weekly class in economic history at the business school.

Grey set about renovating a small spare room that had been used for storage. He scraped and polished the floor, built shelves, and painted the walls pale apple green with the ceiling and moldings glossy white. They had once called this room the lumber room. Now they referred to it as the nursery. On the top of one of the shelves Grey put his collection of glass-encased bird's nests. He already had in mind a child who would go on nature hikes with him.

As for Billy, she grimly and without expression submitted herself to the number of advances science had come up with in the field of obstetrics.

It was possible to have amniotic fluid withdrawn and analyzed to find out the genetic health of the unborn and, if you wanted to know, its sex. It was possible to lie on a table and with the aid of an ultrasonic scanner see your unborn child in the womb. It was also possible to have a photograph of this view. As for Grey, he wished Billy could have a sonogram every week, and he watched avidly while Billy's doctor, a handsome, rather melancholy South African named Jordan Bell, identified a series of blobs and clouds as head, shoulders, and back.

Every month in Jordan Bell's office Billy heard the sound of her own child's heart through ultrasound and what she heard sounded like galloping horses in the distance.

Billy went about her business outwardly unflapped. She continued to teach and she worked on her dissertation. In between, when she was not napping, she made lists of baby things: crib sheets, a stroller, baby T-shirts, diapers, blankets. Two months before the baby was due, she and Penny went out and bought what was needed. She was glad she had not saved this until the last minute, because in her ninth month, after an uneventful pregnancy, she was put in the hospital, where she was allowed to walk down the hall once a day. The sense of isolation she had cherished—just herself, Grey, and their unborn child—was gone. She was in the hands of nurses she had never seen before, and she found herself desperate for their companionship because she was exhausted, uncertain, and lonely in her hospital room.

Billy was admitted wearing the nice black dress Penny had made her buy and taken to a private room that overlooked the park. At the bottom of her bed were two towels and a hospital gown that tied up the back. Getting undressed to go to bed in the afternoon made her feel like a child forced to take a nap. She did not put on the hospital gown. Instead, she put on the plaid flannel nightshirt of Grey's that she had packed in her bag weeks ago in case she went into labor in the middle of the night.

"I hate it here already," Billy said.

"It's an awfully nice view," Grey said. "If it were a little further along in the season I could bring my field glasses and see what's nesting."

"I'll never get out of here," Billy said.

"Not only will you get out of here," said Grey, "you will be released a totally transformed woman. You heard Jordan—all babies get born one way or another."

If Grey was frightened, he never showed it. Billy knew that his way of dealing with anxiety was to fix his concentration, and it was now fixed on her and on being cheerful. He had never seen Billy so upset before. He held her hand.

"Don't worry," he said. "Jordan said this isn't serious. It's just a complication. The baby will be fine and you'll be fine. Besides, it won't know how to be a baby and we won't know how to be parents."

Grey had taken off his jacket and he felt a wet place where Billy had laid her cheek. He did not know how to comfort her.

"A mutual learning experience," Billy said into his arm. "I thought nature was supposed to take over and do all this for us."

"It will," Grey said.

Seven o'clock began visiting hours. Even with the door closed

Billy could hear shrieks and coos and laughter. With her door open she could hear champagne corks being popped.

Grey closed the door. "You didn't eat much dinner," he said. "Why don't I go downstairs to the delicatessen and get you something?"

"I'm not hungry," Billy said. She did not know what was in front of her, or how long she would be in this room, or how and when the baby would be born.

"I'll call Penny and have her bring something," Grey said.

"I already talked to her," Billy said. "She and David are taking you out to dinner." David was Penny's husband, David Hooks.

"You're trying to get rid of me," Grey said.

"I'm not," Billy said. "You've been here all day, practically. I just want the comfort of knowing that you're being fed and looked after. I think you should go soon."

"It's too early," said Grey. "Fathers don't have to leave when visiting hours are over."

"You're not a father yet," Billy said. "Go."

After he left she waited by the window to watch him cross the street and wait for the bus. It was dark and cold and it had begun to sleet. When she saw him she felt pierced with desolation. He was wearing his old camel's hair coat and the wind blew through his wavy hair. He stood back on his heels as he had as a boy. He turned around and scanned the building for her window. When he saw her, he waved and smiled. Billy waved back. A taxi, thinking it was being hailed, stopped. Grey got in and was driven off.

Every three hours a nurse appeared to take her temperature, blood pressure, and pulse. After Grey had gone, the night nurse appeared. She was a tall, middle-aged black woman named Mrs. Perch. In her hand she carried what looked like a suitcase full of dials and wires.

"Don't be alarmed," Mrs. Perch said. She had a soft West Indian accent. "It is only a portable fetal heart monitor. You get to say good morning and good evening to your baby."

She squirted a blob of cold blue jelly on Billy's stomach and pushed a transducer around in it, listening for the beat. At once Billy heard the sound of galloping hooves. Mrs. Perch timed the beats against her watch.

"Nice and healthy," Mrs. Perch said.

"Which part of this baby is where?" Billy said.

"Well, his head is back here, and his back is there and here is the rump and his feet are near your ribs. Or hers, of course."

"I wondered if that was a foot kicking," Billy said.

"My second boy got his foot under my rib and kicked with all his might," Mrs. Perch said.

Billy sat up in bed. She grabbed Mrs. Perch's hand. "Is this baby going to be all right?" she said.

"Oh my, yes," Mrs. Perch said. "You're not a very interesting case. Many others much more complicated than you have done very well and you will, too."

At four in the morning, another nurse appeared, a florid Englishwoman. Billy had spent a restless night, her heart pounding, her throat dry.

"Your pressure's up, dear," said the nurse, whose tag read "M. Whitely." "Dr. Bell has written orders that if your pressure goes up you're to have a shot of hydralazine. It doesn't hurt baby—did he explain that to you?"

"Yes," said Billy groggily.

"It may give you a little headache."

"What else?"

"That's all," Miss Whitely said.

Billy fell asleep and woke with a pounding headache. When she rang the bell, the nurse who had admitted her appeared. Her name was Bonnie Near and she was Billy's day nurse. She gave Billy a pill and then taped a tongue depressor wrapped in gauze over her bed.

"What's that for?" Billy said.

"Don't ask," said Bonnie Near.

"I want to know."

Bonnie Near sat down at the end of the bed. She was a few years older than Billy, trim and wiry with short hair and tiny diamond earrings.

"It's hospital policy," she said. "The hydralazine gives you a headache, right? You ring to get something to make it go away and because you have high blood pressure everyone assumes that the blood pressure caused it, not the drug. So this thing gets taped above your bed in the one chance in about fifty-five million that you have a convulsion."

Billy turned her face away and stared out the window.

"Hey, hey," said Bonnie Near. "None of this. I noticed yesterday that you're quite a worrier. Are you like this when you're not in the hospital? Listen. I'm a straight shooter and I would tell you if I was worried about you. I'm not. You're just the common garden variety."

Every morning Grey appeared with two cups of coffee and the morning paper. He sat in a chair and he and Billy read the paper together as they did at home.

"Is the house still standing?" Billy asked after several days. "Are the banks open? Did you bring the mail? I feel I've been here ten months instead of a week."

"The mail was very boring," Grey said. "Except for this booklet from the Wisconsin Loon Society. You'll be happy to know that you can order a record called 'Loon Music.' Would you like a copy?"

"If I moved over," Billy said, "would you take off your jacket and lie down next to me?"

Grey took off his jacket and shoes, and curled up next to Billy. He pressed his nose into her face and looked as if he could drift off to sleep in a second.

"Childworld called about the crib," he said into her neck. "They want to know if we want white paint or natural pine. I said natural."

"That's what I think I ordered," Billy said. "They let the husbands stay over in this place. They call them 'dads.'"

"I'm not a dad yet, as you pointed out," Grey said. "Maybe they'll just let me take naps here."

There was a knock on the door. Grey sprang to his feet and Jordan Bell appeared.

"Don't look so nervous, Billy," he said. "I have good news. I think we want to get this baby born if your pressure isn't going to go down. I think we ought to induce you."

Billy and Grey were silent.

"The way it works is that we put you on a drip of Pitocin, which is a synthetic of the chemical your brain produces when you go into labor."

"We know," Billy said. "Katherine went over it in childbirth class." Katherine Walden was Jordan Bell's nurse. "When do you want to do this?"

"Tomorrow," Jordan Bell said. "Katherine will come over and give you your last Lamaze class right here."

"And if it doesn't work?"

"It usually does," said Jordan Bell. "And if it doesn't, we do a second-day induction."

"And if that doesn't work?"

"It generally does. If it doesn't, we do a cesarean, but you'll be awake and Grey can hold your hand."

"Oh what fun," said Billy.

When Jordan Bell left, Billy burst into tears.

"Why isn't anything normal?" she said. "Why do I have to lie here day after day listening to other people's babies crying? Why is my body betraying me like this?"

Grey kissed her and then took her hands. "There is no such thing as normal," he said. "Everyone we've talked to has some story or other—huge babies that won't budge, thirty-hour labors. A cesarean is a perfectly respectable way of being born."

"What about me? What about me getting all stuck up with tubes and cut up into little pieces?" Billy said, and she was instantly ashamed. "I hate being like this. I feel I've lost myself and some whimpering, whining person has taken me over."

"Think about how in two months we'll have a two-month-old baby to take to the park."

"Do you really think everything is going to be all right?" Billy said.

"Yes," said Grey. "I do. In six months we'll be in Maine."

*   *   *

Billy lay in bed with her door closed reading her brochure from the Loon Society. She thought about the cottage she and Grey rented every August in Jewell Neck, Maine, on a lagoon. There at night with blackness all around them and not a light to be seen, they heard hoot owls and loons calling their night cries to one another. Loon mothers carried their chicks on their back, Billy knew. The last time she had heard those cries she had been just three months pregnant. The next time she heard them she would have a child.

She thought about the baby shower Penny had given her—a lunch party for ten women. At the end of it, Billy and Grey's unborn child had received cotton and wool blankets, little sweaters, tiny garments with feet, and two splendid Teddy bears. The Teddy bears had sat on the coffee table. Billy remembered the strange, light feeling in her chest as she looked at them. She had picked them both up and laughed with astonishment.

At a red light on the way home in a taxi, surrounded by boxes and bags of baby presents, she saw something that made her heart stop: Francis Clemens, who for two years had been Billy's illicit lover.

With the exception of her family, Billy was close only to Grey and Penny Stern. She had never been the subject of anyone's romantic passion. She and Grey, after all, had been fated to marry. She had loved him all her life.

Francis had pursued her: no one had ever pursued her before. The usual signs of romance were as unknown to Billy as the workings of a cyclotron. Crushes, she had felt, were for children. She did not really believe that adults had them.

Without her knowing it, she was incubating a number of curious romantic diseases. One day when Francis came to visit wearing his tweed coat and the ridiculously long paisley scarf he affected, she realized that she had fallen in love.

The fact of Francis was the most exotic thing that had ever happened in Billy's fairly stolid, uneventful life. He was as brilliant as a painted bunting. He was also, in marked contrast to Billy, beautifully dressed. He did not know one tree from another. He felt all birds were either robins or crows. He was avowedly urban and his pleasures were urban. He loved opera, cocktail parties, and lunches. They did not agree about economic theory, either.

Nevertheless, they spent what now seemed to Billy an enormous amount of time together. She had not sought anything like this. If her own case had been presented to her she would have dismissed it as messy, unnecessary, and somewhat sordid, but when she fell in love she fell as if backward into a swimming pool. For a while she felt dazed. Then Francis became a fact in her life. But in the end she felt her life was being ruined.

She had not seen Francis for a long time. In that brief glance at the red light she saw his paisley scarf, its long fringes flapping in the breeze. It was amazing that someone who had been so close to her did not know that she was having a baby. As the cab pulled away, she did not look back at him. She stared rigidly frontward, flanked on either side by presents for her unborn child.

The baby kicked. Mothers-to-be should not be lying in hospital beds thinking about illicit love affairs, Billy thought. Of course, if you were like the other mothers on the maternity floor and probably had never had an illicit love affair, you would not be punished by lying in the hospital in the first place. You would go into labor like everyone else, and come rushing into Maternity Admitting with your husband and your suitcase. By this time tomorrow she would have her baby in her arms, just like everyone else, but she drifted off to sleep thinking of Francis nonetheless.

At six in the morning, Bonnie Near woke her.

"You can brush your teeth," she said. "But don't drink any water. And your therapist is here to see you, but don't be long."

The door opened and Penny walked in.

"And how are we today?" she said. "Any strange dreams or odd thoughts?"

"How did you get in here?" Billy said.

"I said I was your psychiatrist and that you were being induced today and so forth," Penny said. "I just came to say good luck.

Here's all the change we had in the house. Tell Grey to call constantly. I'll see you all tonight."

Billy was taken to the labor floor and hooked up to a fetal heart monitor whose transducers were kept on her stomach by a large elastic cummerbund. A stylish-looking nurse wearing hospital greens, a string of pearls, and perfectly applied pink lipstick poked her head through the door.

"Hi!" she said in a bright voice. "I'm Joanne Kelly. You're my patient today." She had the kind of voice and smile Billy could not imagine anyone's using in private. "Now, how are we? Fine? All right. Here's what we're going to do. First of all, we're going to put this IV into your arm. It will only hurt a little and then we're going to hook you up to something called Pitocin. Has Dr. Bell explained any of this to you?" Joanne Kelly said.

"All," said Billy.

"Neat," Joanne Kelly said. "We *like* an informed patient. Put your arm out, please."

Billy stuck out her arm. Joanne Kelly wrapped a rubber thong under her elbow.

"Nice veins," she said. "You would have made a lovely junkie.

"Now we're going to start the Pitocin," Joanne Kelly said. "We start off slow to see how you do. Then we escalate." She looked Billy up and down. "Okay," she said. "We're off and running. Now, I've got a lady huffing and puffing in the next room so I have to go and coach her. I'll be back real soon."

Billy lay looking at the clock, or watching the Pitocin and glucose drip into her arm. She could not get a comfortable position and the noise of the fetal heart monitor was loud and harsh. The machine itself spat out a continual line of data.

Jordan Bell appeared at the foot of her bed.

"An exciting day—yes, Billy?" he said. "What time is Grey coming?"

"I told him to sleep late," Billy said. "All the nurses told me that this can take a long time. How am I supposed to feel when it starts working?"

"If all goes well, you'll start to have contractions and then they'll get stronger and then you'll have your baby."

"Just like that?" said Billy.

"Pretty much just like that."

But by five o'clock in the afternoon nothing much had happened.

Grey sat in a chair next to the bed. From time to time he checked the data. He had been checking it all day.

"That contraction went right off the paper," he said. "What did it feel like?"

"Intense," Billy said. "It just doesn't hurt."

"You're still in the early stages," said Jordan Bell when he came to check her. "I'm willing to stay on if you want to continue, but the baby might not be born till tomorrow."

"I'm beat," said Billy.

"Here's what we can do," Jordan said. "We can keep going or we start again tomorrow."

"Tomorrow," said Billy.

She woke up exhausted with her head pounding. The sky was cloudy and the glare hurt her eyes. She was taken to a different labor room.

In the night her blood pressure had gone up. She had begged not to have a shot—she did not see how she could go into labor feeling so terrible, but the shot was given. It had been a long, sleepless night.

She lay alone with a towel covering one eye, trying to sleep, when a nurse appeared by her side. This one looked very young, had curly hair, and thick, slightly rose-tinted glasses. Her tag read "Eva Gottlieb." Underneath she wore a button inscribed EVA: WE DELIVER.

"Hi," said Eva Gottlieb. "I'm sorry I woke you, but I'm your nurse for the day and I have to get you started."

"I'm here for a lobotomy," Billy said. "What are you going to do to me?"

"I'm going to run a line in you," Eva Gottlieb said. "And then I don't know what. Because your blood pressure is high, I'm supposed to wait until Jordan gets here." She looked at Billy carefully. "I know it's scary," she said. "But the worst that can happen is that you have to be sectioned and that's not bad."

Billy's head throbbed.

"That's easy for you to say," she said. "I'm the section."

Eva Gottlieb smiled. "I'm a terrific nurse," she said. "I'll stay with you."

Tears sprang in Billy's eyes. "Why will you?"

"Well, first of all, it's my job," said Eva. "And second of all, you look like a reasonable person."

Billy looked at Eva carefully. She felt instant, total trust. Perhaps that was part of being in hospitals and having babies. Everyone you came in contact with came very close, very fast.

Billy's eyes hurt. Eva was hooking her up to the fetal heart monitor. Her touch was strong and sure, and she seemed to know Billy did not want to be talked to. She flicked the machine on, and Billy heard the familiar sound of galloping hooves.

"Is there any way to turn it down?" Billy said.

"Sure," said Eva. "But some people find it consoling."

As the morning wore on, Billy's blood pressure continued to rise. Eva was with her constantly.

"What are they going to do to me?" Billy asked.

"I think they're probably going to give you magnesium sulfate to get your blood pressure down and then they're going to section you. Jordan does a gorgeous job, believe me. I won't let them do anything to you without explaining it first, and if you get out of bed first thing tomorrow and start moving around you'll be fine."

Twenty minutes later, a doctor Billy had never seen before administered a dose of magnesium sulfate.

"Can't you do this?" Billy asked Eva.

"It's heavy-duty stuff," Eva said. "It has to be done by a doctor."

"Can they wait until my husband gets here?"

"It's too dangerous," said Eva. "It has to be done. I'll stay with you."

The drug made her hot and flushed, and brought her blood

pressure straight down. For the next hour, Billy tried to sleep. She had never been so tired. Eva brought her cracked ice to suck on and a cloth for her head. The baby wiggled and writhed, and the fetal heart monitor gauged its every move. Finally, Grey and Jordan Bell were standing at the foot of her bed.

"Okay, Billy," said Jordan. "Today's the day. We must get the baby out. I explained to Grey about the mag sulfate. We both agree that you must have a cesarean."

"When?" Billy said.

"In the next hour," said Jordan. "I have to check two patients and then we're off to the races."

"What do you think," Billy asked Grey.

"It's right," Grey said.

"And what about you?" Billy said to Eva.

"It has to be done," Eva said.

Jordan Bell was smiling a genuine smile and he looked dashing and happy.

"Why is he so uplifted?" Billy asked Eva after he had dashed down the hall.

"He loves the OR," she said. "He loves deliveries. Think of it this way: you're going to get your baby at last."

Billy lay on a gurney, waiting to be rolled down the hall. Grey, wearing hospital scrubs, stood beside her holding her hand. She had been prepped and given an epidural anesthetic, and she could no longer feel her legs.

"Look at me," she said to Grey. "I'm a mass of tubes. I'm a miracle of modern science." She put his hand over her eyes.

Grey squatted down to put his head near hers. He looked expectant, exhausted, and worried, but when he saw her scanning his face he smiled.

"It's going to be swell," Grey said. "We'll find out if it's little William or little Ella."

Billy's heart was pounding but she thought she ought to say something to keep her side up. She said, "I knew we never should have had sexual intercourse." Grey gripped her hand tight and smiled. Eva laughed. "Don't you guys leave me," Billy said.

Billy was wheeled down the hall by an orderly. Grey held one hand, Eva held the other. Then they left her to scrub.

She was taken to a large, pale green room. Paint was peeling on the ceiling in the corner. An enormous lamp hung over her head. The anesthetist appeared and tapped her feet.

"Can you feel this?" he said.

"It doesn't feel like feeling," Billy said. She was trying to keep her breathing steady.

"Excellent," he said.

Then Jordan appeared at her feet, and Grey stood by her head. Eva bent down. "I know you'll hate this, but I have to tape your hands down, and I have to put this oxygen mask over your face. It comes off as soon as the baby's born, and it's good for you and the baby."

Billy took a deep breath. The room was very hot. A screen was placed over her chest.

"It's so you can't see," said Eva. "Here's the mask. I know it'll freak you out, but just breathe nice and easy. Believe me, this is going to be fast."

Billy's arms were taped, her legs were numb, and a clear plastic mask was placed over her nose and mouth. She was so frightened she wanted to cry out, but it was impossible. Instead she breathed as Katherine Walden had taught her to. Every time a wave of panic rose, she breathed it down. Grey held her hand. His face was blank and his glasses were fogged. His hair was covered by a green cap and his brow was wet. There was nothing she could do for him, except squeeze his hand.

"Now, Billy," said Jordan Bell, "you'll feel something cold on your stomach. I'm painting you with Betadine. All right, here we go."

Billy felt something like dull tugging. She heard the sound of foamy water. Then she felt the baby being slipped from her. She turned to Grey. His glasses had unfogged and his eyes were round as quarters. She heard a high, angry scream.

"Here's your baby," said Jordan Bell. "It's a beautiful, healthy boy."

Eva lifted the mask off Billy's face.

"He's perfectly healthy," Eva said. "Listen to those lungs." She took the baby to be weighed and tested. Then she came back to Billy. "He's perfect but he's little—just under five pounds. We have to take him upstairs to the preemie nursery. It's policy when they're not five pounds."

"Give him to me," Billy said. She tried to free her hands but they were securely taped.

"I'll bring him to you," Eva said. "But he can't stay down here. He's too small. It's for the baby's safety, I promise you. Look, here he is."

The baby was held against her forehead. The moment he came near her he stopped shrieking. He was mottled and wet.

"Please let me have him," Billy said.

"He'll be fine," Eva said. They then took him away.

The next morning Billy rang for the nurse and demanded that her IV be disconnected. Twenty minutes later she was out of bed slowly walking.

"I feel as if someone had crushed my pelvic bones," Billy said.

"Someone did," said the nurse.

Two hours later she was put into a wheelchair and pushed by a nurse into the elevator and taken to the Infant Intensive Care Unit. At the door the nurse said, "I'll wheel you in."

"I can walk," Billy said. "But thank you very much."

Inside, she was instructed to scrub with surgical soap and to put on a sterile gown. Then she walked very slowly and very stiffly down the hall. A Chinese nurse stopped her.

"I'm William Delielle's mother," she said. "Where is he?"

The nurse consulted a clipboard and pointed Billy down a hallway. Another nurse in a side room pointed to an isolette—a large plastic case with porthole windows. There on a white cloth lay her child.

He was fast asleep, his little arm stretched in front of him, an exact replica of Grey's sleeping posture. On his back were two discs the size of nickels hooked up to wires that measured his temperature and his heart and respiration rates on a console above his isolette. He was long and skinny and beautiful.

"He looks like a little chicken," said Billy. "May I hold him?"

"Oh, no," said the nurse. "Not for a while. He mustn't be stressed." She gave Billy a long look and said, "But you can open the windows and touch him."

Billy opened the porthole window and touched his leg. He shivered slightly. She wanted to disconnect his probes, scoop him up, and hold him next to her. She stood quietly, her hand resting lightly on his calf.

The room was bright, hot, and busy. Nurses came and went, washing their hands, checking charts, making notes, diapering, changing bottles of glucose solution. There were three other children in the room. One was very tiny and had a miniature IV attached to a vein in her head. A pink card was taped on her isolette. Billy looked on the side of William's isolette. There was a blue card and in Grey's tiny printing was written "William Delielle."

Later in the morning, when Grey appeared in her room he found Billy sitting next to a glass-encased pump.

"This is the well-known electric breast pump. Made in Switzerland," Billy said.

"It's like the medieval clock at Salisbury Cathedral," Grey said, peering into the glass case. "I just came from seeing William. He's much *longer* than I thought. I called all the grandparents. In fact, I was on the telephone all night after I left you." He gave her a list of messages. "They're feeding him in half an hour."

Billy looked at her watch. She had been instructed to use the pump for three minutes on each breast to begin with. Her milk, however, would not be given to William, who, the doctors said, was too little to nurse. He would be given carefully measured formula, and Billy would eventually have to wean him from the bottle and onto herself. The prospect of this seemed very remote.

As the days went by, Billy's room filled with flowers, but she spent most of her time in the Infant ICU. She could touch William but not hold him. The morning before she was to be discharged, Billy went to William's eight o'clock feeding. She thought how lovely it would be to feed him at home, how they might sit in the rocking chair and watch the birds in the garden below. In William's present home, there was no morning and no night. He had never been in a dark room, or heard bird sounds or traffic noise, or felt a cool draft.

William was asleep on his side wearing a diaper and a little T-shirt. The sight of him seized Billy with emotion.

"You can hold him today," the nurse said.

"Yes?"

"Yes, and you can feed him today, too."

Billy bowed her head. She took a steadying breath. "How can I hold him with all this hardware on him?" she said.

"I'll show you," said the nurse. She disconnected the console, reached into the isolette, and gently untaped William's probes. Then she showed Billy how to change him, put on his T-shirt, and swaddle him in a cotton blanket. In an instant he was in Billy's arms.

He was still asleep, but he made little screeching noises and wrinkled his nose. He moved against her and nudged his head into her arm. The nurse led her to a rocking chair and for the first time she sat down with her baby.

All around her, lights blazed. The radio was on and a sweet male voice sang, "I want you to be mine, I want you to be mine, I want to take you home, I want you to be mine."

William opened his eyes and blinked. Then he yawned and began to cry.

"He's hungry," the nurse said, putting a small bottle into Billy's hand.

She fed him and burped him, and then she held him in her arms and rocked him to sleep. In the process she fell asleep, too, and was woken by the nurse and Grey, who had come from work.

"You must put him back now," said the nurse. "He's been out a long time and we don't want to stress him."

"It's awful to think that being with his mother creates stress," Billy said.

"Oh, no!" the nurse said. "That's not what I mean. I mean, in his isolette it's temperature controlled."

* * *

Once Billy was discharged from the hospital she had to commute to see William. She went to the two morning feedings, came home for a nap, and met Grey for the five o'clock. They raced out for dinner and came back for the eight. Grey would not let Billy stay for the eleven.

Each morning she saw Dr. Edmunds, the head of neonatology. He was a tall, slow-talking, sandy-haired man with horn-rimmed glasses.

"I know you will never want to hear this under any other circumstances," he said to Billy, "but your baby is very boring."

"How boring?"

"Very boring. He's doing just what he ought to do." William had gone to the bottom of his growth curve and was beginning to gain. "As soon as he's a little fatter he's all yours."

Billy stood in front of his isolette watching William sleep.

"This is like having an affair with a married man," Billy said to the nurse who was folding diapers next to her.

The nurse looked at her uncomprehendingly.

"I mean you love the person but can only see him at certain times," said Billy.

The nurse was young and plump. "I guess I see what you mean," she said.

At home William's room was waiting. The crib had been delivered and put together by Grey. While Billy was in the hospital, Grey had finished William's room. The Teddy bears sat on the shelves. A mobile of ducks and geese hung over the crib. Grey had bought a secondhand rocking chair and had painted it red. Billy had thought she would be unable to face William's empty room. Instead she found she could scarcely stay out of it. She folded and refolded his clothes, reorganized his drawers, arranged his crib blankets. She decided what should be his homecoming clothes and set them out on the changing table along with a cotton receiving blanket and a wool shawl.

But even though he did not look at all fragile and he was beginning to gain weight, it often felt to Billy that she would never have him. She and Grey had been told ten days to two weeks from day of birth. One day when she felt she could not stand much more Billy was told that she might try nursing him.

Touch him on his cheek. He will turn to you. Guide him toward the breast and the magical connection will be made.

Billy remembered this description from her childbirth books. She had imagined a softly lit room, a sense of peacefulness, some soft, sweet music in the background.

She was put behind a screen in William's room, near an isolette containing an enormous baby who was having breathing difficulties.

She was told to keep on her sterile gown, and was given sterile water to wash her breasts with. At the sight of his mother's naked bosom, William began to howl. The sterile gown dropped onto his face. Billy began to sweat. All around her, the nurses chatted, clattered, and dropped diapers into metal bins and slammed the tops down.

"Come on, William," Billy said. "The books say that this is the blissful union of mother and child."

But William began to scream. The nurse appeared with the formula bottle and William instantly stopped screaming and began to drink happily.

"Don't worry," the nurse said. "He'll catch on."

At night at home she sat by the window. She could not sleep. She had never felt so separated from anything in her life. Grey, to distract himself, was stenciling the wall under the molding in William's room. He had found an early American design of wheat and cornflowers. He stood on a ladder in his blue jeans carefully applying the stencil in pale blue paint.

One night Billy went to the door of the baby's room to watch him, but Grey was not on the ladder. He was sitting in the rocking chair with his head in his hands. His shoulders were shaking slightly. He had the radio on, and he did not hear her.

He had been so brave and cheerful. He had held her hand while William was born. He had told her it was like watching a magician sawing his wife in half. He had taken photos of William in his isolette and sent them to their parents and all their friends. He had read up on growth curves and had bought Billy a book on breast-feeding. He had also purloined his hospital greens to wear each year on William's birthday. Now *he* had broken down.

She made a noise coming into the room and then bent down and stroked his hair. He smelled of soap and paint thinner. She put her arms around him, and she did not let go for a long time.

Three times a day, Billy tried to nurse William behind a screen and each time she ended up giving him his formula.

Finally she asked a nurse, "Is there some room I could sit in alone with this child?"

"We're not set up for it," the nurse said. "But I could put you in the utility closet."

There amidst used isolettes and cardboard boxes of sterile water, on the second try William nursed for the first time. She touched his cheek. He turned to her, just as it said in the book. Then her eyes crossed.

"Oh, my God!" she said.

A nurse walked in.

"Hurts, right?" she said. "Good for him. That means he's got it. It won't hurt for long."

At his evening feeding he howled again.

"The course of true love never did run smooth," said Grey. He and Billy walked slowly past the park on their way home. It was a cold, wet night.

"I am a childless mother," Billy said.

Two days later William was taken out of his isolette and put into a plastic bin. He had no temperature or heart probes, and Billy could pick him up without having to disconnect anything. At his evening feeding when the unit was quiet, she took him out in the hallway and walked up and down with him.

The next day she was greeted by Dr. Edmunds.

"I've just had a chat with your pediatrician," he said. "How would you like to take your boring baby home with you?"

"When?" said Billy.

"Right now, if you have his clothes," Dr. Edmunds said. "Dr. Jacobson will be up in a few minutes and can officially release him."

She ran down the hall and called Grey.

"Go home and get William's things," she said. "They're springing him. Come and get us."

"You mean we can just walk out of there with him?" Grey said. "I mean, just take him under our arm? He barely knows us."

"Just get here. And don't forget the blankets."

A nurse helped Billy dress William. He was wrapped in a green and white receiving blanket and covered in a white wool shawl. On his head was a blue and green knitted cap. It slipped slightly sideways, giving him a raffish look.

They were accompanied in the elevator by a nurse. It was hospital policy that a nurse hold the baby, and hand it over at the door.

It made Billy feel light-headed to be standing out of doors with her child. She felt she had just robbed a bank and got away with it.

In the taxi, Grey gave the driver their address.

"Not door to door," Billy said. "Can we get out at the avenue and walk down the street just like everyone else?"

When the taxi stopped, they got out carefully. The sky was full of silver clouds and the air was blustery and cold. William squinted at the light and wrinkled his nose.

Then, with William tight in Billy's arms, the three of them walked down the street just like everyone else.

EDITOR'S AFTERNOTE

In her junior year of high school, Laurie Colwin's English class was assigned to write short stories and submit them to the Atlantic Monthly competition. Colwin was the only one who didn't receive an honorable mention. At the time of her death in 1992 at age forty-eight, however, she had ten books to her name, among them the novels *Happy All the Time* and *A Big*

Storm Knocked It Over, and had become one of the most beloved authors of the baby-boomer generation.

Readers credited her with genius, comparing her to Jane Austin, but Colwin refused this descriptor, many times citing her numerous deficiencies with characteristic amusement. "For instance, I can't sew," she once said. "There's a woman upstairs who makes all my kid's nightgowns. I can't speak a foreign language, I don't understand deconstructionism . . . I went to the bank the other day and realized that by accident I had actually balanced my checkbook! It was so unusual I told a perfect stranger."

She was devoted to her family. That, in turn, imbued her popular collections of food essays, *Home Cooking* and *More Home Cooking,* with warmth and a sense of home.

Speaking of her afternoon ritual, which began at the Manhattan apartment where she, her husband, and her daughter, Rosa, lived, she said, "I have this little dog trot that I do. I go from here to Rosa's school to the L&S Dairy, a tiny little store, where we have our ice pop . . . We sit at a little table, and that's our tea, that's our little teatime."

Becoming a Mother
Ally Sheedy

Becoming a mother
makes me think
of my parents' divorce.

Being a little girl and knowing
it was my fault.
Cleaning my room obsessively
Trying to be good
to make it better
to put everything back neatly safely
like it was.

Becoming a mother
makes me remember
loneliness
and fear.
Not having friends
wearing a pigtail
giving my money to the man on the corner
who threatened me.

Becoming a mother
makes me recall
copying words out of a book—
a poem about a turtle, I believe—
tearing out the printed page
and stuffing it under the radiator
so she would never find it.
Telling her I wrote it myself.
Wanting her to believe me desperately more than
life itself.

Becoming a mother
makes me recall
cutting out clumps
of mats from my hair
and hiding them around my room.
Hoping against hope no one would discover
tangles
on my head
and tug and tear and yell
about the waste of time.
I wanted to be a little girl that didn't
Have these aberrations
Who didn't grab on someone's day
and throw it away
on my mistakes.

Becoming a mother
makes me remember
hating asparagus
running away from home
throwing the boiled egg yolks from kosher
    chicken soup
out the window to watch them bounce
being afraid for my brother and sister
scrubbing the toilet on Wednesdays

feeling too small to fight anyone
and too big to cry.

Becoming a mother
makes me think
of the pain of childhood
of the loneliness, of the powerlessness
of being weak in the world.
It fills me with anxiety and dread
having to go through it all again
from the other side.
But some hope—faint hope—I suppose, too
That this time it won't be like that
That I will make it different for my baby
I will heal it
I will transform it
This time it will change.
And so will all my memories.

But honestly—then—
I don't think—
I can really—
believe that.

EDITOR'S AFTERNOTE

While she is prominent as an actress for her roles in *St. Elmo's Fire*, *The Breakfast Club*, *Betsy's Wedding*, and the recent improvisational films *Chantilly Lace* and *Parallel Lives*, many people don't realize that Ally Sheedy has a strong connection to the literary life. Her articles have appeared in *Ms.* and *The Village Voice*, and a collection of her poetry, *Yesterday I Saw the Sun*, was published in 1991 by Summit Books.

What's more surprising is that she wrote her first book at age twelve, the best-selling children's book *She Was Nice to Mice*.

Clouds Across the Moon
Kathryn Lynn Davis

Scottish Highlands
1870

The first thing Morna noticed when she woke was the silence. So strange and unnatural in the wake of the pain and exhaustion, the blindness that had come upon her like the mist at gloaming.

She moaned and opened her eyes as memory cracked the shell that sleep had formed around her. Terrified, she stared at the rumpled, bloody sheets and the wild, damp tangle of her hair, until the pain in her battered body made her remember. She closed her eyes and shook her head in disbelief and denial.

"Aye, 'tis alive ye are, *mo-ghraidh,* though I brought ye back from the edge more than once. Forbye, I doubt ye'll be thanking me for that. At least no' yet."

Slowly, the voice penetrated her tightly closed eyes, and Morna recognized the soothing inflections of Braida, the midwife and healer.

"But look ye at this, and mayhap 'twill change all."

Morna had not yet found her way out of the fog when she felt a weight against her chest and opened her eyes to see Braida reaching out with a small swaddled bundle in her arms. For an instant, Morna shrank back, remembering too vividly other arms that had reached for her in need. She hadn't been strong enough to carry that burden, and was not certain she wanted this one. She was afraid, deep down afraid, as she had never been before.

It was too quiet.

Before she could protest, the baby was in her arms and she looked into its wee, scrunched face and something split open inside her vulnerable heart, which beat sluggishly, weakened by the battle of a difficult delivery, drained by the birth of the baby she had not meant to conceive. She was only sixteen, and lost.

But when she reached out gingerly to touch her daughter's cheek, her tightly curled fist, the veins that pulsed beneath her skin, an unfamiliar rush of feeling overwhelmed Morna. The baby turned its head and Morna looked into the small dark eyes just like her own; emotion consumed her. She let it overtake her, body and soul, staring in wonder, in gratitude, in panic at the child in her arms. She held it cautiously, possessively against her heart. Several long minutes passed while silence fell in transparent curtains between the three people in the room, holding each apart from the other.

In a trance, Morna looked up, startled by her reflection in a nearby mirror. Her ordeal must have transformed her more than she thought. She stared at the image of her face until it came to her that this was not a mirror, but a portrait her husband had painted of her months before. She frowned. Was that curiously lovely and strangely disquieting woman really her? For the first time since waking, she thought of Bran, hovering in the shadows, watching, waiting in silence. She wanted to share her exultation with him, and turned to find him staring at her with a peculiar and unreadable expression. His pallid face and absolute stillness unnerved her.

Trying to fight free of the bands of pain and confusion that bound her, Morna lifted their child toward him.

Bran waited until the midwife backed away from the bed, then, one step at a time, he moved toward the bundle held tightly in his wife's hands. Without a word, he bent to look inside the hand-woven blankets at the tiny squirming body. His stiff, blank face softened when he touched the baby and her fingers closed around his. His pale eyes blazed with sudden warmth, and his hand trembled uncontrollably as he brushed the red down on the baby's head. "She's fair, like me. Will her hair turn blond do ye think?" His own blond hair was long enough to brush his daughter's cheek, and his reddish beard the color of her short, fine curls. Then his fingers froze above a discoloration on the baby's temple, a small tracery of fragile veins, a pattern of color and pulse of blood that did not belong on that red, wrinkled face.

He turned to the midwife accusingly, distraught. "What have ye done? I ken what the people say about ye—that ye 'see' things and cast your spells over man and beast." He sounded more afraid than angry.

Braida glided forward and gently stroked the light blue veins. "'Twas no' me, but the fairies putting their mark on her at birth. 'Tis a sign your child is special, chosen. Though all will no' see it that way. Some will fear her in their ignorance and superstition." She peered intently at Morna's husband. "Would ye be one of those, Mr. Campbell?" She had to tilt her head back to see his face. Surely his ancestors had been the Norsemen who'd conquered and abandoned the Scottish isles long since. He was so tall and lean and fair and his eyes so cool and blue that she could not read them.

Bran straightened to his full height. "I'm twenty-five years old, and well educated. I'd no' be sharin' the superstitions of pagans who live in the past among kelpies and fairies." He leaned down to kiss his wife and new daughter, to prove he meant it, but still he seemed uneasy.

Braida smiled with knowing compassion.

Morna saw the smile and guessed what the midwife was thinking. Bran was not as free of superstition as he claimed. But Morna wondered if it was merely a lingering wisp of superstition that made her husband wary, or something else, something more disturbing.

The baby flailed her arms, demanding her mother's attention. Delicately, with more devotion than she'd ever felt before, Morna bent her head, enclosing the child in the cloak of her long dark hair, and caressed the pattern of veins on her daughter's temple. Each breath she took ached in her chest. To her, this small flaw made the child more vulnerable, and therefore more precious. She felt her heart begin to beat rapidly in answer to the beat of her baby's heart, her blood to flow in concert with her baby's blood. She had never felt so alone or so connected, so frightened of failure, or been overwhelmed by a love so fierce and tender.

The fire collapsed inward, sending a shower of sparks up the chimney. Automatically, Bran rose to put more peats on the faltering flames.

March had been so cold and wet and gray that day bled into night and night into morning. Inside the Campbell croft, the fire in the rough stone hearth cast animated images across the clay that layered the thick stone walls. Generations of soot had accumulated in the creases and crevices, emphasizing the subtle patterns in the clay. The light from the two oil lamps on the press and the ancient oak table barely penetrated the gloom.

Bran Campbell, who often sought the darkness with its powerful and melancholy currents that inspired his sketches and paintings, yearned now for simple daylight. Hands moving restlessly on the open book in his lap, he contemplated the intimate tableau of his wife seated on the rag rug, legs bent so her skirt did not cover her bare feet, her dark head bowed over their new daughter, Megan. Above her hung a painting of a moor in a storm that Bran had done last spring. The effect would have been somber, except for the luminous quality of light that glowed among the blades of grass, an incandescence that rose from the earth itself. The baby began to cry and Morna whispered, "Hush, little one. Go to sleep and dream ye of the fairies in their ferny grottoes, where the burn is touched with bronze." She rocked Megan rhythmically, kissing the birthmark at her temple. Mother, daughter, and painting were caught in the smoldering firelight, transformed by the orange-gold radiance that surrounded them.

Holding his breath, Bran watched his daughter reach blindly for her mother's hair with tiny wiggling fingers. He was amazed by those fingers, by Megan's grasping hands, by her soft pale skin and downy hair. He was fascinated and terrified by the daughter he had made; she was so small, so ineffably fragile. And the Highlands were not kind to small and fragile things.

To stop the thought from going further, he eyed the painting critically. It, and the portrait of Morna that hung in the loft, were two of the few works he had not burned in a frenzy of self-loathing at his own ineptitude.

He swallowed dryly, wishing it were late spring or summer, the days long and filled with magnificent variations of shadow and light, when he climbed to the shieling on the mountain where he kept his oil paints and canvasses. He was alone there for hours, sometimes days, as he made real the fantasies that swirled in his head. Where was the spring light with the capacity to lift him away from this melancholy croft with its small, low windows covered with shutters and a thick leather curtain to keep out the winter cold? Though the damp and mist crept in nonetheless, diffusing what meager light there was.

Often he wondered why he stayed in this inhospitable place. He told himself he had nowhere else to go, that this croft alone belonged to him; it was his refuge. But sometimes, in brief flashes of self-honesty, he admitted it was safer to stay. His brother had gone to America in search of new adventures and new wealth. Bran could have followed, but he hadn't, because he was a coward. He did not dare to take the risk of failing. The thought humiliated him, and he turned it away like an unwelcome visitor. He had chosen the glen, and to the glen he would always return, despite his desire for new and tantalizing knowledge.

Besides, he had a great deal more than many. He was grateful for his woolen clothes, which, though worn, were as fine as a gentleman farmer's. Bran made his living as a tutor, and had fortunately secured a post as instructor to the laird's children. When there were enough of the crofters' bairns not needed for collecting peats or sewing oats and barley or caring for the animals, Bran Campbell was also the schoolmaster in the glen. He put great stock in his appearance, and was frugal and determined enough to look always like a gentleman.

Bran flipped the pages of his book on astronomy in boredom and frustration. He hated to waste time; usually when he could not paint, at least he could improve his mind. But not tonight. He could not shut out the sound and sight of his wife and daughter amusing themselves in the firelight.

"Morna, are ye no' daft with carin' for that child? How long is't since ye picked up a book, or did aught to make ye use your mind as 'tis meant to be used?"

His wife did not raise her head. "I've no' much energy for that," she lied softly. Her husband did not realize she had no desire to read or expand her mind. It was her heart that concerned her just now. "I'm happy seein' to Megan."

Bran watched Morna with their child. Every time he held his diminutive daughter, he became intimidated and uncertain. He wanted her to know how awed he was by the miracle of her birth, by the remarkable fact that he was her father, but she could not understand words, and words were all he had to give. Yet Morna seemed to communicate with her silently, by touch and the look in her warm dark eyes. Bran was both amazed and envious. He was as solitary as he'd always been, but now it hurt more, because he could see what it was to belong to someone, body and soul, as Megan did to his wife. It would have been like that with him and Morna, except the baby had come to steal his young bride away.

He thought wistfully of the first time he had spotted Morna alone in an isolated clearing.

He'd stood watching from the shelter of the trees for a long time. She looked very young in her simple muslin gown, the skirt tangled around her knees, her slippers cast aside. Her hair was long and dark; it fell loose and wild about her shoulders, though discarded ribbons and pins beside a straw hat told him she had not left home in this delightfully disheveled state. He caught only glimpses of her face, veiled by her hair, but he could see that she was pretty, though not beautiful. Her skin was brown from the sun, her nose slightly irregular, her eyes dark with thin black lashes that did not sweep against her cheeks or conceal her thoughts. He'd liked her at once for her informality in a rigid and formal society; the quality of the fabric and the cut of her gown marked her as a gentleman farmer's daughter. He also admired the graceful curve of her sun-browned neck bent forward while she chewed on the end of her pen, scribbling in a small leather book. Her gaze had been fixed on her writing, her concentration absolute. She frowned as she worked, smiling now and then, as though she'd found a word or phrase that particularly pleased her. Once, when she looked up, staring thoughtfully and wistfully into the distance, he was intrigued by her expression— naïve and strangely wise at once.

He'd pulled his sketch pad from his pile of books and drawn her quickly. He had not touched his charcoal for a long time, and thought his muse had deserted him. But he found her again that day.

From that moment, it was as if he had been bewitched. Bran had been exultant when he'd brought Morna here a year later as his handfast wife. To him, she was a gift and a revelation, a child/woman who made him feel things he had never thought to feel—joy, a sense of belonging, devotion, respect, and more than anything else, hope. He had lost those things long before he lost his muse. She shared his delight in exploring new ideas, his faith that they could do anything, no matter how impractical or unlikely. She *wanted* to learn, to imagine and create, to be more than a gentleman farmer's daughter. He had never thought to find a partner, a worthy partner, until he'd come upon her in that copse. It was difficult for him to tell her this, so he'd simply given her all he had to give or teach.

Once back at home—he could use that word now, she had made it true—he soon learned she was even more intelligent than he'd guessed, and she'd learned quickly from the many books he'd asked her to read, so she would better understand the world, and Bran himself. Books on science and medicine and language, on philosophy and history and the changing world outside the glen. Novels and treatises and works of great antiquity; Morna had devoured them all. She had worked hard, trying to please him, and her passion made him feel powerful and worthwhile.

He smiled.

Sometimes he would sit watching her when she did not know he was there, as he had that first day. He took pleasure in the sight of her head bent over a book, brow furrowed in concentration, her fingers moving deftly across a scrap of paper.

He watched her now, but her hands cradling the baby or wringing out wrappings or enfolding her child in a long soft plaid made him feel empty. She had changed since Megan's birth. Tonight she wore a pale green linsey-woolsey gown he did not recognize, and her hair hung down her back in a thick dark braid. Her feet were bare, the bottoms stained and dirty. Bran stared moodily into the fire, longing for the girl he had found in the clearing.

Morna also watched the fire, entranced by a shower of sparks that she thought beautiful, like glimmering fireflies fleeing up the rough stone chimney and into the starless night. She settled into the glow of the oil lamps, which cast soft, gilded pools of light about the room. Outside, the wind raged, carrying rain and mist on its back, but Morna felt safe in the sturdy croft, made cozy by the lamps and the seductive light of the fire. She was drowsy and contented as she cradled her daughter. She was also aware of Bran's gaze and his silence. He seemed to look deep inside her, searching for something she could not guess at, and to shut her out at the same time. She curled herself around Megan and sighed. Bran wore that unsettling expression more and more often of late. And his silences had become distressingly frequent.

Morna would have been lonely, except for her child and the healer, Braida, who had become her friend. Morna shifted, trying to untangle the skirts of her pale green gown without disturbing Megan. She was grateful to Braida for bringing her the flowing, comfortable gowns. She did not care that they were not as attractive as her own and did not flatter her figure, still swollen from the baby's birth. She did not care that they rarely stayed clean for long, what with moving about on the packed-dirt floor and the milk the baby spit up regularly on Morna's shoulder or her bodice or in her lap. Morna was not interested in what she wore, so long as she could tend her daughter easily. She had never been concerned with what others thought of her clothing anyway.

But Bran cared. She had been here only a month when he hired a woman from the nearest town to teach his wife to put up her long hair in chignons and French twists that made her look older, more like a woman than a girl. Then Bran had hired a seamstress to make her new gowns, not of velvet or satin, but elegant, with fine lines and narrow skirts and cuffed sleeves. Morna enjoyed wearing them at first. Her new clothes and upswept hair made her feel graceful and mature. She would never forget the first time she had come upon him with her hair up, wearing a dove gray gown and kid slippers. Bran had looked stunned for a long moment, and then he had smiled.

" 'Tis very bonnie ye are, my Morna. Beautiful and refined. You're becomin' all I knew ye could be."

The admiration in his voice and eyes had lingered with her for days. But as the novelty wore off, Morna realized the gowns and hairstyles were not as comfortable as her old clothes and loose, flowing hair had been. The woman she saw in the mirror might be beautiful, but Morna was only pretending to be her.

Briefly, she wondered what Bran would think if he knew it was Braida who brought the clothes Morna wore now. No doubt he would not approve.

The people in the glen were leery of Braida; they believed she was a seer, which gave her power and the ability to cast curses upon them. Yet they were quick enough to call her when someone was ill and they needed the herbs and wisdom of a healer. It had always angered Morna that they spit on her and crossed themselves against the evil eye in public, but in private, they begged her to heal their sick. Braida herself did not seem to mind. She had a serenity of spirit that Morna envied.

She touched the baby's brow, ran her finger along the soft white flesh of Megan's cheek. Morna flattened her palm against her daughter's chest and felt the pulse of her heart that echoed Morna's own, the rush of her blood that was also her mother's. Each time Morna touched her child in this way, she felt a tug in her chest, a joy so deep it left her breathless, a bond with the tiny baby woven of centuries of instinct. She held Megan close, inhaling the scent of just-washed skin and the honeysuckle powder that kept her dry. She could feel the minute throb in the baby's throat as Megan lay her head, pulse to pulse, against her mother's neck. Morna was hardly aware of the storm outside and felt no chill from the mist that drifted through the room whenever the rain ceased. Megan was warm, so Morna was warm.

She did not think Bran would understand, and sometimes she pitied him, because he could not experience this miraculous feeling.

Morna adjusted her gown when her daughter had nursed and fallen asleep. Gingerly, she put the baby into the nest of warm sheets and blankets in the old hand-carved cradle she had found in a tumble of forgotten things at the back of the croft. Attempting to brush long tendrils of hair from around her face, she looked longingly at her husband. "The babe is asleep."

Morna went to sit in the chair beside her husband. "I miss ye, *mo-charaid*." But other thoughts and feelings she kept to herself, because she felt fragile and lonely and vulnerable tonight. Most of all, she needed his companionship.

"I miss talking to ye and sharing stories. I love our bairn, but she's no' much for conversation, and her hands are no' as wise or tender." She put her warm hand on Bran's cool arm. The fine golden-red hairs glowed in the firelight, sending a ripple of heat down her body, but Bran did not respond. He was staring moodily into the fire. Pensively, he rested his elbows on the arms of the chair and pressed his palms together.

The image of those hands in the flickering light made Morna ache as she remembered other hands in other drifts of shadow and light.

On the day she had left home, Bran had taken her to the clearing where they'd first met, where the burn rushed by and the light fell through the leaves in dappled patterns on the green, green earth. Morna had been weeping, oblivious to the beauty that usually gave her solace. She had been thinking of her lost sister and her mother's grief.

"Morna-my-heart, ye must listen," Bran had said, gripping her hands tightly, possessively. "I've asked ye to become my handfast wife this day."

Morna was surprised into silence, aware, all at once, of the pounding of her heart and her hands cupped warmly in his grasp. She closed her eyes and breathed deeply of the pine-scented air, making a silent vow. She would not think of what she was leaving behind. She would think only of Bran and the future. He was twenty-four and she only fifteen; he made her feel safe.

Looking up into his face, she remembered clearly how he'd emerged that first day like a wraith from among alder and oak and silver fir. She had not been alarmed. She had learned to expect apparitions that formed in the mist and the soft rain, people who appeared from wood or water or cloudy sky. Later, she'd told him without embarrassment that she'd been spellbound by his blue eyes full of wisdom and turbulence and mystery. She'd admired the blond hair that curled around his collar, the disorder of his wild reddish beard, the promise of his long, thin body and artist's hands. He was the first she'd ever known who shared her own tumultuous feelings.

Now he had asked her to become his wife. She smiled into his eyes, then turned away, frowning. Her family would not come; they would not even speak her name. And both clans were supposed to agree to a handfast marriage. "What of your family?" she asked shakily. "Will they no' be angry if ye come home with a wife?"

His gaze became vacant. "The people who bore me and their

*other son are no part of me, Morna Ramsay. I'd not know them
nor them me if we met on the road to the northern glen."*

*Morna was shocked and stepped back, taking her hands from
his. In the Highlands, family and history were everything. It had
torn her apart to leave behind her own past, her own blood, but
she'd known she had to or she would suffocate in sorrow. She
was numb, enveloped in a protective cocoon. Only this morning
she had left her parents' house, and though she was no farther
than the clearing halfway down the burn, already she was very
far away, her feelings numbed by the sheltering cloak woven
around them. She hoped she was farther still when the pain
finally struck, and the cloak fell away, exposing her damaged
heart. She was not entirely certain she could survive that
moment. Except that she had Bran beside her. Bran, who spoke
of his family in a toneless voice, as if speaking of strangers.*

*He stood cold and distant in his well-cut but well-worn
doublet of tartan, his hat and linen shirt and wool trousers,
much finer than the homespun trousers of the crofters. He wore
boots instead of brogues. He was not poor, then. But what was
he? Who was he? She had never wondered before, had simply
followed instinctively her desire and her delight, until he had
offered to become her husband. Now, for the first time, she
actually considered the future. Until this moment, she'd thought
only of survival. Suddenly, she was very much afraid. "Where
will we go, then? Will we live among strangers?"*

*Her urgency woke him from the trance that had taken him
away. He rested his hand lightly on her shoulder. "I've a house.
The only thing my family left me besides bitterness. A fine stone
croft that's weathered many winters, with a loft so big I had to
build a staircase to reach it."*

*Morna said nothing. She wanted to believe him, needed to
believe. He was all she had, and she loved him. He knew her as
no one else could or cared to, the dark corners as well as the light.
He made her realize how stifled she had been before he came,
how much she could do once she was free. He made her believe in
miracles. No boy or man had ever shown an interest before,
while Bran said he was intoxicated by her, enchanted. He*

showed her so with his tender concern and his desire. She trusted him. She was willing to go anywhere with him. But she could not let go of her past so easily.

"Will ye have me for your husband, mo-charaid? *Will ye declare yourself my wife before the ancient gods of water, air, and land?"*

A year and a day. If both declared it, they would be man and wife for a year and a day. If there were no bairn on the way or in her arms by then, they could decide they did not suit and leave one another to find different partners. She could not bear to think of leaving Bran and his wit, his energy, his tender hands and gentle lips.

"Aye," Morna whispered.

They knelt in the grass beside the burn, faced one another and pressed their palms together. "I, Morna Ramsay, promise, as the men and women of old have promised, that so long as this burn runs, I will be faithful to ye and only to ye. And so I call ye my husband."

Bran stood, their hands still clasped, and held them high in the air, as if in victory. "I, Bran Campbell, hereby declare that we be man and wife. And so it is."

Since that day, one year and one half past, Morna had learned to know her husband better—he who had become legally bound to her in the eyes of the law when the year and a day came and she was carrying his child. The croft was comfortable enough, though she could not ignore the ghosts of his family that she felt in the air of a mist-swathed gloaming. In the early days, she had enjoyed his instruction, for she knew he was much wiser than she. She loved reading, studying, learning of other worlds and other lives and other miracles. And the books kept her from thinking of the family she had left behind.

Most of all, she wanted to please Bran, because she feared always that he would leave her. He was a vagabond, restless when caught in one place. She knew that. Knew too that above all things, she needed stability, a home, a place to belong. And she loved Bran so much, so wildly and unwisely. She could not understand why he had chosen her, taken the time to free her from her childhood burdens and offer her a life, a world.

Gradually, she'd realized Bran's expectations were so great that even he could rarely fulfill them. He was often frustrated at his own inadequacy. He wanted to know everything, to need no one. He was haunted by a fierce and perpetual creativity that churned inside him. Sometimes she feared that he would be consumed by the blaze of his own emotions.

While she studied, Bran had painted large canvases of disturbingly brilliant colors—fantasy landscapes that were somehow familiar and portraits of Morna that were tender or angry, distorted or softened, but which always somehow captured the heart of her.

Sometimes the heavy books Bran gave her and his constant challenges and questions became tiresome. Night after night they discussed the books she had read that day, analyzing, dissecting, inhaling the knowledge like fresh Highland air that they needed to survive. Occasionally, when he was pleased with her, he would leave a sketch on her pillow. She'd cradle it like a treasure and trace the charcoal lines in the flickering light of an oil lamp, smiling, forgetting her irritation.

One day he was passionate and would not leave her side; the next he was lost in an intellectual solitude that had no place for her.

As he was tonight, when he sat tapping his lean fingers together, ignoring her touch.

Morna leaned closer, lips parted in longing and desire, unabashed passion in her eyes. Long wisps of curling hair softened her face, and her hand was warm, beseeching, on his arm. She did not try to hide what she felt, nor did she hesitate to ask.

Bran turned, saw the expression in his wife's eyes, which lured him back from a very long distance. Deliberately, he leaned toward her, and Morna shivered with pleasure when his lips met hers. He took her hand to lift her up and onto his lap, where she rested her head in the hollow of his throat, mesmerized by the pulse that throbbed there. Morna raised her head, he lowered his, and they kissed like lovers who've been long apart and have long thirsted for the sight and heat and touch of one another.

The sun touched Morna's cheek as she awoke, but she knew the rain would soon return. She smiled into the fleeting light as she remembered making love with Bran when they'd woken before dawn. Her husband had wise, beguiling hands that had aroused her body slowly from the last remnants of sleep, then made her quiver with pleasure until her fever was too great, and she clutched him close while color and fire spun in her head. He'd moaned his own release into her ear, and they'd held each other, naked in the darkness.

Instinctively, she reached for the cradle beside the bed and lifted her red-faced daughter into her arms. Megan had been fretful of late, so that Morna held and soothed her more frequently. After whining and shifting restlessly for a while, Megan finally settled at her mother's breast, where the baby suckled, fists curled tight under her chin. Morna turned back to her husband for a kiss, but his half of the heather bed was empty.

She glanced idly toward the curtain where the chamber pot was kept, but stopped, startled, when she saw Bran lying face down, naked on the floor. Morna felt a flicker of apprehension, and her throat was dry when she asked, "What are ye doin'? Did ye fall?"

"No," he said. "I'm resting." He did not turn his head to look at her and his voice was toneless, flat.

Morna chose to ignore the chill that ran down her spine. "Ye'd be more comfortable in bed, and warmer, ye ken."

Again he did not look at her as he answered, "I wanted to be away from there."

Morna's apprehension turned to cold, engulfing fear, but she would not give in. "Usually, ye like to lie here pressed close to me to keep away the chill."

"Do I? But then, this morning your hands were too cold and your body too heavy." He gave a little shudder. "I wanted to be away."

Turning the baby in her arms, Morna looked down at her breasts swollen with milk, her stomach not yet slimmed and taut as it had been before the birth. She knew Bran was speaking literally; her body *was* heavy and unattractive. That frightened her more than it should have. These changes happened to a woman when she bore a child. Bran should have known that. But Morna could not forget that little shudder of revulsion. Her body disgusted him. Deftly, she transferred the fidgety baby from one sore breast to the other, then raised her head obstinately. "But ye made love to me."

"Aye."

A single word uttered woodenly.

"Ye used my body to satisfy your need, but ye could no' bear to lie beside me afterward." Her voice quivered with anger and fear.

Bran did not answer, did not turn his head or meet her gaze. Though she did not want to admit it, Morna was mystified and panicked by her husband's bizarre behavior. There was a long, uncomfortable silence, broken only by the whimpering of the baby, who had sensed the tension in her mother's voice.

Bran acted as if his wife were not present, but she could not know that the image lingering in his eyes was of Morna turning away after they made love, taking her warmth and the pleasure of her quivering body, turning her back on her husband and reaching out to touch her child. She had done it unconsciously, without thought or hesitation, caressing Megan with a warm hand that Bran could no longer reach. He knew she would never turn to him with that same instinct, the inborn need to shield from harm, that kind of unquestioning and powerful love. In the moment of his abandonment, he'd recognized a bond between mother and daughter that he could not understand, or ever have for himself.

Morna was more angry now than she was frightened. "If ye lie there too long, ye'll make yourself ill." Her voice was not quite steady, and she hated that. Hated letting him hear her vulnerability. A part of her, the core of rage deep inside, said "Let him go." But she couldn't. "Come ye back to bed and get warm." Despite his rigid body and dispassionate voice, she was trying to reach him, but she could feel him slipping away.

Bran rose slowly, stretching his long, lean body in the path of the sunlight, as if oblivious to the cold and to his wife. Languidly, he gathered his clothes from the cupboard, apparently unaware of his daughter's fretting and small cries.

Morna clenched her teeth as he dressed with his back to her. He was going out; she could tell. But she would not ask him where. She'd deny him *that* satisfaction at least.

Without haste or a backward look, he moved toward the top of the stairway that led down from the loft.

Despite her resolution, Morna called out—a sound, not a word. An inarticulate expression of mingled hurt and trepidation.

Bran paused, watching her expectantly.

All at once, Morna was desperate to keep him from leaving her. She loved the child at her breast, but she needed Bran, too. She loved him. He had shown her how to find herself. "If ye wait just a moment, I'll change Megan and put her off to sleep. Then we can lie here and talk about what's worryin' ye."

Bran shook his head. He was as distant as if he'd already gone.

"Then mayhap we can read together. I've missed that, ye ken."

Her husband had missed it too, though he would not tell her so. He missed her listening raptly, the firelight gilding her lovely face as he read to her, or seeing her bowed head as she lost herself in the classics. He loved the curve of her bare white neck bent over an open book. But she had other interests now, more pressing and fulfilling. "Naught would interest me just now."

"We could take a walk together, leave the baby with Braida." Morna despised herself for her desperation.

"Today I'd walk alone."

"Is there aught ye'd do with me this day?"

Bran considered, head tilted. "The only thing I care to do wi' ye is to play chess."

His wife recoiled as if he'd slapped her. Chess: a game with a table between them, and a board, and two mythical armies fighting to destroy each other. A game that made the players not simply opponents, but enemies. A game of strategy and calculation. Morna disliked those things; to her they were cold and mechanical, not food for her imaginative nature. But Bran loved chess, so she'd learned to play—for him. She was not very good; her attention wandered often to the pattern of frost on the windowsill, the flash of warm sunlight on cold crystal snow. She played, but she hated chess. And Bran knew it.

Her husband looked at her with a challenge in his eyes. "I'd like to watch how ye think and plan."

Morna's daughter whimpered as her mother lashed out, "Ye mean *if* I think at all." She held up the baby, cradling her head. "Ye think I only feel now, listen only to my heart. But ye're wrong. And even if 'twere true, I'd rather a soft heart than a cold, ruthless mind."

Shrugging with a studied nonchalance that hid his disappointment but did not warm the cold place at his side where Morna belonged, Bran said, "Will ye play chess with me or no'?"

"No!" she snapped. Megan began to cry, and Morna held her close, murmuring reassurance, brushing her lips over her daughter's cheek. When Bran turned to go, she called out, "Why? Why are ye treatin' me so cruelly?"

He whirled toward her. "Look at ye." He pointed to her tangled hair, the linsey-woolsey gown that lay across a chair, the shoes she had not worn for a week. "Ye've forgotten everything I taught ye. Ye'd no even wash your feet before bed if I didn't remind ye."

Despite the pain of rejection, Morna refused to be broken. "Ye *chose* me because I'd no' dress like the others, because I preferred common sense and comfort to their rules. Ye told me how much courage that took, how much ye admired me for it. And now ye berate me?"

"That was before ye were my wife and I showed ye how to be more. I thought ye'd become a woman, no' a child any longer." His voice was reproachful, but he remembered with painful clarity that when he'd first known her, he had found her slippers abandoned on a rock beside the burn. He'd peered through the leaves of hawthorn and oak, fir and pine until he saw her walking in the middle of the whispering burn, skirts gathered around her thighs, hair tumbling down her back. She'd been oblivious to the long curled ends floating behind her on the water, oblivious to everything but the notebook in her hand. She'd been writing intently while the pale green light of the woods embraced her.

Morna had been free then, and happy. He'd envied her that freedom and that happiness. He brushed the thought away like a wisp of cobweb that clung to his fingertips. "Ye never try to make yourself pretty anymore." He glanced at the cupboard where the gowns he had bought her hung, discarded and forgotten, and felt a small sharp pain between his eyes.

His wife stared at him. "I've no' time for such things."

Bran looked pointedly at the notebook on the stool beside the bed. "Ye never write now. Ye've no' opened your notebooks since Megan was born." It was an accusation.

"Long before that, ye kept me too busy reading, listening, learning all the things ye wanted me to know." But that was only part of the truth. Since she'd left home, it was too painful even to touch the covers of her old notebooks; she could feel the memories through the bound leather. Morna used to love writing down thoughts and descriptions and little stories to distract herself and her sister. The thought brought tears too near the surface and an ache to her dry throat. She had taken no pleasure in her little books since she'd lost Annie.

She and her sister used to share their fantasies, like children. Now, too suddenly, Morna was an adult who had to care for her own child, whimpering pitifully in her arms. Wistfully, she remembered the days when she'd been free to wander loch or burn to cool her feet and weave her stories. That's why she kept the notebook near but never opened it. She wanted the good memories close so she'd not forget them.

Appearing bored, Bran shrugged again and left without a word. Morna sat like stone for a very long time. She wanted to pack her clothes, take Megan and go, leaving Bran and his elegant image of a well-trained wife. Except that she had nowhere to go. Tears of helpless rage and humiliation trickled down her cheeks onto her daughter's face.

Megan's whimpers turned to sobs. Morna had thought the child was upset by the turmoil around her, but now she looked more closely and saw that the baby's skin was flushed, her forehead over-warm, her eyes rimmed in red. Morna forgot Bran and his cruelty. She forgot everything but the baby. So concentrated was she on Megan's hot cheek against her own, that she didn't hear the door slam as her husband left the croft.

Several days later, Morna closed her eyes and nearly drifted into sleep, but Megan's cry jolted her upright. At first the baby had had only a cold. She had lain quiet, pale and weak, with barely any appetite. But it was winter, the house was draughty and the child frail at only three months. Soon the cold had become bronchitis, and the baby coughed and burned with fever. Braida had been by nearly every day to bring marjoram to help with the fever, peppermint tea to clear Megan's head, wild carrot for the cough and the bronchitis. But Megan continued to grow more ill with every hour that passed. Early this morning, Braida had called in Cathal Mackensie, the only doctor in the glen. This had frightened Morna deeply: healer and doctor were natural enemies, and she knew her daughter's condition must be very serious if Braida had asked for Mackensie by choice.

The two had conferred together, listened to Megan's chest and her breathing, appraised her rising fever, and declared that she had inflammation of the lung. Braida had made barley water and balm for the fever and inflammation, comfrey for the baby's chest. Cathal Mackensie had given Morna liniment to rub on, and shown her how to make a poultice with Braida's balm and mustard powder and other things she did not wish to name.

For four days, Morna stayed by the baby's side, unwilling and unable to sleep, cooling her tiny body with a soft wet cloth, giving her infusions of yarrow tea to make her perspire so the fever would abate, decoctions of ragwort and comfrey, rubbing liniment into her chest to ease the congestion, to reduce the inflammation in Megan's lungs and soothe the hacking cough that tore through Morna's body as if she herself were bearing the pain. As, indeed, she was. For the baby was of her blood, and she felt its pain as deeply, perhaps more so, than she felt her own.

She held Megan constantly, trying to make her comfortable, keeping a large pot full of water suspended over the fire, kept always hot for the teas and decoctions, a smaller pail of cool water for the fever. Morna's eyes were red and raw, and her arms ached. Every part of her ached. There were dark shadows beneath her eyes, and she began to drag her feet as she moved from the bucket of cool water to the baby to the hearth to the sorted herbs and back again.

Bran sat nearby, just out of reach of the light that fell across the floor through the clear icy air beyond the windows. He sat in silence and in shadow, watching and waiting, trying to read, but his eyes, his attention, his concern, were drawn repeatedly to Morna and Megan. At his wife's unconscious sigh of weariness, he looked up and smiled a tentative smile that his wife saw but did not feel.

"I'm sorry I've not been more help to ye," he said.

Numb with apprehension for her child and her own fatigue, Morna waved away the apology. When the child began to cough, strangling on the congestion in her throat, Morna turned her gently upside down over one knee and patted Megan on the back in an effort to loosen the phlegm in her lungs. When the coughing fit eased, she turned the baby over and spread some liniment on her chest, laid her in the cradle among linen sheets and plaid blankets, and warmed a new mustard poultice to cover the foul-smelling, greasy liniment.

Bran observed the intricate process, then rose to crouch next to the cradle, where Megan tossed about fitfully, trying to dislodge the poultice. He looked awkward, with his long legs bent oddly, and his arms resting unnaturally on his knees. He stared at his daughter's face, and the thought that he had made her touched him so deeply that it frightened him.

Sensing Bran's distress through the haze of her own anxiety, Morna glanced up, but when Megan began to cry, the tears heart-wrenching when mingled with the agony of her coughing, Morna turned back to her daughter and picked her up, smelly poultice and all. She held the baby against her shoulder, cupping her head tenderly, then offering milk from her swollen breasts. Megan's spasm of coughing and her tears stopped, at least for the moment. She fell silent and reached up to touch her mother's warm flesh.

Bran crouched nearby, unable to quell the momentary panic at his own inability to help their daughter. Yet his wife, still an unformed child herself, whom *he* was shaping into a woman, knew intuitively what to do. She alone had the nourishment the baby needed; he could not feed his daughter even if he wanted to. The fact threatened him, and he could not admit it to his overburdened wife, so it became, instead, an irritation. She was obsessed with the sick child; there were no other sounds, colors, people in her life. He sometimes wondered if Morna remembered that he was in the room, or in her heart.

Ignoring the pang of love and envy, he touched Morna's cheek when he saw her heartsick expression. She too needed comfort, certainly more than he. " 'Tis a selfish bastard I am, my Morna, leaving ye on your own like this. 'Tis just that I don't know what to do. 'Twas awhile before I understood that she needed ye more than me." Pausing, he ran his fingers through the curly strands of his beard, his blue eyes earnest and intense. "I recognize now how much she means to me, and to ye. I want ye to forgive me, Morna, and let us start again."

Morna nodded numbly. She was too tired to question his unexpected change of heart, his confession of inadequacy; her mind was webbed and cloudy from weariness. She could no longer see Megan's face, even when she held it close. The shafts of light crisscrossing the room were not enough to penetrate the shadows that hovered about her. Pushing her sweat-soaked hair back from her beaded forehead, she saw that the baby had ceased to suckle after only a few half-hearted tries. Morna went to the cool bucket of water and wrung out the cloth with one hand. She could feel the heat of her daughter's body even through the layers of sheets and the woven blanket.

Eventually, Megan fell into a restless sleep.

Bran stared down at his only child, his daughter with the mark upon her forehead. The illness had made the birthmark darker, the blue veins more distinct. He could see the blood pulse through her temple. He repressed a shudder. Morna could not know that he had always feared having a deformed child. "Mayhap 'tis a curse after all, that mark. A curse that's made her ill." He sounded bleak.

Morna blinked in disbelief, and the gray haze cleared for a moment. "Braida was right. Ye do believe in the old superstitions." Perhaps he believed Megan was cursed, and therefore her parents were cursed as well. Morna squinted at her husband with a sense of premonition that disturbed her deeply. She had no defenses left. Megan had used them all up in the last few torturous days.

"Ye're wrong," Bran murmured. " 'Tis only that it weakens her. If she were no' so frail, she'd no' have become so ill." He needed a reason, an explanation; otherwise, this was too cruel to all of them.

"All babies are delicate. They gain strength as they grow. Ye're only usin' the mark as an excuse." Morna had to struggle to find the words to fight one more battle that she knew she could not win. It came to her that in the two years she had known her husband, he had shown over and over that he could not tolerate ineptitude in another or himself. She wondered why. Just now, his eyes were tinged with distaste, but his fear showed more brightly still.

" 'Tis a flaw, a malformation," Bran argued, his face pale. " 'Tis no' as God intended it to be. 'Tis an abomination to Him." He met and held his wife's glazed and disbelieving eyes. "That my child should be marred—" He broke off as blood suffused his face.

"Ye said ye didn't believe in God," Morna cried, her strength momentarily restored. Both were on their feet, facing each other over the hanging cradle. She trembled in an effort to hide her hurt and dismay that he should call their child an abomination. "I think 'tis an abomination to *ye*. *Your* child should be perfect. *Because* she is yours."

Bran did not deny it. But as she watched him try to control

himself, she realized that to him, the birthmark represented, not curses or abominations, but a physical symbol of human frailty. He had condemned such helplessness in Morna, and now in their child. Why was it that Bran feared weakness so much?

Morna froze when she saw the peculiar expression with which her husband was regarding the baby. It held her rigid, that intense observation, as if by some trick of the fairies in which he did not believe, he had taken away her ability to move or speak.

Bran stood unmoving for a long time, though he knew Morna was watching. He could feel her apprehension like a cold hand on his arm, and took an odd satisfaction in refusing to meet her eyes. That's what his secret fear had done to him—reduced him to feeble manipulations in order to restore his faith in himself. When he was ready, when he saw out of the corner of his eye how white and bloodless was his wife's hand on the cradle, he turned.

The spell was broken and Morna moved awkwardly as if she had only just learned to use her legs. She knew what Bran was doing in standing so tall and remaining so still and silent; he would tell her nothing, but make her ask. She was too upset to care. "What were ye thinkin' just now?" she murmured shakily.

Bran frowned and rubbed his fingers through his wild red beard. "It came to me that if Megan were to die, I could mourn her forever. She'd never have the chance to change."

A shudder ran through Morna's body. "Ye mean she'd no' be able to disappoint ye? If she were dead, ye could idealize her without a flawed child to disillusion ye."

"I've not said that."

"No, but ye thought it." Morna shivered as a memory came to her so distinctly that the present seemed to disappear. She had been lying in bed bleeding while the baby struggled to be born, and Braida looked on in concern. Bran had held Morna's hand so tightly, too tightly. He seemed to fear that if he let go, if he broke the contact between his long cool fingers and her damp swollen ones, that she would slip away from him forever. Or had that been why his grip was so strained? That moment—Bran's expression and the hurtful squeezing of her hand—was the only clear memory in a blur of pain and blood and the tearing of her body. He had been staring at her wistfully, with a wrenching sadness, speculatively. As he'd looked at Megan a moment before.

" 'Tis no' the first time ye've had that thought, is it?" Morna asked, profoundly chilled. "Ye thought of mourning me when I was birthin' your baby and Braida was no' certain *I* would live. Did ye wonder then, just for an instant, if 'twould be better if I didn't?" If he'd lost her, he could have nursed his grief and magnified it till it became a shrine to the power of his sorrow, embalmed forever, unchanging, endlessly able to fill his need for turmoil and inspiration.

Bran did not answer, merely stared at her oddly, as if surprised by her perception.

Morna was appalled at his eyes, which were cold, silver, and blank. She was more frightened still that she understood what he really meant, though he had not said the words aloud.

She backed away. She did not know this man with the eyes of a stranger. They had been lovers, man and wife, had conceived a child together, yet she didn't really know him.

Curled around her daughter's cradle as if shielding Megan from the demons Bran had conjured in her imagination, Morna was delirious, uncertain if the flames at her back were hot or icy, the room her own or the croft of a stranger who had taken her in out of pity. Her eyelids were heavy, so gritty from lack of sleep that she had to struggle to keep them open. She did not dare sleep. The baby lay resting, one hand beneath the blankets, one gripping her mother's finger. Morna put her hand on Megan's chest and was reassured by the tiny heartbeat echoing her own. Her head so light that she felt she was spinning, she let her eyes drift closed for just a moment. She relaxed her aching body, curled tight around the cradle, and her breathing grew quiet and regular.

Morna heard a distant dulcet sound and looked up to find the room filled with billowing mist, tinted soft violet, soothing and alluring. The mist thickened to a cloudy vapor that enveloped her; within the swirl and eddy was a sweet, silvery melody. Within the melody, a voice she could not ignore. Compelled by some force other than her will, she drifted through the luminous fog that called her and consoled her. She stepped through the warped doorway as she would have moved through the soft edges of a dream, to follow the captivating voice in the mist.

Soon she saw a figure ahead—a woman, cloaked in green. She recognized Braida from her lissome body as gracefully, silently, she made her way through thick-growing bushes that seemed to part before her.

Morna knew she was dreaming, that the violet mist and a distant song had mesmerized her, but the cotton grass brushing her ankles felt so real that it left a ring of dew on her flowing skirt. The fir and pine needles crunched beneath her feet, and she could feel the supple skeletons of bare winter trees, see their shadows in the moonlight. It was all so beautiful, so achingly real.

Braida glided, head tilted back, eyes closed, listening to voices Morna could not hear, absorbing their sound and their beauty and their strength. The farther they wandered from the tiny group of crofts, the more easy and lithe Braida's movements became. It was as if she were shedding a skin and leaving it behind to be picked up later and reworn, shedding the fears and superstitions of the people among whom she lived.

Eventually, Braida reached the edge of the cliff above the sullen waters of the loch. Slowly, attentively, she lit a small fire, as if the placement of each twig mattered as much as the light and heat the fire would bring. She scattered dried herbs through the curls of smoke from the newborn flames, chanting liltingly in Gaelic while her body swayed to ancient rhythms. She raised her head, the hood of her cloak fell back, and her red hair rose and fell on the wind.

Morna watched, spellbound, drawn by the wise woman's voice into the turmoil of the gray-blue loch beyond. The branches of Douglas and silver fir, of Caledonian pine and rowan, larch and oak rustled above her, undulated with the sound and motion of the water below. Beyond the cliff and the swaying leaves, the clouds moved in the darkening sky, changing, shifting, rolling over one another like the endless breaking waves. Morna stood motionless while three seas roiled around and above her, whispering, calling, bleeding slowly one into the other.

Braida turned at last, green eyes glittering in the firelight. She took a step forward, hand outstretched toward Morna, who felt a tearing inside, a single moment of anguish. She gasped in astonishment at what Braida held in her hand. Somehow this woman had reached inside and grasped Morna's pain, which she held now on her open palm. The pain was like a jewel, a silver thread, a piece of gold whose value she could not gauge.

As Morna stared, Braida whispered softly, "'Tis glad I am ye've come, *mo-run,* for the ancient gods are about tonight, and the fairies are watching. 'Tis they who beckoned us to the water." She paused, head canted to one side, and regarded Morna's rigid body. "But ye don't like the loch, do ye?" She was surprised until she looked deeper and saw another buried grief glimmering in Morna's eyes. "Neithe, god of waters, used to call, and ye answered, did ye no'? Ye loved the loch, the burn, the waterfalls." She gazed into Morna's gaze and stiffened. "Then the loch took something from ye, someone who was part of your soul and your blood. Your other half, your mirror." Braida paused, confused and powerless to penetrate further the barricade Morna had built around her loss. "A child?"

"No," Morna answered finally, though she did not wish to speak the words; they were drawn from her against her will. "'Twas my sister, my twin. And 'twas my fault."

Braida shook her head emphatically in disbelief. "Ye drowned her?"

"No, but I let her go alone." For the first time in two years, Morna could not shut out the remembered sound of her sister's voice.

"I want to go down to the loch," Annie Ramsay had said. *"But 'tis windy today, and I'd no' go alone."*

"I have to study," Morna had replied irritably.

"To impress Bran," Annie snapped with unusual bitterness. *"Ye care more for him than ye do for me."*

Before Bran came, the sisters had been together every day, wandering the glen, weaving fantasies about the loch, following the burn to find where it met the sea. Annie was so delicate that Morna worried about her, guided her, let her sister lean on her when she was afraid or depressed or in need.

"You're the strong one," Annie used to say. "I'd not be knowin' what I'd do without ye."

That last day, Annie had tugged on Morna's arm. "Come with me. There's a storm comin', but I must be away. Come with me. Please. Don't leave me alone." Her voice had been plaintive, full of hurt. "Let's be one again, ye and me. I need ye."

How often had Morna heard those words? How often changed her plans because she feared to leave her sister alone? She loved Annie. How could she not, when they shared more than their parents' blood, but a bond that was stronger than sister to sister? Yet sometimes she felt she could not breathe for the weight of Annie's spirit in her chest. She turned to reach out to her twin, but Annie had slipped away.

Morna never saw her again.

Braida stared at her friend's face, transfigured by guilt, and felt stunned and helpless. Gently, she guided Morna to the ground, then sat beside her and took her hand. "Would *ye* have gone alone to the loch?"

"Aye, I did it often. But Annie was no' like me, even if she was my twin. She was no' strong, but lovely and impractical." She had not spoken of her sister in two years, and the pain was still hot and sharp. "She'd no' walk the earth, but float; she was so frail and fey. 'Twas like she was caught halfway between this world and another, where the fairies lived. I cared for her, watched out for her. I should have gone with her that day, and then she might have lived."

Braida spread out Morna's hand, uncurling her fisted fingers and tracing the lines on her open palm. "Mayhap 'tis true and mayhap not. Ye could not know that then. Were ye to follow her all her life, protecting her from harm?"

Without thinking, Morna answered, "As long as she needed me."

"That would have been forever. Ye know that in your heart."

"Aye, I know." Morna was obstinate. "But she *did* need me and I let her down."

Braida could not bear the misery in her voice. "Were ye to give up your own life, your own needs to keep her safe?" she murmured, green eyes dimmed by a cast of gray. "Do ye really believe she'd have asked that of ye?"

Morna sat on a bed of fir needles and loam, knees drawn up, arms wrapped around them. "She might have," she said, "and it tears me apart."

Again Braida was silent, staring into the flames. "I think that mayhap all your life ye've carried the weight of others, yet ye yourself are little more than a child, even now, with a bairn of your own. Outside, ye seem capable and brave, but inside, your heart flutters like the wings of a captive bird."

For a time, the crackle of the flames, the sough of the wind in the pines, the whisper of the loch on the beach below, filled the night. Morna listened and heard things she had never known before.

"To keep yourself safe and unburdened, ye sat at the loom and wove yourself a cloak of many colors—bright, vibrant, and pure—to hide your human frailty and your pain.

"So fine was the weave, so pure the thread that the others could no' see the cloak, but the old ones and the fairies were drawn to the colors, to the oft-repeated pattern. Their spirits settled on your shoulders and drifted about your head and hid your heart, for the many-colored cloak had power and magic that ye do not understand." Braida paused for a moment, an eternity.

"Your husband shared your frustration and need, and saw beneath the concealing cloak. He saw in ye his destiny fulfilled, no' as the girl ye are, but as the woman he thought ye could be.

"And now, birdeen, another, weaker heart beats next to yours beneath that many-colored cloak. Together, ye'll see strange and dazzling things, things that shimmer in the air, things so beautiful ye'll both tremble at their power, because the cloak ye've woven has a magic that ye don't yet understand."

Braida reached out a second time to show Morna the knot of pain in the palm of her hand, incandescent as a jewel.

The moon rose slowly in the dark purple sky, spinning a fleeting silver path across the wind-whipped water, before the clouds curled over and around it. Morna stared, and Braida followed her gaze. She shook her head slightly.

"You'll no' be findin' the answers ye seek in Mena, goddess of the moon. For her face, when 'tis clear and unsoftened by clouds or mist, is blank and cold like a distant silver disc. She is the essence of mystery, for while ye can no' stare at the sun with its blinding light, ye know that the golden heat brings life and color to the earth. Yet ye can gaze upon the moon forever, and still never know the woman behind that changing face. Ye can admire Mena, fear her, even worship her, but ye'll never understand her."

"Bran likes the moon when 'tis white and untouched by cloud or shadow. He says 'tis purest then, and chaste." Morna's voice echoed over the loch.

Braida stared up into the sky. "Bran Campbell," she said musingly. "What of his family, who share that name? I've never caught sight nor heard a tale of a single one."

"He turned away from them long ago."

"Then he must be very lonely. He hasn't much to cling to, if he discards so easily his blood and his past." Braida took Morna's hand and held it long enough for the heat from her palm to penetrate the chill of Morna's rigid fingers. "He is more tender than ye think, your Bran, and more afraid."

Morna shook her head in disbelief, remembering Bran's reaction to Megan's birthmark and the look in his eyes when he'd murmured, *If Megan were to die, I could mourn her forever.* She shuddered and Braida touched her shoulder. "I can feel your hurt and apprehension on my skin like a chill. I'd not be knowin' what happened between ye—"

"I thought ye saw everything," Morna interrupted.

Braida regarded her sadly. "I 'see' only what they would have me see. Sometimes 'tis no' enough, and sometimes I can no' understand what I see. But I do know this: Bran will no' harm ye or your daughter. No' in the way ye fear. He wishes her no ill. 'Tis only, mayhap, that he wishes for too much he can no' have. I'd ask ye to remember that before ye decide."

Perplexed, Morna looked up. "Decide?"

"You're making a choice, *mo-run,* whether ye see it or no'. 'Tis why ye came tonight."

Morna held the seer's limitless green gaze. "Mayhap I came because Megan is very ill."

"Aye, that she is, puir bairn."

Swallowing dryly, Morna whispered, "Will she—"

Braida looked away while mist and smoke entwined themselves around her. "I told ye, they let me see only what they wish. I've no answer for ye. I can tell ye only this. Whatever choice ye make, the sorrow will be great, and the loneliness. So great that sometimes ye think 'twill consume ye. But even then ye will go on. Ye are resilient and will survive. This I swear by the sun and the moon, by flame and wind and water, by the dew that is no' rain nor river and the twilight that is neither day nor night."

"And then will the struggle be over?" Morna asked.

Braida shook her head. Her eyes were full of a sad, haunted knowledge. "I forget how very young ye are, for there's age and wisdom in your eyes. Life is always a struggle. 'Tis the nature of man's heart and his restless soul. Peace is a rare and precious thing which few ever glimpse at all. Fewer still can make it last. But do not grieve. For if ye catch it for only an instant, 'tis so beautiful that ye exult and weep at its fragile, shimmering radiance. For such moments, such miracles, are we born onto this earth. Remember that, Morna. Will ye remember?"

Morna nodded silently, in silence answered, "I will."

Morna stirred and opened her eyes, automatically reaching for the baby, who lay in her cradle with a hacking cough. Morna herself must have drifted off to dream a dream of fire and loch and moonlight. Yet it had seemed so vivid, each detail so clear, that she had thought it real. She frowned and tried to shake away the eerie feeling that the night had followed her inside. Then she felt the grip of Megan's fingers around hers; the child had not let go of her mother's hand.

Morna was comforted by the unbroken connection with her child, though her weariness was greater than before, as if the dream had drained the last of her energy. She roused herself awkwardly, her hands clumsy, red and raw from preparing poultices and decoctions and trying to cool Megan's heated body. Morna warmed some milk, added a little brandy in a cup, then lifted the tiny spoon to Megan's mouth. As she sat back on her heels, she dropped the cup on the hearth, where it shattered. From somewhere in the shadows she heard movement, but her vision was misty and she was trying futilely to gather the shards of the cup in her palm.

"Let me take it," Bran said gently, prying her fingers loose from a fragment that had cut her.

Somewhere in the dim recesses of her mind, she knew she should pull away from him, but her muscles had melted into her bones and she could not move. She watched blearily as her husband took the broken cup away and brought her another, which he held to her lips until she drank the fragrant tea. "Chamomile," he told her. "Ye said 'twas soothing and healing both."

When she finished, he bathed her bloody palm and found that the cuts were slight. He wrapped her hand in his handkerchief and held it there while Morna strove to speak.

"I know what ye must think of me," Bran said. "Because I know what I think of myself. I'm sorry I talked so daft, my Morna. 'Tis just that I'm wild with bein' helpless. I'm sorry, *mochride*." He paused to let the words sink in, for she stared as if from a long way away while she tried to make sense of what he was saying. "Do ye believe me?"

To her own surprise, she nodded. Even through the fog that was winding through her brain and sapping her body of vitality, she could see that this was Bran, her husband, come back in place of the cold, distant stranger.

The hand not bound by Bran's handkerchief lay on Megan's forehead, and Morna realized her daughter was once again burning hot. She reached for the bucket of cool water, pulling her hand from her husband's grasp, and tried to dip the square of linen in the water. She stumbled when she turned toward the cradle with the cool rag, and her legs collapsed beneath her.

She was so tired she could not hold the rag, which was too heavy for her to grasp. Bran caught it and began to brush it over his daughter's flushed face, tenderly. Morna wanted to take the baby in her arms, but her hands were shaking, her vision blurred.

When Bran took Morna's shoulders and guided her away, she had no stamina to fight him. "Ye've pushed yourself for too long," he said. "Ye need to rest, before ye hurt her or yourself." He pointed to the handkerchief that had come loose from her injured hand.

"Don't be worryin' yourself, *mo-run,* I'll see to Megan. You're swayin' on your feet, you're so tired. 'Tis rest ye need. Go now and sleep. Sleep now and dream. Dream, and in your dreams your strength will come to ye again."

She wanted to gather all her energy to protest, but she could not do it. Somewhere in the fog of her exhaustion, she heard Braida's reassuring voice. *Bran will no' harm ye or your daughter. He wishes her no ill.* She trusted Braida. Morna sagged with relief against her husband.

He continued to speak as she wept for the loss of the baby's slight weight from her arms. Bran spoke but she did not understand the words, only the soothing inflection of his voice, which lulled her, cradled her as she had cradled their child. The words lay like fine, soft weights upon her eyelids, until she let the sounds enfold her and she drifted beyond the darkened room, beyond the fatigue too great to bear, beyond the fear for her whimpering child.

Morna fell into dreams that curled about her, caught her softly as she slid into the colored light. She drifted, aimless, free of burdens for the first time in many days and nights, unfettered by thoughts or worries or shadows from the past. She drew her knees up to her body and rocked—protected, safe, invisible.

* * *

Morna awakened abruptly in her own bed with the quilt twisted about her sweat-damp body. She looked around frantically. How had she gotten here? She should have been at her place beside Megan's cradle, but it was downstairs, beyond her reach. She frowned, remembering the hypnotic sound of Bran's voice, luring her toward sleep. She must have been more weary than she realized if she had not felt his arms about her or the motion as he carried her up the narrow stairs. But what had woken her? She felt a sense of urgency and rose, her night rail wrinkled and clinging to her body. Her heart was pounding in the cadence of an ancient Celtic warning drum, and her breath came in short gasps as she stumbled down the stairs.

When she reached the bottom, she was struck by a blast of cold air that stopped her, turning her body to ice and dread. The fire had gone out, and the smell of peat ash was heavy in the air. Bran sat in the rocking chair beside the cradle, his head drooping against his chest. The smell of sickness and stale herbs filled the room like smoke. Morna ceased to breathe when she saw her daughter thrashing in the cradle, hitting her hands and feet on the hard wooden sides. Her head was thrown back, her mouth open in a gasp or scream as her body jerked about. She was deeply flushed, choking for air.

Morna moved so fast she did not seem to move at all. She took the baby in her arms, and Megan's tiny hands struck Morna's face again and again. Terrified and trembling, she tried to capture those hands and hold them still, but Megan was too strong. She flailed wildly, jerking her body into unnatural positions as she twisted and turned.

Before Morna could move or think, Megan arched upward. Her eyes rolled back in her head, there was an eerie gurgle in her throat, and she went limp in her mother's arms. The baby was very white and very still. Morna had been too late.

Morna's heart stopped, and the flow of her blood. There was no floor to hold her upright, no walls to keep out the winter blasts, no roof to keep away the freezing rain. There was no sun, no light, no air, no warmth to keep her from turning to stone where she stood with her dead child in her arms. There was only desolation, cold and bleak and without hope.

Slowly the feelings returned to Morna's barren body—grief, wild and raw; terror, all-consuming; rage, savage and primitive. "No!" she cried like an animal, head thrown back in a plea to a power above that was as useless now as she. She stared at Megan's hands flung outward. "Reaching for me," she said in anguish, "reaching into empty air."

She gasped for breath, though she did not wish to breathe. She could not bear the pain, the agony inside as every part of her tore itself away from where it belonged. She prayed for numbness, for all things to cease that supported or protected or gave her life. She prayed for emptiness, nothingness to blot out the suffering.

Bran had risen bolt upright at her cry, but she did not feel him touch her shoulder or see him stare at the baby's white, white body. She did not see his horror, the blood that drained away as he opened his mouth in a silent howl. She began to moan incoherent words and phrases. Appalled, Bran shook her until she looked up and saw his face, bleached of color, pale and free-floating, like the moon in total darkness.

"'Tis my fault," she groaned. "I should no' have left her." She focused on her husband's pallid face. She had been seduced by the lure of Bran's melodic voice, seduced into placing her daughter in his hands. He had told her he did not know what to do, had admitted his inadequacy, but still she had let him entice her with the oblivion sleep had promised. She forced herself to look at Megan, cold and limp in her arms. Morna could not comprehend the enormity of the absolute silence, or the meager-ness of that tiny body with its outflung empty arms.

'Tis the punishment for your sins, a voice in her head whispered. *So many sins. Too many.*

Bran stood immobile, transfixed by the grief that ravaged her face. Then the baby stirred and her eyes rolled down, glassy as a mirror, while she coughed violently. "Not dead," Bran said with a violent flash of hope. "She's no' dead at all."

Morna fought her way out of the darkness as the baby began to move again. Her heart raced and her head spun as realization struck her. For the first time, she really heard her husband's voice. "Ye bastard," she screamed, "go ye and get help, ye who slept while your daughter suffered. Get Cathal Mackensie, and get him *now*." Bran reached for his greatcoat, but Morna was wild, out of control. "GO! Don't ye understand? It could happen again. We have to stop it. GO."

Morna's dark eyes glittered feverishly as she tried to think what to do. She heard the door creak open and closed, but the thought of the doctor did not calm her. She could feel the labored rise and fall of Megan's breath, the beating of her heart, the shuddering of her body as she choked and tried to suck in air. Her skin was burning and she struggled in her mother's arms. Morna felt impotent, crazed with the need to help her child when she did not know how.

Her eyes were huge with relief and cold fear mingled. Megan was not dead, but she had been close. Too close.

She prayed to the ancient Celtic gods to spare her child once more. She wanted Braida, needed her, but she could not risk taking the baby outside in the cold. When the gasping and coughing ceased for a moment, she pressed her daughter's cheek to her own and felt the hot flush of fever. She did not know what to do, what had happened, what to pray for. All she knew was that she was frenzied, raving, mad with dread.

She reached for a stick to force the dying fire to life, and noticed the bottles of herbs, untouched on the hearth. The water in the bucket was coated in ice. She whirled and saw the cold mustard poultice tossed aside by a restless baby and not put back in place. There was no smell of liniment. Megan's chest was dry, the vial of liniment lying on the floor beside the rocking chair. Clutching the baby so tightly that Megan began to weep, Morna stood stunned and uncomprehending, leaning for support against the cold stones of the hearth.

There Braida found her when she appeared in the doorway a few minutes later. "I heard ye calling, *mo-run,* so I came."

Gratefully, Morna gave up Megan to Braida's strong arms. The healer touched the baby's hot skin, heard the cough from deep in her chest and frowned. "Tell me what happened."

Morna searched for coherent words. "I went to sleep, and when I woke, she was thrashing like a daft thing in her cradle. I picked her up to try and soothe her, but she went limp in my arms. I thought—I thought she had left me," she ended raggedly.

Braida shook her head, once, twice, three times, then gave the child back to Morna and began to bustle about. When Cathal Mackensie appeared with Bran close behind him, Braida sighed with gratitude. She told him briefly what she knew. Bran hovered worriedly behind them, his eyes bleak with misery.

"Convulsions from the fever," the doctor said without inflection. Morna knew from the look on his face that the danger had not passed. He took the baby from her.

"Tell me what to do!" she cried. "I'll do aught ye say, only tell me."

Her eyes were wilder than before, and her body shook from head to toe. There were deep shadows along her cheekbones and beneath her eyes. Her hands trembled so badly that she could not wrap her plaid about her to ward off the chill.

"Bran," the doctor ordered, "build up that fire and bring a new bucket of water."

Bran looked from Morna to Megan, torn between them, but he did as the doctor told him.

Cathal Mackensie met Braida's eyes across the baby's worn out body. They would have to work together to try to save the child. There would be no petty bickering in the croft this day about the old ways and the new. "I think we've all else we need, except quiet."

"I've said I can help," Morna repeated. "Tell me how."

"Ye'd help us most by takin' yourself off to bed to get some sleep. Braida and I can do this between us."

Morna was chilled by the grim expressions on their faces. "Don't send me away. I want to help. I have to."

"Ye've nothin' to do now but rest," Braida said. "How many days and nights have ye no' slept so ye could stay by Megan and care for her?"

Morna shook her head, but Braida persisted. "How many? I can see how ye've worn yourself down to try and save her. But 'twill do her no good if she lives and ye die of exhaustion." She touched Morna's tangled hair gently. "Besides, she feels your terror, this little one born of your blood. She breathes in your fear like winter air and it weakens her. Take ye away to rest, Morna. 'Tis best, I promise ye. We'll do all we can, Cathal and I. Go."

Morna hesitated. It was so hard to tear herself away from her tiny defenseless child. She would not have gone, except for Braida's warning that Megan would absorb her mother's panic, and it would further weaken her. Morna could not risk that.

As she slowly, laboriously climbed the stairs, she heard the words, "Quinine," and, "Both lungs inflamed. But the fever's the danger just now. We must break it at once." Morna's feet barely moved; each step was an agony, because it took her farther from her daughter. She knew she would not sleep, but she no longer had the will to stand; so she staggered across the room and fell onto the bed. She did not believe Megan would live, and the knowledge blocked her throat. She could not speak; she could not find release in tears.

She had never seen such gravity on Cathal Mackensie's face, nor Braida's—she who usually hid her thoughts so well. They were just as frightened as Morna, just as certain that there was no hope.

'Tis the punishment for your sins. So many sins. Too many.

Morna winced, bent double, and put her hands over her ears, but the voice would not go. She could not bear it, not when she knew it spoke the truth. She had abandoned her daughter and now the child would die. Bran had promised to care for Megan or Morna would not have let him coax her from her vigil. He might have tried to see to the baby's illness before he fell asleep, but Morna should have known not to leave her daughter in his hands. She should have been strong enough to rend the thick woven veil of her weariness and find the stamina to keep her baby safe and alive. Now Morna wanted nothing more than to follow her daughter into death, but she didn't even have the strength to find a means for that. If Bran's straight razor were lying now within her grasp, she would have picked it up and slid it slowly, deeply, gently across her throat. All she wanted was peace that would silence her guilt and torment and grief, lift them from her shoulders and give her a fleeting moment of tranquillity.

She lay rigid while pain coursed through her, through every vein and pore, until she shook with it and the thought of the razor gleamed in her head. When she closed her eyes, it was there, bright with promise; when she opened them, she imagined it lying on the pillow by her cheek. For a long time she drifted, and then, at last, she fell asleep to the soothing image of her own blood flowing, making a bright, clean pool of red on the pillow beside her.

When she awoke, she knew what she had to do.

The first thing she noticed was the silence. So strange and unnatural in the wake of the shouting and the anguish. She had expected cold, dark stillness as she descended the stairs. But the leather coverings had been tied up, the peat fire burned cheerfully, and the first violet hints of gloaming slipped in through the windows. In the kitchen, Morna could hear the clink of cups and the swish of water. Reluctantly, she took the last step and stood paralyzed, face to face with her husband. Bran stood near the fire, holding Megan in his arms. In the pale shadows of gloaming, his skin looked brittle, yellowed with age, his eyes colorless, bereft of vitality. For one appalling moment, Morna thought the child was dead, and though she had expected it, her body went numb and she started to fall.

Braida was there at once, her hand under Morna's elbow to steady her.

Then she saw that Bran was speaking to his daughter quietly, consolingly. The baby's breathing was less labored and her skin tinged pale pink instead of angry red. She was alive.

Bran looked up at his wife, every angle of his body sharp with remorse. "I'm sorry, Morna. Forgive me. I'd no' blame ye if ye thought I did it on purpose, but I swear."

"No need to swear," his wife said, hardly aware that she was speaking. "I do believe ye." The sight of her daughter had drained her dry, made her head spin with shock. First the certainty of death and now this precious gift of life. It was too much for a sixteen-year-old girl to understand. She leaned against the healer and stared.

"Aye," Braida murmured, "she lives. She's still quite weak, and she'll want constant care."

"She'll be all right?" Morna had asked that question once before.

"The worst is past, but she'll need everything ye have to give." For the second time, Braida had not really answered.

"I'll help," Bran said, his sincerity palpable. His body sagged, though the arms that held his daughter were firm. It was clear that he was as devastated as Morna. At the realization, something cracked inside her and shattered.

"He's already been a great help this day. We'd no' have done it without him," Braida said.

Morna gasped at a wash of pain that left her weak.

Braida saw, and grieved because her visions were not always true, because often she did not understand. But she understood the look in Morna Campbell's eyes.

"What he did today," Braida whispered, "'tis no' enough, is it?"

Eyes filmed with tears, Morna replied, "No. Not anymore."

Two months had passed, while Megan fought to regain her strength, before Morna crept quietly down the rough stairs into a frightening new morning. In one hand, she balanced two bags— one filled with clothes and a notebook of blank pages, the other with Megan's things. In the crook of her other arm, she held the baby. She would never forget the moment when Bran had first put Megan back into her arms and she'd felt again her daughter's heartbeat. Morna's elation had been fierce and immutable as the blood raced through her veins, restoring her color, her energy, her life. Her arms did not tremble; she would not let her daughter

fall again. She'd felt then as she had the day Megan was born—
consumed by love and tenderness and the passionate need to
protect. She was still alarmed by the baby's frailty, by her skin,
yellowed by illness and oddly translucent, though free of fever at
last. Morna breathed in deeply, willing the heat and vigor of her
own breath into Megan's wee body.

Bran had heard his wife packing and was sitting alone and
dejected beside the ashes of the fire, his hair uncombed, his eyes
red from sleeplessness.

He had closed tight all the leather coverings so the light could
not get in. He sat in semidarkness, staring at Morna, wanting her
so much that the breath would not move through his constricted
lungs. He did not notice that he was shivering from the cold, that
his teeth chattered as he spoke. "I need ye," he said softly,
penitently, like a child who had misbehaved and sought
forgiveness from his parent. "Ye don't understand how much I
need ye." He saw that she did not believe him. He could not
really blame her. He had judged her, belittled her, pushed her
away, and very nearly destroyed the one she loved most in the
world.

Bran swallowed dryly, in pain, his hands clasped like a vise in
his lap. He had not thought it possible for Morna to love anyone
more than him. After all, he had found her in the wilderness,
taught her, given her the gift of his age and his wisdom. But it had
not been enough. He had thought to bind her to him inextrica-
bly, but instead he had bound himself to her. He needed her love,
her unquestioning adoration, her respect. He needed her like a
drug to hold together the fragile pieces of his shattered ego. He
had thought a moment like this impossible; unthinkable, that she
should choose the needs of another over his, that she should
cease to love him. He looked up frantically. "I love ye, Morna. I
can no' say how much."

Morna dropped her bags, hesitated, pressed her forehead hard
against the doorframe. She had already let so many down. Then
Megan gurgled and tangled her fingers in her mother's hair.
Morna clenched her teeth, afraid she would say something

intolerably cruel. Every moment she was aware of the image of her husband sleeping, head drooping, while his daughter lay nearby in convulsions. She had determined she would not use that against him, though she knew without a doubt he would have used it against her. But she was Morna, not Bran. That was why she was going.

If Megan were to die, I could mourn her forever. Morna knew she could not stay, not only for her own sake, or her daughter's, but for Bran's. "Ye don't even know me," she said, "except as a potter knows his clay. When ye found me, I was the color, the texture ye thought ye needed. But I am already Morna, and was when I first met ye. I thought I could be someone else, the woman that ye wanted, but I can no' do it. I can't, Bran Campbell."

Bran bent forward, folded in upon himself. Didn't she know that his loss had been nearly as great as hers, except that his guilt was greater. She had to forgive him. He'd convinced himself she would. "Please don't go. Don't be leavin' me like ye did the others."

Morna cried out, and beneath Megan's body, pressed her hands across her middle as if he'd struck her with a knife and she knew no other way to stop the blood from flowing.

She had stood, chilled and empty, in the stone house farmhouse where she'd been born. Her mother, Clara Ramsay, had leaned on her daughter heavily, as if the physical contact would somehow fill the void left by the death of her other child. "I need ye near me," she'd said in a voice shaky with grief, "to talk to, to weep with. Ye're the only one who understands how deep the pain goes, how it rends and weakens me. Ye are the strong one. Ye took care of Annie—"

Morna was frozen where she stood. "Annie's dead." The horror of her sister's death filled her with sorrow and anger and guilt that spun inside her head until she thought it would burst. She was barely fifteen and had lost her closest friend, her other half, her ally and responsibility. She did not know how to stop the hopelessness and emptiness, to ease the ache in her chest, so she might breathe without pain. The weight of her guilt and her grief was so heavy that the young girl walked like an old woman, bent and crippled.

Clara Ramsay did not notice Morna's silence or bowed shoulders, her waxy face or shaking hands. "Don't leave me alone with my grief." She waved away her husband, the neighbors and family who would come sit with her if she asked. "The others don't know what 'tis like to hurt like this, and I'd no' want to burden them with my loss."

Ye'd no' burden them, *Morna cried silently,* only me. *She could not stop the resentment that flared within her. She looked at her mother's swollen, desolate face, at her empty hands, and was overwhelmed by Clara Ramsay's need.* Ye're supposed to take care of me, *she wanted to cry.* I'm your child, and I need solace too. *She did not speak her thoughts aloud; she knew it would break her mother, this one more failure to protect the children she had borne.*

Gently, she took her mother's hand. "Ye want me to grieve wi' ye, and ye think 'twill make it easier. But ye're wrong. We'll only suffer together, weep each others' tears and stand face to face like reflections in a mirror. That mirror will magnify the sorrow and shadows, so the shadows expand and grow and fill the room, and we're left in total darkness." *As her mother stared at her in incomprehension, the walls seemed to move inward, thickening the stale air. The covered windows deepened the gloom until Morna thought she would choke. She could find no breath of air to fill her empty lungs, no light to remind her that outside was life and growth and freedom.*

"I can no' bear to live in the darkness, Mama. I can no' do this thing." *She could barely speak; her mother's misery was drawing her into anguish deeper than her own.*

"Ye must leave," *Bran said later as she lay shivering in his arms.* "They don't mean to hurt ye, but still, they'll drain ye till ye're empty, mo-charaid. Ye don't deserve that, Morna. Ye deserve all this and more." *He indicated the thick green wood with its ceiling of leaves, the long cotton grass, starflowers, and bluebells, and the burn rushing over smooth bronze stones.*

He held her and stroked her and painted her sorrow, and in painting it, made it beautiful, so she could look on it without turning away. "Ye must go," he'd repeated. "Ye've no other choice."

When Bran shifted in the peat-scented dimness of their croft, Morna turned away from the past and the farmhouse she had left behind. She faced her husband, who was chiding her now for something he had urged upon her not so long ago. But that knowledge did not help, or the sense that his cruelty came from desperation.

Every muscle in her body was crying out in pain. He had struck where she was weakest, knowing she could not be heartless. Perhaps, after all, she could not leave him. She did not have the strength this time; her husband had drained it from her as he'd warned her her mother might do, as the child had drained her blood at birth, until there was too little left. *He is more tender than ye think, your Bran, and more afraid*, Braida had said. It was true after all.

"I need ye," he repeated.

He was weeping, and she wanted to shut out the muffled sound of his sobs. Though he was not touching her, his tears were a weight on her heart just as the baby was in her arms. All at once he seemed equally defenseless. Each tear was a thread binding her close, as her love for her sister and her mother had before.

Morna wanted to weep her own pent-up tears. She had loved Bran in her way, loved him still, because he had seen things in her that she'd never known were there. He had courted her, made her feel beautiful, painted lovely and disturbing portraits of her. He had used his talent to create images that had touched her inside, touched and named feelings she had never dared explore before he painted them on canvas. He had transformed her with his vision and the beauty of colorful paints from a girl into a woman. But the wonder was gone now, the vibrant hypnotic hues that had once held her fast. Bran had killed the beauty with his anger, his bitterness, his eyes closed tight against the fragile miracle of their child.

"Please." His voice was hoarse with tears. "I'm thinkin' I can't go on if ye leave. I chose ye for your strength, ye ken," he said. "I knew ye'd no' let me shatter."

How many times would they plead with her to help them, cling to her as if she had the strength to heal their wounds? Were they all so blind, her sister and her mother and her husband, that they really believed she was the strong one? She was not strong, she thought in anguish. She was broken and torn and weak inside, with barely enough determination to keep herself and her small baby alive. And perhaps not even enough for that. Yet they asked so much of her, every one of them. Why, when she had so little to give?

To keep yourself safe and unburdened, ye sat at the loom and wove yourself a cloak of many colors to hide your human frailty.

She shook her head, confused and bewildered, and took a step toward the door.

"Don't go!" Bran cried, staring at her and into her, beneath her skin to her soul and her beating heart. "Don't leave me!"

Your husband shared your frustration and need, and saw beneath the concealing cloak. He saw in ye his destiny fulfilled. She wanted to shut out the sound of Braida's voice, but she could not. Morna straightened to face Bran one last time. She owed him that at least. "I can't leave ye—because in your eyes, this woman, Morna, was never here. The girl who lived here was someone ye invented. Whatever ye saw through your eyes, she was, or tried to be. The only time I was *me*, Morna, was when I held my daughter in my arms."

Bran stared at her blankly.

Odd, she thought, how she'd always believed he knew so much, that the bounds of his knowledge were endless and eternal. Yet he could not conceive of a truth so elemental.

Bran glared at the bundled baby. "Ye've known ye were going all along, have ye no'? Ever since—" he stuttered, "that awful day. Ye've waited till she was well so ye could leave me. But Morna, I need ye as much as Megan."

She shook her head. "Ye need someone, some*thing;* I know that now. But I'd no' be knowin' what. I look in your eyes today and see the emptiness that ye thought I could fill." When he put his hand on her arm, she did not shake it away. " 'Twon't work, Bran. I'm not the one. I can no' make your demons go. Don't ye see, ye've made me a ghost as well. Only Megan makes me real. To her I am no more than exactly what I am, and 'tis enough for her. 'Twould never be enough for ye."

She was hardly aware of the tears streaming down her cheeks. She'd always thought he'd be the one to leave her and, for so long, had lived in fear of that moment. But once she'd held her baby in her hands and thought her dead, Morna had known there could never be another moment as terrible as that.

"To ye I've always been a fantasy, a dream ye wove in your sleep then tried to give breath and life through me. Ye're wakin' up now, 'tis all. The dream was never real."

Before he could say anything more, before he could touch her, taking back the courage she had fought so hard for, she slipped out the door with Megan bundled tight against her chest.

Morna forced her body into numbness so she would not feel the pain of separation, the agony of Bran's harsh, wrenching sobs that followed her down the hill. The sound did not dissipate as the distance widened between her and the small thatched croft. Instead it lingered, clinging about her shoulders, ringing in her ears, when she sought only silence, silence and peace and the whisper of her baby's breath. She moved forward slowly, one step at a time, until she had gone too far to turn back. But she could never turn back now; she knew that. She had failed Bran like the others. She could only look forward and pray to the god she had forsaken long ago that she would not also fail her child.

Morna was not certain where she would go, alone, poor, and with a small baby. She'd received a letter from her mother in the last few days. Clara Ramsay had sought her missing daughter until she found her again and asked for her forgiveness. Morna had wept with compassion for her mother. Now she had a child of her own and understood what it meant to lose one. But she was not yet ready to go home. Perhaps someday, when she'd become a woman of her own creation. *Not yet,* a voice inside her whispered, *not yet*. Instead, she found herself making her way along the path she had followed after Braida that long-ago night. As the two stood on the cliff top, concealed by mist, then revealed as the wind swept the moist white cloak away, Braida had told Morna of a place at the foot of the loch, an isolated place, reached only by boat, where few ever went: ". . . except women of our kind, yours and mine, when our spirits are fading and we need to find the core of them again, to remember what 'tis to be all that we are, whether we choose to be so or no'." Blindly, Morna headed for the boat landing. Because she knew of nowhere else to go, she would find this place, with her daughter in her arms.

On the boat that carried her over the wind-whipped water of the loch, Morna dreamt a dream that lifted her beyond the pain of parting and her own troubled thoughts about an uncertain future.

She dreamt, and the dream was of a time when she carried within her the seed of a child. The chill left her body and her blood, which now flowed warm through the tiny beating pulse of the unformed baby's heart. In the dream she felt strong and contented, for she knew the child she carried would be her gift to a cold and barren world where she had not yet found her place.

In her dream she saw that the child lying safe and warm inside her was her own gift—her freedom. She carried it within herself. She knew, as a priest knows his vocation or a nun her sacred vow, that she was changed forever by the beat of that frail heart—a life, a child, a victory that could never be denied her.

She walked past the shell of her childhood home, past the loch that had taken her sister into its storm-tossed waters, past her husband's cabin with the curtains closed against the light. And yet she felt no sorrow or regret. She touched her stomach, swollen with the weight of her unborn child, and knew that her pain and the knowledge it had brought her were also her strength and her prize. She knew that it would be all right.

When she awakened to the chill of morning and the fresh

Highland wind on her face, the dream lingered until she took up her notebook, untouched for so long, and wrote a story about a child. It was quiet and still in the misted light of dawn as the words welled up from a long winter silence. Peace rose with the sun, stirring her briefly with the warmth of early spring.

When she was finished, and the pages nearly full, the story had no ending and the child had no name.

EDITOR'S AFTERNOTE

While Morna's tale in "Clouds Across the Moon" is an empowering one, resurrection collects its sacrifice. Her marriage to Bran is threatened, tested, and eventually found unlivable after the arrival of her baby. Morna's creator, Kathryn Lynn Davis, however, disagrees with any notion that romance and motherhood are mutually exclusive.

"I believe if a woman has a strong and loving relationship with her mate, a child can enhance and enrich that relationship."

Lest we overlook it, Davis recommends we consider the possibility that "there is definitely a kind of romance to motherhood itself: the intense blood bond between mother and child awakens instincts and emotions previously unimagined. The love a mother feels for her child is unconditional and, it has been said, closer to the sacred than any other human emotion."

Davis's first book, *The Dakotas: At the Wind's Edge*, made national news when it was banned in the town that provided its setting, Medora, North Dakota. Since then, she has written six additional historical novels and is currently working on her eighth, a sequel to *All We Hold Dear*. A frequenter of national best-seller lists, Davis is an active speaker in public schools, promoting literacy.

Which Is More Than I Can Say About Some People

Lorrie Moore

I t was a fear greater than death, according to the magazines. Death was No. 4. After mutilation, three, and divorce, two. No. 1, the real fear, the one death could not even approach, was public speaking. Abby Mallon knew this too well. Which is why she had liked her job at American Scholastic Tests: she got to work with words in a private way. The speech she made was done in the back, alone, like little shoes cobbled by an elf: Spider is to web as weaver is to *blank*. That one was hers. She was proud of that.

Also, *blank* is to heartache as forest is to bench.

But then, one day, the supervisor and the A.S.T. district coordinator called her upstairs. She was good, they said, but perhaps she had become *too* good, too *creative*, they suggested, and gave her a promotion out of the composing room and into the high-school auditoriums of America. She would have to travel and give speeches, tell high-school faculty how to prepare students for the entrance exams, meet separately with the juniors and seniors and answer their questions unswervingly, with authority and grace. "You may have a vacation first," they said, and handed her a check.

"Thank you," she said doubtfully. In her life she had been

given the gift of solitude, a knack for it, but now it would be of no professional use. She would have to become a people person.

"A *peeper* person?" queried her mother, on the phone from Pittsburgh.

"*People,*" said Abby.

"Oh, those," said her mother, and she sighed the sigh of death, though she was strong as a brick.

Of all Abby's fanciful ideas for self-improvement (the inspirational video, the breathing exercises, the hypnosis class) the Blarney Stone, with its whoring barter of eloquence for love— "O gift of gab" read the T-shirts—was perhaps the most extreme. Perhaps. There had been, after all, her marriage to Bob, her boyfriend of many years, after her dog, Randolph, had died of kidney failure and marriage to Bob seemed the only way to overcome her grief. Of course, she had always admired the idea of marriage, the citizenship and public speech of it, the innocence rebestowed, and Bob was big and comforting. But he didn't have a lot to say. He was not a verbal man. Rage gave him syntax—but it just wasn't enough! Soon Abby had begun to keep him as a kind of pet, while she quietly looked for distractions of depth and consequence. She looked for words. She looked for ways with words. She worked hard to befriend a lyricist from New York—a tepid, fair-haired, violet-eyed bachelor. She and most of the doctors' wives and arts administrators in town. He was newly arrived, owned no car, and wore the same tan blazer every day. "Water, water everywhere but not a drop to drink," said the bachelor lyricist once, listening wanly to the female chirp of his phone messages. In his apartment there were no novels or bookcases. There was one chair, a large television set, the phone machine, a rhyming dictionary continually renewed from the library, and a coffee table. Women brought him meals, professional introductions, jingle commissions, and cash grants. In return, he brought them small, piebald stones from the beach, or pretty weeds from the park. He would stand behind the coffee table and recite his own songs, then step back and wait fearfully to be seduced. To be lunged at and devoured by the female form was, he believed, something akin to applause. Sometimes he would produce a rented lute and say, "Here, I've just composed a melody to go with my 'Creation' verse. Sing along with me."

And Abby would stare at him and say, "But I don't know the tune. I haven't heard it yet. You just made it up, you said."

Oh, the vexations endured by a Man of Poesy! He stood paralyzed behind the coffee table, and when Abby did at last step forward, just to touch him, to take his pulse, perhaps, *to capture one of his arms in an invisible blood-pressure cuff!* he crumpled and shrank. "Please don't think I'm some kind of emotional Epstein-Barr," he said, quoting from other arguments he'd had with women. "I'm not indifferent or dispassionate. I'm calm. I'm romantic, but I'm calm. I have appetites, but I'm very calm about them."

When Abby went back to her husband ("Honey, you're home!" Bob exclaimed), she lasted only a week. Shouldn't it have lasted longer—the mix of loneliness and lust and habit she always felt with Bob, the mix that was surely love, for it so often felt like love, how could it not be love, surely nature intended it to be, surely nature with its hurricanes and hail was counting on this to suffice? Bob smiled at her and said nothing. And the next day she booked a flight to Ireland.

How her mother became part of the trip, Abby still couldn't exactly recall. It had something to do with a stick shift: how Abby had never learned to drive one. "In my day and age," said her mother, "everyone learned. We all learned. Women had skills. They knew how to cook and sew. Now women have no skills."

The stick shifts were half the rental price of the automatics.

"If you're looking for a driver," hinted her mother, "I can still see the road."

"That's good," said Abby.

"And your sister Theda's spending the summer at your aunt's camp again." Theda had Down's syndrome, and the family adored her. Every time Abby visited, Theda would shout, "Look at you!" and throw her arms around her in a terrific hug.

"Theda's, of course, sweet as ever," said her mother, "which is more than I can say about some people."

"That's probably true."

"I'd like to see Ireland while I can. Your father, when he was alive, never wanted to. I'm Irish, you know."

"I know. One-sixteenth."

"That's right. Of course, your father was Scottish, which is a totally different thing."

Abby sighed. "It seems to me that *Japanese* would be a totally different thing."

"*Japanese?*" hooted her mother. "Japanese is close."

And so in the middle of June they landed at the Dublin airport together. "We're going to go all around this island, every last peninsula," said Mrs. Mallon, in the airport parking lot, revving the engine of their rented Ford Fiesta, "because that's just the kind of crazy yuppies we are."

Abby felt sick from the flight, and sitting on what should have been the driver's side but didn't have a steering wheel suddenly seemed emblematic of something.

Her mother lurched out of the parking lot and headed for the nearest roundabout, crossing into the other lane only twice. "I'll get the hang of this," she said. She pushed her glasses farther up on her nose, and Abby could see for the first time that her mother's eyes were milky with age. Her steering was jerky, and her foot jumped around on the floor, trying to find the clutch. Perhaps this had been a mistake.

"Go straight, Mom," said Abby, looking at her map.

They zigged and zagged to the north, up and away from Dublin, planning to return there at the end, but now heading toward Drogheda and the N1, Abby snatching up the guidebook and then the map again and then the guidebook, and Mrs. Mallon shouting, "What?" or "Left?" or "This can't be right, let me see that thing." The Irish countryside opened up before them, its pastoral patchwork and stone walls and chimney aroma of turf fires like something from another century, its small stands of trees, and fields populated with wildflowers and sheep dung and cut sod and cows with ear tags, beautiful as women. Perhaps fairy folk lived in the trees! Abby saw immediately that to live amidst the magic feel of this place would be necessarily to believe in magic. To live here would make you superstitious, warmhearted with secrets, unrealistic. If you were literal, or practical, you would have to move—or you would have to drink.

They drove uncertainly past signs to places unmarked on the map. They felt lost—but not in an uncharming way. The old, narrow roads with their white markers reminded Abby of the vacations her family had taken when she was little, the cow-country car trips through New England or Virginia—in those days before there were interstates or plastic cups or a populace depressed by asphalt and French fries. Ireland was a trip into the past of America. It was years behind, unmarred, like a story or a dream or a clear creek. I'm a child again, Abby thought. I'm back. And just as when she was a child, she suddenly had to go to the bathroom.

"I have to go to the bathroom," she said. To their left was a sign that said "Road Works Ahead" and underneath someone had scrawled, "No, it doesn't."

Mrs. Mallon veered the car over to the left and slammed on the brakes. There were some black-faced sheep, haunch-marked with bright blue, munching grass near the road.

"Here?" asked Abby.

"I don't want to waste time stopping somewhere else and having to buy something. You can go behind that wall."

"Thanks," said Abby, groping in her pocketbook for Kleenex. Already she missed her own house. She missed her neighborhood. She missed the plentiful U-Pump-'Ems, where, she often said, at least they spelled "pump" right! She got out and hiked back down the road a little way. On one of the family road trips thirty years ago, when she and Theda had had to go to the bathroom, their father had stopped the car and told them to "go to the bathroom in the woods." They had got out and wandered through the woods for twenty minutes, looking for the bathroom, before they came back out to tell him that they hadn't been able to find it. Their father had looked perplexed, then amused, and then angry—his usual pattern.

Now Abby struggled over a short stone wall and hid, squatting, eying the sheep warily. She was spacey with jet lag, and when she got back to the car she realized she'd left the guidebook on a stone and had to turn around and retrieve it.

"There," she said, getting back in the car.

Mrs. Mallon shifted into gear. "I always feel that if people would just be like animals and excrete here and there rather than in a single agreed-upon spot, we wouldn't have any pollution."

Abby nodded. "That's brilliant, Mom."

"Is it?"

They stopped briefly at an English manor house, to see the natural world cut up into moldings and rugs, wool and wood captive and squared, the earth stolen and embalmed and shellacked. Abby wanted to leave. "Let's leave," she whispered.

"What is it with you?" complained her mother. From there they visited a Neolithic passage grave, its design like a birth in reverse, its narrow stone corridor spilling into a high, round room. They took off their sunglasses and studied the Celtic curlicues. "Older than the pyramids," announced the guide, though he failed to address its most important feature, Abby felt: its deadly maternal metaphor.

"Are you still too nervous to cross the border to Northern Ireland?" asked Mrs. Mallon.

"Uh-huh." Abby bit at her thumbnail, tearing the end of it off like a tiny twig.

"Oh, come on," said her mother. "Get a grip."

And so they crossed the border into the north, past the flak-jacketed soldiers patrolling the neighborhoods and barbed wire of Newry: young men holding automatic weapons and walking backward, block after block; their partners across the street, walking forward, on the watch. Helicopters flapped above. "This is a little scary," said Abby.

"It's all show," said Mrs. Mallon breezily.

"It's a scary show."

"If you get scared easily."

Which was quickly becoming the theme of their trip—Abby could see that already. That Abby had no courage and her mother did. And that it had been that way forever.

"You scare too easily," said her mother. "You always did. When you were a child, you wouldn't go into a house unless you were reassured that there were no balloons in it."

"I didn't like balloons."

"And you were scared on the plane coming over," said her mother.

Abby grew defensive. "Only when the flight attendant said there was no coffee because the percolator was broken. Didn't you find that alarming? And then, after all that slamming, they still couldn't get one of the overhead bins shut." Abby remembered this as if it were a distant, bitter memory, though it had only been yesterday. The plane had taken off with a terrible shudder, and when it proceeded with the rattle of an old subway car, particularly over Greenland, the flight attendant had gotten on the address system to announce that there was nothing to worry about, "especially when you think about how heavy air really is."

Now her mother thought she was Tarzan. "I want to go on that rope bridge I saw in the guidebook," she said.

On page 98 in the guidebook was a photograph of a rope-and-board bridge slung high between two cliffs. It was supposed to be for fishermen, but tourists were allowed, though they were cautioned about strong winds.

"Why do you want to go on the rope bridge?" asked Abby.

"*Why?*" replied her mother, who then seemed stuck and fell silent.

For the next two days, they drove east and to the north, skirting Belfast, along the coastline, past old windmills and sheep farms, and up onto vertiginous cliffs that looked out toward Scotland, a pale sliver on the sea. They stayed at a tiny stucco bed-and-breakfast, one with a thatched roof like Cleopatra bangs. They slept lumpily, and in the morning, in the breakfast room with its large front window, they ate their cereal and rashers and black-and-white pudding in an exhausted way, going through the motions of good guesthood. "Yes, the troubles," they agreed, for who could say for certain to whom you were talking? It wasn't like race-riven America, where you always knew. Abby nodded. Out the window there was a breeze, but she couldn't hear the faintest rustle of it. She could only see it silently moving the dangling branches of the sun-sequinned spruce, just slightly; it was like looking at objects hanging from a rearview mirror in someone else's car.

She charged the bill to her Visa, tried to lift both bags, and then lifted just her own.

"Good-bye! Thank you!" she and her mother called to their host. Back in the car, briefly, Mrs. Mallon began to sing "Toora-loora-looral." "Over in Killarney, many years ago," she warbled. Her voice was husky, vibrating, slightly flat, coming in just under each note like a saucer under a cup.

And so they drove on. The night before, the whole day ahead could have shape and design. But when it was upon you, it could vanish tragically into air.

They came to the sign for the rope bridge.

"I want to do this," said Mrs. Mallon, and swung the car sharply right. They crunched into a gravel parking lot and parked; the bridge was a quarter-mile walk from there. In the distance dark clouds roiled like a hemorrhage, and the wind was picking up. Rain mizzled the windshield.

"I'm going to stay here," said Abby.

"You are?"

"Yeah."

"Whatever," said her mother in a disgusted way, and she got out scowling and trudged down the path to the bridge, disappearing beyond a curve.

Abby waited, now feeling the true loneliness of this trip. She realized she missed Bob and his warm, quiet confusion; how he sat on the rug in front of the fireplace, where her dog Randolph used to sit; sat there beneath the five Christmas cards they'd received, and placed on the mantle—five including the one from the paperboy—sat there picking at his feet or naming all the fruits in his fruit salad, remarking life's great variety or asking what was wrong (in his own silent way) while poking endlessly at a smoldering log. She thought, too, about poor Randolph, at the vet with his patchy fur and begging, dying eyes. And she thought about the pale bachelor lyricist, how he had once come to see her, and how he hadn't even placed enough pressure on the doorbell to make it ring, and so had stood there waiting on the porch, holding a purple coneflower, until she just happened to walk by the front-room window and see him standing there. *O poetry!* When she invited him in, and he gave her the flower and sat down to decry the coded bloom and doom of all things, decry as well his own unearned deathlessness, how everything hurtles toward oblivion except words, which assemble themselves in time like molecules in space, for God was an act—an act!—of language, it hadn't seemed silly to her, not really, at least not *that* silly.

The wind was gusting. She looked at her watch, worried now about her mother. She turned on the radio to find a weather report, though the stations all seemed to be playing strange, redone versions of American pop songs from 1970. Every so often there was a two-minute quiz show—Who is the president of France? Is a tomato a vegetable or a fruit?—questions that the callers rarely if ever answered correctly, which made the show quite embarrassing to listen to. Why did they do it? Puzzles, quizzes, game shows. Abby knew from A.S.T. that a surprising percentage of those taking the college-entrance exams never actually applied to college. People just loved a test. Wasn't that true? People loved to put themselves to one.

Her mother was now knocking on the glass. She was muddy and wet. Abby unlocked the door and pushed it open. "Was it worth it?" Abby asked.

Her mother got in, big and dank and puffing. She started the car without looking at her daughter. "What a bridge!" she said finally.

The next day they made their way along the Antrim coast, through towns bannered with Union Jacks and lines from

Scottish hymns, down to Derry with its barbed wire and I.R.A. scrawlings on the city walls—"John Major is a Zionist Jew." ("Hello," said a British officer, when they stopped to stare.) Then they escaped across bandit country, and once more down across the border into the south, down the Donegal coast, its fishing villages like some old, never-was Cape Cod. Staring out through the windshield, off into the horizon, Abby began to think that all the beauty and ugliness and turbulence you found scattered through nature you could also find in people themselves, all collected in them, all together in one place. No matter what terror or loveliness the earth could produce—winds, seas—a person could produce the same, lived with the same, lived with all that mixed-up nature swirling inside, every bit. There was nothing as complex in the world—no flower or stone—as a single "hello" from a human being.

Once in a while Abby and her mother broke their silences with talk of Mrs. Mallon's job as office manager at a small flashlight company—"I had to totally rearrange our insurance policies. The dental and major-medical were eating our lunch!"—or with questions about the route signs, or the black dots signifying auto deaths. But mostly her mother wanted to talk about Abby's shaky marriage and what she was going to do. "Look, another ruined abbey," she took to saying, every time they passed a heap of medieval stones.

"When are you going back to Bob?"

"I went back," said Abby. "But then I left again. Whoops."

Her mother sighed. "Women of your generation are always hoping for some other kind of romance than the one they have," said Mrs. Mallon. "Aren't they?"

"Who knows?" said Abby. She was starting to feel a little tight-lipped with her mother, crammed into this space together like astronauts. She was starting to have a highly inflamed sense of event: a single word rang and vibrated. The slightest movement could annoy, a breath, an odor. Unlike her sister Theda, who had always remained sunny and cheerfully intimate with everyone, Abby had always been darker and left to her own devices; she and her mother had never been very close. When Abby was a child, her mother had always repelled her a bit—the oily smell of her hair, her belly button like a worm curled in a pit, the sanitary napkins in the bathroom wastebasket, horrid as a war, then later strewn along the curb by raccoons who would tear them from the trash cans at night. Once, at a restaurant, when she was little, Abby had burst into an unlatched ladies' room stall, only to find her mother sitting there, in a dazed and unseemly way, peering out at her from the toilet seat, like a cuckoo in a clock.

There were things one should never know about another person.

Later, Abby decided that perhaps it hadn't been her mother at all.

Yet now, here she and her mother were, sharing the tiniest of cars, reunited in a wheeled and metal womb, sharing small double cots in bed-and-breakfasts, waking up with mouths stale and close upon each other or backs turned and rocking in angry-seeming humps. *The land of ire!* Talk of Abby's marriage and its possible demise trotted before them on the road like a herd of sheep, insomnia's sheep, and it made Abby want to have a gun.

"I never bothered with conventional romantic fluff," said Mrs. Mallon. "I wasn't the type. I always worked, and I was practical, put myself forward, and got things done and over with. If I liked a man, I asked him out myself. That's how I met your father. I asked him out. I even proposed the marriage."

"I know."

"And then I stayed with him until the day he died. Actually, three days after. He was a good man." She paused. "Which is more than I can say about some people."

Abby didn't say anything.

"Bob's a good man," added Mrs. Mallon.

"I didn't say he wasn't."

There was silence again between them now as the countryside once more unfolded its quilt of greens, the old roads triggering memories as if this were a land she had travelled long ago, its mix of luck and unluck like her own past; it seemed stuck in time like a daydream or a book. Up close the mountains were craggy, scabby with rock and green, like a buck's antlers losing their fuzz. But distance filled the gaps with moss. Wasn't that the truth? Abby sat quietly glugging Ballygowan water from a plastic bottle and popping Extra Strong Mints. Perhaps she should turn on the radio, listen to one of the call-in quizzes or to the news. But then her mother would take over, fiddle and re-tune. Her mother was always searching for country music, songs with the words "devil woman." She loved those.

"Promise me one thing," said Mrs. Mallon.

"What?" said Abby.

"That you'll try with Bob."

At what price? Abby wanted to yell, but she and her mother were too old for that now.

Mrs. Mallon continued, thoughtfully, with the sort of pseudo-wisdom she donned now that she was sixty. "Once you're with a man you have to sit still with him. As scary as it seems. You have to be brave and learn to reap the benefits of inertia," and here she gunned the motor to pass a tractor on a curve. "Loose chippings," said the sign. "Hidden dip." But Abby's mother drove as if these were cocktail-party chatter. A sign ahead showed six black dots.

"Yeah," said Abby, clutching the dashboard. "Dad was inert. Dad was inert except that once every three years he jumped up and socked somebody in the mouth."

"That's not true."

"It's basically true."

In Killybegs, they followed the signs for Donegal City. "You women today," Mrs. Mallon said. "You expect too much."

"If it's Tuesday, this must be Sligo," said Abby. She had taken to making up stupid jokes. "What do you call a bus with a soccer team on it?"

"What?" They passed a family of gypsies, camped next to a mountain of car batteries they hoped to sell.

"A football coach." Sometimes Abby laughed raucously and

sometimes not at all. Sometimes she just shrugged. She was waiting for the Blarney Stone. That was all she'd come here for, so everything else she could endure.

They stopped at a bookshop to get a better map and inquire, perhaps, about a bathroom. Inside there were four customers: two priests reading golf books, and a mother with her tiny son who traipsed after her along the shelves begging: "Please, Mummy, just a wee book, Mummy. Please just a wee book." There was no better map. There was no bathroom. "Sorry," the clerk said, and one of the priests glanced up quickly. Abby and her mother went next door to look at the Kinsale smocks and wool sweaters—tiny cardigans that young Irish children, on sweltering summer days of seventy-one degrees, wore on the beach, over their bathing suits. "So cute," said Abby, and the two of them wandered through the store, touching things. In the back, by the wool caps, Abby's mother found a marionette hanging from a ceiling hook and began to play with it a little, waving its arms to the store music, which was a Beethoven concerto. Abby went to pay for a smock, ask about a bathroom or a good pub, and when she came back her mother was still there, transfixed, conducting the concerto with the puppet. Her face was arranged in girlish joy, luminous, as Abby rarely saw it. When the concerto was over, Abby handed her a bag. "Here," she said, "I bought you a smock."

Mrs. Mallon let go of the marionette, and her face darkened. "I never had a real childhood," she said, taking the bag and looking off into the middle distance. "Being the oldest, I was always my mother's confidante. I always had to act grown-up and responsible. Which wasn't my natural nature." Abby steered her toward the door. "And then when I really was grown-up, there was Theda, who needed all my time, and your father, of course, with his demands. But then there was you. You I liked. You I could leave alone."

"I bought you a smock," Abby said again.

They used the bathroom at O'Hara's pub, bought a single mineral water and split it, then went on to the Drumcliff cemetery to see the dead Yeatses. Then they sped on toward Sligo City to find a room, and the next day were up and out to Knock, to watch lame women, sick women, women who wanted to get pregnant ("Knocked up," said Abby) rub their rosaries on the original stones of the shrine. They drove down to Clifden, around Connemara, to Galway and Limerick—"There once were two gals from America, one named Abby and her mother, named Erica. . . ." They sang, minstrel speed demons around the Ring of Kerry, its palm trees and blue and pink hydrangea like a set from an operetta. "Playgirls of the Western World!" exclaimed her mother. They came to rest, at dark, near Ballylicky, in a bed-and-breakfast, a former hunting lodge, in a glen just off the ring. They had a late supper of toddies and a soda bread their hostess called Curranty Dick.

"Don't I know it," said Mrs. Mallon. Which depressed Abby—it was like a tacky fixture in a room—and so she excused herself and went upstairs, to bed.

It was the next day, through Ballylicky, Bantry, Skibbereen, and Cork, that they entered Blarney. At the castle the line to kiss the stone was long, hot, and frightening. It jammed the tiny winding stairs of the castle's suffocating left tower, and people pressed themselves against the dark wall to make room for others who had lost their nerve and were coming back down.

"This is ridiculous," said Abby. But by the time they'd reached the top, her annoyance had turned to anxiety. To kiss the stone, she saw, people had to lie on their backs out over a parapet, stretching their necks out to place their lips on the underside of a supporting wall where the stone was laid. A strange-looking, leprechaunish man was squatting at the side of the stone, supposedly to help people arch back, but he seemed to be holding them too loosely, a careless and sadistic glint in his eyes, and some people were changing their minds and going back downstairs, fearful and inarticulate as ever.

"I don't think I can do this," said Abby hesitantly, tying her dark raincoat more tightly around her.

"Of course you can," said her mother. "You've come all this way. This is why you came." Now that they were at the top of the castle, the line seemed to be moving quickly. Abby looked back, and around, and the view was green and rich, and breathtaking, like a photo soaked in dyes.

"Next!" she heard the leprechaun shouting.

Ahead of them a German woman was struggling to get back up from where the leprechaun had left her. She wiped her mouth and made a face. "That vuz awfhul," she grumbled.

Panic seized Abby. "You know what? I don't want to do this," she said to her mother. There were only two people ahead of them in line. One of them was now getting down on his back, clutching the iron supports and inching his hands down, arching at the neck and waist to reach the stone, exposing his white throat. His wife stood above him, taking his picture.

"But you came all this way! Don't be a ninny!" Her mother was bullying her again. It never gave her courage; in fact, it deprived her of courage. But it gave her bitterness and impulsiveness, which could look like the same thing.

"Next," said the leprechaun nastily. He hated these people, one could see that. One could see he half hoped they would go crashing down off the ledge in a heap of raincoats, limbs, and traveller's checks.

"Go on," said Mrs. Mallon.

"I can't," Abby whined. Her mother was nudging and the leprechaun was frowning. "I can't. You go."

"No. Come on. Think of it as a test." Her mother, too, gave her a frown, then a lunatic scowl. "You work with tests. And in school you always did well on them."

"For tests you have to study."

"You studied!"

"I didn't study the right thing."

"Oh, Abby."

"I can't," Abby whispered. "I just don't think I can." She breathed deeply and moved quickly. "Oh—okay." She threw her hat down and fell to the stone floor fast, to get it over with.

"Move back, move back," droned the leprechaun, like a train conductor.

She could now feel no more space behind her back; from her

waist up she was out over air and hanging on only by her hands clenched around the iron rails. She bent her head as far back as she could, but it wasn't far enough.

"Lower," said the leprechaun.

She slid her hands down farther, as if she were doing a trick on a jungle gym. Still, she couldn't see the Stone itself, only the castle wall.

"Lower," said the leprechaun.

She slid her hands even lower, bent her head back, her chin skyward, could feel her windpipe pressing out against the skin, and this time she could see the Stone. It was about the size of a microwave oven and was covered with moisture and dirt and lipstick marks in the shape of lips—lavender, apricot, red. It seemed very unhygienic for a public attraction, filthy and wet, and so now, instead of giving it a big smack, she blew a peck at it, then shouted, "Okay, help me up, please," and the leprechaun helped her back up.

Abby stood and brushed herself off. Her raincoat was covered with whitish mud. "Eeyuhh," she said. But she had done it! At least sort of. She put her hat back on. She tipped the leprechaun a pound. She didn't know how she felt. She felt nothing. Finally, these dares one made with oneself didn't change a thing. They were all a construction of wish and string and distance.

"Now my turn," said her mother with a kind of reluctant determination, handing Abby her sunglasses. As her mother got down stiffly, inching her way toward the stone, Abby suddenly saw something she'd never seen before: her mother was terrified. For all her bullying and bravado, she was proceeding, and proceeding badly, through a great storm of terror in her brain. As her mother tried to inch herself back toward the Stone, Abby, now privy to her bare face, saw that this fierce bonfire of a woman had gone twitchy and melancholic—it was a ruse, all her formidable display. She was only trying to prove something, trying pointlessly to defy and overcome her fears—instead of just learning to live with them, since, hell, you were living with them anyway.

"Mom, you okay?" Mrs. Mallon's face was in a grimace, her

mouth open and bared. The former auburn of her hair had descended, Abby saw, to her teeth, which she'd let rust with years of coffee and tea.

Now the leprechaun was having to hold her more tightly than he had the other people. "Lower, now lower."

"Oh, God, not any lower," cried Mrs. Mallon.

"You're almost there."

"I don't see it."

"There, you got it?" He loosened his grip and let her slip further.

"Yes," she said. She let out a puckering, spitting sound. But then, when she struggled to come back up, she seemed to be stuck. Her legs thrashed out before her, her shoes loosened from her feet; her skirt rode up revealing the brown tops of her pantyhose. She was bent too strangely—from the hips, it seemed—and she was plump and didn't have the stomach muscles to lift herself back up. The leprechaun seemed to be having difficulty.

"Can someone here help me?"

"Oh, my God," said Abby, and she and a man in line immediately squatted next to Mrs. Mallon to help her. She was heavy, stiff with fright, and when they had finally lifted her and got her sitting, then standing again, she looked stricken and pale.

A guard near the staircase volunteered to escort her down.

"Would you like that, Mom?" Abby asked. Mrs. Mallon simply nodded.

"You get in front of us," the guard said to Abby in the singsong accent of County Cork, "just in case she falls." And Abby got in front, her coat taking the updraft and spreading to either side as she circled slowly down into the dungeon dark of the stairwell, into the black, like a bat new to its wings.

In a square in the center of town an evangelist was waving a Bible and shouting about "the brevity of life," how it was a thing grabbed by one hand and then gone, escaped through the fingers. "God's word is quick!" he called out.

"Let's go over there," said Abby, and she took her mother to a pub called Brady's Public House for a restorative Guinness. "Are you okay?" Abby kept asking. They still had no place to stay that night, and though it remained light quite late and the inns stayed open until ten, she imagined the two of them temporarily homeless, sleeping under the stars, snacking on slugs. Stars the size of Chicago! Dew like a pixie bath beneath them! They would lick it from their arms.

"I'm fine," Mrs. Mallon said, waving her daughter's questions away. "What a stone!"

"Mom," said Abby, frowning; she was now wondering about a few things. "When you went across that rope bridge, did you do that okay?"

Mrs. Mallon sighed. "Well, I got the idea of it," she said huffily. "But there were some gusts of wind that caused it to buck a little, and though some people thought that was fun, I had to get down and crawl back. You'll recall there was a little rain."

"You crawled back on your hands and knees."

"Well, yes," she admitted. "There was a nice Belgian man who helped me." She felt unmasked before her daughter and now gulped at her Guinness.

Abby tried to take a cheerful tone, switching the subject a little, and that reminded her of Theda, Theda somehow living in Abby's voice, her larynx suddenly a summer camp for the cheerful and slow. "Well, look at you!" said Abby. "Do you feel eloquent and confident, now that you've kissed the stone?"

"Not really." Mrs. Mallon shrugged.

Now that they had kissed it, or sort of, would they become self-conscious? What would they end up talking about? Movies, probably. Just as they always had at home. Movies with scenery, movies with songs.

"How about you?" asked Mrs. Mallon.

"Well," said Abby, "mostly I feel like we've probably caught strep throat. And yet, and yet—" here she sat up and leaned forward. No tests, or radio quizzes, or ungodly speeches, or brain-dead songs, or kookie prayers, or shouts, or prolix conversations that with drink and too much time always revealed how stupid and mean even the best people were, just simply this: "A toast. I feel a toast coming on."

"You do?"

"Yes, I do." No one had toasted Abby and Bob at their little wedding, and that's what had been wrong, she believed now. No toast. There had been only thirty guests, and they had simply eaten the ham canapés and gone home. How could such a marriage go right? It wasn't that such ceremonies were important in and of themselves. They were nothing. They were zeros. But they were zeros as placeholders; they held numbers and equations intact. And once you underwent them you could move on, know the empty power of their blessing, and not spend time missing them.

From here on in, she would believe in toasts. One was collecting itself now, in her head. She gazed over at her mother and took a deep breath. Perhaps her mother had never shown Abby affection, not really, but she had given her a knack for solitude, with its terrible lurches outward and its smooth glide back to peace. Abby would toast her for that. It was really the world that was your brutal mother, the one that nursed and neglected you, and your own mother was only your sibling in that world. Abby lifted her glass. "May the worst always be behind you, may the sun daily warm your arms. . . ." She looked down at her cocktail napkin for assistance, but there was only a cartoon of a big-chested colleen, two shamrocks over her breasts. Abby looked back up. *God's word is quick!* "May your car always start. . . ." But perhaps God might also begin with tall, slow words: the belly bloat of a fib, the distended tale. "And may you always have a clean shirt," she continued, her voice growing gallant, public, and loud, "and a holding roof, healthy children, and good cabbages—and may you be with me in my heart, Mother, as you are now, in this place, always and forever, like a flaming light."

There was noise in the pub.

Blank is to childhood as journey is to lips.

"Right," said Mrs. Mallon, looking into her stout in a concentrated, bright-eyed way. She had never been courted before, not once in her entire life, and now she blushed, ears on fire, lifted her pint, and drank.

~

EDITOR'S AFTERNOTE

Lorrie Moore, a professor of English at the University of Washington, has been quietly building a reputation as one of America's finest new writers. Playwright Wendy Wasserstein calls Moore's work, "witty, sharp, and very moving." She has authored two collections of short stories, *Self-Help* and *Like Life,* and two novels, *Anagrams* and, her latest effort, *Who Will Run the Frog Hospital?* Her short fiction is often adapted for stage productions and continuously singled out for accolades, prominent among these, inclusion in several *Best American Short Stories* anthologies, as well as 1994's *Prize Stories: The O. Henry Awards.* She is also a 1991 recipient of the Brandeis University Creative Arts award.

She is currently working on her third collection.

The Mothering Blackness
Maya Angelou

She came home running
    back to the mothering blackness
    deep in the smothering blackness
white tears icicle gold plains of her face
    She came home running

She came down creeping
    here to the black arms waiting
    now to the warm heart waiting
rime of alien dreams befrost her rich brown face
    She came down creeping

She came home blameless
    black yet as Hagar's daughter
    tall as was Sheba's daughter
threats of northern winds die on the desert's face
    She came home blameless

The Girl Who Gave Birth to Children

Jessica Amanda Salmonson

Keedy, the youngest daughter of three in a poor, undereducated family, early learned to evade her drunken father's fists and caresses and her ignorant mother's whining and complaints. Within their crowded little house, she managed by some marvelous method of introspection to remain reclusive and to live her life alone and in books. She had acquired the mystic power of invisibility, although, for many years, she thought only that she had learned to be ignored.

Her horrid mother, thin as a stick despite her inactive existence, smoked cigarette after cigarette, read Harlequin romances, spent most of her days in bed, and ate endless boxes of cherry cordials that the children weren't allowed to touch except maybe on Christmas. Every tooth in her head was long and rotten.

The two sisters painted their faces, arranged their hair, and dated grunting, broad-shouldered anthropoids. Between them they smoked as many packs a day as their mother. They strove violently to restrict Keedy from spending any daylight hours in their shared bedroom.

Keedy's eyes were always swollen and red from the constant exposure to cigarette smoke. Her throat was always sore. She was susceptible to colds, and other children in the neighborhood teased her for her runny nose.

Somehow, she carried on. She even managed, unbeknownst to her older sisters, to stay in the shared bedroom—while in her invisible state—during which moments Lisa and Marianne would be convinced they'd chased her out. Keedy would climb onto her very own bed, which was the only place in the house that she felt was really and truly somewhat her own territory, and sit in the very center of the rumpled bedspread, quietly reading. No one would even notice she was there.

The books were acquired at a nearby branch library, surreptitiously taken from a drugstore rack, or obtained from the paperback exchange a few blocks away on the main highway. She could trade ten of her mother's discarded romances for one or two books more to her own liking—often Mentor classics, because these were cheapest. In a private stash under the bed were badly worn copies of old-fashioned adventure novels, wherein Keedy discovered magic worlds of ideal or morbid beauty. She liked best those stories with historical settings and which were tragic but heroic, such as written by H. Rider Haggard, the Baroness Orczy, and Charles Dickens, each of whom her young mind thought had similar styles, contents, and intentions.

When she was in her fourteenth year, she calculatedly chose a lover. He was three years older than she, quite worldly by her impression, but still too young to have become cynical or cruel. He was very beautiful in face and body. She liked his wavy hair and his brown sleepy eyes. He was like an artist's dream of a sweet angel, an effeminate Gabriel, though such beauty would never last beyond adolescence. His balding father was as vile as her own; his mother as uselessly pathetic. His older brothers, after years of going through phases that alternated between extracurricular sports and thievery, had at long last gone away to join the military.

Beneath their families' noses, without being detected, Keedy and her beau explored the far-most reaches of one anothers' bodies. At age fifteen, as though for a birthday surprise, it was discovered she was pregnant. This had not been part of her calculation. She'd assured herself time and again that it wouldn't be possible to get pregnant until she was at least eighteen.

Angered parents softened in the short run and saw these children wed. He dropped out of high school a few months shy of graduation and went to work in a fast-food restaurant as night manager. He came home late and tired and smelling of hamburger grease and never talked to her about anything more interesting than how many kinds of frozen french fries the wholesalers had. She took care of the newborn girl in their stuffy studio apartment that got much too much hot sun and sat next to a noisy highway.

Soon after, she was carrying a second child. In time she gave birth to a son, while her husband worked his way rapidly to district manager, the youngest man in the franchise to have reached this level of success, although they still paid him very little.

When he became abusive, she left. It was easy to do. She'd only agreed to marry him in the first place so that her parents would stop yelling at her and so she could get away from them. But if he was going to yell and hit her, well, she might just as well have stayed home and gotten banged by her drunken father.

Most girls have trouble leaving such a situation. Their emotions trap them, as does their lack of self-esteem. But for Keedy, it was no problem. You can never change your past, but you can always change your future. That was her belief. After leaving, she contacted nobody for a long time, sought help from no one, figuring everything out on her own. She hitchhiked around the country for a while, dressed in a smart suit and heavy jacket that had belonged to her husband and passing for a scruffy-haired boy. Eight months later she called her mother collect and was informed she was a goddamned whore to have abandoned her children.

"I'm not completely heartless," said Keedy, "but I had to get away."

"Where would you be, young lady, if I had walked out on your father? Do you think that I didn't want to get away?"

She made no reply. Instead, she listened to her mother's loud abuse, and completely forgot whatever it was that had prompted her to make the call in the first place. Keedy learned, in between the nastier accusations, that her husband was in the process of divorcing her on the grounds of abandonment. He would inevitably be awarded custody of the children and had already dumped them on his mother to raise on his behalf.

"It may not be too late to stop the proceedings," said Keedy's mother. "He might take you back if you begged for his forgiveness."

"That's okay, let it be final."

"Don't you miss your children?"

"I miss them. But I'm only sixteen myself."

"You should have thought of that before!"

"I know, I'm no good."

"You're worse than no good, Keedy. You're in the clutches of the Devil."

"Yes, I know."

She never called her mother again. Never.

In Chicago she took to writing poetry and reading it aloud in different places. She had several pamphlets published on fine paper by letterpress publishers, in limited editions of from fifteen to a hundred copies. She was a cause célèbre in her immediate neighborhood. For money, she worked temp, office shitwork the regular secretaries wouldn't do. No one would give her a steady job, supposing she had wanted one, because she dressed in leather and black lace with extravagant earrings and her hair tied in weird knots.

Secretly, she was working on a novel about a girl in a rock-and-roll band who was in actuality an Israeli secret agent, and who saved the world from neo-Nazis who had built a death camp in Idaho to burn Indians, queers, communists, and Jews. She finished it when she was nineteen, and it was even more awful than the premise. But within two more years she finished her second book-length work. This one was about a girl who traveled around the Midwest disguised as a boy and had a bizarre romantic relationship with an eighty-year-old homosexual who fed her and housed her but was impotent and never even tried to feel her up, so he never knew the final heartthrob of his existence was a girl. It, surprisingly, found a good publisher, was reviewed in several important places, and its author was declared a prodigy.

Her novels thereafter fit no pattern or genre, thus she was taken seriously. Her second published novel was declared a work of art and even had a second printing in hardcover. She managed to get one short story in *The New Yorker* and two in *The Paris Review*. She had a fresh turn of mind and a cynical, abrupt manner of speech that made her a welcome interviewee on radio and local late-night television. She considered herself a feminist, but didn't like mainstream feminism, so she was often called on by the *Tribune* to give her quotably negative opinion on whatever women's issue was currently unfashionable to nay-say. Lots of people hated her as a result, and she thought that was great. It was all bullshit anyway.

Suddenly, when she was just shy of thirty years old, a fourteen-year-old girl called her on the phone and said, "Is this Keedy Osborne? I'm in town and I'm your daughter."

"Come on over if you want."

She met her daughter for the first time in all those years. She was stringy-haired, pig-eyed, overweight, and dirty-smelling. She had abominable taste in clothes, artificial fibers of pink and orange. She chain-smoked, stinking up the apartment, all the while trying to make Keedy feel guilty and ashamed.

"You gave birth to me. Doesn't that mean something to you?"

"I always liked to imagine that somewhere I had a daughter who was going to be a writer or a singer, or even a lousy poet, or save rare species of birds and mammals from extinction."

"Are you saying I'm not good enough?"

"My point is that there has to be something admirable before I can admire someone. It isn't enough to just be related."

"If I had a gun, I'd shoot you! I know where I can get one, too!"

"You've won me over after all," said Keedy.

"All right, I'll go, and you won't have to see me ever again. Can you give me any money?"

"Why should I give you money?"

"Because you didn't raise me. You owe me."

"What about your father?"

"He didn't raise me either. I ran away from Grandma. She's too strict. So just give me some money and I'll leave."

"I have barely enough to live on," said Keedy.

"You're a writer! You have lots of money!"

"Writers are paid very little. You'd be surprised."

"Well, you must have something, so give it to me."

"I have a heart of stone. You can't have even that."

Her daughter stormed out. Keedy got busy on a new book project that required a lot of library research. Late in the evenings she sat in a coffeehouse handwriting rough drafts or talking to friends. She had barely any time to think of her unpleasant, pig-eyed daughter. When she did think of her, she felt a mild degree of sadness, but not much else.

Keedy often wondered how people without talent—without something inside themselves that was special to hold on to—how they managed to survive. As for herself, she had never wanted to be close to her parents; she had spent the majority of her childhood being invisible to them. She had found private worlds instead and, to a degree, had grown up to make elements of those private worlds reality. But what of a child hurting and confused who had nothing inside herself to cling to? No love of literature, no imagination, no artistic ability?

A week later the girl called on the phone and said, "Have you thawed out? It must have been interesting to meet me."

Keedy couldn't think that it had been interesting at all. It had been mildly disappointing. She had given birth to an unattractive child very like almost anyone in her repugnant family, grasping and needful and hating all at the same time. It would have been nice if her loins had issued something of a finer substance.

"Listen," said Keedy, "I have never understood family feeling. I choose my friends on the basis of their individual merits, their artistic vision, and their willingness to put up with me."

"Aren't you feeling guilty? Aren't you feeling any pain?"

"I guess I'm not. Are you?"

"I'm feeling confusion."

"It's the old myth that blood is thicker than water that has you confused. People have to have something in common to like each other. You and I are strangers with nothing in common. I, for instance, am in love with books. Do you read?"

"Sure I read."

"What do you read?"

"Oh, Stephen King I guess. I've seen his movies anyway."

"You see, we have no meeting ground. I made a lot of mistakes and you'll make a lot of mistakes. Maybe you'll end up a wonderful individual in the end, maybe not. For me, my art is what matters, my writing. The reason families quarrel is they try to stick things out with one another, even when no one has any real liking for anyone else, nothing to go on except mutual bitterness and disappointment in life. It's destructive the way families pretend some vital thread connects them when all that keeps them together is fear and conventionality and mutual dislike. For some reason, I was able to turn my back on all that."

"But you're my mother. You should want me."

"I am moved, like anyone, by the pain of children, but I don't see that any genetic relationship gives you priority in my emotions. If that makes me so horrid, you should want to avoid me."

"I'm not blaming you for anything," she said in a wheedling voice. "Do you think you could loan me any money?"

"I could mail you five dollars."

"Oh. Well, good-bye."

A week later she got a long-distance phone call.

"Is this Keedy Osborne the writer?"

"You bet. Who's this?"

"It's your son."

"What a surprise."

"My sister came home this week and told me about you. I never knew I had a novelist mother. I thought you might like to know I write books, too."

"I guess it's in the blood."

"Could you tell me how to sell my novel?"

"You're thirteen, right? Look, it's too early to sell your novel."

"It's about a drug deal and some kids that solve the crime, and it has guns in it, too. I think it's pretty good."

"Okay, send it around to a few publishers."

"Could you do it for me?"

"No; you have to do that yourself."

"Could I mention your name?"

"I'd rather you didn't. I assure you it wouldn't help."

"Well, how does someone become a writer?"

"You keep writing for ten years without selling anything, without making any money, without anyone caring if you succeed or not. If you've got the stamina to keep doing it without any rewards, at the end of ten years someone publishes one of your books, and a year after that, it disappears."

"I have to wait ten years?"

"You don't wait ten years, you work ten years. And all that work is thrown away, because it's garbage."

"I don't think I'm writing garbage. Could I send it to you?"

"Writers are solitary. A good writer never asks his mother to read his book."

"What should I do?"

"Get a business degree. Or learn auto mechanics. But if for the next ten years you can ignore such excellent advice, then maybe you're cut out to be a writer."

"You won't help me get my book published?"

"I told you, if you think it's good enough, submit it to publishers in New York."

"Do you think I could get an agent?"

"You're not listening to me. You write and write for ten years, then you see what happens. A thirteen-year-old boy would have to be awfully precocious to write a publishable book."

"I'm pretty grown up."

"Writers usually read a lot. Do you read?"

"Yeah."

"How many books have you read since the year began?"

"I read *The Deer Hunter* and *The Odyssey*."

"What besides what your teacher made you read?"

"Oh, uh, I like movies."

"Then be a filmmaker."

"I don't know how."

"But you know how to write a book?"

"I've written one almost."

"Do you watch television?"

"Sure I do."

"How many shows did you watch last night?"

"Three or four, I don't know."

"Look, since the year began, you've read two books because your teacher made you. But yesterday alone you watched four shows on TV. Writers never watch television."

"Never?"

"Maybe I exaggerate a little. But writers are obsessed with words. You can't write if you don't read."

"I'd like to meet you sometime. Will you ever come to this town?"

"That's not very likely."

"Why not?"

"Why should I?"

"To see your kids."

"I've seen enough."

"Don't you like us?"

"I don't know you. How could I like you?"

"Because we're your kids."

"That's called circular logic and it's dumb."

"You must think about us sometimes."

"I used to think about the little babies I lugged around, and I rather liked them. But they no longer exist. Now they are teenagers and they're completely different from my memories."

"But since you're my mother, you should love me and help me publish my book."

"If I have a responsibility to love you on general principle, and to do you favors, then why don't you have an equal responsibility to be a more interesting kid or something?"

"I'm interesting."

"This call's not interesting."

"Then why are you talking to me?"

"Because you called me. It would be rude of me to hang up. Listen, if you want to write so badly, just remember, nobody is going to help you get started. Everyone will tell you to give up your dream. And that's the best thing anyone *can* do for you. If you've got the talent and the persistence, that's exactly what it takes to be a writer. No one can give that to you. You give it to yourself. So send me a copy of your first book after it's published and don't bother me in the meantime, all right?"

"You think I'm a bad writer, but you haven't even read my book."

"Can you play the piano?"

"No."

"Well, why not write a whole concerto right this minute? A kid playing the piano for the first time is going to sound awful. Should it be recorded and sold in the record shops? Maybe later he'll be good enough for that, but probably he never will be. It's the same with books. You don't just sit down and do good work. It takes practice, and a lot else that can't be explained."

"Grandma's paying for this call, so I guess I should go."

"Fine. Just remember not to ask any favors of people. Make yourself so good that you don't have to ask any favors. You'll be doing them a favor to let them buy your book, when you're good."

"I'll remember that."

"You're welcome."

Keedy was in a café with a latte and her best friend Winnie. "It's great to see you again. I still can't believe you've moved all the way to New York. There's no one else I can talk to like this."

"It sounds like you're taking it well," said Winnie. "I'd be climbing the walls, if it was me."

"The worst part," said Keedy, "is now I have to live with the fact that I gave birth to two totally ordinary people. If a random child called you up and asked you to send her money, or to publish his book, what would you do? You'd tell them to stop playing with the phone, then you'd hang up. But these two kids were related to me, even though they were strangers, and the societal myth is that because I gave birth to them, I have some continuing responsibility for their dreams, their greed, their everything. And if I fail them, then all the screwups of their entire lives will automatically be my fault. If mothers are so fucking the cause of everyone's troubles, then people should be glad not to have one."

"I had a kid once, when I was twelve," said Winnie. "I had to give her up for adoption. I don't know how I'd feel if she called me up. I suppose, if she ever gets in touch, I'll be glad to find out how she did. I guess I do feel some kind of inherent responsibility."

"Where there are responsibilities, there are rights. Doesn't a mother cat have a right to *eat* her babies if she wants? Humans are more civilized than cats. We have no inherent rights, therefore no responsibilities. Now, if you meet a perfect stranger who is just a little kid, and he or she has a lot of talent, it's easy to say, 'That's pretty damned good, kid. I'm surprised.' But when it's just an ordinary child who shoves garbage in your face, what are you supposed to do, lie? If you're honest, you're being cruel. Me, I wasn't cut out to be friends with stupid people, let alone their mother, because I've never learned to call a dog's turd a rose; I either clam up entirely or I tell the truth. There's no in-between. They don't like that I gave them life? Let them go kill themselves if it stinks so much!"

"You're annoyed because you'd been nurturing an illusion," said Winnie. "Now the illusion is shattered. You'd been hoping all those years that your children, despite that they were being raised by boring clods, were living inside themselves with imagination and awareness, just as you managed to do. As it turns out, they weren't aware of anything except their own anger and pain; they're clods among clods, and they think it's your fault life's not better. As an artist, it's hard for you to face the fact that not everything you've created was aesthetically conceived."

"It's true I was alarmed they were so commonplace. My mother, my father, my sisters, everyone in my family, are really unpleasant people. They're drunkards, child abusers, welfare frauds, and have no sense of aesthetics. A mathematician or numbers racketeer would never have given good odds for those two children turning out any different than the rest of the family."

"You should write a book about it."

"No thanks. I'll leave the investigation of banality to others."

Before dawn, Keedy awoke, hearing someone prying at the dining room window. She vaguely recalled having left it unlocked. She sat up and grabbed a bathrobe to cover her nude body, then sat perfectly still and listened.

They were whispering. "Is this the right place?"

"Of course. I wouldn't forget."

The second voice was a girl's.

Far, far away an ambulance or fire engine screamed through the night.

They came tiptoeing through the dark apartment. The boy was holding a gun, aiming it in front of himself, his hand shaking, his finger resting on the trigger.

"I don't know if I can do it," he whispered.

"You can. Just do it."

They were in her bedroom, looking at her bed.

"She's not there."

"Remember what Daddy said? Sometimes she's invisible. Shoot the bed."

"I can't do it."

"Give me the gun then."

"No, I can't do it."

He turned and ran back down the hallway to the window in the dining room. For a moment the young girl stood in the bedroom gazing from one shadow to another. She said, "We'll get you yet. You just wait." Then she followed after her brother.

Keedy sat there a long while after they were gone. Then she stood and walked to the dining room, staring out the open window. In the street, lamplight gleamed in a moist gutter. In an alley, a snoring man in a torn coat was a dark lump huddled in his dreams.

A weird little smile played across Keedy's lips. Those kids had come to Chicago with a gun and they'd worked out the whole plan. They weren't so ordinary after all. It was a perversely comforting discovery.

The man in the alley was rousing. Dawn spread her bloody illumination against the Chicago skyline. Keedy sauntered to the kitchenette to heat water for coffee, a chapter of a book seething from the edges of her subconscious.

～～

EDITOR'S AFTERNOTE

Jessica Amanda Salmonson is a versatile and prolific writer, whose books include *Phantom Waters: Northwest Legends of Rivers, Lakes and Shores, The Eleventh Jaguarundi and Other Mysterious Persons,* and *Mr. Monkey and Other Sumerian Fables.* Her short fiction wins praise, as well, with "Namer of the Beasts, Maker of the Souls" being cited by Arthurian specialist Phyllis Ann Karr as the most important Arthurian tale since Tennyson. Currently, she is editing the complete supernatural tales of the Victorian romantic Harriet Prescott Spofford.

Of her teenage character's "rather crippled motherhood" in "The Girl Who Gave Birth to Children," Salmonson has this to say, "Keedy is accepting and empathetic, but selfish and irresponsible. She found strength sufficient to abandon a culture of poverty, abuse, and ignorance. Yet by not allowing one childhood error to inform the rest of her life, she inevitably perpetuated the generations of neglect. She had unjust choices—to save herself or to save no one."

Salmonson believes "It can be a poison-bad world and we should all receive better survival kits when little."

I Must Go Down to the Sea Again

Nancy Holder

To Hannah, hanging up the phone was the sole miracle of the day. She managed the handset's descent from her ear toward the rest of the phone somewhere far below, only by moving slowly and being very, very careful. Her face prickled and felt as if it were stretching, until it lost all form, becoming weightless, floating at the surface of the sea, that endless Sargasso Sea, while the receiver sank into the cradle.

In the aftermath of the call, as she braced herself for the ropy vines to wind themselves around her limbs and pull her under, she found that this time she couldn't even take a breath, so massive was her sense of helplessness. Not an arm flailed; she didn't even blink. Dully she realized she was prepared to greet the undertow as an old friend, and thought, *Another death, this time of hope.*

Another.

Another.

Another.

And down she sank, nearly enjoying it, because it would be much worse on the surface, a building storm of sobs and shrieks and the furies of falling-down grief that crashed whitewater frozen and black and killing. Down in the dullness she could pretend she was still floating, still buoyant and lighter than air. Yet it wasn't fair to surrender yet. She, too, had promises to break before she slept.

Pushing upward through the thickness into the panic, hating it there, wanting to be done with her business and down again, she grabbed up the phone in the living room of their condo and punched in her husband's work number.

He answered at once, tersely, his name, their name. "Mandell."

"Hi, it was negative." No softening, no working up to it. They had learned that that was worse. No long, lingering deaths, but quick, like an execution.

"Oh, Hannah. Oh, I'm sorry." As if it were his fault. But Peter at forty was fine; he worked. Their first doctor, whittling away at the vast forest of their supposed fecundity, had told him his sperm was "Olympian." In her misery she had hated Peter for being so proud of it, although she had kept that to herself. When he'd said, "Well, thank God we don't have a male factor on top of everything else," she'd nodded mutely and climbed inside the little box the doctor had carved for her, large enough for Peter, too, who climbed inside with her out of love, out of choice.

"It's *our* fertility problem," he had promised her. "*We* are trying to get pregnant."

Now he said, "Honey, I'm so sorry."

"I'm sorry," she echoed.

"It's not your fault. It's no one's fault."

"Yes, I know." But if that were true, why was he proud of the quality of his sperm? And why had Dr. Covey, their third and current doctor, praised her for having produced such a wonderful uterine lining in which to implant these latest never-to-be children? And why had she flushed happily and watched the ultrasound monitor reveal this wonderful lining with such pleasure, basking in his approval like a good girl?

"Do you want me to come home?"

"No, it's all right. I pretty much knew this time."

"It was just a bad cycle. We just had bad luck."

The thing about her infertility was this: It was like buying lottery tickets, only when she had bad luck, she really *lost*. Each time she was not pregnant, she was not back to zero. She was not a little wistful, a little disappointed yet hopeful and back in line for more tickets. She was less than she had been. Something was taken away, as if in this lottery you had to decide what was most precious to you and stone it to death with your own hands—your job, your marriage, your health—because you clearly couldn't have it all the way fertile people did. The gods required sacrifices of you, just because. They insisted that everything you owned became chipped and bruised, for the sake of the children you still did not have.

There was not much more left of her battered world, of her. "Hannah?"

"It's all right," she said again. "It's almost one o'clock. You'll be home soon anyway." As she spoke, the words automatic and unconsidered, her mind stretched ahead to the future wherein their luck never changed, never, and because she was then too old and tired and broke, no one would give her a baby to adopt, either.

Up toward the surface, to the storm, to the blackwater panic—
Be still, be calm, she told herself. *There are always answers.*
No. No, there are not.

Because with Dr. Covey's, "Sorry, Hannah, I'm so very sorry," there had been another—another another another—death in her family.

The dream children:

The first one, for whom she and Peter had had the Big Talk and decided it was time. The giggling and endearingly awkward fumbling of sex without birth control for the first time ever, though they had been together a good long while. Blurring from one gender to the other, one age—an infant, an adolescent—to another, the first dream child was a perfect, splendid amalgam of all that was good and pure and beautiful about each of its perfect and splendid forebears. This was the child for whom she reread Gibran ("your children are not your own"). The child for whom she bought, shyly, the pregnancy and baby-name books and the first gossamer infant treasures: a silver picture frame, a tiny rattle, a suit (what do they call those strange one-piece garments?) of ducks. Why not assume, presume? Hannah was only thirty-four.

The death of that child came all at once, a huge shock, though she had mourned him and her and him again in bits and pieces, in ebbs and red flows, as gradually she and Peter began to suspect that something was wrong. By the time the confirmation of that wrongness was diagnosed, she had folded and refolded the little suit of ducks so many times, held it against her chest so tightly and whispered, *"Please,"* begged, *"Please,"* so often that by the time the HSG results came in, she could see the crease marks and tear stains on the soft fabric even in the dark.

And upon hearing that her tubes were blocked and that she must go to a fertility center, that one death telescoped back into the past to many deaths, each month a ridiculous, ignorant failure, so that she felt that she had lost perhaps a dozen children in those first two years of "trying," as everyone so quaintly put it: "You must be having so much fun!"

The death of the sexual act, or of the need for it: Peter's Olympian sperm washing like the tide into her unworking body, except for the times when he must give it to the fertility clinic's lab, in a cup. He had asked her to "help" him, though saliva and lubricants of any sort were forbidden; and she had sat on her freezing ass in front of him, writhing naked or half-clothed on the floor of a sperm bank or other "collection room," seething with resentment and shame. Until she told him she couldn't do it anymore: the death of marital lasciviousness.

"All right, then, if you're sure."

Hannah started. She had forgotten Peter was on the line. She said, "It's all right."

He used to come home without asking. Out of meetings, out of racquetball games, out of lunches with clients. He would fly into the house with tears streaming down his face—he cared as much, he wanted it as much—and hold her so hard she couldn't breathe. They kept each other's heads above the water; eventually, in some way they grieved their way to shore, touching bottom en route back to the doctor's office to discuss their bad test results or "failed cycle." That combined strength, coming together like sperm and egg to form a child of resilience, used to be the miracle that sprang out of what now appeared to be the lack thereof, the lack of miraculous good luck. And now, even that strength appeared to be gone. Perhaps after five cycles, that was what one should expect.

She should be fair. He was in middle management and now feared daily for his job: the firm had just been purchased and his department was redundant. They had spent over forty thousand dollars on tests and lab fees and cycles. Their charge cards were loaded, their savings nearly depleted.

Oh, my child, my children.

Each time, as she sat on the hospital bed and filled out forms, generally for the benefit of the anesthesiologist and the hospital's legal department, the curtain would pull back and she would see Dr. Covey in his scrubs, a sight that gave her a sharp, quick thrill. *He is the best doctor in his field, he wants to win, and we are doing something of substance today, he and I.* She understood and completely concurred with the religious notion of heroic conception, births from foreheads, from the sea, from swans and golden mists and holy spirits; she on the table, sometimes awake, sometimes sedated; he with his medical instruments and his tremendous knowledge; his handpicked embryologist in her lab next door, handing him a chalice of precious embryos, machines in the background oddly clicking. A strange but sacred trinity. And Peter, waiting and pacing, a strange sort of add-on, like Joseph, although possessed of heroic and very necessary seed.

If this particular cycle was a "stimulation" cycle, Hannah would have been given drugs to make her release many eggs for the lab to fertilize with Peter's sperm. Of course, not all of them would "take." So two days later, Dr. Covey would then tell them, in front of the opened curtain of the hospital room, the number and quality of embryos (for they were graded in much the same way as diamonds—symmetry, clarity, and so on). There would be guarded happiness if the numbers were good, more tension if they were not.

If it was a frozen cycle, he would tell them how many the lab had had to thaw to get the amount they wanted. Not all made the thaw. The extras, if there were any, continued to float in their subzero sea; souls on ice, they were called, lives that might or might not happen.

Then Dr. Covey would hand Peter and Hannah a color photocopy of the embryos he would transfer into her uterus. They would marvel at the blobby things; these were their potential children at cellular level. Baby pictures for infertile couples.

She had five such pictures now. She had kept them all, staring at each embryo, missing it, pressing her womb where they had swum in search of the liquid lining of her uterus, her own Oceanus Maternicus, not finding it, or not remaining there. The twenty who were gone, the six who had not made the thaw.

One remained frozen. They had one extra because it was reckless to put in more than four. With more, the chances of multiples went way up. Triplets were often born prematurely and afflicted with birth defects; one woman had recently miscarried hers at five months. Sometimes selective reduction was called for: the aborting of the one-or-two-too-many, an agony of riches after the anguish of abject pennilessness.

Her best friend Jane from the infertility group, RESOLVE, had undergone this procedure a month previous. Still pregnant with twins, Jane mourned the embryo that (who) had been "selected." She grieved, with life inside her, for the death. Hannah had sat *shiva* with her, nervous, envious, terrified that it would happen to her or that it might never happen to her. The death of tranquility, security, and certainty: it was a well-documented fact that the stress level of female infertility patients exceeded that of female cancer patients, even terminal cases.

Give me children, or else I die, Rachel had begged Jacob. And the prophet had replied, *Am I in God's stead, who hath withheld from thee the fruit of the womb?*

It made little sense to transfer just one embryo, Dr. Covey had explained before this last transfer. "But we'll talk about that later. We still have options. It's good we have that one," he added, with his smile that sometimes reassured Hannah and sometimes did not.

"You know I love you," Peter finished, and she was startled again. Hadn't he wondered at her long silence?

Or perhaps she had been wordless (childless) only a single, frozen second. Time was racing for her, and time was standing still. The tests and preparatory surgeries—HSG, FSH and estradiol levels, fertility panels, semen analyses, swim-up, laparoscopy, hysteroscopy—took months; the transfers, fifteen minutes per, half an hour max. The hour following the last transfer she had had to lie on the operating table with her feet elevated because someone else was lying on a gurney in the recovery room with her feet elevated, and there was no room for Hannah. On the way to the operating room, Hannah had seen the feet of the other patient in there, just her feet in their baby-blue hospital booties peeking from the towel-like blankets. It was one of the few times she felt herself in a cattle call: *so many others, and the odds always, always against us.*

"I love you, too," she said, in case she hadn't already.

This time it was easier to hang up, though not less painful.

There were other calls to be made; each time, she and Peter told fewer people, but some always knew. Others didn't, and things were becoming increasingly uncomfortable because of it. It was more difficult to get time off from her job for the myriad appointments—consults, ultrasounds, blood work, the three days of lying flat in bed following each transfer. Hannah worked in the research department at one of the networks. Before the discovery of her infertility, she had been ambitious, with schemes to produce any number of documentaries, including one on Samuel Taylor Coleridge, the author of *The Rime of the Ancient Mariner.* ("You lit majors," Peter had teased her once. "Who the hell is that?" She had explained to him that the *Ancient Mariner* was a retelling of the Flying Dutchman legend, about the captain of a ghost ship doomed to sail the seas for eternity with his crew of the dead. He hadn't heard of the Flying Dutchman, either, but told her it sounded great.)

Now her friends pointed out, quite logically, that she could produce an entire series on infertility, which was "hot." But that was another death to be mourned: she simply did not have the resources to work on anything. Checking facts was not work, it was make-work, and that she could do.

She could also lift the big folders in the photo morgue now, she thought vaguely. She could lift anything she wanted to. You only had to be careful until the negative pregnancy test. She knew her office mate, Alix, had always been skeptical of her "bad back." Now Hannah had to take a couple of days off every two months or so because it had gone out again. Alix was twenty-six, had one child, and had recently had an abortion. Hannah had cried all night after Alix came in to work and blithely announced that the deed was done.

Water, water, everywhere, and not a drop to drink. Other women got pregnant when they didn't even want to. Hookers got pregnant. Drug addicts got pregnant.

She stared at the phone. Her mother, who did not understand ("just relax and it'll happen"), would want to know. Her sisters, one in Toronto and one in Florida, would call her if she didn't call them. Her brother's wife. Her best friend who, despite everything, had an occasional "empathic failure," as Dr. Covey's social worker termed it. Her RESOLVE friends: Chris, who was negotiating with a surrogate into whom her embryos would be placed and who mourned the death of any hope of pregnancy of her own. Barb, whose husband refused to consider using a sperm donor or pursuing adoption. Carol, veteran of six miscarriages, whose second adoption had just fallen through. So few with families, with babies, with kids. Hardly any.

Hannah began to shake. Bulleting toward the surface, where the sea raged, she closed her eyes and imagined herself caught in the Sargasso Sea. How much more manageable the depression, how terrifying the catharsis found only on the surface. She sucked in the thick water of her unshed tears and let herself drown, sluggishly, into that good ocean. Into that good ocean.

The womb a cradle of life, the doctor a maker of life, the lab and its magic, animating clicks and whirs. The lives of the clinicians going on, calling other women, comforting some and congratulating others. (Did anyone really get pregnant?) Her husband, her love, who was at work. Lives that went on.

At once she fell to her knees, searching for purchase as she contracted with dry heaves. *No, no, no* the loudest in her mind but beneath it, *Please, oh, please,* as if her need would change the phone call, the lab results—*Golly, we're sorry; we called you with Jane's results! Why, she's not pregnant after all. You are!*— Wretched woman to think that, to hope that, to wish that.

Give me children.

Give me *children.*

On her hands and knees, the full brunt of her loss washed over her, the stormy crash of it, the wailing of banshee winds, waves flashing and the deck thundering. Praying for a capsize; she did not want to be here, to do this; this was not her ghost ship, this vessel of dead children. She saw them, pink babies slightly transparent, heard their insistent, newborn cries like dolls, tossed like dolls against the bulkheads, dangling above her from the sails. The ship, careening from side to side; she fell onto her side and curled up, resisting, resisting, trying with the last vestige of thought to remind herself that afterward it would be better. Afterward, afterward. There could be no afterward; there could be no now.

She threw back her head and the storm roared inside her mouth, inside her body. No gentle drowning, this; this was a murder, this was a rape; no kind intent, nothing, nothing—

—she was nothing—

The pain too intense. She grabbed her abdomen and shouted, "Come back!"

And the storm roared in, tidal wave, wall of redwater, into every orifice and crevice and all the holes in her heart; all gone, all dead—

She screamed; no sound came out as she whirlpooled in a vortex, as it fell in on her from all sides and was one unending surge of despair. She was blind and numb and frozen and dashed to bits, broken, more broken than she was, distorted, deformed, damned, and—

—no sound came out but a voice shouting her name, shouting "Hannah!"

And Peter was there on the floor beside her, throwing his arms around her. In her confusion she resisted: there was nothing to be comforted about, to be protected from. He forced her arms around himself in the pitch and roll of their living room and, gasping, dragged her against his body and held her. He rocked her, sobbing against her shoulder, saltwater tears, and warm.

"Oh, Hannah, oh, my poor baby."

At last, desperately, he was embraced. He rocked her, was heartbrokenly rocked.

Sound came out. It was his name: *Peter*. Their name. His life. Their life. For the moment, for the need, for the choice and love, coming together like sperm and egg.

"I needed you," he whispered. "I couldn't handle it at work. I wanted to come home. I wanted . . ."

"Ssh, ssh." She held him, held on to him, her eyes shut tight with gratitude that she had survived after all to feel this living thing that was theirs.

She cried, more quietly, for about an hour.

He comforted her as he wept. They comforted one another.

Shadows lengthened on the wall. The phone rang; the machine got it: her mother, sounding falsely cheerful: "How are *you* today?" Another call. Peter and Hannah lay unmoving on the floor, tears streaming down their faces.

The room darkened. Cars of returning workers susurrated on the highway, traffic surf. Their next-door neighbor came home and switched on the news.

With one voice they each whispered to the other, terribly frightened, terribly hopeful, "We have one left."

The sea beckoned; the Sargasso Sea of vines and forgetting and closed bedroom doors and closed curtains. The seabirds wheeled; the breezes tantalized.

Hannah thought of Dr. Covey's inscrutable smile and said, "I'll call the clinic for an appointment."

"I'll call your mother," he offered.

She kissed him softly on the lips, the third miracle of her day. For a short time longer they drifted, surrounded as if with water lilies by their children, by their little ones bobbing cradled by the foam as in a Pre-Raphaelite painting, crowns of flowers in their hair, their gossamer, heroic smiles, and then, in the starry night and quite alone, she and Peter made for shore.

For the Bad Luck Club: Alyson, Ginger, and Debbie. I love you all very much.

EDITOR'S AFTERNOTE

This unusual take on a mother coping with the death of a child was prompted, writes Nancy Holder, "because some of my nearest and closest friends are infertile. They are at this moment immersed in a hellish existence of medical treatments, adoption classes, hoping, waiting, exhilaration, and agony. It was for them that I wrote this story, and for all the infertile people everywhere."

Adds Holder, "Studies show that women suffering from infertility struggle with the same amount of stress as terminal cancer patients, and yet they do not receive the same amount of compassion and support. Instead, the reality of their pain is often denied by those closest to them, as well as by society at large."

With eighteen novels and sixty short stories behind her, Holder is a four-time winner of the Bram Stoker Award, a yearly accolade voted on and presented by members of the Horror Writers Association. She also authors best-selling romance fiction and, as an interesting sideline, occasionally writes television commercials for Japan. Holder and her husband, Wayne, live in San Diego.

Free Parking
Faye Kellerman

All of our family traditions are stupid, but at least, this one's harmless. And just maybe Great-granny enjoys it, although she never says so to me. At eighty-seven, Great-granny doesn't say much of anything. Not that she's senile. She knows all her children, her grandchildren, and her great-grandchildren, but she just doesn't talk anymore. Mom says she never talked much to begin with, so I suppose the adjustment was an easy one.

Great-granny has been in an old-age home for about six years now. It's called the Golden Years and it's a nice place, especially in the summertime. It has a fenced backyard that holds a sweeping lawn outlined with beds of jeweled marigolds. Behind the fence sits Taylor's Woods full of sweet-smelling leaves and crunchy bark that decays into soft ground that sinks beneath your sneakers. The backyard also has an old playset off to the side. When I was younger, I used to pass the time swinging. Even back then, the seat—a black leather strap—was cracked and dry, and the chains that held it creaked as I rose and fell. The rusty rhythm used to rock me into a trance, making the visiting hours go quickly.

But now I'm twelve and too old to swing, too old to play explorer in the woods. Mom expects more. Not that she makes me come. But if I'm going to come, I have to behave like an adult, whatever *that* means. I never liked the way adults act around old people. They're uncomfortable with them, like being elderly is contagious. They're freaked out by the palsies, and the bladder bags, by the toothlessness and drool. None of that stuff bothers me, but maybe that's because I've been visiting Great-granny forever. Besides, it isn't that much different from my school-mates, with Emma Tolosky munching on her hair, or David Robertson squeezing his zits, or the worst . . . Jason Rathers picking his nose and rubbing it in his history book. I'll take Granny over Jason any day of the week.

My family is considered a good one by the staff. We visit Great-granny with prune-eating regularity. Twice a week my grandma, my two great-aunts, and my mom trudge down to the home. It has become such a routine, it's been ritualized—Tuesday after-noon there are the soaps, Thursday morning is the Monopoly game, and then there's the bimonthly brunch picnic with all the aunts and cousins, weather permitting of course. I'm only obligated to go to the picnics, because I'm in school. But this particular Thursday, some kind of teacher's conference was called at my school, so I'm off.

Then Mom suggests that I might do a good deed and come with her. In an unusual burst of generosity, I say okay. I put down my book, put on my shoes, and climb way back in the van to make room for Grandma and her two sisters. Since we own a big car, Mom drives carpool.

My great-aunts have daughters, too, but *my* mom is the only one who visits Granny on a regular basis. Which gives my grandma lots of brownie points over her sisters. My great-aunts have tried to disparage mom's visits, Kate saying things like: "I'm so happy that Allison has so much free time. Connie works so hard as a lawyer."

Or sometimes, Great-aunt Renee would say, "Allison is such a caring girl. She should really think about becoming a social worker like my Judy."

My mom, who takes a very Zen approach to life, always chooses to ignore the barbs. Rather, it's like she never even hears them in the first place. *Nothing* ever bothers her. Not me and my mouth, not my klutzy older sister, not even my hypochondriac father, who has yet to figure out how he got from football hero to middle-age man. My mom has always been the eye in the swirling storm. All activity centers around her, but she never seems to get caught up by it. Always calm but caring, even if she is a space cadet. It's better than Emma's mom, who yells all the time.

Grandma, on the other hand, is not one to let things pass. Whenever her sisters would throw verbal daggers at my mom, Grandma Lion would get this steely look in her eyes and say things like:

"Your shmocial worker Judy has time for everyone except her family."

Or:

"And your Connie has *plenty* of time to go to the gym, but not to visit her own flesh and blood?"

Then Mom would take a deep breath and put on a serene smile and say, "Mom, Connie is Connie and I'm me."

Then Grandma would add, "Thank goodness for that." Otherwise, Granny would never have any visitors under sixty.

Of course Great-aunt Kate would have to defend her progeny. "Connie needs a way to burn up her frustrations at work, Ida."

"So let her lead an aerobics class for the people here at the home," Grandma would snap back.

Then Guru Mom would say in a calm voice, "Everybody has their own strengths."

"Your daughter is very wise," Great-aunt Kate would state with authority.

And Renee would agree and that would be that until the next time. Until the next visit when Mom would show up again and their daughters wouldn't. And the whole thing would repeat itself in some variation or another.

When *I* show up, well, it's almost too much for them to bear.

How sweet for Christy to come.

Isn't she a special girl.

What a little love you have there, Allison. She must take after you!

Meanwhile, I'm getting the chilly looks. My cousins might hate me. Except *I* have the computer and the CD-ROM and the modem. If they want to get their E-mail, they'll just have to put up with my mom and her quotes from *Zen and the Art of Motorcycle Maintenance,* which is an old book that beatniks used to read. Or was that Jack Kerouac?

Anyway, today Grandma wears a pink, polyester suit complete with matching plastic purse. Renee has on a bulky mustard sweater over black stretch pants. Kate chooses a multicolored caftan and dangling wooden earrings.

Kate has been married three times. Last time she took the plunge, she wanted an alternative ceremony. My second cousin Sandy, her grandniece, played the recorder as Kate danced down the aisle and threw autumn leaves and dried rose petals from a basket she had made in her junior college art class. She and her husband, Hubert, made vows to the Earth Goddess, Ceres, and prayed for the release of the Mother Spirit. My great-granny had raised her daughters Baptist, but if she disapproved of Kate's wedding, she never says so.

This morning, both Mom and I wear jeans, T-shirts, and sneakers. My T is red, Mom's is white. Mom made a vow to always wear white in some form or another because she says it symbolizes purity. She got that idea from one of the Eastern religion books on her nightstand. *I* think she wears white Ts because they're easy. Just throw on a Hanes special and you're dressed for any occasion.

We all arrive at the home around ten in the morning, time for Granny's mid-morning snack. Great-granny has her own semiprivate dining room composed of four round tables, six chairs per table. Granny is about four foot five and weighs about one fifty, down from her former weight of two hundred plus. She started losing pounds a while back, and everyone panicked that she was sick. It turned out to be a case of ill-fitting dentures.

Today, the snack is ice cream, so Great-granny's in seventh heaven. The dining room's jammed, staff working fast and furious, so we're expected to give a hand. I take to feeding Mr.

Zarapata. Carefully, I give him measured spoonfuls of orange sherbet. But he becomes impatient with me.

"You feed me like a baby," he croaks out testily. "Give me more."

I give him a bigger spoonful. Of course, he starts coughing. I wipe spittle off his mouth. "Told you so," I say.

"You little snot," he retorts.

"Yeah, yeah. Open your mouth."

He complies, then complains once again that I'm feeding him like a baby. And on and on it goes until he polishes off his sherbet and snack time's over. By the time I finish wiping his mouth, plumping his pillow, and adjusting the footrests of his wheelchair, Great-aunt Kate has set up the board on one of the cleared tables. Great-aunt Renee wheels Great-granny over, and Grandma pulls up five chairs. Mr. Zarapata asks if he can play, too, but tradition demands that only blood relatives play. He calls us all snots— and worse—until finally, a nurse wheels him away.

"We had enough tokens for eight," I say to Grandma.

"Rules are rules," she answers.

"Yeah, but who makes up the rules," I contest. "We do. So that means we can change them."

"Rules are rules," Renee answers.

"That's right," Kate agrees. "Rules are rules."

"Rules are a state of mind," my mother interjects. "In the universe, there are no absolutes."

"I want the thimble," Renee states.

"You had the thimble last week," Grandma says.

"No, I had the hat," Renee corrects.

"You had the thimble," Grandma repeats.

"Kate had the thimble," Renee says. "I had the hat."

I reach over and grab the thimble. "Here, Renee."

Renee takes the thimble. "I had the hat last week. You're thinking two weeks ago."

"Who wants to go first?" I say.

"Wait, Christy," Grandma says. "I even don't have my token yet. I think I'll be the iron."

"I was going to be the iron," Kate says. "Why don't you be the rocking horse? You had good luck with that last week."

"No, I had good luck with the shoe," Grandma says. "Okay, you be the iron, I'll be the shoe."

"I'll be the race car," I say. "I'll roll first to see who goes first."

"Wait, wait," Grandma says. "Your mother doesn't have her token. And nobody has any money. Who's the bank?"

"I can be the bank," my mom says.

"Mom, I'll be the bank," I say, picking up a stack of apricot-colored five-hundred-dollar bills. "By the time you count out the money, it'll be dark."

My mom gives me a gentle rap on the shoulder. "Have a little patience."

"You're so impatient, Christy," my grandma chides.

"It's because she's young," Renee pronounces.

"I know she's young," Grandma says. "But she's also impatient. Allison isn't impatient."

"That's because Allison has time," Renee mutters out loud under her breath.

"That's because her husband makes a *good* living and she doesn't have to work," Grandma mutters even louder under her breath.

I start doling out the cash. "Mom, did you choose a token yet?"

"You choose one for me."

I hand her the wheelbarrow. At this point, Mom closes her eyes and puts on her Buddha smile.

"You're not going to *chant* first, Allison." Renee turns to my grandma. "Ida, she's not going to chant, is she?"

Grandma reaches out and touches my mother's arm. "Allison, honey, we don't have time for the chant, today. Renee has a hairdresser's appointment."

Kate says, "Why are you going to the hairdresser's, Renee?"

My grandma gets a teasing look on her face. "She's got a date tonight—"

"Oh, hush up," Renee scolds. "It's not a date."

My mother says, "I refuse to play without some acknowledgment of the Higher Spirit."

"Oh, for goodness' sakes!" Renee mutters.

Grandma says, "Hush up. How about the hands' thing, Allison?"

"The universal hand circle would be lovely," Mom states. "Let's all join together and give praise to our spirits and souls."

We all take each other's hands. I'm sitting next to Great-granny. Her hand is dry, knobby, and liver-spotted. I give it a small kiss and Great-granny smiles. Slowly, she strokes my face with a crooked finger. I kiss her again and admire her nails. They are clean and manicured—courtesy of her daughters.

My mother closes her eyes and says, "Heavenly Being, we thank You for the opportunity to address You, and for the many blessings You have bestowed upon this family. Please bless the game we are about to play."

Mom opens her eyes and says, "Great-granny, do you want to be the hat?"

Great-granny grunts. Mom picks up the hat and places it on go.

"I'll roll first," I say. "Just to see who goes first."

"Just go, Christy," Grandma says. "I can see you're very impatient."

I roll the dice. I get a five. I buy a railroad.

Kate says, "Mom, you can be next." She rolls the dice for her and says, "Mom, do you want to buy Oriental?"

Great-granny grunts. Kate buys Oriental. She says, "So, Renee, tell me about this date that isn't a date."

Renee says, "There's nothing to tell."

Kate says, "So tell me the nothing. Who is he?"

"He's William the ex-insurance agent," Grandma says.

"Not ex," Renee clarifies. "He's retired."

"Did I ever meet him?" Mom wants to know.

Renee says, "He insured your house, Allison. Don't you remember?"

"I remember someone." She thinks for a moment. "I'm usually good at faces. What does he look like?"

"It's someone's turn," I state. "Whose turn is it?"

Grandma says, "He's nice-looking. Except for the beard. The beard has to go."

"I like the beard," Renee says.

"It's too white."

Renee says, "He's old, Ida. Of course, it's white."

Grandma says, "It looks like someone threw a pie in his face."

"I don't think I know him," my mother says. "Of course, David usually deals with the insurance agents."

"Whose turn is it?" I say in a singsong voice.

Nobody knows. Mom shrugs. "I'll go."

She rolls a seven and lands on Connecticut. "I think I'll buy . . . no forget it. I'll pass."

"Why?" I ask.

"Because if I buy the property, Great-granny can't get a monopoly."

I stare at her. "Mom, that's why you should buy the property. You want to block anyone else from getting a monopoly."

My mom smiles at me and whispers, "Christy, don't you know that Great-granny always wins?"

I frown. "You mean the game is fixed?"

"We prefer to think of it as predetermined."

Grandma says, "You're upsetting Christy's bile, Allison. Buy the property. Trade it to Great-granny later."

"It's okay if I buy it, Great-granny?" Mom asks.

"I don't believe this," I say to myself.

Great-granny grunts. Mom buys the property. It's Renee's turn. She rolls the dice and lands on my railroad. I make her pay me the twenty-five dollars.

"Such avarice," Renee states handing me five five-dollar bills.

"It's the rules," I say.

"I know it's the rules. It's just that you ask me for money with such relish!"

"She's young," Kate states. "So where are you and William, your nondate, going to go, Renee?"

"Probably The Submarine Station for a tuna sandwich."

"That's your date?" I say to my great-aunt. "A tuna sandwich at The Submarine Station?"

"I told you it isn't a date." Renee talks to me like I'm a child.

"Then why are you getting your hair done?" I ask.

"Because she wants to look nice," Grandma says as if I'm a moron. "Why are you going to The Submarine Station instead of The Salad Shop?"

"Because The Submarine Station is closer."

"Two blocks closer," my grandma says.

"Two blocks is two blocks," Renee says.

"Whose turn is it?" I'm dying of boredom.

Grandma picks up the dice and rolls. "I still don't understand why you'd want to go to The Submarine Station. I thought you like plate food."

Renee says, "I do like plate food."

"So do I," Kate pipes in. "I never could understand the breast of chicken sandwich. I like chicken on a plate, with a fork and a knife and nice glass of tea. Chicken does not belong in a sandwich."

"I can even understand the chicken sandwich," Grandma states. "But meatballs? Meatballs belong on spaghetti—"

"Or on rice," Renee interrupts.

"I'll give you rice," Grandma concedes. "But meatballs definitely do not belong in a sandwich. Like in Gardilucci's on Third. I don't understand these Italian restaurants."

"I agree that meatballs belong on a plate," Kate says. "But that's not true of all chopped meat. Take hamburgers, for instance. I like hamburgers in a sandwich, not on a plate."

"Hamburgers belong in a sandwich," my mom agrees.

I say, "Grandma, you landed on Chance. You're supposed to pick a card."

She picks a card, but doesn't read it. "So if you like plate food, Renee, why are you going to a sandwich place?"

Renee says, "Because sandwiches are easier to eat than plate food. I always spill on the first date."

Kate says, "I thought you said it wasn't a date."

"It isn't a date," Renee says. "But I still don't want to spill."

"You can spill with a sandwich," Grandma says. "Especially the big ones they make at The Submarine Station. You take a bite and it comes smushing out the other end."

I take the card from my grandmother, read it, and pay the fine with her money. "Grandma, you've got to roll again. You got doubles."

Grandma looks up. "I rolled doubles?"

"Yes."

"You're the boss, Christy." She rolls the dice absently. She gets doubles again.

"You want to buy State, Grandma?" I ask.

"Certainly I want to buy State! What do you think?" Grandma hands me two hundred dollars. "Give me change, honey."

Kate says, "You don't wrap your sandwiches in a napkin, Ida? I always wrap up my sandwiches. When I eat sandwiches. Mostly, I like plate food."

"Except hamburger," I mutter.

"Exactly," Kate agrees.

I give her change. "You rolled doubles again."

"Christy, hold on," Grandma says. "You're giving me a headache."

"Just trying to move the game along," I say with a strained smile.

"Then what?" Renee says. "We finish and I have to wait three hours for my hair appointment. Ida, roll the dice. You're making Christy antsy."

Grandma gets a ten and lands on Free Parking. "Where's my money? Christy, honey, you forgot to put the money for Free Parking."

"That's not in the rules," I state.

No one says anything, but I sense hostility. "You guys play with one hundred or five hundred?" I say, taking both bills from the bank.

Grandma smiles. "Now you're catching on. Monopoly isn't life, Christy. In life, there's no such thing as Free Parking."

Kate says, "To me, Free Parking symbolizes stagnation. You don't go anywhere, you don't do anything. You just sit there."

"Or it could be the elusive respite we're all looking for," Mom says. "The opportunity to meditate without interference."

"To me, Free Parking is family," Grandma says.

"The whole game is a metaphor for family," Kate states.

"It is?" I ask.

Grandma pats my hand. "You'll understand when you have your own children."

I nod as if I understand her.

"In the meantime, I'll take five hundred bucks." Grandma snatches the bill from my hand.

Renee says, "You know, Allison, if Christy hurries up and has a baby, you can have five generations of Hathaway women."

"I'm only twelve," I say.

"Say you have a baby at twenty-two," Kate says. "Not so impossible."

"Not at all," Grandma agrees.

"That means Mom has to make it to ninety-four," Renee says.

"Mom has longevity in the family," Kate says.

"It would be better to have the baby at twenty," Renee states.

Grandma says, "Mom, didn't your mother live to ninety-two?"

Great-granny grunts twice.

"Ninety-three, excuse me," Grandma states.

Renee says, "So split the difference and have a baby at twenty-one, Christy."

"Thanks for planning my life," I say.

"Oh, Christy." My grandma waves me away. "Can't you take a joke?"

I don't say anything because I know she's not joking. "Whose *turn* is it?" I say angrily.

"Mom, is it your turn?" Renee says.

"Great-granny had her turn," I say. "She bought Oriental, remember?"

"I'll take a turn," Renee says. "Unless you want to go ahead of me, Kate?"

I blurt out, "How do you guys *ever* finish anything? You move so slowly and talk so much, it'll be Easter by the time we're done."

Five pairs of eyes stare at me. Even *Granny* is looking at me. I suddenly feel embarrassed by my outburst. No one knows what to say, and I mutter an apology.

Renee pats my arm. "Aw, youth."

"It's hard being with a bunch of old ladies," Kate says.

"No, really, it's not," I say. "I'm just impatient." I pick up the dice and give them to Renee. "Your turn."

At first, everyone is real quiet, and I feel very bad. But after a few minutes, the chatter starts. I bite my lip and endure it. The rest of the afternoon moves *slowly*. I try to understand them, I try to be patient, I even try to contemplate the true meaning of Free Parking. But I fidget and squirm and probably make everyone feel uncomfortable. Two hours later, the game is still going. Renee checks her watch and says it's time for her hairdresser's appointment. Without ceremony, we clean up the board, get up, and kiss Great-granny good-bye. They will meet again for the game next week. I'm sure they'll be happy that I'll be in school.

After Mom has dropped off her kin, I turn to her. "How do you stand it week after week?"

"Stand what?"

"The game, Mom. They move so slow. It's so *boring!*"

"It depends what you want out of the game, Christy. For you, the outcome is important—who wins, who loses. For your grandma and her sisters, it's the process. The game is just an excuse for them to get together and chat."

"So why don't they just get together and chat?"

"Because then Great-granny wouldn't be included."

"She's hardly included now. They move her pieces, they talk around her. All *she* does is an occasional grunt."

She smiles at me and kisses my cheek. "You'll understand when you get older."

"Yeah, just like I'll understand the philosophy of Free Parking."

My mom pauses for a moment. "Some people race through life, Christy. Some people stroll through it. Whatever suits you, suits me. Just remember, whether you walk or run, it doesn't matter much. The finish line is still death."

I frowned. "What a morbid thought."

"Not if you have beautiful children like I do."

I stare at her. "That isn't a hint, is it?"

"A hint?"

"You guys kept talking that I should have a baby at twenty-one. They didn't really mean that, did they?"

"Of course not," she says. "They were just doing some idle talk."

"A lot of idle talk."

My mom kisses me. "Have a little patience, Christy."

"You sound like Grandma."

"I am her daughter. Maybe one day, you'll sound like me."

A scary thought. I say nothing.

"After all, we are four generations of Hathaway women." She smiles. "And maybe one day, when you're willing . . . and the Higher Spirit is willing . . . it will be five generations."

"But *not* at twenty-one," I say.

"I agree," Mom says. "No sense rushing things. Besides, it could all be for naught. You just might have a boy."

EDITOR'S AFTERNOTE

Though religion does not play an obvious role in Faye Kellerman's "Free Parking," it does for the main character of her nine best-selling mysteries, Peter Decker, to whom family is paramount. Unusual within the structure of a mystery, Decker's role as father, husband, and a man adjusting to life as an orthodox Jew, receives almost as many pages in *Sanctuary*—one of her most recent—as the detecting.

Given this, I asked Kellerman to rate religion's importance to her as a factor in maintaining the bonds between mother and child, as well as motherly bonds down through the generations.

She states, "As an observant Jew, I believe in two fundamental relationships—person to God and person to person. The mother/child bond is a subset of person to person. Our holy books devote many pages to how our foremothers related to their offspring; serving as teachers and guides from generation to generation. Our sages tell us it was the righteousness of the women—defying Pharaoh and having babies—that merited the Jews freedom from slavery and Egypt."

Married to novelist Jonathan Kellerman, Faye Kellerman lives with him and their four children in Los Angeles.

Ready

Paul Gervais

I haven't been in the States in over a year. People ask, "Sam, aren't there things you miss? Fanny Farmer Chocolates? The *CBS Evening News?*"

I eat well in Italy; I get the news. If my mother weren't in the midst of a crisis just now I really wouldn't be coming back at all.

Cliff called the other evening. "They've put her in the hospital," he said. "She doesn't eat. She's dehydrated. She can't do anything for herself anymore. They won't release her until we find a place for her to go. In fact, she's tied up; or at least she tells me she is. She calls ten times a night. I've got my hepatitis back, and it's her fault."

Sometimes I wonder if Cliff doesn't invite these problems that make his life miserable. Maybe he'd actually wanted that rare tropical eye infection he got swimming in Puerto Rico. Maybe he'd actually wanted to have the motorbike accident in Greece when he broke his leg and ended up getting hepatitis from a dirty needle. Maybe he wants this relapse. Some people thrive on troubles; they're made that way. When you say to them, How are things? the last thing they want to tell you is, Couldn't be better!

Five days later, I'm in Boston, standing beside my luggage at Cliff's front door in the South End. Gazing down at sand clogged between sidewalk bricks, I recall how it gets there: orange D.P.W. trucks spew the stuff out to icy streets the way a peasant in Tuscany seeds a plowed field.

Cliff comes to the door in sweatpants. He has coarse, coiling hair and a beard of the same short length. He's apparently been to a tanning studio again. The lines that fall from the corners of his nose to his lips are hard and deeply shadowed. He doesn't say hello, he just breathes out and his sallow cheeks shudder. A diminished fall sun shines through a stained-glass fanlight over-head (it shows a brig in high seas) and washes the walls of the entry with pinks, yellows, purples.

I'm afraid to say, "How're you doin', Cliff?" I'm afraid to touch him, shake his hand, kiss him the way brothers in Italy kiss after not seeing each other in a long, long time. Cliff and I don't act out emotions; we're full of attending feelings which, like seas, advance and ebb but always hold themselves just back a bit, minding their place. And Cliff's obvious anger makes me shy. I know that he feels abandoned, left to care for Meg all alone, and that he holds my absence against me and always will.

Inside, upstairs, Danny's in the shower. Alone now in the living room, I hear spraying water; then it stops. The phone rings. Cliff comes back into the room. "Now it starts," he says.

"That's her?" I say.

"Of course it's her."

"How do you know?"

"Who else is it?" he says.

"Well, answer it," I say.

Cliff goes to the phone. "Hi," he says, then listens. "I was at work where I always am!" His voice is brittle, sickly, but its volume expands, gaining wind. I stand there quietly, watching his clouded eyes, and then he hands me the phone. "She's calling from prison," he says.

"Hi," I say.

"Who did this to me?" Meg says.

"Did what?"

"Put me in prison."

"In prison?" I say, laughing.

"In jail!" she says. "I'm in jail and I just want to ask you one thing. Why am I here?"

"You're not in jail," I tell her. "You're in the hospital."

Her speech gets clipped. "I am *not* in the hospital." Her voice picks up with emphasis. "You know damn well I'm not!"

"What language!" I say, winking at Cliff.

"I'm not the same," she says. "Who would be? I don't care. I'm in jail in North Tewksbury and who knows what they'll do. They could bop me over the head and take my money. They have me tied up." She starts to cry. "I can't believe it. I can't believe this is happening to me."

"Tell her to read what it says on the sheets," Cliff says.

"I'm coming to see you tomorrow," I tell her.

"It's written on the sheets," Cliff says. "St. John's Hospital. Just tell her to read it."

I don't want to go through all this stuff about the sheets, build a whole case and work on convincing her that she's in the hospital and not in jail like she thinks. This is Cliff's approach. I'd have my own.

Cliff went to business college in Boston, then settled for a dull, secure job with a big bank. Bow ties make Cliff happy. Dinners at The Whistling Oyster in Ogunquit July nights. Barbara Cook concerts at the North Shore Music Tent. February cruises in the Antilles. I'd always wanted more than that. I studied enology at Davis so I could work in wine country anywhere, get out of Boston once and for all.

"I'll be coming in to see you tomorrow morning," I say. "Can you hold out till then?"

Meg stops crying. "What time?" she asks.

"Early," I say. "Just wait for me there."

"Wait for you!" Meg laughs. "I'm all tied up. Wait for you! Jeesh!"

"How did you do that?" Cliff says, once I've hung up.

"Do what?"

"Get rid of her so fast."

"I don't know," I say. I take off my necktie and sit on the smooth beige couch that goes with the chair Cliff's sitting on, his feet pulled up under him.

Danny comes in. I stand and shake his hand. Danny's from Argentina; he has clear blue eyes going to white at the irises and a tightly trimmed beard just like Cliff's. In the corner of the living room is a wicker daybed, and Danny sits on it with his ankles crossed. "Was that her?" he asks.

"Of course it was her," says Cliff.

"I unplug the phone after a while," says Danny. "Cliff can't handle it. He's been very sick with this hepatitis thing. He needs a rest."

"She brought it on," Cliff says. "She's driving me nuts. I haven't got a moment's peace. I haven't had a vacation in a year and a half because I'm afraid to go away and leave her. My doctor's prescribed Valium . . ." There's an incantatory rhythm to Cliff's speech, highs and lows on a regular beat. "And now she's in the hospital!"

"Tell me what the doctors are doing," I say.

"Her doctors are all jerks," he says.

"Oh?"

"They had a neurologist in."

"What did he find?"

"Brain damage," he says. "That's all they can tell me. Irreversible brain damage."

"But do they think that cancer is the cause?" asks Danny, whose words are separated by spaces as on a printed page.

"Years of hard drinking is the cause," I say, looking around for reactions. "Last year, her oncologist told me that her liver was injured because she tends to have 'too many cocktails.' That was the way he put it. Because her liver isn't doing its job of purifying the blood, brain cells are getting killed off."

"But she never had a drinking problem," says Danny. "Did she, Cliff?"

"Of course she did," I say. "She's an alcoholic. She's been an alcoholic for thirty years. When we were kids living at home, she was drunk every night."

Danny looks at Cliff as if expecting him to disagree.

"It's true," says Cliff. "She drank in the kitchen. She blocked off the door with a heavy stuffed chair so nobody sitting on the living room couch could look through the hallway and see her drinking by the sink."

"I never knew that," says Danny.

I'm surprised. Danny and Cliff have been together for years. Why doesn't Danny know all there is to know about Meg?

Danny gets up, climbs the stairs to the loft, and turns on the TV. I hear canned laughter and the voice of an American child getting smart with her mother, saying the clever words adults wrote for her.

"I'll start dinner," Cliff says, then goes to the kitchen.

"Want to watch TV?" Danny calls down.

I climb the carpeted wooden stairs, which creak and move under me like a living thing. Danny's lying flat out on the couch in his stocking feet, his arms wrapped up around his head. I duck down under the low ceiling and, feeling as if I've come into a temple, take off my shoes and sink to the floor cross-legged, my eyes on the light of the TV screen.

"This sitcom's one of the biggest hits of the season," Danny says.

I'm not really watching, but pretending. I'm not listening, not following the story. The lacquered stovepipe behind my head heats up and snaps and I smell chicken getting cooked with gas. In a minute Cliff comes upstairs and sits on the floor beside the couch. Danny puts his arm around him, and I wonder if I'm imagining that Cliff's heavy expression changes, just a little, to a lighter one, and that it lingers there at least until the telephone rings and it's Meg again.

It's five-thirty A.M. I slept on a spare bed in the loft. Now I'm up and it's tricky getting dressed all stooped over under the low ceiling.

I find Cliff downstairs in the bedroom ironing a shirt for work. Hung on a closet door behind his back is one of Meg's nightgowns, with a frilly collar and a bow at the throat.

"Will you take that to her?" says Cliff, tossing his head back. "I washed it."

I gaze at the nightgown hanging loose and flat, clean and pressed; how tiny it looks, as if it belongs to a little girl.

Danny's still in bed. He's on sabbatical from his teaching job at Wellesley College and spends his days fixing up a house in Roxbury that he and Cliff just bought. "Hey, Cisco," Cliff calls out, saying it the way Poncho always did in the last scene of *The Cisco Kid*. Danny stirs, curling himself up under the dark blue down comforter for a final doze. Cliff finishes pressing his shirt, giving it a stiff, human form like a suit of armor. I'm grateful to be seeing Danny asleep, to be watching Cliff iron his shirt, to have seen more deeply into their things, the insides of their closets stuffed with camping gear, the old toboggan we had as kids that I haven't thought about in years.

"Hey, Cisco!" Cliff calls, louder this time.

Volunteers with untidy makeup jobs and pink smocks work the front desk at the hospital. They all know me—Meg started volunteering here when I was in the fifth grade. It's not visiting hours, but the ladies tell me to go on upstairs just the same.

"I *thought* that was you," Meg says as I walk in. "I recognized your footsteps." Her hair is matted and her eyes are wide and outsized like a baby's. She's wearing a robin's-egg-blue robe and white terry slippers that the hospital supplies.

"You know," she says. "I was just looking in my pocketbook. I only have thirty dollars. That's crazy. Supposing the girls come by and want to go out to lunch. I'll feel like two cents if I can't pay."

I notice it. It's like a white vest with only a front, and there are straps at the four corners. The straps go around the back of her chair and then they're tied together with bows like shoelaces. "I don't think you'll be going out to lunch," I say. "You're in the hospital. They don't let patients go trotting off to restaurants with their friends."

"I'm in the hospital?"

"Yes," I say.

"I'm not in North Tewksbury?"

"You're in St. John's Hospital in Lowell."

She looks to the window, then to the door. "Is this my room?"

"Yes," I say.

Something connects in her mind, as if a plug, loose in its outlet, got pushed back in. "Oh, of course," she says, and smiles. "Those are my flowers. That's my snowman."

"It's cute, the snowman."

"Cliff gave it to me." She thinks a minute. "Then where are my clothes?"

There are two closets. "In there, I guess," I say, pointing. I get up and open one of them. There's a green linen sport coat and a Polo shirt on a hanger. On the floor is a pair of running shoes, toes facing out, with white cotton socks stuffed inside.

"That's all?" she asks, losing patience.

"That's all *here*," I say.

"Then where are the rest of them?" she says.

"At home."

"In North Tewksbury?"

"You live in Andover," I explain.

"*I* know I live in Andover," she says, offended. "Jeesh! Don't you think I know things?"

I sit.

"That's all I hear from Cliff," she says. " 'You don't remember anything! Your mind is gone!' I'm forgetful, that's all. So what of it?"

A girl in white comes in with a menu for tomorrow's meals and a yellow half-sized pencil. "Oh, *there* you are!" says Meg. She looks back at me, a smile coming to the left side of her face. "They hate me, these girls," she says. The girl's legs are as big around as Meg's waist (I can't get over the fat in the States). "You all hate me," Meg says, "don't you?"

The girl laughs and makes some little remark in an understanding tone.

Meg puts her hand to the side of her mouth. "Well, they're apt to tie you up, you know," she whispers.

The girl leaves, smiling.

"But I fooled them, once," Meg says. "I untied myself. They couldn't get over it. 'How'd you do that?' they said. Well, I did it, by gosh! Oh, I was going all over the place!"

I laugh, then feel a certain other kind of laugh coming on, one that comes from the center of the heart. It's like having drunk a concentrate of all funny things ever shared with Meg, all the absurd situations we'd ever found ourselves in together.

She opens her meal stand; it's become a toilet case containing topless lipstick, liquid makeup, a hairbrush. She takes the teeth out of her mouth and fumbles with a tube of denture paste. Her hands shake as she squeezes out the pink adhesive.

"When am I going home?" she says, once everything's in place again.

"Well . . . this is the question," I say.

"Why?" she asks.

"We have to find a place for you to live," I tell her. "A place where you can have care."

She gets angry. "Oh, so I'm going into a nursing home," she says. "Is that it?" Obviously, Cliff has been preparing her for this.

"There are nice ones," I say. "I think you could be happy in a nice one."

"Cliff wants me to go into the Prescott House. He says they have to dress for dinner every night." She gets excited and almost shouts. "I don't have the clothes for that! I'd have to get long velvet dresses. I don't want to wear long dresses!"

"It's not like that," I say. "You misunderstood."

There's a moment of silence. "So I'm never going home again," she says, breaking it. "Is that what you mean?"

I'm afraid to say, "Yes, that's it. You're never going home again. You'll never see your apartment again, your things, your cat." I can't bring myself to tell her straight out; instead, I sit silently, my eyes lowered.

"You mean this is it for me now, isn't it?" she says. "This is it for the rest of my life. This room. This chair." She puts a hand to her face and begins to cry. Her chin trembles. Her eyes squeeze shut.

*   *   *

I'm going to the nursing home where "Grampa," Meg's father, died. Even though most things I pass look different, a few familiar landmarks lead the way: Shedd Park, where I used to play in the summer, and a colonial saltbox I once coveted, where, on weekends, a perfect family, so different from mine, tended banks of impatiens along a white split-rail fence, or raked leaves together beneath a towering elm.

The social services director at the Beaconhurst graduated from high school with my young second cousin whom I'll always think of as a little boy. "Does she have problems staying put?" she asks me after we've discussed Meg's condition. "Is she apt to wander?"

"Maybe," I say.

"Well," she says, "our wanderers here are fitted out with electronic signaling devices which they wear at all times, strapped to their ankles. When they go through the door, an alarm sounds and we nab them. We have one woman who's especially bad. Goes out at all hours."

She takes me on a tour and when the notorious wanderer goes by, holding on to the chrome-plated lifting rigs that line the hallways, the social services director points her out to me. "There she is," she says, "the escape artist." The woman has a white, dusty complexion, and wayward, dim eyes. She looks familiar in spite of the vague expression of terror. Isn't it Mrs. Burns, my Cub Scout den mother? I stop, following her face with my gaze as she passes slowly by; then I drop my eyes to the flesh-colored signal box strapped to her ankle.

"You're not minding your friend," says the social services director to a passing attendant. She points to the wanderer and smiles.

The nurse takes the woman's hand, "Come along now, Mrs. Burns," she says.

Meg's apartment was done by a decorator friend of Cliff's. I never saw it until after my father's death and I couldn't picture him reading the paper in one of those white slipcovered chairs with the African fan hanging behind his head and the West Indian basket-style hammock leaning against the wall by his side. Meg, on the other hand, always looked content there, as if she were on vacation in a rented condo in Florida.

In the hall I meet a neighbor, Mrs. Drake. "How's your mother?" she asks.

"Not so well," I say.

"We've been so worried about her," says Mrs. Drake. She's wearing a black raincoat and carries an electric heating pad and a bunch of other things under her arm.

The Drakes are my mother's age and yet their minds run smoothly. They go to Florida five months out of the year. They drive to Michigan together to visit their daughter. Seeing Mrs. Drake now, I ask myself, Why couldn't Meg have lived differently, been sober and minded her health so that things might be better for her now? I'm angry that Meg isn't like this woman who's taken careful, dignified steps along her route to old age.

"You're putting her in a home, your brother tells me," she says.

"I think she's beginning to realize herself that it's the only answer," I say. "Daily life is tough."

"Well, it's a good thing she feels that way," Mrs. Drake tells me. "I had to *force* my mother to go. I took her to the home myself and I left her there. I could hear her screaming as I drove out of the parking lot, and I can still hear her screaming, in my mind, right this very minute. But there comes a time—maybe it will happen to you, maybe it won't—when you have to walk away and leave them there. And I want to tell you, Sam, when that moment comes, you'd just better be ready for it, that's all."

Meg always says that her cat, Beatrice, hates men. When a man walks into her apartment, the cat hides and doesn't come out until he's gone. But I made friends with Beatrice during my last visit, coaxing her out from under one of the draped end tables beside the couch. I even got her to purr beneath my hand, and roll over playfully.

I can't believe the smell when I open the door to Meg's apartment. Cliff has been coming in to feed Beatrice, but he hasn't cleaned out her box. If her box is soiled, she goes in the bathroom sink or on the living room chairs. But even if the cat behaved herself and went in her cat box, the apartment would still be filthy, the air used up and close. For security, there are broom handles in the tracks of Meg's sliding glass doors. She lacks the agility to bend down, the dexterity to take the broom handles out so she could slide open the doors and let in fresh air.

Sitting on the wobbly piano bench, I look around and see this apartment in a new, different way. No longer my mother's home, it is the unlivable space in which a disaster has occurred; it is the dead center of all my hurt. I see these furnishings of hers not as a collection of still-good, functional things which might serve human needs in daily life, but as negated objects, soiled by a dreadful accident, which have to be disposed of.

In the afternoon, I visit two other nursing homes, better, more expensive ones, and decide that the second is the one I like best. Is it just because the social services director is so attractive, so well dressed, someone I know Meg would find cute and so might be happy to see every day? Maybe. But still, it seems like a good place, family run, spotless, with pink tablecloths in the dining rooms and waiters in bow ties.

At five I go back to the hospital to see Meg, who's now angry and even more confused. "Where have you been?" she shouts, furious to have been left alone for the afternoon.

"I've been visiting . . ." I don't want to say "nursing homes." "I've been looking at places for you to go to," I say.

"Do you know what I think?" she whispers, onto something. "I think Cliff is up to no good. I just heard that he's always off in Boston with my cancer doctor. Someone from here told me. They're thick as mud, the two of them. And here I am in jail. You think about this for a minute. What are they up to anyway? Oh, I *hate* Dr. Field. Honest to God, I hate that man for doing this to me."

"For doing what to you?" I say.

"I'm old now," she shouts. "You don't do this to old people."

"But this is a hospital," I explain, "not a jail."

"Oh, don't you tell me such nonsense. I'm in jail in North

Tewksbury and I'm fed up with it." Her chin crimps up and reddens, and she starts to cry again.

I have an idea. Wouldn't she understand she was in a hospital if she could step out into the corridors she knew so well as a volunteer?

"Let's take a little walk," I say, getting up.

Meg looks at her feet, then searches for her bag. I untie the restraint and it falls to the floor. "What's that?" she says.

"Nothing," I say, tossing it on the bed.

I help her into the robe my cousin Mary brought in—it's so long it drags on the floor behind her like a train. She hooks her Gucci bag over her arm, picks up a black wooden cane (I have no idea where it came from), then takes my arm. As the two of us step out of her room, tears, caught in the folds beneath Meg's eyes, reflect the bright overhead lights, and her cheeks rise in a poised smile like the one she must have worn as a volunteer delivering newspapers from ward to ward on Friday mornings. Suddenly, she is the woman everybody looked forward to seeing as she made her rounds: patients, nuns, orderlies, candy stripers.

Meg and I turn the corner, heading out of the ward, and pass three old men, restrained in wheelchairs. "Off for a little galli-vant," says Meg to their gray, stone faces.

But after a few steps, she's sad again. "I never thought it would come to this," she says. "Oh, gee . . ."

"To what?" I ask.

"Going into a nursing home." She sighs, stepping on. "Oh, well! I suppose I just have to face it, don't I?"

Did she really say that? I wonder. Does she really feel this way?

"I wish I'd known," she says. "I would have said good-bye to my cat, at least given her a last hug." Her face draws in.

There's something under my foot. I stop and bend down. It's a nurse's aide's plasticized ID with a photograph on it. I show it to Meg. "Do you know her?"

"No," she says.

"She lost her ID," I say, then invent a mission to distract Meg. "This is terrible! Without her ID, she might not know who she is. We'd better see if we can find her. Study this image well!"

Meg laughs and moves faster. She holds the cane under her arm as if it were an umbrella she'd made the mistake of carrying on a sunny day. We come to the station of the next ward, where there are two nurses whose faces are white-blue in computer light. I look at the ID, show it to Meg, then look at the nurses. "Is she there?" I whisper.

Meg laughs. "Course not," she says. The nurses are watching. "He's silly," she says, and gives me a little shove.

There's an old woman in a wheelchair beyond, and as we pass she reaches out to me. Her open palm is shriveled and flaked; I start to go to her and give her my hand, but I don't. I stay back.

"She wants you," says Meg, nudging me.

I hold up the ID to give Meg a look. "Is it her?" I say.

Meg laughs.

Down the hall we meet a patient, a woman, much younger than Meg, with dyed blond hair and traces of old makeup around her anxious eyes.

"Good evening," says Meg, her smile expanding.

"Greet'ns," says the woman.

"When are *you* going home?" asks Meg.

"Tamorrah," says the woman. She wears a floor-length white robe, as if she were already at home, en route from the bedroom to the kitchen for a glass of milk. "And you?" she says.

"Oh, I'm not going home," Meg tells her, confidently. "I'm going into a nursing home."

The woman steps back and frowns at me. Her face grows small and fierce. I feel despotic, ashamed to hold this ugly power over the small lives of others. "Nursin' home!" she says. "Holy Mother o' Gawd! Nobody's evah gonna put me in a gawddamn nursin' home. They'll have to chain me up first!"

I look at Meg, whose smile is all but gone. I want to get her away from this woman before she ruins everything. I take Meg by the arm. "We have to go along," I say. "Important job to do." I slip the lost ID into her hand. "Bye for now," I say, "Okay? Bye-bye!"

"Nevah say good-bye," the woman says. "Say so long."

"Good-bye," Meg says.

A few steps later, I feel confident that Meg isn't at all affected by the woman's feelings about nursing homes. Who knows what she's thinking about, but it isn't that, I'm sure.

All of a sudden, Meg laughs. "Imagine," she says, " 'so long.' I've never said 'so long' in my entire life. I'm not about to start now."

I go to dinner at a trendy new place in Andover. At the bar, I read the menu and nothing appeals to me; not the two enchiladas, not the blackened redfish, not the junior steak. I overhear people using expressions Cliff and I used as kids: "Whattaya, weird?" and "Whattaya, soft o' somethin'?" and in a moment I find myself alone with Cliff on a hot spring day, beyond the Gazecks' mown field, down at the bottom of Mill Hill where we skied in the winter, across the Garabedians' broad cornfield, and down, down a fern-covered, steep slope, bathing in Burr Brook, in its cold water, bending to dunk our elbows beside slippery black stones. Suddenly, someone else is there, way off there in the woods where we know no one ever goes. I see a shadow on the water which isn't Cliff's, isn't mine. I look up. It's Meg, so far away from the house, with a watermelon under her arm, with plates and napkins and knives and forks, standing, in shorts, with her legs spread wide apart (like a wrestler, my father always said).

The waitress lays out a paper place mat in front of me, gives me a glass of ice with a little water in it. "Yes?" she says.

I feel the way I felt when I first went to Italy and didn't know the language. I don't understand the customs anymore; I don't know what's expected of me. Across the bar a businessman, all alone, raises his beer and, looking at me, says, "Cheers," but I think he must be toasting someone else, someone behind me, in the scant reddish light. I don't dare turn around and look.

In the morning, I search for the impossible, the one-of-a-kind pre-chain, pre-big-business diner where I might find a fresh pot of coffee and a homemade bun, but have to settle instead for a microwaved muffin at Pewter Pot.

Back at my mother's place, the phone rings. It's Cliff. "Where have you been?" he says. "That guy Simon from Andover Manor has been trying to get you. They have an opening. They can take her on Monday morning."

I'm thrilled. No one at these homes seemed very confident about finding Meg an empty bed. "That's fantastic," I say.

"It is?" says Cliff. "What's the place like?"

"It's the best I've seen," I tell him. "It's very airy and has a pretty setting."

"Does she get a room of her own?"

"Ah . . . no," I say. "They're all doubles."

"You mean she'd have a roommate?"

"I'm afraid so."

"Oh, great," he says, laughing. "She's gonna love that."

"But her problem is loneliness, Cliff," I say. "No one to talk to. How do you know? She might love the other gal."

A silence.

"Well, I want to check it out," he says. "Call and see if you can get an appointment for tomorrow morning."

"Sure," I say.

It's Sunday. I put on a suit and tie for Mr. Simon. Cliff turns up on schedule with Danny, and they're both dressed in hunting outfits. Cliff, in a thickly stuffed, signal-orange quilted pullover, looks ruffled and bushed. Whenever he's with me, he seems to hold his mouth in a narrow, sour frown, but I can tell he's feeling this hepatitis relapse. He doesn't want to put Meg in a home any more than I do, and this, too, has him down.

Look, Cliff, I want to say to him. It's not your fault, not our fault, but just the fault of time, nothing more. And I do say something like this, but the words that come out don't seem to sound so good as the ones I put together in my mind, words like: Hours and days go by, Cliff, years and years. None of us can go ahead at the same pace forever. We tire somewhere along the way, all of us do.

Cliff isn't cordial to Mr. Simon. He barely looks him in the face, doesn't speak to him, doesn't ask questions the way Danny does, questions about the home's obligations to the "guest," legal points. Mr. Simon leaves us in the conference room to fill out the application.

When the door closes, Cliff says, "He's nothing but a shyster!"

"Shush," I say.

"I don't care," says Cliff. "He's just a moneygrubbing—"

"Shut up!" I shout. My echoing voice in the bare room sounds like that of a child.

We're all silent now, reading the prospectus. Cliff gets his calculator and starts figuring out whether or not Meg can afford this.

"Well?" I say. "Do we do it or not?"

Looking off, Cliff considers. "Yes," he finally says, softly.

I nod. "Okay," I say.

We have lunch together at The 99. I pick at my cheeseburger, knowing I can't digest all that fat. Cliff eats quickly, dutifully, in silence, now and then setting a crumpled paper napkin to his lips, and looking to the side at Danny. "You know, we're supposed to be in London on vacation," Cliff says. "But how can I go on vacation? What if something happened?"

"We're doing this, in part, for you, Cliff," I say. "With people looking after her, you don't have to worry anymore. Go next week. Go ahead. Make your reservations now."

"You don't know what I've been going through."

"He's really pretty sick," Danny says.

"Eventually, you have to decide that this can't destroy you, Cliff. We do our duty. We do all we can, but we have our own lives to lead, and the fact that we go on with these lives of ours has nothing to do with the scope of our love for Meg—"

Cliff pounces. "Oh, that's easy for you to say! You go off to Italy and I'm the one who's stuck here with the abuse!"

I don't snap back like I always did as a kid, or like I might have done up until just a few years ago. Instead, I look at Cliff and nod as if to say, Yes, you're right. Go on, Cliff. I deserve it.

"Want another beer?" Danny asks.

"No thanks," I say. I begin to think of all the things that have to be done: Meg's clothes to be gone through, her apartment to be broken up. And the cat? "You won't take the cat?" I say.

"We can't live with shredded furniture," says Danny.

"I don't blame you," I say. "But let's try to find her a home. Couldn't we?"

At the apartment, Danny and Cliff go through Meg's things. They take the silver plate flatware and linens. I gaze at a photograph of Meg on a boat in Acapulco, a picture I've always hated because it shows a woman whose mind is nearing death. Cliff had a rough trip with her there two years ago. In the photo, a mustached pirate holds an old Spanish pistol to Meg's head and threatens to shoot as she, grotesquely, crooks down the corners of her lips. When Cliff and Danny go, I'll destroy it.

On Monday morning I select, from Meg's immense wardrobe which contains doubles of everything, a warm outfit for her to wear: a tweed jacket with suede patches at the elbows, a cotton shirt with a bow at the neck, a forest-green woolen skirt. Cliff said it ought to be my job to take Meg to the nursing home, and I figured that seemed fair since I'd done so little for Meg over the years. Cliff is no good at times like these; he can't block out sorrow the way I block things out.

Meg, already dressed in the clothes she arrived in two weeks ago, is sitting in a chair waiting for me as I come in. Her bed is stripped. Her snowman is tucked in a plastic bag beside her chair.

"But you can't go out like that," I say.

"Like what?"

"A linen jacket and a short-sleeved shirt? It's cold now. Look at me. I've got a coat on, see? It's fall."

I have her change into the outfit I brought, but let her keep on the running shoes.

"And what is this place you're taking me to?" she says.

"Andover Manor," I tell her.

"What kind of a house is it?" she asks. "Are you sure about this? I'm happy to stay *here*, you know. This is a nice place, fixed up cute. Is this my room?"

"This *was* your room," I say. "But you're leaving now."

Jean Young, one of Meg's friends, a fellow volunteer, comes in to say good-bye, and Meg looks up and brightens.

"I think it's the best thing for you, to go over there," Jean says. "I've heard nothing but good about it. We'll come and see you, take you out to lunch." She looks at me. "Your mother loves the lunches, you know."

Meg tries to cover up her sadness with a quick change of subject. "Oh, you know who just came in, Jean?" she says. "That high-society gal, you know? Always in the paper." Her voice wavers and tears rush down her cheeks.

"High society?" says Jean. "I didn't know we had any high society in Lowell." She glances at me and winks.

I carry Meg's flowers; from out of a plastic bag marked "Personal Items" their blossoms unfurl. Jean, with the snowman, will come with us to the car, walking beside the girl who pushes Meg in a wheelchair. As we pass the desk, nurses go to Meg one at a time. Their puffy, bare arms engulf her and they kiss her on the cheek. They are sad to see her go. No doubt Meg will always have a way of pulling people into her life.

"Bye-bye," says Meg with a sort of laugh. "I knew I was going to cry. I'm going into a nursing home, you know! Good-bye," she cries.

"No one will ever find me here," says Meg, "surrounded by woods. What's through *there*, anyway?"

"It's a bird sanctuary," I explain, knowing, of course, that Meg has always thought of birds as nothing more than dinner for her cats. "You can take nature walks."

"With who?" she says. "I have no one to take walks with."

"With the other people who live here," I say.

We're met at the door by a young woman with a clipboard, not the attractive girl who took me through on my first visit but another one—"I'm Audrey"—who isn't Meg's type of person at all, too big and strong, high-shouldered and chinless.

A group of people, all with snow-white hair, sit in the lobby in wing-back chairs, and Meg studies them as we're led past to the room she will share with Mrs. Forbes, who, Audrey explains, "comes from a very fine old Andover family."

Mrs. Forbes is much older than Meg. She is well dressed and

handsomely groomed. Graciously, she receives her new roommate, then takes my hand and looks into my eyes. "How lovely!"
she says. "Oh, how lovely to see you!"

Meg stays back in the doorway, just managing a smile.

"And you'll, of course, be doing this for all of us, won't you?"
says Mrs. Forbes.

"Doing this?" I say. I glance at Audrey for help.

"Forget it," Audrey whispers. "She's confused."

We leave our coats on the chair to take a walk. In the hallway,
Meg grabs my arm and pulls me back. "Oh, I don't like this
place," she says. "Do you? Do you like this?"

"Well . . . I think it's very nice," I tell her. "You haven't seen it
yet. Let's have a look around before you decide whether or not
you like it."

Meg, wrought up, struggles to modulate her shout. *"Did you
see those people in the lobby?"* she says. "Oh, Sam, I've *had* a
look around."

Audrey falls back and listens in. Meg speaks to her politely.
"You have a beautiful place here," she says, "but I'm old. I can't
just throw myself into something like this. I'm going to have to
think about it for a while. It was very nice to have met you."

"Well," says Audrey, "the best way to think about it is by
spending the night." She's employing a trusted argument. "Then
you'll have a better idea about what it's like. Come, let me take
you around."

We walk, Audrey out ahead. Meg pulls me back. "I'm not
spending the night here with that old lady," she says, whispering
forcefully. "Are you crazy? Oh, I don't like it. This is an awful
house! Come on now. I've seen it. Okay. Let's go." She gives me a
quick-before-anybody-sees-us look.

My confidence breaks. The situation is out of my control.
Blood seems to abound in my system, then suddenly go cold in
my veins. Drops of perspiration fall away from my underarms and
skitter down my sides. I never expected this, never dreamed she'd
refuse to stay, refuse care, companionship, things she seemed to
understand she needed. I expected to have trouble with her cat.
I've been preparing myself for that morning when, before the

movers arrive to take the furniture off to Cliff and Danny's rental property in Roxbury, I'd have to coax Beatrice out from under the tented end table and, gradually taming her, take her up in my arms—hoping she won't sense the terrified beat of my heart— then quickly slip her into the Cat Caddy. I've been preparing myself for that struggle, for that painful refusal, but not for this one.

Meg stands with her legs spread, ready to go forward or back according to the strength of my insistence, taking short, frightened breaths, her small, unsteady hand against her forehead. All at once, I'm struck by a different kind of grief, one that has nothing at all to do with sentiment: it's about the struggle against mortality.

"Aren't you coming?" says Audrey.

"Where are my car keys?" says Meg, desperately. "Where's my coat? I'm getting out of here."

"But they were going to give us lunch," I say.

She bursts. "Okay," she shouts, "then *you* stay! If you like this so much, *you* stay here in this damn place!"

"Weren't you going to introduce us to some of the guests?" I say to Audrey with a weakened voice.

Two women pass on their way to the dining room. Meg pulls herself together.

"Ladies," says Audrey. "Just a moment. This is a new resident." She gestures with her clipboard to Meg, then to the others. "This is Mrs. O'Neill, Mrs. Dillon."

"Oh, I'm not staying," says Meg with a quivering smile. "I'm just looking. It's a beautiful place, this one. But I've got some others in mind. I have to look around for the right house. I'm old now, and this is the rest of my life."

The ladies walk off chatting in lowered tones, looking back.

"I'd like to take you now to one of our visiting rooms," says Audrey, "where we can talk about this in private." As we turn a corner and head up a ramp Meg bows her head and climbs.

Audrey gets me aside. "I think you should leave," she whispers.

"When?" I say.

"Like *now!*" she says.

I'm thrown off. I'd never considered this: just leaving her there, disappearing the way Mrs. Drake did with her mother, leaving her there like a package dropped at the right address. I want to set Meg free, bring her through electronic barriers, sirens bellowing, attendants rushing, help her young heart escape to what passion or conquest there is left in this dwindling life of hers. I want to take her, now, into my arms, the way Italian sons embrace their mothers, and press my cheek against hers, and hug and hold her and keep her near, always. But I can't.

In the visiting room, Meg, trembling, holds her head and breathes feverishly. "Oh, Sam," she repeats. "Can't I go home? I still have a home, don't I?"

Another young woman, wearing a gray suit, comes in followed by a waitress carrying lunch: a cake of glutinous scrambled eggs with ham bits inside, cut in the shape of a pound of butter.

"Why don't you give us a chance?" says the woman in gray. "Let us show you what we can do."

Meg's shaking hand breaks the geometry of her eggs with the side of her fork.

I excuse myself to go to the bathroom, but instead, want to find a telephone, want to call Cliff. Audrey, following me out, takes me to her office.

The fumes of business coffee, reduced to sediment, bore a hole in the wall of my stomach. Nausea sets in. Audrey picks up her phone and presses 9 for an outside line, then pushes it in front of me.

I will say something like, "We have to make a decision, you and me, Cliff. We have to decide something together, the two of us, right now."

Audrey, sitting across the desk from me, looks into my eyes. "You can still leave, you understand," she says. "We're professionals. We're used to taking care of these things."

I pick up the phone and dial. Cliff comes on the line. "Cliff," I say, "we're here at Andover Manor . . ." I'm crying and my voice shows it; it weakens and snaps back in the middle of words, a disconcerting sudden burst of volume like bad TV reception.

"And?" says Cliff. There's a trace of hope in his low tone.

I gaze out the window behind Audrey's head. In a bit of walled-off ground, a maple tree stands on a round carpet of its own crimson leaves. I see something of myself in the lone migratory bird paying a call here en route to its winter home. My whole life with Meg is contained within this landscape, contained in this moment, a moment I am all at once ready for.

"They just gave us lunch," I tell Cliff, "and . . . everything's fine. Don't worry," I say. "I think she'll be happy here. Really, Cliff, I couldn't be more sure of it."

EDITOR'S AFTERNOTE

Some say there comes a time when an aging parent becomes the child and the child becomes the parent. I asked Paul Gervais if he agreed, and if so, whom the transition is harsher for, the mother or the father?

"The mother becomes the child when she's alone and needy," Gervais says, "and when her child makes decisions that alter her daily life: where she lives and how, etcetera. The father becomes the child even sooner: when he loses his paternal authority."

Gervais feels, "Women endure pain—and perhaps even sorrow—with more courage and internal equilibrium than do men, yet a mother's suffering is more acute than a father's; a woman might have the strength you need to deal with hurt, but she has an equal measure of a kind of tenderness men don't usually possess."

A finalist for the PEN/Faulkner Award for his book *Extraordinary People,* Gervais is at work on his newest novel, *Love in the Eyes of God.* Born in Maine and raised in Massachusetts, he now resides on a farm in the Tuscany region of Italy, where he has lived since 1982.

Growing Boys

Robert Aickman

*What, you deny the existence of the supernatural, when
there is scarcely a man or woman alive who has
not met with some evidence for it!*
LUCIAN

*It is, indeed, singular that western man, while refusing
to place credence in anything he cannot see, while
rejecting absolutely omens, prophecies, and visions,
should at the same time, as he so often does, deny
the evidence of his own eyes.*
OSBERT SITWELL

The first time it occurred to poor Millie that something might
really be wrong was, on the face of it, perfectly harmless and
commonplace.

Uncle Stephen, the boys' great-uncle, had found the words,
conventional though the words were. "You're much too big a
boy to make messes like that, Rodney. And you too, of course,
Angus."

"*Angus* wasn't making a mess," Rodney had retorted. "There's
no need to bite his head off too."

"Keep quiet, boy, and clean yourself up," Uncle Stephen had rejoined, exactly as if he had been father to the lads, and a good and proper father also.

In reality, however, Uncle Stephen was of course a bachelor.

"I'll take you up to the bathroom, Rodney," Millie had intervened. "If you'll excuse us for a few moments, Uncle Stephen."

Uncle Stephen had made no effort to look pleasant and social. Rather, he had grated with irritation. When Millie took Rodney out of the room, Uncle Stephen was glaring at her other son, defying him to move, to speak, to breathe, to exist except upon sufferance.

It was certainly true that the boys lacked discipline. They were a major inconvenience and burden, overshadowing the mildest of Millie's joys. Even when they were away at school, they oppressed her mind. There was nowhere else where they were ever away, and even the headmaster, who had been at London University with Phineas, declined to accept them as boarders, though he had also declined to give any precise reason. When Millie had looked very pale, he had said, as gently as he could, that it was better not to enter into too much explanation: experience had taught him that. Call it an intuition, he had explained. Certainly it had settled the matter.

She had supposed that, like so many things, the headmaster's decision might have related to the fact that the boys were twins. Twins ran in her family, and the two other cases she knew of, both much older than she was, did not seem to be happy twins. None the less, until the coming of Rodney and Angus, and though she would have admitted it to few people, she had always wished she had a twin herself: a twin sister, of course. Mixed twins were something especially peculiar. She had never herself actually encountered a case, within the family, or without. She found it difficult to imagine.

Now, Millie no longer wished for a twin. She hardly knew any longer what she wished for, large, small, or totally fantastic.

All that notwithstanding (and, of course, much, much more), Millie had never supposed there to be anything very exceptional about her situation. Most mothers had troubles of some kind; and there were many frequently encountered varieties from which she had been mercifully spared, at least so far. Think of Jenny Holmforth, whose Mikey drank so much that he was virtually unemployable! Fancy having to bring up Audrey and Olivia and Proserpina when you had always to be looking for a part-time job as well, and with everyone's eyes on you, pitying, contemptuous, no longer even lascivious!

But upstairs in the bathroom, it came to Millie, clearly and consciously for the first time, that the boys were not merely too big to make messes: they were far, far too big in a more absolute sense. Rodney seemed almost to fill the little bathroom. He had spoken of Uncle Stephen biting his head off. That would have been a dreadful transaction like . . . But Millie drew back from the simile.

Of course, for years no one could have failed to notice that the boys were enormous; and few had omitted to refer to it, jocularly or otherwise. The new element was the hypothesis that the irregularity went beyond merely social considerations. It existed in a limbo where she and her husband, Phineas, might well find themselves virtually alone with it, and very soon.

Millie had read English Language and Literature and knew of the theory that Lady Wilde and her unfortunate son had suffered from acromegaly. That appeared to have been something that ran in Lady Wilde's family, the Elgees; because Sir William had been quite stunted. But of course there were limits even to acromegaly. About Rodney and Angus, Millie could but speculate.

When all the clothes had been drawn off Rodney, she was appalled to think what might happen if ever in the future she had to struggle with him physically, as so often in the past.

Reentering the drawing room, Rodney pushed in ahead of her, as he always did.

Angus seized the opportunity to charge out, almost knocking her down. He could be heard tearing upstairs: she dreaded to think for what. It mattered more when her respected Uncle Stephen was in the house.

She looked apologetically at Uncle Stephen and managed to smile. When her heart was in it, Millie still smiled beautifully.

"Rodney," roared Uncle Stephen, "sit down properly, uncross your legs, and wait until someone speaks to you first."

"He'd better finish his tea," said Millie timidly.

"He no longer deserves anything. He's had his chance and he threw it away."

"He's a very big boy, Uncle Stephen. You said so yourself."

"*Too* big," responded Uncle Stephen. "Much *too* big."

The words had been spoken again, and Millie knew they were true.

Uncle Stephen and Millie talked for some time about earlier days and of how happiness was but a dream and of the disappearance of everything that made life worth living. They passed on to Phineas's lack of prospects and to the trouble inside Millie that no doctor had yet succeeded in diagnosing, even to his own satisfaction. Millie offered to show Uncle Stephen round the garden, now that it had almost stopped raining.

"It's quite a small garden," she said objectively.

But Uncle Stephen had produced his big, ticking watch from his waistcoat pocket, which sagged with its weight. There was this sagging pocket in all his waistcoats. It helped to confirm Uncle Stephen's identity.

"Can't be done, Millie. I'm due back for a rubber at six and it's five-eleven already."

"Oh, I'm terribly sad, Uncle Stephen. Phineas and I have raised the most enormous pelargoniums. Mainly luck, really. I should so much like you to see them." Then Millie said no more.

"My loss, Millie dear. Let me embrace my sweet girl before I go."

He crushed her for a minute or two, then stepped back, and addressed Angus.

"Stand up and give me your hand."

Angus soared upwards but kept his hands to himself.

"I mean to shake your hand," bawled Uncle Stephen, in his quarter-deck manner; even though he had never mounted a quarter-deck, except perhaps on Navy Day.

Angus extended his proper hand, and Uncle Stephen wrenched it firmly.

When Millie and he were for a moment alone together in the little hall, something that could not happen often, Uncle Stephen asked her a question.

"Have you a strap? For those two, I mean."

"Of course not, Uncle Stephen. We prefer to rely on persuasion and, naturally, love."

Uncle Stephen yelled with laughter. Then he became very serious. "Well, get one. And use it frequently. I've seen what I've seen in this house. I know what I'm talking about. Get two, while you're about it. The Educational Supply Association will probably help you."

"Phineas will never use anything like that."

"Then you'd better consider leaving him, Millie dear, because there's trouble coming. You can always make a home with me and bring the boys with you. You know that, Millie. There's a welcome for you at any time. Now: one more kiss and I must vamoose."

As soon as the front door shut, Angus, who had been watching and listening to the scene through the hole the twins had made in the upstairs woodwork, almost fell on her in every sense.

Back in the drawing room she saw that Rodney, released from thrall, had resumed his tea, and had already eaten everything that had been left. Noting this, Angus began to bawl.

It might be all right later, but at that hour Millie was afraid lest the neighbors intervene: Hubert and Morwena Ellsworthy, who were ostentatiously childless.

"Don't cry, Ang," said Rodney, putting his arm tightly around Angus's shoulder. "Uncle Stephen always hogs the lot. You know that."

Angus's rage of weeping failed to abate.

Rodney gave him a tender and succulent kiss on the cheek.

"We'll go to the Lavender Bag," he said. "I'm still hungry too. I think I've got the worms. I expect you have as well. Race you. Ready. Steady . . . Go."

As the race began on the spot, the picking up and clearing up for Millie to do were not confined to the tea things.

The Lavender Bag was a café at the other end of the Parade. It was run by the Misses Palmerston, four of them. It was a nice enough place in its way, and useful for the release through long lunchtimes and teatimes of high spirits or low spirits, as the case might be. Millie went there often, and so did her friends, though soon she would have no friends. Some of them distrusted her already because they knew she had a degree.

Now Millie suddenly set down the cake tray she was holding. She took care not to let the large crumbs fall to the carpet.

"Oh God," gulped Millie, sinking to the edge of the settee and almost to her knees. "God, please, God. What have I done to be punished? Please tell me, God, and I'll do something else."

Only some outside intervention could possibly avail.

She had never been very good at having things out with anyone, not even with girl friends, and Phineas had undoubtedly weakened her further. All the same, something simply had to be attempted, however recurrent, however foredoomed.

To make a special occasion of it, she put on a dress, even though it had to be a dress that Phineas would recognize: at least, she supposed he must. The boys were still rampaging about at the Lavender Bag, which in the summer remained open for light snacks until eight P.M. They liked to run round the tables wolfing everything that others had left on plates and in saucers. The Misses Palmerston merely looked on with small, lined smiles. Simultaneously the boys were normal children and flashing young blades.

"Why *should* you feel at the end of your tether?" enquired Phineas. "After all, every day's your own. Certainly far more than my days are mine."

If only one could give him a proper drink before one attempted to talk seriously with him; that is, to talk about oneself!

"It's the boys, Phineas. You don't know what it's like being at home with them all day."

"The holidays won't last for ever."

"After only a week, I'm almost insane." She tried to rivet his attention. "I mean it, Phineas."

Millie knew extremely well that she herself would be far more eloquent and convincing if Phineas's abstinence had not years ago deprived her too, though with never the hint of an express prohibition, but rather the contrary. When she was reading, she had learned of the Saxons never taking action unless the matter had been considered by the council, first when sober and then when drunk. It was the approach that was needed now.

"What's the matter with the boys this time?" asked Phineas.

Millie twitched. "They're far too tall and big. How long is it since you looked at them, Phineas?"

"Being tall's hardly their fault. I'm tall myself and I'm their father."

"You're tall in a different way. You're willowy. They're like two great red bulls in the house."

"I'm afraid we have to look to *your* family for that aspect of it. Consider your Uncle Nero, if I may venture to mention him."

"I don't like him being called that."

"But you can't deny he's bulky. There's no one of his build anywhere up my family tree, as far as I am aware. For better or for worse, of course. There are more troublesome things than sturdiness, especially in growing boys."

Millie did not have to be told. She had often reflected that Phineas, sleeping tiredly over the settee at the end of the day's absence, was like an immensely long anchovy, always with the same expression at the end of it; and in the next bed it was, of course, far worse.

"Then you're not prepared to help in any way? Suppose I have a breakdown?"

"There's be no danger of that, Millie, if only you could persuade yourself to eat more sensibly."

"Perhaps you could persuade your sons of that?"

"I shall try to do so when they are older. At present, they are simply omnivorous, like all young animals. It is a stage we go through and then try to pass beyond."

"Then you do admit that they *are* like animals?"

"I suppose it depends partly upon which animals."

Millie knew perfectly well, however, that for her they were not like animals, or not exactly; and despite what she had said to Phineas. They were like something far more frightening.

"Uncle Stephen was very upset by them before you came home."

Phineas merely smiled at her. He had all but finished the lactose drink which he consumed every evening before their meal.

"Uncle Stephen said we ought to see what discipline could do."

"Discipline would hardly prevent the boys growing up," observed Phineas.

And it was still a matter of hours before it was even sunset.

The boys could be heard approaching in what had become their usual way. They stumbled in through the open French window.

"Got any good grub in your pockets, Dad?" shouted Rodney.

With a smile, Phineas produced a dun-colored bag of huge, gluey toffees: something he would never have put into his own mouth.

The boys fell into chairs and began to pass the bag from hand to hand.

"Mum going to cook supper soon?"

"I expect so, Angus."

"What's it going to be, Dad?"

"Better ask her, Rodney."

It was not, she knew, that he aimed to instill manners. It was merely that he could not care less.

One thing Millie had particularly resented was that every single evening she had to produce two very different meals, and then be silently sneered at if she herself chose the more exciting one, or consumed any scrap of it.

Now Millie was past resentment. Panic had taken its place.

"We need food, Dad. You don't want us to outgrow our strength."

"Besides, we're twins," said Angus.

It was hard to see where that came in, but Millie knew quite well that somewhere it very much did.

Everything was fundamentally her own fault. She was perfectly well aware of that. Everything always is one's own fault.

"Our reports come yet, Dad?"

"I don't think so, Rodney."

"You can't put them on the fire this time, because it's summer, but you *will* put them down the *topos?*"

"Unopened, Dad?" put in Angus. He was half on his feet again, and redder than ever.

"*Unopened*, Dad," insisted Rodney, though perhaps more calmly.

"Torn up, if you like," said Angus.

"We shall have to see," said Phineas. "Shan't we? When the time comes, that is."

He rose from the settee and walked quietly from the room.

"Oh, Mum," said Rodney, jumping up and down. "Do get on with it."

The patience of the young is soon exhausted.

"We're hungry," Angus confirmed. "Remember, we only had salad for lunch. Muck, we called it."

It had been a cut-up which Phineas had not eaten the previous evening. One could not simply throw it away; and Phineas would never accept such things unless they were completely fresh. It was the trouble with food of that kind that no one ever wanted it all, and it then became useless. Nor was the household made of money. Phineas not only lacked prospects: he lacked a suitable income also. Unhappily, Phineas was an intellectual without either creativity or judgement. Millie had realized it even during those early days in the Camargue, when Rodney and Angus were being conceived.

In the kitchen, she was shaking so much she gashed the index finger of her left hand. It would, of course, have mattered more if she had been lefthanded, as were Phineas and the boys; but it was a nasty enough cut, which bled far too much, so that fair-sized gouts fell on the newly prepared vegetable matter, which thereupon had to be slowly picked over a further time. Blood oozed through Millie's handkerchief and spotted the dress she had specially put on.

At the same time, the big fry-up for the boys was beginning to run out of fat.

In the end, they came charging in. Millie was weeping, of course, and in more and more of a muddle. Once, she had never muddled things, but quite the contrary: perhaps that was why she wept now.

"For God's sake, Mum! We're hungry. We told you."

"Hungry as hunters."

What had that originally meant? A kind of horse? A kind of tiger? A kind of man?

"What is it, Mum? What are we getting?"

"Chops and liver and bacon and things," replied Millie in a very low voice, possibly inaudible above the sizzle. "I've hurt my finger."

"We could eat the entire animal," said Angus.

Phineas always lay on his bed while a major meal was in preparation, and Millie had to ascend and summon him, because the boys simply did not do it, however often she asked them.

Four days later, Millie's finger was as bad as ever, and her left hand almost unusable. She knew that incurable illness often first manifested itself through minor injuries which failed to clear up.

"Oh, Mum, do get better!" admonished Angus at breakfast when she let slip the teapot.

"It's entirely a matter of eating the right things," observed Phineas mildly, "though, naturally, it'll take some months before you can expect to enjoy the benefits."

Phineas himself was eating a small quantity of muesli in skim milk. He always used a tiny teaspoon for such purposes.

The flap of the front-door letter-box was heard: presage everywhere of Charon's final shoulder-tap, bone against bone.

The boys made a dash, as they did each day; but this time Millie had reached the door of the room before them. She stood there facing them.

"We're going for the post, Mum."

"I'm going for it this morning. You both sit down, please."

"It may be our reports, Mum."

"I'm going this morning, Angus."

They were only a foot or two away, but before they could lay hands on her, she had not merely whipped open the door but also snatched the key out of the lock, flashed from the room, and managed to lock the door on the other side: all this with the real use of one hand only.

For the moment she had proved as effective as she used to be, but there had been something strange about the incident; which had all begun with a vivid dream she had had the previous night, so vivid that she remembered it (or imagined it) still, and in detail: a small dream really, but prophetic.

For the moment Phineas had been left to manage the two roaring boys. The French window was in the drawing room, but soon the boys would be out through the dining-room casements and making mischief of some kind. Happily, the big drawing-room window was never opened until after breakfast. The boys had never as yet intentionally smashed their way in or out, but Millie dreaded to see their huge faces gazing at her, diminishing her, from the world outside.

None the less, Millie paused for a moment, and quite consciously.

Much was at stake if her dream could be taken at all seriously.

It could. Millie had advanced into the hall and the delivery had proved to consist of two accounts rendered and a packet with the school crest upon the envelope.

Millie went back into the drawing room, and, sitting down, even straightened the crease in her jeans. Then, while in the locked room the abominable hubbub raged on, she calmly opened the boys' reports.

Reports they had been in her dream, and dire ones: at once a burden, but also, in certain ways, a release, or a faint hope of release. The actual packet proved, however, simply to contain a letter, together with some appeal forms for reconditioning the school chapel. The letter, addressed to Phineas, was from the deputy headmaster. Millie read it.

Dear Mr. Morke,

    I know you will forgive my writing on behalf of the Headmaster, who has unfortunately been in Hospital since the middle of the Spring Term, as you may possibly have heard from your Sons.

    I very much regret to tell you that the Trustees, to whom the matter has been referred in the absence of the Headmaster, take the view that no useful purpose would be served by the return of your Sons to the School at the commencement of the Term now ahead, that is to say, the Autumn Term.

    It is the view of the Trustees, in which I am bound to say I fully concur, that the Boys are too physically mature to benefit from the ordinary course of Tuition in Class, however excellent. Perhaps they may be regarded as outside and beyond the normal school disciplines.

    In the circumstances, there would seem no advantage to our delivering the usual Reports upon the conduct of the Boys during the Summer Term, just past. Doubtless you will have drawn your own conclusions from the Reports relating to previous Terms, and will scarcely be surprised by the Decision which the Trustees have reached.

    It is the custom of the School to extend Best Wishes to all its Old Boys when finally they move towards New Fields of Endeavour; and I am sure that the Headmaster, with whom, as I understand, you are on terms of long-standing and personal friendship, would wish me to make no exception in the present cases.

    May I venture to remind you of the Outstanding Account in respect of the Boys' attendance during the Summer Term, and including a number of important Extras? The Bursar requests me to take this opportunity of remarking that he would be most grateful for a settlement during the next seven days, as he is keeping his Books open for this single item, and is being pressed by the School's Honorary Accountants. I am sure you will understand.

Yours sincerely,
PHILIP DE SODA
(REVD., M.A., B.D.)

Millie rose, unlocked the door, and reentered the dining room, holding the letter high above her head.

"There are no reports, Phineas. They've been expelled."

When the boys had been much younger, it might have availed to hold the letter up there, but now it was pointless, because they were far taller than she was, as well as in every way more brawny. The letter was out of her hands in a flash.

It was very unlikely that they could understand it, and doubtful if they could even read all of it, but she herself had provided the clue, and at least they could take in the signature.

"It's the Sod!" cried Angus. "The Sod wrote it."

"Give it here," commanded Rodney. Within seconds the floor was littered with tiny scraps of paper, and the boys were standing shoulder to shoulder against the world, completely obscuring the framed photograph of their mother on a horse.

"What are you going to do now, Phineas?" enquired Millie.

Phineas was, as always, making a point of being undisturbed. He continued to chase the last particles of saturated muesli with his toy teaspoon.

"Well?" enquired Millie. "Our sons have been expelled from their school. You'll have to do something with them."

"Was the term *expulsion* actually employed in the letter?"

"Of course not. Schoolmasters don't use it nowadays. They're afraid of libel actions."

"Well then, we mustn't exaggerate. It's not all uncommon for a headmaster to reach the view that a boy would fare better in some other school. Nowadays, there's no question of a stigma at all. The change in itself is often entirely beneficial."

He drew a crispbread from the packet, broke it in half,

returned one half to the packet, and began to break up the other into reasonably symmetrical pieces on his plate.

Each of the boys now had his arm round the other's shoulder, in the style of Tweedledum and Tweedledee. But they had no other resemblance to Tweedledum and Tweedledee.

"If you don't do something, Uncle Stephen will," said Millie.

The boys extended their thick red tongues at her, but Phineas's eye was glancing at the *Guardian* which lay on the table for him alone to read and take to work.

Millie went upstairs, locked the door of the bedroom, and began looking through her old address book. It had little to offer, apart from varying shades and intensities of nostalgia and regret.

She lay down on her unmade bed, turning her back on Phineas's unmade bed.

She could not think while the boys were in the house, or, for different reasons, Phineas either.

She could hear birds singing, and, from the next house, screeching music for early housewives. She knew that they were supposed to choose the records for themselves.

Then, duly, there was the din of the boys leaving. At the moment their craze was to do something with dogs in the local wood—any dogs, as she understood it.

She had no idea what it was that they did, nor did she wish to know. The wood was of course deserted on a weekday morning, apart from the usual misfits straying about, and unlikely to present much of a problem to boys such as Rodney and Angus.

Millie gave it a little longer, lest she walk into Phineas, then she unlocked the door and went down.

Phineas had departed for work, with all the others. She had feared that the letter from Mr. de Soda might have held him back. She began to collect the torn pieces into a small plastic bag that was lying about, because she proposed to keep them. It was a surprisingly long job: she could not but remember that the mills of God tear exceeding small. Then she began to clear up, and, later, to wash up. She could count on a little tranquility until the boys returned, raging for their midday meal.

But the bell rang, and then there was that same flop from the

letter-box: somewhat less menacing, however, when it is presumably a matter not of a postal delivery, but more probably of a
harmless circular.

Millie went out quite calmly. Duly, it was a publicity leaflet, a
throwaway.

Your Fortune is in your Hands
Consult
Thelma Modelle
NOW

Modern Palmistry
Absolutely Private and Confidential
Normally no need for an appointment
Nothing spooky Nothing embarrassing

4 The Parade
"There is no reason why the human hand
should not provide as good a guide to
individual destiny as any other."

The concluding quotation was unascribed. Millie fancied that
it came from Aldous Huxley. She seemed to remember encoun-
tering something of the kind when trying to read one of Huxley's
works at Oxford. The leaflet was inexpensively produced in
simple black on simple white. It was quite small.

Millie had almost finished her immediate chores. There was
little incentive to embellish the tasks. She stuffed the bag of torn-
up paper into her handbag, because she could think of nothing
else to do with it at the moment and set forth for 4 The Parade.
Reason and careful thought had proved alarmingly unfruitful.
The moment had come to give the subliminal a trial; if that was
the applicable word. An omen was an omen, and there were few
of them.

Number 4 The Parade was her own fish shop, selling rough
vegetables and packet cheese as well. She had never previously

had occasion to heed the number. Upstairs had lived the rheumatism lady, who went round all the old folk in her little car. Millie was aware that lately the rheumatism lady had moved to a proper clinic, paid for by the ratepayers, because everyone was talking about it. Now at the foot of the stairs there was an arrow, with a curious curve in it pointing upwards, and the name THELMA MODELLE newly painted at the heart of it in gray. Plain THELMA would, perhaps, have been too much like an unregulated fairground; and changing times were rendering the title "Madame" obsolete even in such cases as this. There was nothing to do but ascend.

Thelma Modelle came out on to the little landing. Her jeans were pale green and she wore a sleeveless gray jumper which looked as if it were woven from used raffia. As promised, there was to be no attempt at formality or mystification.

Thelma Modelle had a smooth dark brown mop, falling over one side of her angular, sallow face; and the enormous, rather empty eyes of the seer or pythoness.

Indeed, at first she stared at Millie for a perceptibly long time without uttering a word.

"Well, come in," she said at last, as if there had been some demur.

They were in the rheumatism lady's small sitting room, though already it looked much more run down. The rheumatism lady's little water-colors had been replaced by wall cards bearing emblems of the zodiac; somewhat stained, and by no means a complete set. There was a round black table in the center of things, with two black composition chairs opposite one another.

"Sit down," said Thelma Modelle, still a little petulantly, "and call me Thelma."

Millie sat, as one does at such times; but Thelma continued to stand. She was observing Millie.

"Would you prefer to smoke?"

"I've given it up. My husband made me stop it."

"Then why are you carrying a packet of Players in your handbag?"

Millie felt that she had turned pale and puce at the same time.

"It's an unopened packet. I suppose you can see that too."

"One thing I can't see is why you're here. What are you looking for?"

"Your leaflet came through my door. Just this moment, in fact. So will you please read my palm, or whatever it is you do?" Millie extended her hand across the table.

"That's the wrong one," said Thelma. "But never mind. It would be no good with you in any case. I'll see what the cards have to say."

She picked up a working pack from the mantel behind her. Millie would have supposed there would be shuffling, perhaps cutting, certainly a careful and symmetrical laying out. But all Thelma did was chuck six or seven apparently random cards across the surface of the table.

"You're in trouble right enough," said Thelma.

"What sort of trouble?" asked Millie steadily.

"You'll know the details best."

"What's going to happen about it?"

"It's going to get worse."

"Yes, I suppose it's bound to do that."

"I should try running away, if I were you. Hide. Change your name. Change your appearance. Change everything."

"Join the raggle-taggle gypsies, in fact?" After all, one must at times seek some proportion in things.

"Please!" exclaimed Thelma. "I *am* a gypsy."

"I'm so sorry." But that was wrong too. "I wasn't meaning to be rude."

"The gypsies wouldn't *have* you."

"Why ever not?" But Millie was by now hardly surprised, hardly capable of surprise.

"You're marked."

"In what way? How am I marked? You don't mean that lacrosse accident?"

"No. Not that."

Millie reflected silently for a moment. If Thelma Modelle would sit down, as consultants normally do, it could be that much easier.

Millie spoke again. "Please tell me more."

"The cards won't go any further."

"Well, something else then." After all, there was a crystal on the mantel too, though Millie had never seen one in her life before (it was smaller than she had supposed); and some sort of large, shapeless thing leaning against the wall.

"If you want to know more, it will have to be sex."

Millie had heard at Oxford of "sex magic" and its alleged dangers.

"I don't think I want that," she said.

"That's quite all right," said Thelma rather nastily. "I shouldn't advise you to find out more anyway."

"Why ever not? Is it really as terrible as all that?"

"It might make you mad."

The familiar Shakespearian phrase was really too much. Millie rose to her feet.

"How much do I owe you?"

Thelma's expression had become very odd.

"No money. Just look in again. While you still have time of your own."

"You've made a mistake there," said Millie. "The boys aren't going back. They've been expelled."

"I've never claimed to be right every time."

Millie managed to smile a little. "Please take some money. I have profited by your frankness."

"Not from you," said Thelma. "I've told you what you can do."

"I'll think about it," said Millie.

"You can come and live here if you've nowhere else to go."

"I can go to my Uncle Stephen. Actually he's pressing me."

"You can do whatever you like," said Thelma.

There was a scuffling up the stairs, and another client appeared. It was Dawn Mulcaster, mature, frustrated, and twittery as ever. She and Millie exchanged very faint smiles but no words. Millie sped downwards.

The curious thing was that, though nothing could have been more depressing and foreboding than Thelma's insights, yet

Millie felt noticeably more buoyant than on her outward journey. As in the matter she had last night dreamed of, the burden was at the same time a release, or a faint hope of release. She was even able to muse smilingly upon a fortune-teller's obvious need of a receptionist; and upon the positively comical discrepancy between this particular fortune-teller's publicity and her performance. Perhaps the discrepancy was mainly in tone. All the same, surely the interview had been "spooky" in the extreme? Dawn Mulcaster would certainly be finding it so. Millie felt that she had done better than Dawn was likely to be doing. In fairness to Thelma Modelle's publicity person, Millie had to acknowledge that she did not feel in the least "embarrassed."

She stopped in the street for a moment. A more precise thought had struck her. Her cut finger was completely healed. Somehow she had even parted with the unpleasant bandage. She smiled, and continued homewards.

The boys stormed back, wolfed their food without a word to Millie, and stormed out again.

Millie washed up after the three of them; circulated round The Parade and The Avenue, shopping, meditating; put together two totally different evening meals; and then went upstairs to lie on her bed, in order to prepare for another confrontation with Phineas. She must keep up the pressure or go mad, as Thelma Modelle had predicted.

Indeed, when Millie fell asleep, she found she was dreaming of Thelma's establishment, where she, Millie, now appeared to have a job of some kind, as she was seated at the toilet table in what had been the rheumatism lady's bathroom, and sorting through hundreds, perhaps thousands, of invoices in the desperate hope of finding her own. The invoices were on paper of different sizes and textures, and in many different handwritings, mostly illegible. Millie was amazed by the mental processes that must lie behind the ways in which many of the bills were laid out. Only those which had been drafted by Uncle Stephen were fully orderly. When Millie awoke, it occurred to her to wonder whether Thelma herself could write at all, or whether she relied mainly on bluff, as did Rodney and Angus though no one ever dared to mention it.

There was the noise of creeping about downstairs. Then Phineas's voice floated up the stairwell: "Millie!" She shrivelled. "Millie, where are you?"

It was far, far too early for his return. Could he have lost his job? That might be yet another burden which was not a burden entirely, but very faintly a forerunner.

Millie threw off the eiderdown, pulled on a jacket, and sauntered downstairs.

Phineas was positively prancing from room to room. It was impossible that he could have been promoted, because, in his position, there was no real promotion. His step seemed light and gay, as with the man in the ballad.

"I've been adopted!" cried Phineas, unable to contain himself until she had reached the ground floor, terra firma.

"Whatever for?"

"As Liberal candidate, of course. At North Zero."

"Where's that?"

"It's in Cornwall and Anew MacAndrew says I should have every chance."

She had been perfectly well aware that Phineas was frequenting the local Liberal Association and bringing their literature home. It was one of various activities of his that resulted in her being so often alone with the boys.

"Does the Party find the money for your deposit, or do you have to do it?"

"I haven't the slightest idea. I haven't thought about it."

"Perhaps the boys can go down and canvass for you?"

"They're too young, as you can perfectly well imagine for yourself. I'm afraid I shall have to sacrifice much of my family life, and leave the boys more in the hands of their mother. I notice that you haven't congratulated me, Millie."

"If it's what you want, I'm pleased for you, Phineas. Provided, that is, that you find a new school for the boys before you set out."

"I haven't been able to think much about that, as you can

imagine. I feel it is something their mother can perfectly well do for them, if the necessity should arise."

"I can and shall do nothing of the kind, Phineas. Finding a school for boys like that is the father's job. I mean it, Phineas."

She was almost glowing with resolution. She realized that to display moral qualities demands practice, just as much as intellectual and manual qualities. She had never really attended when, down the years, such truths had been hammered into her. But she also knew that much of her relied upon the boys being out of the house.

"I had hoped you might be pleased for me," said Phineas, entering the sitting room, and draping himself. "Could I have my lactose, please?"

"It's too early. It's only just past teatime." Phineas eschewed tea, because of the tannin, which affected both his colon and his autonomic structure.

"I'm going to get myself a cup of tea," said Millie. "And then I want to go on talking seriously."

In her heart, she was not in the least surprised to find, when she returned, that Phineas had taken himself off. Perhaps he had gone out to look for the boys. He liked to delude himself that he could "join in" their play, though Millie knew better, knew that he was accepted on the very thinnest of sufferance, for short periods only, and only for ulterior reasons. In the boys' eyes, there was very little to choose between Phineas's status and hers. She knew that, even if he did not.

Millie took her little tray upstairs, locked the bedroom door, took off her jacket once more, and wriggled beneath the eiderdown. She had brought up the Family Size packet of Playmate biscuits, really meant for the boys.

But, contrary to expectation, Phineas drifted back in no time. Elation at the thought of the new and more fulfilling life that lay before him had probably made him restless. Soon, he was tapping at their bedroom door.

"Let me in, please."

"I'm having a rest. I'll come out when it's time for your supper."

"Where are the boys?"

"In the wood with the dogs, as far as I know."

"It might be better if they were encouraged to stay more in their own home."

"That's their father's job."

"Millie, what are you doing in there?"

"I'm lying down, and now I'm going back to sleep." She knew that by now there was not a hope of it, though she had spoken as positively as she could.

So positively, indeed, that there was quite a pause. Then Phineas said, "I might as well have my lactose now. I've had a lot to think about today."

Grumpily, Millie emerged. Rest and peace had gone, as well as slumber.

"Let me carry the tray," said Phineas. "It's right that I should do these things when I'm here."

He was not at all used to the work, and had to descend the stairs very slowly, like a stick-insect.

"What is going to happen to your job?" asked Millie, as soon as the tray was on the sink-surround, more or less in safety.

"That must come second. In life, one has to make such decisions."

"Meanwhile, what pays the boys' school fees? They won't have them at the ordinary local school. You know that."

"I shall have my Parliamentary salary in the end, and shall of course make you an allowance for things of that kind. Could I please have my lactose?"

"So you propose quite calmly to live entirely on me. On my little income from Daddy's estate?"

"Not if you do not wish it. You and the boys can do that, if necessary; and lucky we are that it should be so. I myself can apply for a maintenance grant."

"Do you mean the dole?"

"Of course not. I refer to the Applecroft Fund for supporting Liberal candidates. I did not intend to approach them but I always can if you lack all interest in your husband's career in life."

"Phineas!" Millie tried to sound positively menacing. "I tell you again that I accept no responsibility for the future of the boys, financial or otherwise. They are out of my hands."

"Well, Millie, in the very, very last resort, that's a matter for the common law, is it not? But there is no need at all for it to come to that."

"It would be bad for your chances, if it did."

"Not nowadays. Your notion of the world often seems antediluvian, Millie dear."

"The boys neither love nor want me. Not that they love or want you either."

Quite unselfconsciously, Phineas smiled. "What boys feel for their father is something a woman cannot understand, not even their mother. It's something that really is antediluvian, Millie."

"If you had any understanding whatever of what goes on around you, you'd know better than to talk such rubbish."

"No one is more concerned than I am about what goes on everywhere in the world."

His eyes were filled with a need for his mission to be understood and appreciated; for the lactose that by now really was due.

Millie set about preparing it.

"Where are the boys?" asked Phineas, as the sun sank in unnoticed glory.

"I expect they're at the Lavender Bag, as they were last night." Millie looked at her watch; the boys having stopped the clock so often that it no longer seemed to her worth paying for repairs. "No. The Lavender Bag will have shut some time ago."

"Perhaps it's some kind of special evening?"

"They would have come here and gorged themselves and then gone back."

"Well, what *are* we to think, Millie? It really might be better if you took more interest in what your sons do. I shan't be able to give so much time to it in the future. You must understand that."

Millie went to the record-player and put on Honegger's *Pacific*

231. The next piece on the record was Mossolov's factory music. Before the record could reach Gravini's *Homage to Marinetti,* Millie turned the machine off.

"Would you like your supper? I should like mine."

"I shall have to take more care over what I eat now that I have so much greater responsibility."

But when, shortly afterwards, the moment came, he seemed to pick and niggle very much as usual. Her own appetite was undoubtedly the more disturbed of the two.

In the end, the police arrived, though not until it was quite dark. Most unusually, it was Phineas who unwound himself and let the man in. For this reason, Millie did not learn his rank: lacked the opportunity to glance at his official card. The man was not in his blues, but dressed overall by a multiple outfitter.

"Good evening, madam. Do either of you know anything of two men named Angus Morke and Rodney Morke? They've given this address."

"They are our two sons, officer," said Phineas.

"Indeed, sir? I should hardly have thought it. Certainly not in your case, madam. These two are fully grown men. In fact, rather more than that."

"Don't be ridiculous, officer," said Phineas. "They are our sons, and we know exactly how big they are."

"I wonder if you altogether do, sir. If you don't mind my saying so, madam. It took a whole squad to get them under any kind of control. And, even then, there are some very nasty injuries which the Court will be hearing about tomorrow, in addition to the other charges. The Sergeant is worried about whether the cells will hold them. The station isn't Parkhurst Prison. It's only intended for quiet overnight cases. But I mustn't do all the talking. I've only come to make the usual routine enquiries. The two men—boys, if you prefer, madam—do really reside here, then?"

"Of course they do," said Phineas. "This is their home."

"If you say so, sir. Now, how old would each of them be?"

"They are twins. Surely you must have realized that? As far as I recall, they are rising sixteen."

"You mean that they're fifteen, sir?"

"Yes, I think that's right. Fifteen."

"It's incredible, if you don't mind my saying so, madam."

"In the course of your work," said Phineas, "you must have realized that some boys grow faster than some other boys."

It was high time for Millie to speak. "What have the two of them done?"

"What are they *alleged* to have done?" Phineas corrected. "If anything, of course."

The officer made it clear that from now on, and whatever the rule book might say, he preferred to deal with Millie.

"I'm afraid the charges are rather serious, madam. In fact, we've never before had anything to compare with it since the station first opened, which of course was when most of the houses like this one were being built. We haven't had much violence in the suburb, *serious* violence that is; though of course it's growing fast pretty well everywhere in the world."

"What have they done, officer? Please tell me. I'm perfectly able to face it." Again, the additional burden that could at the same time be a further remote prospect of freedom!

"Remember," put in Phineas, "that it's still only mere allegation. It is well known that the police exaggerate; sometimes very greatly. I speak as an adopted Parliamentary candidate."

"Do you indeed, sir? For somewhere round here, that is?"

"No, not locally. But it makes no difference."

"Well, madam," said the officer, with professional quietness, "as for the charges, they include a long list of assaults, fifteen at least so far, and we are expecting more. Some of those we already have are very serious indeed. Not what we're used to round here, as I have remarked. More like the Glasgow docks in the old days, I should have said. Then there's a lot of damage to property. A lot of damage to a lot of property, I should have put it. Doors stove in and roofs ripped about and ornaments smashed. There are a couple of attempted rapes expected to be reported soon, from what the other officers say. A couple at least."

"In these times, there's no such thing as *attempted* rape," objected Phineas. "It's a rape, or it isn't a rape, and most people are very doubtful about it even if it's supposed to be proved."

"And that's not to mention the injuries inflicted on the officers, which we don't like at all, madam, especially in a quiet district like this."

"No," said Millie soberly, "I'm sure not."

"Now, if I could have a few details of the education these lads have had? Supposing them to have had any, of course. But it's no matter for joking, all the same. It's an offence too, not to educate a child."

Millie realized that the night air was coming in through the front door which Phineas had left open: the night air of a hot summer. Phineas made no move, and Millie did not care to leave him just then even for a single moment. Besides, closing the outer door might lead to new suspicions.

By the end of it, and indeed long before that, Millie knew perfectly well that Phineas should have produced the whisky, but that, thanks to Phineas, there was no whisky in the house. Most assuredly she could not be absent long enough to make tea, even supposing the officer to be interested in tea at that hour.

"If the accused really are what the law calls minors," said the officer, "then a parent will be required to attend the Court."

"Of course my husband will attend the Court," said Millie.

"Perhaps you too, madam? A mother can often influence the Justices more than a father."

Millie smiled. "I shall remember that, officer."

"Not that a case of this kind is likely to remain with Petty Sessions for long. It will be simply a matter of a quick committal, as far as I can see."

"I'm sure you are once more greatly exaggerating, officer," said Phineas, smiling in his turn.

"You'll be there to hear for yourself, sir," replied the officer, entirely reasonable.

When he had gone, Millie found it almost impossible even to speak to Phineas.

"I'm not sharing a room with you," she managed to say.

"Please yourself," said Phineas. "After today's news, I've still a great deal to think about and plan, as anyone but you would see at once."

Next morning, and really quite early next morning, the child-less Hubert Ellsworthy was the first with the local news; or with a bit of it.

In his old yachting jumper, with part of the club name still on it, and shapeless gray bags splashed with oil from his garden workshop, he stood there trying to arrange his scattered locks. "I thought I ought to tell you first, Phineas, as, after all, we are neighbors. I've heard that there are two sex maniacs on the loose. Apparently, the authorities feel we should warn one another to keep everything bolted and barred. What times we live in! Eh, Phineas?"

Millie, who had overheard this in her nightdress, could already see, from the bathroom window, Morwena Ellsworthy sealing every aperture with passe-partout, despite the season, and even pulling down blinds.

The next arrival was young Graham, the local weekly's cub reporter, as people described him, and the only one who left the office very often. Girls tended to tell him that they liked the name Graham.

That time, Millie opened the door.

"May I come in for a few moments, Mrs. Morke? It's really rather important."

Millie had never before spoken to him, though, like everyone else, she knew who he was. He was a nice young lad, everyone said. In any case, he was by now sufficiently practised in his profession never to take even the hint of negation as an answer.

"Well, what is it?" asked Millie. "Do sit down."

Phineas, having dealt with Hubert Ellsworthy, had gone back to bed. In the marital bedroom: Millie had spent the night on the lounge sofa-convertible which, at the time of hire-purchase, she had, consciously or subconsciously, made sure really was long enough and wide enough to live up to its brochure.

"You've heard the news, Mrs. Morke?"

"What news in particular?"

"The police station in The Approach has been completely wrecked. I've never seen anything like it," said young Graham very seriously.

"Well, what can I do? Would you like a cup of coffee?"

"Not just at the moment, Mrs. Morke, though thanks all the same. The thing is that the Station Inspector tipped us the wink that your two boys were being held for all that damage last night. And now, presumably, they've made a getaway. Would you care to give me a statement?"

"No," said Millie.

"Are the boys here, Mrs. Morke? After all, it's their home."

"I have nothing to say," said Millie, hoping she had the formula right.

"Then, presumably, they *are* here? Don't worry, I shan't give them away. Nor do *you* have to give them away. You can just say whatever comes into your head. It doesn't much matter what it is, really."

Millie could see that he was only trying to be kind.

"Nothing. So would you please go? I'm sorry to turn you out, but I'm sure you'll understand."

"Rum tykes, aren't they? Sorry, I suppose that's not a very nice way of talking to their mother. My kid brother told me about the month or whatever it was they spent in the under-seven. They made a mark there all right, from what Matheson had to say. Marked everyone, in fact. Do please give me a statement of some kind, Mrs. Morke. Anything you like. Just anything."

"I'm sorry," said Millie. "I really am. I know you're only doing your job."

"Well, I suppose there's not much more I can do this time, but you're famous now, Mrs. Morke, and there'll be others coming fast in my footsteps. Not that I've missed a scoop. Not personally, that is. I don't suggest that."

"I'm glad," said Millie, meeting his generosity at least half-way.

"And I'm sorry you're in trouble, Mrs. Morke. I really am. You're still a very nice-looking girl. If I may put it that way."

"I don't see why you shouldn't," said Millie. "Well, that's it, wouldn't you say?"

Millie opened her handbag and carefully combed her hair. She went upstairs.

Phineas lay there, reading Minutes.

"Phineas! I'm leaving you."

"Oh, please calm down, and let's have breakfast."

"Get it yourself. I'm packing and going. I'll collect the rest of my things as soon as I can. The things that are left. Before the boys smash them too."

"Millie!" cried Phineas, while she bustled around with a quiet efficiency she had not known for years. "Millie, don't you realize that this is the moment in all their lives when our sons are likely to need their mother most? Surely you must see that for yourself? The moment in their lives when *I* need you most too?"

"I've done all I can," said Millie. "You're full of educational theories. Now's the time for you to give them a real trial. You. Not me."

"At least come with me to the Court? Let's have breakfast quietly and consider what line to take. I'm sure the whole thing is quite grossly exaggerated. The police do that, you know. I keep saying so."

"It would be difficult to exaggerate in any way about the boys."

"But you're their mother, Millie!"

"Perhaps that's how I know. You learn nothing."

Replete and bursting though it was, she shut her suitcase with new strength. It still bore her maiden name: MELANIE PIGOTT. Why should she not return to that? When in due course she had left Uncle Stephen's abode and started a life of her own? The green suitcase had been a joint present from her parents on her twenty-first birthday. At the time, she had wondered how long the family name would still be hers; but now it might be hers once more, and for a very indefinite period. When empty, the suitcase was delightfully weightless; when full, delightfully substantial.

"I'm not going to bother with good-bye," said Millie.

Phineas clutched at her physically. His overlong arm was as the tentacle of an undernourished octopus.

"Millie, do at least try to be sensible. Just get breakfast, and we'll talk it all over as much as you like."

She threw his elongated hand back on the bedspread.

As she bore her packed suitcase briskly up The Drive, she reflected that two days ago she could hardly have lifted the thing from the bedroom floor.

She wondered how long it would be before the inevitable reaction and collapse.

Uncle Stephen saw to it that Millie wanted for nothing.

Every morning he brought her the loveliest, most fragrant breakfast in bed. Every evening he lingered in her room, tucking her in, adjusting the ventilation and positioning of the curtains, putting away any clothes she had left about, gossiping about the small events of the day, taking away her shoes in order to give them a rub.

He prepared most of the other meals too. As he pointed out, he would have had to feed himself in any case, and having to feed her too made the whole thing into a work of joy. He had many outside engagements: bridge, bowls, the rifle and revolver ranges, the committee of the small amateur soccer club, the British Legion, the Skeleton A.R.P., the Patriotic Alliance (which was often in a state of inner schism, and therefore particularly demanding); but Millie could never for one moment doubt that she constituted the primary demand both upon his heart and even upon his time. The undiagnosed trouble inside Millie had ceased even to demand diagnosis.

"You do spoil me, Uncle Stephen. It's lovely." She lay on the settee in lounging pyjamas and matching surtout (as the manufacturers termed it). She had never been able to bother with garments of that kind before, but now Uncle Stephen had bought them for her at Katja's in the new Vanity Market, and had helped to choose them too. She had rather looked down on such shops and on such clothes, but that had been ignorance and the wrong

kind of sophistication. It was almost impossible to believe that
Phineas lived only eleven and a half miles away as the crow flew,
if any crow should be so misdirected.

"I like being spoilt, Uncle Stephen," said Millie.

"I love to do it, girl. You're all I have, you know that, and
always have been."

That must have been what Phineas would have called an
exaggeration, but it was true that Uncle Stephen, so far as was
known, had at all times "looked after himself." Now he had a
thick mop of silky white hair, like a wise old lion, and the same
green eyes as his sister, Millie's mother, and as Millie herself.

"All the same, I can't stay for ever," said Millie coyly.

"Why on earth not? First, *I*'ll look after *you*, and do it with
love in my heart. Then, when I'm past it, *you*'ll look after *me*—
well, some of the time. In the end, I'll leave you all I've got. I've
no one else. Remember that. It's not much. But it will be
enough."

"I'll remember, Uncle Stephen, and thank you. All the same, a
woman nowadays is expected to lead a life of her own. I was all
set to do it."

"You've tried that sort of thing once, girl, and you've seen
what happened." Uncle Stephen's eye wandered away from her,
which was unusual. "I wish I could put a hand to one of the
rattans I used to have."

"What are they, Uncle Stephen?" asked Millie, though really
she knew fairly well.

"Disciplinary instruments, my love. Disciplinary instruments.
Never had one out of my right hand during all the years I was in
the Archipelago."

"I wonder if anything's happened by now?" Millie spoke a little
drowsily. The wine at dinner had been South African, and she
had fallen badly out of practice.

"You let sleeping dogs lie. Never trouble trouble until trouble
troubles you."

She smiled at him. It would be absurd to argue about anything.

"Carry me to bed, Uncle Stephen."

* * *

She dreamt that she and Thelma Modelle were climbing Everest together. They were both garbed in the latest chic, waterproof, windproof, coldproof clothing, and carried little axes, silvery in the sun. Thelma, the gypsy, was deputizing as a Sherpa. It was all exceedingly enjoyable, and not at all too steep for Millie's new energies. The summit lay straight ahead. They might have tea when they arrived there; or Thelma might have to have ideas of her own about a suitable gypsy celebration.

How many months later was it when Millie opened the *Daily Telegraph* and saw the familiar headline: LIBERAL LOSES DEPOSIT? Apparently the sitting member for North Zero had fallen over a cliff, or at least been discovered by children dashed to pieces on the rocks below. The coroner had returned an open verdict, and a by-election had followed. Previously Millie's eyes must have glided over these events.

Uncle Stephen brought her the *Daily Telegraph* or the *Sunday Telegraph* with her early-morning tea; and *The Imperialist* every time there was a new issue. That day, when a little later he came up with her breakfast, two small, heavenly-smelling kippers and the perfect toast upon which she could always rely, she was pensive.

"Uncle Stephen, tell me. Did they ever catch those boys? I suspect you know all the time."

"I know nothing that you don't know, little girl."

She eyed him. "What exactly does that mean? Do you know the answer to the question I asked?" She spoke quite roguishly.

"I do not. I know what my answer would be if I only had the chance. Now eat your scrap of porridge, or it'll go cold. I'll sugar it for you."

Millie dragged herself upwards. She really preferred to eat in a sprawling position, but Uncle Stephen liked to see more of her.

"Tell me, Uncle Stephen, have there been any more happenings? Like the one on the night before I left. I simply don't read the reports of things like that."

"That's the self-protective instinct, my little love, and you could do with more of it, not less."

"But have there, Uncle Stephen? I'd rather like to know."

"Nothing that anyone could get a grip on. Or nothing that's come my way. I don't spend all day reading the newspapers. It can get hold of you as poisonously as the television, if you once let it."

"You're hiding something, Uncle Stephen."

"That I am not. There are these violences all over the world every minute of the day. Everyone's a villain without proper discipline. I haven't noticed the names of your two lads in particular."

"And you haven't heard anything locally either?"

"Not a word. I'd be out in no time if I had, after what's been done."

The last words very nearly convinced Millie.

"Let me pour your chocolate," said Uncle Stephen.

But immediately he spoilt it all by speaking further.

"They'll have shot up a lot further by this time," he observed. His eyes were searching round the room, as they always did when the subject of the boys arose.

"Thank you, Uncle Stephen," said Millie, as he stopped pouring. "It's a beautiful breakfast. When I've finished it, I'd like to sleep a little more. Then I'll come down and give you a hand."

He took the hint quite quietly. He merely said, "I see now that you're looking pale. Don't you worry about helping me. I can easily bring up your little lunch when the time comes."

"You *are* good to me, Uncle Stephen."

But, as soon as he had left the room and closed the door, Millie began to heave; and in no time, while trying to muffle the noise, she was being copiously sick into the article provided in well-found houses for that and other purposes: as sick as she had been, without cessation as it had seemed, during the long months before the two boys were born.

Really there could be no question of Millie even attempting to lead a life of her own as, like so many women, she had originally, in a vague way, intended. She was afraid to leave the house, and even more so after what Uncle Stephen had so casually said.

That she had good reason to lie low was confirmed by the episodes that followed.

It was more than a year after Millie had left Phineas, and the gold of summer was fast dissolving into the copper of autumn, when one night Millie stirred in her sleep to see a big face pressed against the panes of her first-floor bedroom window. Whether it was Angus's face or Rodney's face, which of their faces, she would probably not by now have known in any case. It was an unseemly blot on the October moonlight, then it ducked.

What was more, her window was open, as at night it always was. The boy was far too big to climb right in, but he could easily have inserted a huge arm, perhaps reached to the bed, and then strangled or humiliated her. Millie had realized from the first that the boys must have a perfectly clear idea of where she was, even though she emerged so seldom, and Uncle Stephen never recommended otherwise. What had decided the boys to reenter her life now? She had seen only one of them, but was sure that the other was there also, because the other always was. She suspected that by now their combined strength could throw down the entire house. And very possibly they were growing still. Boys by no means always cease to grow at sixteen or seventeen.

She drew on her kimono and ran to Uncle Stephen's room. She knocked at his door, as she had done before when hungry during the night, or when merely lonely.

"Come in, girl. Come in."

"Uncle Stephen. The boys are back. One of them has just looked through my window in the moonlight. I think I'm going to be sick again."

"Come in with me, little love. I'll look after you and protect you. That's what I'm doing in your life. That's what I'm here for. You know that."

Fortunately, it was a very large bed. Uncle Stephen had brought it back from the East; from gorgeous, sanctified Goa, now forever lost.

"When I was young, I could never in my life have even imagined anything so frightening," said Millie. "Not until the boys were born. Or actually a little before that. When Phineas and I were on our honeymoon. In France, and then in the marshes behind Ariano. I never dared to read horror stories and ghost stories." She snuggled towards Uncle Stephen.

"No man and no woman knows anything of the troubles they are going to meet with in life. Or I take it they'd succeed in dodging them," said Uncle Stephen. "They're supposed to be sent to form and mould us, but my idea is to form and mould *them* whenever possible. Remember that."

"You're the most wonderful uncle," Millie murmured, though she was still shivering and gulping.

"I'll stay with you ten minutes while you calm down and arrange your pinafore, and then I'm going hunting."

"No, Uncle Stephen! It's too dangerous. They're watching the house. They're *immense.*"

"Many times in my life I've been under siege. Each time, in the end, I burst out and destroyed everything in sight. I'm hard to hold, Millie."

"Things have changed since those days, Uncle Stephen. It's sad, but it's true. Even *The Imperialist* admits it. That was the bit I read you, when you ordered me to stop. There's nothing for either of us to do nowadays but escape. A fortune-teller told me that last year, and now it's come true."

"I know all about times changing, none better," said Uncle Stephen, holding her close. "The fact remains that *I* have *not* changed. I am older, unfortunately, but otherwise exactly the same. Also I have weapons, I have strategy and tactics, and I have experience. I am going to give those cubs the lesson they've needed since their first birthday. I learned, my little love, to deal with growing boys in a harder school than Eton and Harrow or any of those places."

"I'm not going to let you try. You're over-confident. Those two are like children of the future." She was appalled. "Perhaps they *are* children of the future?"

"I'll admit that they're too big for their boots," said Uncle Stephen drily.

"If you go anywhere near them they'll harm you. We're just going to wait for the daylight. I'll stay with you if you'll let me.

Then we'll steal away somewhere for a bit. Somewhere nice. You've always said you could afford it, if only circumstances had been different. Well, circumstances *are* different, whether we like it or not. We could go and stay in an hotel at Southampton and you could look at the different ships going to places. You would like that, wouldn't you?"

"And if everyone behaved in that way?" enquired Uncle Stephen. "If everyone did, what would become of our country? Things are rough enough already. You're as bad as that so-called man of yours, Millie." But he spoke affectionately, none the less, cuddling and caressing her, not meaning his comparison very seriously.

"Uncle Stephen, don't be silly. They're not ordinary boys you can either pamper or stand in the corner. They're *enormous*. I told you what the man from the police station said. They're quite beyond handling by any single individual."

"All I know is that they're boys, and that's quite enough. I don't want to leave you alone, as you know perfectly well, my little pet, but I'm going. You just lie in my bed until I'm back. And don't worry. I'm here to keep you from all harm. And I have weapons. Remember that."

He squeezed her hand, and clambered out into the night.

Soon he was on the roof, directly above her. She could hear the slotting of iron into iron, or was it nowadays steel into steel? When she had lived beside the Heath as a small child during the Second World War, the A.T.S. girls operating the anti-aircraft unit concealed among the evergreen gorse had made that noise all day as they took the long guns to pieces and put them together again. Uncle Stephen possessed artillery of his own. It was included in the weapons he had mentioned; nor did it consist in a couple of squat, serio-comic muzzle-loading Peninsular War mortars, looking like pugs. On the contrary, Uncle Stephen could mount at least three quite modern-looking pieces, painted not black but dark green as gorse, and palpably requiring expert knowledge to discharge satisfactorily; the kind of knowledge that the girls on the Heath had been acquiring during the daytime. He had explained to Millie that these guns were designed by the authorities primarily for withstanding a concerted rush. She wondered when he had managed to dismantle at least one of them in the room downstairs and reassemble it on the roof of the house without her hearing or noticing a thing. She might have been impressed by his foresight, but instead resurrected her suspicions that Uncle Stephen had all along known something that he had failed to pass on.

There was a flash and a crash: quite startlingly like six-thirty or seven-thirty P.M. when Millie had been but a tot.

Another and another. Millie fully realized that this could not continue for long; not in the modern world. Somehow it would be stopped, however justified it might be, even by the narrowest legalistic standard of self-defence and of protecting an unarmed mother.

Concurrently, Millie was subdued by a confused melee of feeling about Angus and Rodney; even though she had never been able within herself to accept that they were authentically her own offspring.

A shadow passed between the moon and the casement. Surely the boys should have been intelligent enough to take cover? How, without doing so, had either of them survived Uncle Stephen's cannonade? Uncle Stephen was the least likely of men to aim and then miss. He kept in continual practice, as in so many directions.

Another flash and crash: though this time in the latter was a curious rending sound, as if the gun barrel were about to burst asunder. Millie had heard of guns soldering up through being fired continuously day and night. Probably Uncle Stephen's gun had not of late been fired often enough to be in prime condition. Millie realized the danger that Uncle Stephen might be running from the gun exploding within itself and shattering into smithereens, as she understood that guns not infrequently did.

But by now the official legions were massing. Millie could hear outerspace blastings of fire engines, of ambulances, of police cars; and between them the insect whinings of television vans and radar. It was much as the moment when an escape from a concentration camp is first notified. She ran to the window.

Functionaries were swarming over and around machines to make sure that nothing remained unaccounted for in the designated area, except criminally. It was an ideal spot for such an operation, as Uncle Stephen's house stood in comparative isolation at a corner of the woods; a public open space owned by the Council.

Millie ran back to her own room. It would be most unwise to turn on a light, and possibly the current had already been chopped at the main. In any case, public lights were beginning to range: brutal searchlights, and the torture-chamber arc lights necessary for television.

Millie tore off her nightdress. She plunged into her jeans and a thick sweater which Uncle Stephen had bought for her at the supply stores where he bought many of his own garments. She had lost her handkerchief and took out a clean one.

For these simple actions the case was cogent enough. But Millie then hesitated. Uncle Stephen had stopped firing, and Millie could but speculate upon the exact reason. She could not possibly bring herself to desert Uncle Stephen, but the thing of which she was most certain was that the two of them could not win. She suspected that Uncle Stephen really knew that as well as she did. So what then?

Cautiously, she reentered Uncle Stephen's bedroom. The beam of light which now filled it illuminated nothing human or real. In her short absence, the room had been killed.

Millie realized that Uncle Stephen was in difficulties. The gun was refusing to fire, as cars sometimes refuse to start. Uncle Stephen was tinkering with it, bashing it, cursing it. Soon, in the nature of things, the functionaries would close in finally, nor would it be a concerted attack of the kind which the gun was designed to ward off. It would be more a matter of irresistible infiltration, worked out long before in every detail, standard practice, precluding all possibility of topographical variation.

Millie ascended the attic ladder to the rooftree. "Uncle Stephen!" she called down to him.

Absorbed though he was in his male task, he looked up at once.

"Go back," he cried out. "Go back, little Millie."

"What's up, Uncle Stephen? What's gone wrong?" Nothing else was possible than to enter into things as he saw them.

"The boys have won this round, Millie. We must admit that. They've put the gun right out of action."

"But how, Uncle Stephen?"

"It's some kind of schoolboy muck. They dropped a whole gob of it into the breech. Clever monkeys, we must admit."

Millie had almost forgotten the boys; incredible though that seemed.

"Where are they now?"

"I'll bet they've made off. They don't have much more to do, just at this moment."

Millie glanced anxiously round amid the confused and inhuman lights. But she knew that for a second she had almost wished the boys had still been there; as some kind of reassurance against all that was developing.

"I said I was here to protect you," affirmed Uncle Stephen, "and I shall do it still. I have always won the last battle. Always and always."

"Come away with me, Uncle Stephen, while there's time."

He went through burlesque bristling motions. "You don't suppose I shall knuckle down to a couple of schoolboys with their pockets full of gum." He expressed it facetiously, but of course he meant it, could hardly have meant it more.

Now that the firing had ceased for some time, the encircling host had begun to relax. Cups of tea were being consumed; ambulance workers were chatting to firemen on familiar subjects, their respective rates of pay and conditions of employment, their pension prospects, the maladies of their dear ones.

"Oh, come on, Uncle Stephen. If the boys have gone, we can go too."

To her consternation, he was not to be budged. "No, girl," he said. "This is my home, my castle, as we used to say; and perhaps by now it's your home and castle too. Wouldn't you say that's very nearly true, Millie?" He had given up fiddling with the gun, and was addressing himself to something even more important.

"The boys will return," she said. "When all the people have gone. And you'll be in endless trouble for firing that gun in any case, even though I know you did it for my sake."

"All my guns are licensed, Millie. I'm a registered holder of firearms. And as for the boys, let them come. I want nothing better. They've won a battle. They won't win the war. They're hulking brutes, but they're still only schoolboys. Look at this." Uncle Stephen displayed the mess on his hands and combat suit.

"We shan't feel the same about the house ever again, Uncle Stephen. You must know that."

"If we were all to let ideas of that kind govern our lives, we'd all be homeless." Uncle Stephen sat back on the semi-dismantled gun. "You mustn't suppose, girl, that I don't know what you mean. It's simply that not one thing in life is ever gained by running away. This is our home, yours and mine, and here we stay."

"I'm afraid of the boys coming back," said Millie. "I'm terrified."

The big lights were being turned out, one after another. It is often noticeable that they are in use only for a few minutes. By now Millie was unsure whether she preferred the crude glare or the deep darkness.

Someone was hammering at the front door. It was of course inevitable, sooner or later. Probably it had been going on at a lesser intensity for some time.

Millie dropped down the attic ladder and flitted through the dark house like a noctambule. She was not going to wait for any nonsense from Uncle Stephen about taking no notice. All the same, at the foot of the stairs she stood and called out. After all, it might conceivably be the boys.

"Who's there?" In the hall, the trophies were shaggy as a tropical forest.

"I'm a police officer, madam. Kindly open the door."

She knew the voice. She slipped the chain and drew the big bolts in a trice.

"We're old friends, officer."

All the same, he showed his card, and said, "Detective-Sergeant

Meadowsweet." Millie smiled. "May we have some light on the scene, madam?"

"Would that be safe?"

"Safe as could be, madam. The two men have been sighted miles away, and we're closing in steadily."

"Oh!" gasped Millie. "So you know?"

"Of course we know, madam. What else did you think we were doing here? Now, I just want you to tell me all that's taken place. After that, I must have a word with the gentleman upstairs who's been treating himself to a little pistol practice."

"I hope he's not done any damage."

"No particular damage that we know of, but that's more by luck than judgement, wouldn't you say?"

"He's got all the necessary licences."

"We know that, madam, but he happens not to have a licence to fire at intruders, because no such licence exists. Jobs of that kind must be left to the police. It sometimes causes hardship, but it's the law, and a gentleman with all those different licences knows better than most what they permit him to do and what not."

"Perhaps I should say," put in Millie, "that the gentleman's my uncle. He kindly took me in after the trouble we had a year ago. A little more than a year, actually."

"I could see at the time that your husband wasn't much help," said Detective-Sergeant Meadowsweet in his inimitable way; and then duly added, "If you don't mind my saying so, madam."

"Oh no, I don't mind," said Millie. "Phineas was utterly wet from first to last. The whole thing was the biggest mistake I ever made. Not that 'mistake' is quite a strong enough word. But do sit down, Sergeant."

"I take it," said the Detective-Sergeant as he did so, "that the two men were attempting to force an entrance? Tonight, I mean."

"They're really only boys," said Millie, "absurd though it seems."

"I don't think we need to go over that ground again, madam. If you remember, we covered it very fully when Mr. Morke was there. So the two of them were attempting to force an entrance?"

"Well, not exactly, as I have to admit. What happened was simply that I saw one of them out on the lawn and rather lost my head. You know what they look like, Sergeant? How enormous they are?"

"Yes, we know very well, madam. Don't you worry about that. The approved school couldn't hold them for a week. The Tower of London would be more the thing, I'd say. So what happened then?"

"They're so strong too. I admit that I'm frightened to think about it. But of course you know about that too."

The Sergeant nodded. He had settled himself on a big black stool from somewhere in French West Africa. Millie had been given to understand that, before the French came, the potentate whose official seat it had been (perhaps even throne) had at times waded through blood almost to the knees. She had difficulty in remembering which of the different regions the different things came from; especially as Uncle Stephen had shifted in mid-career from the fairly Far East to Africa, and then back to the East. The legs of the stool were decorated with small projecting bones and teeth, inserted into the woodwork. Above the Detective-Sergeant's head flapped a faded rushwork curtain originally intended, Uncle Stephen had said, to deter the flesh-eating birds and bats from entering one's room during the night.

"So what happened then, madam?"

"I admit that I completely lost my head, and ran in to my uncle, who took steps to defend me. No more than that."

Another voice broke in. "I take full responsibility, officer."

Uncle Stephen had appeared at the top of the stairs. He had changed into his usual sharply pressed trousers and camel-hair jacket. "The situation was extremely menacing. I was protecting my own flesh and blood against a couple of thugs."

"Yes, sir, they're a nasty enough pair, according to all the evidence. The police are fed to the teeth with them, I can tell you that."

"Very good of you to confirm what I say, officer. I am sorry I had to take the law into my own hands, but you'll agree that I had every justification. I've spent most of my life in places where you have to think quickly the whole time, or you find yourself dead. Worse than dead. May I suggest that we say no more about it? Let me give you a stiff whisky before you go?"

"We're not supposed to drink while we're on duty, sir."

"Of course not," said Uncle Stephen. "I have served with the police myself. In several different parts of the globe."

A little later, when the three of them were sitting amicably together, Millie began to feel intensely sad.

"I cannot help feeling partially responsible," she blurted out. "Do you think, Sergeant, there's anything to be done? Anything, even in theory, that *I* could do? Any possibility?"

At once Uncle Stephen shouted out, "Clap them in irons, I should hope. Use straitjackets, if necessary. Though you'd have to have them specially made big enough. And then you've got to lay hold of the boys first. Eh, officer? They won the first round against *me*, you know."

"We'll manage that all right, sir," replied Detective-Sergeant Meadowsweet. "The police don't fancy having the mickey taken out of them by two overgrown kids. Which is what you and Mr. Morke both said they were, madam."

"But what can be done *then?*" persisted Millie, though somewhat against the grain, as she was perfectly well, although confusedly, aware. "Is there *anything* that I could do?"

"All I am permitted to say is that it will then be a matter for the proper authorities." The Detective-Sergeant thought for a few seconds and, in his characteristic way, he added, "I wish them the best of British luck with it."

Unfortunately, it soon proved that the Detective-Sergeant had been mistaken at the precise point where he had shown most confidence: his conviction that Angus and Rodney would be finally apprehended in virtually no time.

A week passed and there was no hint or rumor of an arrest. On the other hand, Uncle Stephen had no further trouble with the authorities. There were questions at the next two Parish Council meetings, but nothing was permitted to come out of them. As for the two young giants themselves, they appeared to have gone into hiding, difficult though that must have been; or perhaps it was that they were passing almost unnoticed amidst the freaks and zanies that people urban and suburban areas in the latter part of the twentieth century. Millie, however, remembering the pair, found that hard to believe; and shivered when recollection fell for a while into full focus.

None the less, she had begun to go out once more: shopping, visiting the library, even attending a lecture on Criminology by an Austrian refugee. Uncle Stephen was fiercely opposed to all these excursions, and, to please him (as she would have expressed it to a confidante), she gave two undertakings: that she would never be parted from a tiny gun he lent her; and that for any longer journey she would take his car and not lightly step out of it or turn off the engine. Before she was married, Millie had driven all the time. Uncle Stephen's car was a beautiful old Alvis. Millie loved muffling herself up in order to drive it; and it had the advantage that then she was not easily identifiable. The gun went into the pocket of her jeans, where it was no more noticeable than a compact. It fired special tiny bullets which, as Uncle Stephen confided, were, strictly speaking, illegal: a steady stream of them, if necessary; and it fired them almost silently. Uncle Stephen was at his best when instructing Millie on mid-week mornings in the small orchard.

These things were advances, and Millie had no doubt about how much Uncle Stephen loved and needed her; but the whole thing amounted to little more than a half-life, when all was said and done. Millie had no very precise idea of what the other half might consist in, still less of how best to go after it; but she missed it none the less, as people do. In the end, she decided finally that there was no sensible alternative to a further consultation with Thelma Modelle.

She had, of course, been aware of this for some time, and had continued to dream about Thelma quite frequently, but it meant returning to the other suburb, the suburb where she had lived for years with Phineas and the boys; so that she had hesitated and hesitated. Uncle Stephen would have had a fit if he had known what she was proposing.

Then one morning it became unbearable, as things suddenly do. It was a premonition or other compulsion.

She tied up her hair in a dark-green scarf, donned heavy-duty garments, and tucked in the ends of her knotted, paler green muffler; all without a word to Uncle Stephen except to the effect that she wanted some different air and would very likely die without it. It was not a very gracious thing to say but it was essential to seem adamant.

"Drive fast," said Uncle Stephen anxiously. "Never slow down unless you absolutely have to. And be ready for anything."

She knew by now what that meant.

"Of course, Uncle Stephen," she said. "I'll be fine."

"I ought by rights to come with you, and look after you, but it's not safe to leave the house on its own. You know how it is, Millie."

"I know."

"Luckily, I went over the car this morning while you were sleeping. She'll go like the wind. See to it that she does. There's a girl."

"That's what I'm going to do." She was trying an *eau-de-Nil* silk scarf round the lower part of her face.

"Good-bye, my sweet."

Through the tight scarf, Uncle Stephen kissed her lips.

She roared away, but really there was a traffic light round the first bend, and always it was red. Uncle Stephen must have known that even better than she knew it.

None the less, she had a perfectly authentic disinclination to linger; and as the other suburb came nearer, one of her hands dropped half-consciously from the wheel and rested for longer and longer periods upon the reassuring object in her pocket.

The Parade, once again; the Lavender Bag; the fish shop! The fish shop was now even more diversified in its wares than when she had seen it last: now there was hardly a fish in sight. Millie felt no nostalgia; nothing but nausea.

She brought the Alvis to rest as unobtrusively as was possible with such a machine and darted upstairs in her full rig. She had no more made an appointment than on the previous occasion.

But this time the visionary did not greet her upon the landing, and the door of the sanctum, once the rheumatism lady's little sitting room, was shut.

Millie hesitated for some little time. After all, she was presumably hidden from observation, and could give a moment or two to thinking and deciding. Most probably, Thelma's practice had grown since those first days, so that by now a client would have to be specially fitted in. Alternatively, Thelma might have failed and gone. Or gone, anyway. Communities are full of neat or braggart labels referring to vanished enterprises.

Millie timidly tapped.

"What is it?" The voice was Thelma's.

How could Millie explain? It was best to open and enter.

Thelma sat on the floor by the rheumatism lady's miniature gas fire. The black table, with its attendant black chairs, had been pushed into a corner. The zodiacal wall cards hung at madder angles than ever. Thelma herself wore what looked like the same green jeans, though they also looked a year and more older; and a battle-dress tunic, dyed dark blue by the authorities. It could be deduced that business was less than brisk.

"Oh, it's you."

Thelma did not get up, and this time it was Millie who stood.

"Yes, it's me. I want to know what's happening now. Exactly, please. What's happening at this very moment, if possible."

"Well, in that case you'd better shut the door."

Millie complied. She perceived that she should have done it in the first place. At least Thelma had not specifically demurred.

"And you'd better take off your clothes."

"Some of them," said Millie, smiling.

She had unwound the silk scarf from her face before entering. Now she climbed out of the heavy-duty garments and threw them on the floor, where they lay like prehistoric monsters, alive or dead, as the case might be. The rheumatism lady had presumably arranged to take away her carpets since Millie had last been there, because now the boards were bare. They were also mottled, but that happens soon and mysteriously in almost any house.

"Leave that," said Thelma sharply, as Millie was about to unwind the dark green scarf which confined her locks.

Millie desisted. Her brow was moist.

"Take off your sweater if you're too hot," said Thelma.

Millie shook her head.

"This time I shall need your money," said Thelma. "You can't depend entirely on my good will. I might need a new dress. Have you thought of that?"

"How much money?" asked Millie, still on her feet.

"How much have you got with you?"

"Can't you see without asking me?"

"Yes," said Thelma. "Forty pounds in fivers, and ten single pounds. You must want to know badly."

"I do," said Millie calmly. For some reason, Thelma, no matter what her words or deeds, never upset her, as so many people did, even when saying or doing very little. Thelma was like Uncle Stephen in that.

"I'll take forty-nine pounds of it. You may need a pound suddenly when you leave." Millie had noticed before that Thelma was surprisingly well-spoken in her own way.

"Only if you tell me what I've asked you to tell me and tell me the truth and the whole truth."

Thelma shot Millie a confusing glance. Though intense, it was not necessarily hostile.

Then she arose from the floor and drew the curtains across the single window. They were not the rheumatism lady's pretty chintz, but heavy, dun, and unshaped. As they were touched and moved, they smelt. It was as if old clothes were being draped before the fairy windows of a wagon.

Thelma locked the door.

"I'm not locking you in. You can leave any time you like."

And Millie could indeed see that the key was still there.

Thelma lifted the crystal and placed it on the floor. Sure enough, it was much smaller than Millie had always supposed such gadgets to be. Perhaps they came in different sizes, according to the purchaser's needs and resources?

The only light was from under the door and from the small yellow gas fire. The room was odorous as well as stuffy.

Thelma signalized this fact by throwing off her dark-blue tunic. Beneath it she wore a fragile pinkish garment with big rents in it, through which her brown skin could be seen by what light there was. Her mop of hair was uncombed and uneven in length.

"Do what I am doing," directed Thelma; and added, "If you really must go on with this."

When Millie made no answer, Thelma wriggled down on the floor until she lay at full length upon her front with the crystal about two inches before her eyes.

She looked ridiculous; or any other woman in her position would have looked ridiculous. Millie had supposed that crystal-gazing was done seated at a table. Moreover, a very suitable table was in the room with them.

"I advised you to take off your sweater," said Thelma. "Why not be more friendly?"

Millie continued calm. Upon the passage to truth, cross-currents are to be expected.

"I'm all right," she said, and lay down upon her front on the diametrical other side of the small crystal. She rested her chin upon her two hands, as Thelma was doing. At these close quarters, Thelma's lupine aroma was very pungent. Millie tried to concentrate upon gazing into the crystal. She assumed that to be the right thing to do. If only the crystal had been proportioned for a mature woman instead of for a waif!

But that matter began to adjust itself, and before Millie had had time even to begin feeling physically uncomfortable. As she gazed through the crystal at Thelma's rock-pool eyes, the yellow light from the gas fire turned blue; and the circumference of the crystal expanded and expanded, as did Thelma's orbs on the other side of it. Indeed, Millie realized quite clearly that it must always have been impossible for her to have seen Thelma's eyes *through* the actual crystal. All anyone could really have seen *through* it, would have been Thelma's nose and a small distance on either side of it.

Incandescent with darting blue lights, the crystal grew until it filled the room, until it *was* the room, and Thelma's eyes were no longer there, as if her face had split vertically down the middle and her eyes had rolled away round the polished sphere, each in a different direction.

But by now Millie was in a room no longer. Nor was she lying inconveniently upon her front. On the contrary, she was in a small woodland clearing and was observing with perfect ease what therein transpired.

The two boys were sitting, rather absurdly jammed together, on a tree trunk. It was not a whole fallen giant of the forest, but a neatly sawn-off section, awaiting the arrival of the timber float and its tractor, or perhaps left there by intention as a nature seat for wooers, an accessory to picnics. In fact, the boys, ravenous as ever, were at that moment engaged upon a picnic of their own.

Each boy held in his hand a very large, very red bone, from which he was gnawing in the frenzied manner that Millie remembered so well.

On the worn, wintry grass before them lay what was left of a human body.

The boys had already eaten their way through most of it, so that it could not even be described as a skeleton or semi-skeleton. The disjoined bones were everywhere strewn about at random, and only the top part of the frame, the upper ribs, remained in position, together with the half-eaten head.

It was Phineas's head.

Things swam.

Millie felt that her soul was rushing up a shaft at the center of her body. She knew that this is what it was to die.

But she did not die.

She realized that now she was lying on her back in the still-darkened room. Thelma must have moved her. The gas fire was as yellow as before, no doubt because there was something wrong with it; and Thelma in her pink rags and dirty jeans was standing before her, even looking down at her.

"You've been out a long time."

"I wish I were still out."

"*You* may, but I don't. I've things to do. You forget that."

Millie hesitated.

"Did you see them too?"

"Of course I saw them. Remember, I asked you whether you really had to go on with it."

"What else could I do?"

"I don't know. I'm not your nursemaid."

Millie sat up. "If you pass me my handbag, I'll pay you."

Thelma passed it. It did not seem to have been rifled during Millie's anaesthesia.

"Perhaps we could have a little more light?" suggested Millie.

Thelma threw on her tunic and, without fastening it, began to draw back or take down the window coverings. Millie did not examine which it was.

She rose to her feet. Had Thelma been behaving differently, she, *Millie,* would have been shaking all over, still prostrate. She seated herself on one of the dusty black chairs. She counted out forty-nine pounds onto the black table in the corner. Then she gazed for a moment straight into Thelma's vatic eyes. At once the sensations of a few moments before (or of what seemed a few moments) faintly recurred. Millie felt dragged out of herself, and turned her face to the dingy wall.

"You can stay if you wish. You know that." Thelma made no attempt to take up the money; though Millie could be in small doubt that the sum would make a big difference for Thelma, at least temporarily.

"You can't expect me to keep open house for you always."

Millie turned a little and, without again looking at Thelma, attempted a smile of some kind.

"I shan't be around much longer," said Thelma. "Surely you can see that?"

Millie stood up. "Where will you go?"

"I shall go back to decent people. I should never have left them."

"What made you?"

"I killed a girl."

"I see."

"I did right."

There was a pause: a need (perhaps on both sides) for inner regrouping. It was a metaphor that Uncle Stephen might have approved.

Millie gathered herself together. "Is that the sort of thing *I* ought to do?"

"How can I tell? Why ask *me?* You must decide for yourself."

Millie gathered herself together a second time. It was difficult to petition. The forty-nine pounds still lay untouched on the hocus-pocus table. "You *can* tell, Thelma. I know you can. They're obscene, monstrous, all those words. You know as well as I do. You're the only one who does. I feel responsible for them. Is it what I ought to do? Tell me."

Thelma seemed actually to reflect for a moment; instead of darting out a reply like the double tongue of a snake, the flick of a boxing second's towel, as she usually did.

"You're not the kind," said Thelma. "It would be beyond you."

"Then what? Help me, Thelma. Please, please help me."

"I told you before. Run away."

Millie stared blankly at the entire, round, empty, world.

"Be more friendly and you can lie up with *me.* I keep saying so. But soon I shan't be here. I have debts."

Millie wondered with what currency Thelma proposed to settle.

"Hurry up and put the money away somewhere," Millie said.

But Thelma again spoke to the point: "I'll place my right hand on your heart and you'll place yours on mine. Then we'll be friends."

Millie glanced at Thelma's ragged pink garment, but all she said was, "It wouldn't be fair." Then she added, "Thank you all the same." What a depraved, common way to express gratitude, she thought.

There was a tapping at the locked door.

"Who's that?" asked Millie, as if she really did live there.

Thelma had leapt upon the money like a cheetah and shoved it hugger-mugger into her jeans.

"It's Agnes Waterfield. She comes every day at this hour."

"God! I don't want to meet *her*," cried Millie.

"Well, you'll have to," said Thelma, and unlocked the door on the instant.

Millie could only snatch her garments and scuttle away like a cat, hoping that Agnes might be too involved in her own troubles and preoccupations to recognize her, though not really believing it.

Outside, it had begun to snow. The big open car was spattered with separate flakes.

Millie sped away. Soon the suburb which had once been home was miles behind.

The straggling and diminishing woodlands touched the road at several places before one reached the main section in which lay Uncle Stephen's house. The ground was hummocky here, and nowadays the road ran through several small cuttings, ten or twelve feet high, in order to maintain a more or less constant level for the big lorries, and to give the tearaway tourists an illusion for a minute or two that they were traversing the Rocky Mountains. There were even bends in the road which had not yet been straightened, and all the trees in sight were conifers.

Thinking only of sanctuary, Millie tore round one of these bends (much too fast, but almost everyone did it, and few with Millie's excellent reason); and there were the two boys blocking the way, tall as Fiona Macleod's lordly ones, muscular as Gogmagog, rising high above the puny banks of earth. It was a busy road and they could only a moment before have dropped down into it. Beneath the snow patches on their clothing, Millie could clearly see the splashes of blood from their previous escapade. The boys were so placed that Millie had to stop.

"Got any grub, Mum?"

Quite truthfully, she could no longer tell one twin from the other.

"That's all we ask, Mum," said the other twin. "We're hungry."

"We don't want to outgrow our strength," said the first twin, just as in the old days.

"Let's search," cried the second twin. Forbearance was extinguished by appetite.

The two boys were now on the same side of the car.

Millie, who had never seen herself as a glamorous mistress of the wheel, managed something that even Uncle Stephen might have been proud of in the old, dead days at Brooklands. She wrenched the car round onto the other side of the highway, somehow evaded the towering French truck charging towards her, swept back to her proper lane, and was fast on her way.

But there was such a scream, perhaps two such screams, that, despite herself, she once more drew up.

She looked back.

The snow was falling faster now; even beginning to lie on the car floor. She was two or three hundred yards from the accident. What accident? She had to find out. It would be better to drive back rather than to walk: even in the modern world, the authorities would not yet have had time to appear and close the road. Again Millie wheeled.

The two vast figures lay crushed on the highway. They had been standing locked together gazing after her, after the car in which there might have been sweets or biscuits; so that in death, as in life, they were not divided. They had been killed by a police vehicle: naturally one of the heavier models. Millie had underestimated the instancy of modernity. The thing stood there, bluely lighted and roaring.

"It was you we were after, miss," remarked the police officer, as soon as Millie came once more to a standstill. All the police were ignoring the snow completely. "You were speeding. And now look what's happened."

"If you ask Detective-Sergeant Meadowsweet, he will explain to you why I was going fast." Millie shivered. "I have to go fast."

"We shall make enquiries, but no individual officer is empowered to authorize a breach of the law."

By the time the usual particulars had been given and taken, the ambulance had arrived, screaming and flashing with determination; but it was proving impossible to insert the two huge bodies into it. The men were doing all they could, and the police had surrounded the area with neat little objects, like bright toys; but anyone not immediately involved could see that the task was hopeless.

The snow was falling more heavily every minute, so that by the time Millie was once more left alone among the traffic surging round the frail barrier, the two boys were looking like the last scene in *Babes in the Wood*, except that the babes had changed places, and changed roles, with the giants.

EDITOR'S AFTERNOTE

Writes the late author's agent, Kirby McCauley, Robert Aickman "haunts his reader by a skillful blending of the supernatural with odd aspects of the modern world or allegory." That flair for allegory, I believe, is the brilliance behind this story, which projects the paradigm for motherhood onto something much larger. By showing us the shock, terror, and frustration of a parent whose boys' growth is unchecked, he illuminates for us the very human consequences of giving birth to an abstract body that can neither be contained nor controlled, such as a nation, or society as a whole.

Aickman crafted over forty-eight stories during his life, served as a drama critic, and founded The Inland Waterways Association, an organization committed to reviving Britain's rivers and canals. The grandson of Edwardian novelist Richard Marsh, he lived in London at the time of his death in 1981.

Variations on a Theme
Chelsea Quinn Yarbro

Once upon a time—and if you'll believe that, you'll believe anything—there was a poor widow whose husband had quarreled with his relatives and then died without adequate health or life insurance and intestate to boot, so that by the time the attorneys and the doctors and the taxmen and the courts had finished collecting their shares, there was very little left for the widow and her two daughters, but the woefully inadequate college accounts the widow's parents had given to the girls the year before they were killed in a pile-up on the interstate.

The poor widow was distraught, for her children more than herself, for she felt that they had been treated shabbily by their father; she knew she had to make sure his memory was respected, to avoid making their trauma worse. So she apologized to the two girls, whose names, incidentally, were Aphra and Zoe, and whose main abilities consisted of being charming when they chose to be, and some skill at sports.

"I don't know what to tell you, girls," said their mother when she got off the phone with the realtor. "I don't like to sell the house, but it's the only thing I can think to do. The mortgage is paid off," she reminded them, thinking that the bank had been wiser than she to demand her husband insure his life for the value of the note they held. "Then I'll have something to invest, and maybe things will turn out better in the future than they are right now."

"Oh, Mother," cried Zoe, "but we'll have to change high schools if you sell the house and that would mean losing all our friends."

"Yes," wailed Aphra, "it's bad enough now, the way they all treat us because Father died so . . . stupidly." She wrung her hands, demolishing her paper napkin in the process. "He didn't have to . . . to—"

"Your father," said their mother, in the manner of one reciting a litany, "loved you very much. He would never do anything to hurt you. He didn't know the gas canister on the barbecue was leaking the way it was, or he wouldn't have tried to test it with a match." In spite of her best intentions, she heard the sharp anger in her voice, and did her best to modify her tone. "If he had known what could happen, he would have been more sensible. He never wanted to hurt himself, or you. You can be sure of that," she added, although she was not.

"I think it was mean of him," said Aphra with all the stubbornness of her two-months-short-of-fifteen years. "I think he didn't care if he blew the whole house up. I think—"

"He should have used a flashlight," said Zoe, as confident of adult inadequacy as any sixteen-year-old.

"Yes," said their mother, "he should have." She looked out the kitchen window toward the backyard, thinking that her girls still didn't understand what had happened to them, not really. She allowed the view to distract her: they had a kidney-shaped swimming pool and the fruit trees she had planted when they moved in eight years ago were just coming into their own, and the climbing roses had spread nicely along the back fence; the small lawn was properly manicured. The realtor had said these plants might help make up for the blackened ruin of the garage.

"Mother," said Aphra, adjusting her black shirt over her jeans. "Is this all right for school?"

"Certainly," said the mother. "Your father hasn't been dead more than ten weeks. You can still wear black for him."

"No, silly," Aphra protested with exaggerated patience, "is it okay to have the second button unfastened?" She gave what she hoped was a good version of a provocative smile, copying the way her favorite singer held her mouth in photographs.

Her mother stared at her. "What are you talking about?"

"My bra shows, just a little," said Aphra. "Is that okay, or are you going to get mad at me again?"

Zoe snickered.

"I won't get mad," their mother said wearily. "If you don't try to lean over every chance you get, so that everyone will see you're wearing a bra." She knew Aphra had felt woefully inadequate when her friends had started to develop breasts before she did, and now that she was beginning to catch up, it was urgently necessary for everyone to notice. "You could get Miz Greyson mad again, though."

"Miz Greyson doesn't have more than an A cup herself," said Zoe, smug in her 32-B. "No wonder she gets mad at Aphra."

Aphra picked up the last morsel of her skimpy breakfast and licked the fork clean. "I have swimming practice after school," she announced.

Her mother regarded her narrowly. "I think . . ." she said, "I better enroll you in that dance class we talked about."

Aphra looked at her as if her greatest dreams had been betrayed. "Mo-*ther!*" she protested.

"A girl who can dance well has a better chance at things," she said vaguely, and rounded on Zoe, who was preparing to go out the door. "That goes for you as well, young lady. Ice-skating practice starts next week. I've signed you up at the rink."

Zoe rolled her eyes heavenward and sighed the sigh of the ill-used. "Why waste the money?" She thought the question was inspired.

"It's not wasting money; it's giving you girls some advantage in the world, so you won't have to fight over that piddling college fund," their mother insisted. "Your father and I discussed your futures often."

The two girls looked pained at what was for them a familiar catechism.

"You're pretty and talented," said their mother. "You could both do very well for yourselves, if you bring yourselves to the attention of the right people."

"She means rich men," said Zoe to her younger sister, who nodded sagely.

"Of *course* I mean rich men," said their mother. "And don't you dare say it doesn't matter, when you've just seen what can happen if the man of the house doesn't take care of you." She glanced at the clock and reluctantly cut her harangue short. "I'll be home at eight-thirty. You know what to put in the microwave." She hated missing dinner with them, but they needed her paycheck. Doing her best not to feel guilty, she reminded the two girls, "Don't make more than one frozen dinner each—we can't afford the cost or the calories for more than that."

"Yes, Mother," said the two in unison, exchanging a secretive glance confirming their plans to stop at the pizza parlor on the way home and blow part of their allowances on gooey, garlicky, oniony, medium deep-dish with *everything*.

As the two girls left the house, their mother watched them, hoping her worry would not add to the lines in her face. Being thirty-seven and a widow was bad enough, but if she began to look haggard . . . She banished the idea from her mind; it was too unpleasant to contemplate. Then she went to change to her simple, beige suit, getting ready for her job from noon until eight, four days a week, at the cosmetics counter at the Macy's in the new mall. Today she had to go in early for an interview with Mister Scholcross; she hoped that her request for more hours would be granted, so that she could get the full-time benefits package.

But Mister Scholcross, while expressing sympathy for her plight, reminded the widow of the sad state of the economy just now, and in the end made her feel grateful that she was not going to be laid off, as thirty-four other part-time workers were. "I know your situation is difficult, Rhonda, and I know what a trying time you're going through. Believe me, if it were up to me, I would give you full-time status in an instant. You're a good worker; we need more like you. But these things are out of my hands, and there's nothing I can do." He spread out his hands on the top of the desk as if to show he had no power to help her.

Rhonda did her best to smile, and fought down the panic that welled within her. "I understand," she said, although she did not. "Thanks for talking to me, Mister Scholcross." She almost backed out of his office. Once she had closed the door, she bolted for the Staff Ladies' room, swallowing hard to keep from crying.

The only other woman in the utilitarian lounge was Mimi Longacre, the thrice-wed doyenne of the leather-goods department; a woman of energetic middle-age, she had weathered the ups and downs of retail for most of her adult life. She surged up to Rhonda and put her arm around her shoulder. "Hey, Rhonda, don't let it get to you. They're all a bunch of shits. They don't give a rat's ass about any of us. They don't deserve your—"

"I won't," said Rhonda abruptly and unsteadily, wishing that she did not have to endure this concern, for it made her control more precarious than she liked.

But Mimi was not willing to be put off. "The thing is, you've got to get *out* more, start *meeting* people. What's it been? three months?"

"Two and a half," said Rhonda. "George died on July eighteenth, after . . . eleven days in the hospital." She blinked twice at the memory of the burn unit where George had lain, where care cost more than two thousand dollars a day.

"Well, it's time you thought about your *future*," Mimi reminded her, in much the same tone Rhonda had used with her own girls that morning. "You can't wait around, hoping Prince Charming is going to ride by and snap you up. That's for kids, not for grown-ups." She put her hands on her hips. "If kids nowadays believe any of the old myths."

Rhonda sighed. "I hate to see them go through this," she said, dabbing at her eyes, hoping her mascara would not run.

"Sure you do," said Mimi, approvingly. "You're a good mother. That's why you're going to start looking around. You need a man in your life." She chuckled. "They're the ones who hold all the cards, Rhonda."

"I know," said Rhonda softly; she blew her nose and set about putting her face in order.

Mimi watched her in the mirror. "Hey, what about Friday night? Why don't you and I go out together? I know some good places to meet guys. Not singles bars, nothing like *that;* you don't want to meet a bunch of tail-chasing drunks," she went on as she saw the doubt in Rhonda's face. "Just good places, like the bowling alley. And," she added when she realized Rhonda was unconvinced, "there's the International Deli. That's a *great* place to meet guys, the ones who keep their boats at the marina."

"But . . ." said Rhonda, reaching into her purse for her lipstick.

"But, nothing," said Mimi. "You've got two girls to think about. They need to have a father, don't they? And you need a husband." She gave a significant nod. "You said you're going to have to sell the house and move to a less expensive place."

"I found a nice, three-bedroom condo, and it's nearer to work," said Rhonda, feeling defensive. "The property taxes are not quite half of what I have to pay on the house."

"Sure," said Mimi. "That'll do for the short run. But what about ten years from now? This place gives lousy retirement for full-time employees; you can't have a lot set aside. You want to have something worthwhile when you think about your old age, don't you? What about when you don't work anymore? Your girls aren't going to be able to take care of you, are they? Especially if you can't afford to send them to college." She managed a grim smile. "You come with me. We'll make sure you find a nice guy with a kid or two himself, who'll understand what you're up against."

Rhonda allowed herself to be persuaded, and on Friday night, after work, she got into the new washed-silk outfit she had splurged on for the occasion and met Mimi at nine at the International Deli. The noise, and brass, and green-and-white tile, all seemed a bit much, and Rhonda said so as they made their way to the counter to place their orders.

"It's part of what makes the place popular," said Mimi. "Make sure you get something worth eating. The guys don't like to see the women picking at little salads. It makes them think they'll get stuck with a *whopping* dinner check, if they stop to talk for too long. Let me order a bottle of wine for us, too; it makes everything *friendlier*." She called out her order to the waiting counterman, and nudged Rhonda.

Rhonda ordered the pâté-and-cheese plate and hurried to the end of the drinks line to get in her order for espresso before making her way back through the crowd to the table she and Mimi had staked out. As she sat down, she noticed a man wearing gold chains against the graying thatch of his chest hair, the buttons of his rayon shirt open almost to his waist; the man smiled at her, and she was about to smile back when Mimi bustled up and said, "Oh, no, no, not that one. He's nothing more than a fancy-man, as they used to call them in my mother's day."

"You mean, he's a con man who targets women," said Rhonda, her face sad with the realization that this might all be a mistake.

"That's right," said Mimi. "And you, of *all* people, can't afford one of those." She nodded to the waiter who brought up the bottle of Pinot Grigio. "We'll have some now," she said grandly, and approved the wine on the first taste. "Not that I know anything about wine," she confided to Rhonda in an undervoice. "But I think it's a good idea to make it look like I do."

"Probably," said Rhonda, finding the blare of conversation distracting. She stared at Mimi, astonished at her vivacity. She knew she would never be able to be so . . . so *out there* as Mimi was. When her meal arrived, she pulled the baguette apart and cut some of the buttery brie. She saw that her hands were shaking a little, and she scolded herself for being a ninny.

"Have some wine. You'll relax," said Mimi, handing Rhonda a glass. "You look like you expect to be nailed to the wall."

"I feel a little that way," said Rhonda, thinking of her girls, who were with the McFarlane family at the Cine 11, for the Friday Nite Horror Fest.

"Well, don't. It puts men off," said Mimi knowledgeably. "Think of something funny to tell me. Do it now."

Rhonda was nonplused. "I . . . I can't think of anything," she said, trying not to panic. "Really, I can't."

"Sure you can," said Mimi. "That ridiculous dog your neighbors have. Hasn't he done *anything* dumb this week?"

"Oh," said Rhonda, and took a sip of wine. "I thought you wanted me to tell you a joke. I don't know lots of jokes and I don't tell them very well."

"Don't worry about it; just tell me about that damned dog," said Mimi, smiling her encouragement. "You said it likes to steal shoes."

"Yes," said Rhonda, relieved, and recounted how the dog had made off with the shoes of a guest of one of the families across the street, and the uproar this theft had caused. Mimi laughed more heartily than the story deserved, and Rhonda felt thankful for her graciousness.

The International Deli stayed open until midnight, and Mimi insisted they remain until the place was closed. When they wandered out to the parking lot, Mimi gave Rhonda a thumbs-up. "You've got your feet wet. That's something."

Rhonda shook her head. "I don't know, Mimi. I don't think I'm very good at this."

"Of course you're not good at it. You're out of practice. It'll be easier next weekend," Mimi assured her.

"Next weekend?" Rhonda cried. "I can't afford another night like this, not for a month."

"Oh, yes, you can, and you better include it in your budget," Mimi admonished her. "You'll come here next Friday with me again. Don't worry. I'll treat. But you *have* to do something or you'll run out of chances." She nodded toward her car, waving as she went toward it. "You know I'm right. Think about it." As she opened the door, she added, "I'll see you at work on Tuesday. We'll make plans."

All the protestations Rhonda wanted to make seemed in vain. As she drove back to the house, she argued with herself about what Mimi had said and could not bring herself to disagree. By the time she parked in the driveway, she had already started to plan how to use her wardrobe most effectively.

By the next Friday, Aphra and Zoe had teased her steadily

about her plans. "Go on," said Zoe, who was still nursing sore muscles from her ice-skating lessons. "You just want to get laid."

"Zoe," protested her mother.

"Well, why not?" said Aphra. "We don't blame you. Just remember to carry condoms and use them."

"For *heaven's* sake!" their mother cried. "I'm hoping to find a good man who can make a nice life for all of us. I don't care about getting laid. There are more important things than sex and all that." It was not quite true; over the last month she had felt the first disturbing stirring of libido since her husband's death.

Aphra looked remote. "You better get the condoms, then. You aren't going to get a man without letting him have a sample. And you want to know what he's like in bed. Betty McFarlane told us all about that. She says that a woman's a fool to go with an insensitive man."

"And what does *she* know about it?" exclaimed their mother. "She's only seventeen."

"Betty knows everything," said Aphra. "She goes to Wilson. You learn everything there."

"So they say," their mother said drily. "Be glad you're still at Hilltop. They don't experiment on the kids at Hilltop."

"They don't do anything but babysit at Hilltop," said Zoe with the total disgust only a teenager can achieve.

"Well, if that's the case," countered their mother, "you should be getting straight As and nothing else."

Zoe flushed and pouted, and glared toward the door. "We have to leave now."

"I'll see you at twelve-thirty, at the Jacksons'. Enjoy the movie," their mother reminded them, and settled down to an hour of housework before getting ready for her job, glad that she did not have to listen to any more suggestions from her daughters.

So for the next two months, Rhonda went out with Mimi every Friday night, and she met half a dozen men who were mildly interesting—Sam, who was a cop; Jerry, who owned an appliance-repair business; Benjamin, who brokered boats; William, who did something with computers; Ed, who was a reporter for the local paper; and Lloyd, who had been a priest and was now teaching philosophy at the local college—but none of whom were eager to get involved with a widow with two teen-aged daughters.

Then she met John Flanders, who designed and installed office security systems. He was a quiet man, withdrawn, but successful, a widower, with a twelve-year-old daughter named Ellen. It was not so much a question of bells ringing or fireworks for either of them, but a sense of relief.

So for the next two months they went out together, to dinners and movies, and once to a play; Rhonda learned to like him, putting up with his quirky ways because he, of all the men she had met, was interested in her children, and he was well enough off to afford them.

Finally John suggested that he should meet her girls, and offered to meet her after work one evening and take them all to dinner at a local restaurant that featured prime rib and fresh fish.

The outing was not a success.

"What a *dweeb*," Zoe pronounced as soon as John left the house.

"Mother, how *could* you?" Aphra echoed in despair.

"He's a very nice man," said their mother, who was already thinking about the packing she would have to do if they got the townhouse; she would know in two weeks.

"He's not anything like Daddy," mourned Zoe, who had been ranking her dead father with the lesser deities in the last month.

"No, he's not," her mother agreed. "He's a lot richer."

Both girls looked eager and guilty at once.

Aware she had their attention at last, their mother went on, "You keep saying you don't want to have to live in the Bel Arbor part of town, though you know I can't afford to keep this place and pay for your skating lessons and dancing classes and all the things you're going to need, not on my salary. You need a future, and the way things are going, I won't be able to give it to you, not without help. So you better get used to the idea that I am going to have to find someone who is willing to take us on, and can do it handsomely. So far, John Flanders is the best bet I've come across." Her face was stern but she felt a certain excitement, because until that moment she had not been certain she wanted to catch this man. Now she knew she would use every trick in the book—though she had to admit that her tricks were a little rusty—to land John Flanders.

Zoe sighed. "If he just were a little more . . . interesting."

"I'm the one who should worry about that, not you," her Mother said sharply, thinking it was true that John Flanders was a trifle dull. She told herself that was why he was good and steady and worthwhile.

"What's his daughter like?" asked Aphra in the voice of doom.

"I don't know. I haven't met her yet." Their mother admitted this with misgivings. The pictures she had seen were of a non-descript youngster, pleasant to look at but lacking spark or verve. Still, she told herself, what could you expect from a girl at twelve, and one who had lost her mother two years before? She probably just needed the chance to come out of herself, a little like her father.

"Well, if she's like her dad, we'll all be bored," Zoe predicted.

"Don't make assumptions," her mother warned her. "You just might like her."

The meeting was arranged for a Sunday afternoon at the Flanders' "Place," as John called it, with a touch of embarrassment.

Rhonda had been told that John was well-off, but she was not prepared for the sprawling, Mediterranean-style villa of 1920s vintage that occupied the brow of a hillock overlooking the ocean. "Goodness!" she exclaimed as she drove through the gates.

"Wow," whispered Zoe.

"Holy shit," exclaimed Aphra.

The drive curved up to the house, to the entry that was framed with trellises of wisteria, now just past their best bloom. John stood in the open door, pointing to the parking area, which proved to face the pool area.

"Glad you could make it," he said as he came to open her

door. "Hi, there, girls," he went on so heartily that even Rhonda felt it was hard to take.

"What a beautiful place this is," said Rhonda as she got out of the car. "You should have warned me."

"It was my late wife's house. She inherited it from her grandmother," he explained. "Let me show you around." He took Rhonda's elbow—which she disliked—and guided her toward the open door, calling out, "You girls come along."

Much as Zoe and Aphra disliked the way he talked to them, they obeyed eagerly, anticipating the delights of the luxurious dwelling.

"The grounds are almost four acres," said John just before he entered the house. "We have eleven rooms, and four baths." He indicated the entry hall. "The stained-glass window is real Tiffany." Then he turned into the living room. "It's eighteen by twenty-six," he said with pride.

"Look at that," marveled Zoe, indicating the fifty-inch television screen on the far side of the tremendous room.

"I'm looking," whispered Aphra.

"The terrace," John went on, waving toward the wall of French doors that opened onto it, "has special paving stones of marble. The pillars are red granite. They don't build anything but government buildings and banks this way anymore." His smile was self-effacing. "It's been restored recently."

"Great," said Rhonda, who was finding John more interesting by the second. She gave him her very best smile and did what she could to look entranced with him instead of his house.

"And here's Ellen," he said, nodding toward the plain child standing in the doorway to the dining room. "Ellen, this is Rhonda and her daughters, Zoe and Aphra."

Ellen smiled with that adamantine sweetness some girls develop early in life. "Hello," she said shyly.

Rhonda was determined to make a good impression, and so she held out her hand to the child and achieved another blinding smile. "Hello there, Ellen. I've been wanting to meet you."

"Mother," sighed Zoe.

Ellen blushed furiously and tried to move away.

"These are our guests, Ellen," said John in a pointed way. "No escaping, now."

Ellen looked as if she would prefer to be drawn and quartered than remain where she was, but she dutifully looked at Aphra and Zoe and asked in a small voice, if they would like to go swimming.

"Yes," said Aphra. "But we didn't bring suits."

"That's okay. We have some for . . . guests," said Ellen.

"Mother, can we?" Zoe inquired, unsure of how to respond.

Rhonda glanced at John. "If it's all right with you."

"It's *fine* with me," John responded, sounding relieved.

Aphra and Zoe hurried away with Ellen, all but squealing with delight.

That evening as they were driving home, Aphra said, "It's too bad he's such a nerd, Mother."

"He's a very good man," said her mother, wishing she could find John more attractive than she did. He was a wonderful catch, she reminded herself.

"Well, he's real rich," said Zoe with practical enthusiasm. "It would be *great* to live there."

"With Ellen?" Aphra asked, the question so laden with angst that it caught her mother's attention.

"Yuck," Zoe agreed.

"What's wrong with Ellen?" their mother demanded.

"She's duller than her dad," said Zoe patiently, "and so *good.*"

"Yuck," Aphra concurred.

"She's shy," their mother explained.

"She's *awful,*" protested Aphra.

"You'll like her better when you get to know her," their mother said, not convincing any of them.

When Rhonda and John became engaged, Mimi was overjoyed. She promised to arrange a wedding shower for Rhonda and predicted Rhonda would be set for life. "Congratulations. You deserve it."

"Yeah," said Rhonda. "And so will the girls."

"Nothing like a rich husband to solve a lady's problems," said Mimi with an exaggerated roll of her eyes.

Rhonda sighed. "Right."

"What's the matter?" Mimi asked. "Not getting cold feet are you?" She prepared to give a stern lecture to Rhonda.

"Not exactly," said Rhonda. "I just wish he turned me on a little. It wouldn't have to be a lot. But—"

"But nothing," said Mimi at her most bracing. "You're doing the right thing, Rhonda. You can't wait around for an ideal husband; this man has money, he likes your girls, and he can take care of you, all three of you. He *wants* to take care of you, for Chrissake! Do you know how lucky you are to find a man who actually *wants* to commit himself?"

"I know," said Rhonda. "I tell myself that every day."

"Good," declared Mimi. "Keep at it. And tell yourself he turns you on. Eventually he will."

Again Rhonda sighed. "Sorry. I can't help feeling I'm . . . selling myself."

"What of it?" asked Mimi. "That's the way the world works, honey." She rocked back on her heels. "The trick is to get a high-enough price. And you're doing that."

"My girls don't like him, or his daughter," Rhonda confessed, as if it were a terrible secret. "They think they're dull."

"They're trying to protect their father's memory, like you'd expect they'd do," said Mimi, dismissing her concern. "Girls always make Daddy their favorite saint. Don't let it bother you. A little time in that house and they'll decide that John Flanders is a real prince."

"I don't know," Rhonda said uncertainly.

"It'll take time," Mimi said. "Like it will for you."

"I guess so," said Rhonda, and took out her pocket calendar to work out the best time for the shower.

The wedding was in the garden, all three girls acting as attendants. Aphra and Zoe giggled through the ceremony; Ellen wept. There were sixty guests, most of them friends and associates of John's. When the ceremony was over, the reception was held in the house, and it was there that Peter Holt, John's attorney, took Rhonda aside for a short chat.

"John has drawn up a new will," he said.

"So I understand," said Rhonda, with a sudden rush of queasiness at the mention of a will at a wedding.

"He's leaving his entire estate to you and your girls," he said, doing his best to sound positive.

Because she knew it was expected of her, Rhonda said, "Isn't that unfair to Ellen, though?"

Peter laughed. "Hardly. Ellen has her grandmother's fortune and estate coming to her. Her grandmother is a very wealthy woman, and Ellen will be, too. She doesn't need John's money."

"What do you mean?" Rhonda asked more sharply than she wanted to.

"Ellen gets everything when she reaches twenty-five. The money, this house, all of it." Peter saw that Rhonda looked shocked, so he added. "He said he'd explained it to you. John's not a pauper, you know. He's got a tidy sum of his own, and some very good investments. Not anything like his first wife's fortune, but you won't go hungry on it." His mouth turned down at the corners.

"Of course he does," said Rhonda hollowly, as the vision of her future grew bleaker and bleaker; all Mimi's good advice now mocked her as the whole weight of her expectations came down on her.

"I thought you understood about Ellen," said Peter. "I told him to explain it to you, in case you were—"

"Fortune-hunting," she supplied for him. "Thanks very much for your high opinion of me. Well, I'm not. I just didn't quite understand about Ellen."

"So I guessed," said Peter in disapproval.

"It doesn't make any difference," said Rhonda gamely, doing her utmost to smile. "I know John is a fine man, and Ellen is a sweet girl."

"Good," said Peter with the first glimmerings of approval. "I wouldn't want to think you'd hold her situation against Ellen. She's been through so much already."

"How could I do that?" Her face was beginning to ache from smiling. "She's just a child."

Peter shrugged. "It can happen."

Rhonda stared at him, wanting to ask him what she was supposed to do now, but the words would not come. She reminded herself that her girls were provided for now and she herself did not face an impoverished old age, but it did not help. Against her own best instincts, she began to hate Ellen, as if the child had deliberately taken all satisfaction from her. She made herself smile and thank Peter for informing her of how things stood.

"My pleasure," he said with a slight bow.

Then John saw them and hurried over, Ellen in tow, and put his arm around Rhonda's waist. "There you are," he said, kissing her once, with affection but without passion.

"Hello, darling," said Rhonda, and dutifully kissed his cheek, aware that Peter was watching.

"I'm glad you've married my father," said Ellen in her soft tones, looking up into Rhonda's eyes in a way that pleaded for support, for inclusion.

"So am I, honey," said Rhonda, her voice brittle as she tried to banish the fury that raged through her. That this child should be so blessed, while she and her daughters so betrayed.

"Great," said John, oblivious to the emotions consuming his bride. "Come on; get your kids and let's all go live happily ever after."

EDITOR'S AFTERNOTE

Intrigued by the wicked stepmother in *Cinderella*, Chelsea Quinn Yarbro asked herself, "Why was she so wicked? Did she start out that way—in which case, why did Cinderella's father marry her—or did she turn wicked over time?" Stepmothers repeatedly get a bad rap from the authors of traditional folktales, who in Yarbro's estimation, "exist for the sole purpose of ruining the lives of the heroines.

"I thought it was about time to tell the story back to front, or inside out," she says, "to find out what made the wicked stepmother so unkind to Cinderella."

A writer for over twenty-seven years, Yarbro has had more than fifty books and sixty short stories in print. Her best known are from the Saint-Germain cycle. She has received the Fine Foundation Award for literary excellence and versatility. An avid opera lover, she is also a composer.

Ms. Carpenter
Andrew Greeley

The next appointment," announced Father Muratori implacably, "is a certain Ms. Mary Carpenter."

"Ms?" said the archbishop. "Of what vintage is this Ms. Carpenter?" He emphasized the *Ms.* both times he used it.

His secretary shrugged. "Her term, Archbishop. I'd say she has at least a year to go before she's twenty."

"Do we know her or what she wants?"

"What she wants is 'personal,' she says, and she looks vaguely familiar to me, but I don't think I know her."

The archbishop sighed. He prided himself on his accessibility, but it was Muratori's job to screen out the nuts from the people who really had something to say to their spiritual leader. He must think this Mary Carpenter was worth seeing, so there was no point in arguing with the dutiful but inscrutable young man about it. It was such a soft May morning with flowers in bloom outside his window. Tulips, he thought. He wasn't up to another confrontation with a feminist today.

Mary Carpenter was shown in. The archbishop realized that Muratori was probably right. The young woman did not look like a nut. Dressed smartly in a gray suit with a plaid scarf at her neck, she seemed a presentable and sensible late-adolescent girl.

Still, there was something slightly "foreign" about her. Her skin was almost olive in color, and her long black hair and deep brown eyes seemed to suggest the eastern Mediterranean. Carpenter was not a Greek name, but maybe it was a translation of something more clearly Levantine.

"Good morning, Ms. Carpenter," said the archbishop, emphasizing the *Ms.* ever so lightly, as he rose from his desk to greet her.

"Good morning, Archbishop," she replied, bowing to kiss his ring—an old Church custom he found embarrassing. Her brown eyes sparkled, and she showed a row of even, white teeth in a quick and somewhat impish smile.

Then he recognized her. The world spun around him. He was on a crazy cosmic roller coaster. He quickly went back to his seat behind the desk and sat down, badly shaken. Ms. Carpenter sat down across from him, a friendly grin lighting up her face. "You recognized me, didn't you?" She spoke delightedly, as if they were playing a wonderful game. Her voice was rich and deep, as though somewhere in the background there was breaking surf.

"Yes. Do you read minds?"

She laughed. "No, not really, but I'm pretty good at reading faces."

"What I want to know is why you look exactly like I always imagined you to look."

More laughter. "But, Archbishop, how else did you expect me to look? Admittedly, if I were going to China—to cite the old example—I would have had to make certain other changes. . . ." Her laughter hinted at wisdom which teenagers didn't have. But then she really wasn't . . .

"How many changes did you have to make for me?"

"Surprisingly few. That's one of the advantages of dealing with a scholar who specializes in the area." The laughter was still in her eyes and smile. What deep dancing eyes. He amused her; she felt no constraint to hide the fact.

He was still shaken. "Would it be proper to offer you some tea?"

"Why not?"

He poured her a cup of Lapsang souchong from the pot on the warmer. She smiled with surprise and pleasure when she sipped it.

"First time?" he asked.

"Only for this brand. You are surprised that I would drink tea?"

"No reason why you shouldn't, actually. We have a doctrine that says you should be able to. But please spare me the shock of asking for one of my cigars."

Now the laughter was explosive. "Well, it wouldn't give me a cancer at any rate!" They laughed together. This was not a dream. Nor was he suddenly out of his mind, but reality was slipping away, like a fading TV signal on a rainy night.

"Uh, what is the proper title that I should use?"

"Oh, I have lots of them, but I think Ms. Carpenter is fun. We had a lot of laughs over that. 'Course, you can always use my first name if it doesn't scare you too much."

It did. "Well, would it be out of order, Ms. Carpenter, to ask what you want—other than to sample my brand of tea?" Get down to business; yes, that was the thing to do.

Her eyes widened. "A favor, Archbishop. What else have I ever wanted? I think my record on that is quite clear."

"A church?"

"Come now, Your Grace, you and I really ought to be beyond that sort of thing. Besides, they have already built one for me here in this country."

"A beautiful church then?"

"I have heard the joke, too, you know. Heaven forgive me, I laughed at it."

"Heaven forgive you? Surely that's an inappropriate phrase?"

"Archbishop, you are a literalist, aren't you?" The same impish grin spread across her lovely face. She looked like he thought she should, but there was a hoydenish quality about her that did not fit his expectations.

"There was a time when you seemed to need beautiful churches."

"Not I, my lord. People wanted to build them, and that was all right. But I never needed them."

"They put up some fine ones, though."

"Yes, and I'm proud of them; but not many after the fourteenth century, don't you think?"

"Quite."

"Do I shock you, Archbishop?" Her voice was frank and unassuming.

"To be honest with you, you do surprise me."

"I don't seem to fit the image of an age-old human symbol."

"Oh, I'm not arguing with the symbol, Ms. Carpenter. If what you reflect is like what you are, then the cosmos is a better place than I thought it was. . . ."

She actually blushed. "A very pretty compliment . . ."

"Yes"—he continued his thought—"better if a little wilder and more unpredictable, and—"

"Better make it good," she murmured.

"—and more filled with playful wonder." Grand larceny with someone else's phrase, but under the circumstances . . . He was on the roller coaster again.

She clapped her hands like a child at a circus. "Oh, very good indeed! May I have more tea?"

He poured the tea. "Now, as to that favor you wanted?"

"So businesslike—just when we were having such a nice conversation. Well, you don't need to look all that serious and solemn. I won't affect your budget at all." She was now a pretty fishwife in a marketplace, promising him a bargain. Oh Lord, he was in trouble. . . .

He put down the teapot with a clatter. "You did read my mind!"

"I told you that's out of bounds for me. I'm just a shrewd bargainer and a good reader of faces. You know my ethnic background." She leaned over his desk, every inch the confidential negotiator.

"You know the cloistered convent up at Docksville?"

"Sure, there's three old nuns in it and one postulant. The order is being suppressed by Rome because it doesn't have more than a score of members all over the world."

"Don't close it down. Leave it open. I told you it wouldn't cost much."

"But why?"

"Now, my lord, you ought to know better than that. People don't ask me that kind of question." In her dizzying spin from mood to mood she now was playing the part of an Italian cardinal.

"To quote yourself, Ms. Carpenter, you and I ought to be beyond that sort of thing."

"Ah-ha, you catch on to the game too quickly. You also ought to know that my kind tend to make up the rules as we go along. Anyhow, I just know that it's very important that the convent be left open."

"Very important, to judge by the status of the messenger."

She shrugged in the ancient gesture of the Near Eastern negotiator. But her answer was twentieth-century New York. "What can I tell you?"

"I've got rules I've got to keep."

"Bend them."

"Orders from Rome."

"Ignore them. The Romans won't know the difference."

"That sounds slightly seditious."

"I'm sure you won't tell on me." She winked. He wouldn't mind the conversation if she wasn't enjoying it so much.

"You do remember the story about the leper from the Hebrew scripture, don't you? I think we improved on it in ours, but you know the lesson. If I asked you for something big, you would cheerfully do it, so I ask for something small and you hesitate."

"I'm not hesitating; I'm just saying I don't understand."

"That's the whole point. You're not supposed to understand. Besides, if I hadn't come, you certainly would have closed it."

"I certainly would have. I can think of no good reason to keep open an expensive and useless convent. Neither can Rome." It was his most archiepiscopal tone, reasonable but firm.

"Keep it open as a favor for me, please?" There was a tone of pleading in her voice.

"How can I say no?"

"I don't take away people's freedom. You can say no by saying no. You can even make a good case that I have no authority to release you from Roman regulations. I am not, as you surely realize, a member of the curia."

"I can't." He sighed, looking at his hands as he always did when he had to say no.

"You won't keep the cloister open?" She wrinkled her nose in disbelief. "Not even for me?" The girl was used to getting her way.

"I'm afraid I can't. I've got the Congregation of Religious in Rome on one side of me and the pastoral council here on the other side. And they both have decided to close it. If I had my way . . ."

Her small hand tightened, the knuckles turning white. Sparks flashed from her eyes. "Don't I have any vote?"

"I'm sure you do, but as you well know, there are legitimate channels of authority in the Church. We all have to go through them. I could arrange for you to talk to the chairman of the priests' senate. . . ."

She rose from her chair and paced back and forth in front of his desk. "Fine chance I'd have with them. They think I belong in a medieval monastery." She was angry . . . but she wasn't supposed to . . .

"Or a Portuguese basilica." He didn't know what made him say that, but it was a mistake.

She turned on him, her face grim, her jaw set, her eyes now blazing. "Archbishop, you're a fool and a coward. You're not really a bad man, as canon lawyers go, but you've balanced so many forces for so long that you've forgotten what you're supposed to be. You don't really want to close that cloister down. You never did. . . ." Her dark skin flushed a dusky rose in anger.

"How do you know that? I thought you didn't read minds."

She dismissed the quibble with an imperious wave of her hand. "Someone who does told me. You like the old nuns, you even believe that cloisters are a good idea. You have compromised so often that you can't follow your own instincts anymore." She stamped her feet impatiently. "Why don't you wake up before you waste your whole life?"

Shock and dismay must have begun to show on his face. She smiled faintly. "You're scandalized because I'm angry. I'm not supposed to get angry, right? Just a plaster statue to light candles for?"

"I am a little surprised," he mumbled.

"Sure, I should not have any human emotions at all, no strong feelings, no concern; you want to make me the kind of person who would be a good archbishop."

"That's not fair. . . . I . . ."

"It is too fair. I may grow angry, but I'm not unfair. You know that."

"Ma'am, you have me trapped."

She sat down in her chair again. "That, my lord, is the general idea. To clear up this point: you don't think someone would have been given my job unless she had powerful feelings, do you? You don't think that I would lose those feelings ever, do you? What kind of a theologian are you?" Her anger seemed to be rising again.

"I just wish I could sign you up for a talk with some of my theological advisers. You'd blow their minds."

"No thanks. Archbishops are bad enough."

He played with his episcopal ring as he always did when making decisions. The flowers were still blooming in the garden outside. The sun was still shining. He could hear Father Muratori's typewriter. It was not a dream. Ms. Carpenter's theology was impeccable. He had never thought the principles should be taken that literally, though. If people like her . . . strange way to put it . . . really cared desperately, then . . .

"Would you have really preferred me, my lord, without passionate concern?"

"No . . . but the force of it surprised me. . . ."

The same impish grin. "A lot of people are going to be

surprised. Now tell me that you are going to fend off the Congregation and the senate and follow your own good instincts about those poor nuns. . . ."

"Woman, you are used to having things your way."

"Solid scriptural grounds for that, too, Excellency." She knew she had him. "Well . . ." She stood up. "It's been a pleasure to do business with you, Archbishop. Now I really must be going."

"Don't try to tell me that you haven't enough time."

"I've already taken too much of yours. You have so many administrative responsibilities." Now she was just plain making fun of him.

As he walked around his desk to see her out he said, "May I be so bold as to point out that having persuaded me to break Rome's rules, you're in no position to say anything about the responsibilities of my office."

The laughter was like an old bell pealing across a French countryside. She knelt to kiss his ring. "I've enjoyed this conversation."

"I guess I have, too, though it will take me a while to get back down to earth."

"A nice pun, if unintentional. Good-bye, Archbishop. Till we meet again."

"We will meet again, Mary?" He finally got out the name.

She beamed. "I don't know the future any more than I can read minds. But, yes, Archbishop, I have a feeling we will meet again."

Father Muratori came into the office after Ms. Carpenter had left.

"Not a kook?"

"Oh, no."

"Didn't look like one. She want anything important?"

"Depends."

Muratori got the signal. He wasn't supposed to ask.

"I can't help the feeling that I've seen her someplace before. Anyone I ought to know?"

The archbishop looked at him steadily. "George, you wouldn't believe it if I told you. Who's next on the visitors' list?"

EDITOR'S AFTERNOTE

"While Pope John is brilliant and devout, he doesn't have the faintest understanding of American Catholics, especially women," Father Andrew Greeley was quoted in 1995, the year of a papal visit by Pope John Paul II to America. Said this Catholic priest of forty-one years, "his shortest chapter is on women, and all he does is denounce feminism. His mind is closed."

Ever controversial, Greeley has taken the heat over his publicly expressed views and, perhaps more noticeably, his more than twenty-five best-selling novels, *Fall From Grace, The Cardinal Sins, Thy Brother's Wife,* and *Irish Gold* among them, which often explore combined themes of sex and religion; oil and water to the church hierarchy.

Author of over one hundred other books, including *Sex: The Catholic Experience* and *The Catholic Myth: The Behavior and Beliefs of American Catholics,* Greeley is a professor of sociology at the University of Arizona and founder of the National Opinion Research Center in Chicago.

Whatever fundamental differences he may have with current church policy, he remains a staunch defender of the Catholic faith in America and a generous benefactor. In 1986 he donated $1 million to establish the Catholic Inner-City School Fund, designed to assist Chicago's financially ailing Catholic schools.

The House on Hester Street

Erika Holzer

Peter was a rock, of course. In fact, he looked like a rock all through the funeral preparations: big, wide, and solid in his neat blue suit, white handkerchief in the breast pocket, nothing out of place except the straight sandy hair he couldn't keep off his broad forehead, his manner that of your genial eager-to-please neighborhood pharmacist even though he was a pretty good lawyer with a healthy practice in the neighboring town of Troy.

He saw to everything except my mother's last dress—she had specified "the pink silk I wore on my fiftieth anniversary, you know the one, Gloria"—and the flowers: I had insisted on a bouquet of my mother's beloved white roses, as big and bountiful as the one in her wedding picture.

We had congregated in my mother's pink-and-lemon-yellow kitchen, my sibs, their spouses, and I: a study in contrasting black. Our fellow mourners had dispersed after the last of the catered cold supper had either disappeared or been desecrated by the under-eight crowd. Peter was the last to leave.

The minute the kitchen door closed after him, my sister Anna said to me, "These days, nobody stands on ceremony. Why don't you save us the airfare and have yours? I'll help you get ready."

"I can't think about a wedding now," I said—too sharply, I

admit. Anna's folded arms tightened; she was as tiny and well-formed as our mother. I sat down, not wanting to tower over her.

"We'll help you, uh, get rid of Mom's stuff," Mark offered. He was a gaunt six-one and towered over all of us.

"Will you be doing any renovating?" John asked, looking around, his practiced architect's eye taking in a swatch of peeling wallpaper. "Damn funny place for an oil painting—the kitchen," he went right on in a disapproving tone even as his glance turned admiring. He gestured at my mother's favorite work of art—a portrait of a stunningly attractive raven-haired woman in turn-of-the-century dress—and turned to his wife, Jan. "How about we banish the still life to your powder room and install *this* beauty over the living room fireplace? Okay with you, Gloria?" he said as Jan bit her lower lip, considering.

My mother, not unexpectedly, had left me the house and furnishings, bearing in mind, no doubt, that the income of my brothers and brother-in-law relegated me, by comparison, to the category of "impoverished." Her only proviso was that each of her children take something—"whatever catches their fancy"—in remembrance of her.

"It's the one thing more than any other that I want of Mom's," I told John with a red face, not knowing until this minute that it was true. "Do you mind?"

John, ever generous, didn't mind. John didn't remember, as I just had, that the portrait had belonged to Grandmother Fanny Frank who, newly widowed and teary-eyed, by all accounts, had bestowed it on our mother.

Mine, now. I don't mind telling you I dreamt about it that night—about her, I mean: the woman in the portrait. Such knowing eyes! And something . . . intriguing in the smile; a woman of secrets, I remember thinking when I woke up. Like my mother, and her mother before her. A woman of the world, judging by the cut and fit of her crimson velvet gown, I decided as I stood before the portrait while my tea went cold. Strange artistic company for the shy, reticent Fanny, I couldn't help thinking.

I forgot all about her in the flurry and detail of family matters and postfuneral arrangements, at once depressing and burden-releasing. I can't say I forgot about the promise I'd made to my mother, but you know how it is when you don't really want to do something—one excuse as good as another. New York City, where my mother had been born and raised, seemed a million light years away instead of a comfortable three-hour ride on an Amtrak train.

It was my brother Mark's sober request, on the eve of his departure for London, for some pictures "from the old days" that propelled me to my mother's ebony hope chest—once full to the top with linens and lace, now a repository of the past. I had put aside a couple of dozen photos, conscientiously digging to the very bottom of the chest even as the dust of the ages sent me into a spasm of sneezing, when an unfamiliar photograph, a wedding picture more brown-and-white than black-, caught my eye. I had spotted something familiar in the bride's smile . . . as if I were still staring at my own reflection, my mother's soft voice urging me on: "Look for yourself, Gloria."

I looked at Fanny Frank, demure in a lace dress, roses covering her hair, filling her arms. My grandfather, trim and elegant in dark suit and bow tie, stared at the bride, his glance a transparent testament to his love.

The third smiling person in the photograph was the raven-haired woman in the portrait that hung in my mother's kitchen.

I left for New York the next day.

Trains have an uncanny, mesmerizing rhythm, a way of lulling and loosening until your locked-up thoughts—painful, threatening—merge with the passing landscape and float free. As the muddy expanse of the Hudson River endlessly filled my window, so did the image of my mother as she lay dying. . . .

Tiny little thing propped up on pillows, one long-fingered hand resting on the steel arm of the twin-size hospital bed I'd had installed in her bedroom. I sat up on her *real* bed—the queen I'd been occupying for the past month—and debated whether to alert my siblings, each in some far-flung corner of the world. "Not yet," my mother had been saying for the past three weeks.

Instead of the phone, I reached for *Old Rose and Silver*, a turn-of-the-century "woman's" novel by a now defunct press: color illustrations, musical bars, silver-leafed white roses embossed on faded leather. We were halfway through it, my mother and I— for the third time, believe it or not.

I picked up where I had left off, my steady narrator's voice one step above monotone—more soothing, I hoped. Ten minutes into it, my mother opened her eyes and looked at me.

"No more," she said.

I closed the book and went rummaging through the pile on our joint night table: *When Knighthood Was in Flower* (Marion Davies Edition, Illustrated with Scenes from the Photoplay); Bret Harte's *The Reluctant Madonna;* Sabatini's *The Romantic Prince*. No more.

"Mom . . ." Her eyes—so brown; not quite seeing me. She had long ago perfected the melancholy inward look, my mother.

"This house is too big for you, Gloria. You should sell it." Seeing me now.

Seeing what? The lines starting to form in the corners of things . . . my mouth, my eyes? The lackluster complexion? The indifferent cut of my too-thick brown hair?

I shrugged. "And go where?"

Faint smile on those incredibly young rosebud lips; I had inherited my father's slash of a mouth. "You know where."

"Peter likes this house." It came out defensive, I'm sorry to say.

"This house, this town," she said, smile fading. "Peter is a decent man."

Translation: Decent but dull. Peter is not the love of your life, Gloria, and if I weren't on my deathbed, I'd make you admit it. Out loud!

Feisty, my mother used to be, and remarkably persuasive. The truth is, I've lost more arguments with her than I've won.

"Thirty-six is still young," she said with a feeble wave.

"You got married when you were twenty-four."

"Too young," she said in a whisper that chilled me.

I went over and wrapped her hand in mine. "You were happy with Dad. I know you were."

"Fifty-four years. . . . I miss him. Your father was—" She

cracked a smile. "A decent man. He always said I'd outlive him. By a year, he said, remember? He was a year off."

No doubt because my mother had insisted she would make it to eighty. She had a week to go. "I'm calling the others," I told her, insistent now. "Today, Mom. You *do* want to . . . see them?"

She didn't seem to hear. "Water, please."

I got it for her. Removed the straw when she frowned at it. She took two birdlike sips, then loosened her grip on the glass.

"Fanny was only seventy when she died."

Fanny was the grandmother I'd been born too late to meet. My mother always referred to her by name, don't ask me why. Like a heroine who'd stepped right off the page of one of my mother's beloved turn-of-the-century romance novels.

"She didn't outlive Papa by more than a month. Fanny was a lost soul without him. You're the only one of my children who looks like her," my mother said with such hard scrutiny that I lowered my eyes, rubbing the knuckles of my right hand.

"Fanny did that all the time," my mother said in the soft tone of reminiscence she invariably slipped into whenever my grandmother's name came up. "There was a shyness, a reticence. You could see it in her smile. . . . Yours, too."

"Mom—" I started to protest.

"Look for yourself," she said, handing me her bedside "porcelain finish" black-and-white photograph of my grandmother, gesturing at the mirror over her gleaming mahogany bureau. "Take a good look, Gloria. And smile."

She was right, of course. Don't think I was unhappy with the comparison. "Did I really look like her?" I pressed.

"You have the same hair. The identical shade of brown."

Unruly and unmanageable . . .

"And tall. You have Fanny's wonderful height."

I suppose five-foot-six is "tall" when you've lived your life as an entrancingly petite five-two . . .

"Eyes more like hers than mine," my mother said. Her own eyes were shining. "Fanny's were so full of secrets . . ."

"You should talk!" I shot back and got a raised eyebrow.

She touched my cheek. "I always thought of you as her gift to me."

"Why on earth would you think—"

"Because of when you were conceived. The day Fanny died." My mother was nodding faintly with the memory. I couldn't speak.

"She didn't want me to marry your father, you know. Not that she ever said as much—she liked John. But I knew just the same. I knew why."

"Why?" I whispered. You have to remember, I loved my father. "Why, Mom? For the same reason you don't want me to marry Peter?"

A sigh—so wistful it wrenched my heart. "I don't want you to settle." *As I did* . . . Is that what her eyes were telling me? She gestured at the night table, at the shelves in the far corner of the room. "Keep my books for me. But don't just read about it, Gloria," she said. "Promise me."

It. "What?" I pressed gently. "You want me to go off in search of the Big Romance?"

Her eyes turned remarkably clear. "Fanny and Papa . . . They found each other in New York, but they never would tell anyone how they actually met—their secret, Papa used to say. But, oh, how Fanny's eyes would sparkle even as she blushed!"

She tried to pull herself up. I helped her, rearranging the pillows, pink satin against the silver waves of her hair.

When she gripped my arm—so hard through the thick sleeve of my cotton sweater that I winced—I have to tell you I thought I was losing her then and there.

"Find out for me, Gloria," she urged. "You're a reporter. Promise me you'll take the train to New York and find out."

I made a harsh sound. For the past five years, I'd been a sort of chronicler for the Mechanicville *Gazette,* if you want to know. "I write about births, deaths, and weddings," I reminded my mother, "so don't go making me out to be some investigative—"

"Fanny's secret was the birth of something," my mother said in that stubborn tone she could slip into. "I want your promise."

"But I can't leave you now!"

"Right after."

I started to cry.

Her delicate features softened a little. "I'm waiting, Gloria. I *knew* I was waiting for something . . ."

I promised.

"Call the others," she said in the next breath.

My sister, Anna, arrived from Mexico the next day, my brothers—John, Jr., from Denver, Mark from London—the day after.

My mother died on the morning of her eightieth birthday.

My first stop via the New York subway—"Little Italy"—shouldn't surprise you; my grandfather's name, after all, was Marsicano. As I stared up at a huge white edifice with Moorish stained-glass windows and, over the door, a couple of angels reaching for the chalice of His Most Precious Blood—the name of the church—I knew, suddenly, that I was wasting my time. No way they'd have a record of my grandparents' wedding; Fanny Frank had been Jewish.

A judge, then. I stepped into a curio shop to ask directions. Glad I'd had the foresight to wear running shoes, I hiked the rest of the way downtown, stomach churning at horns and shouts and undecipherable chatter, brushing elbows when I couldn't avoid them and, programmed for familiar faces, trying not to stare into the eyes of strangers. To think my mother had grown up on these giddy, garrulous streets!

The spread of buildings along Foley Square—some massive, some skyscraper-tall, all of them courthouses, I was told—left me speechless. I approached the Supreme Court, a simple neo-Classical structure as befits the lowest court on New York's judicial ladder, with trepidation, knowing things could go either way: the real beginning of my search, or the end of it.

Before you go pronouncing me an accomplished sleuth as, twenty minutes later, some clerk in Records handed over a copy of the marriage license of Joseph Marsicano and Fanny Frank, bear in mind that I was the recipient of an extraordinary stroke of luck. On the back of the photograph in my mother's hope chest, someone (my grandfather?) had written in lyrical black-inked script: "Oh happiness! June the tenth, in the Year of Our Lord, 1901."

The date unlocked yet another door: the presiding judge on that particular day and year of our lord. Marriage ceremonies performed in chambers are usually a cut-and-dried affair, the clerk informed me, but Judge Angelo Costantino, it turned out, characteristically had indulged in a touch of whimsy. He had marked the occasion of *his* ceremonies with a group photograph, his own smiling presence an unofficial stamp of approval, with the name and address of the beaming participants meticulously recorded on the back. With shaking hands, I went looking for my grandparents. I found them standing center stage, the judge flanking the bride, the sole witness half turned to the groom.

She was even more enigmatic in semiprofile, the lady in the portrait. Her name was Reba (short for Rebecca?) Luskin, and her address was as steeped in Manhattan's ethnic history as Ellis Island. "Hester Street," I said out loud with a kind of wonder.

Not sure of my next step, I opted for the familiar. A cab driver took me to the main branch of the public library—everyone here seems to know where it is. When I got to Fifth Avenue and Forty-second Street, I ran up a small mountain of stone steps, stopping only once to cast an admiring glance at the leonine keepers of the gate.

Thanks to my sometime job with the Mechanicville *Gazette,* I don't find microfilm machines daunting—sort of like feeding spools of thirty-five-millimeter film into a projector and then cranking by hand until you find what you're looking for and freeze it on-screen. I went hunting with nothing to go on but a gut feeling that Reba Luskin was too lush a lady for those innocent times, the kind who makes waves, not ripples. I scrolled to "June tenth, 1901" and, after debating a few minutes, went forward chronologically.

Almost fifteen years passed before my eyes when hunger pains brought me to a halt. This morning's "brunch" had consisted of black coffee and Amtrak's version of powdered-sugar doughnuts.

The dinner hour loomed. I stared out the window, watching lights go on, and knew I'd have to find a place, spend the night, play this thing out in the morning. I wanted to turn the machine off but couldn't make myself do it—and not because I'm dogged. I confess it was more a touch of the obsessive-compulsive; never ever quit in the middle of something, my mother used to counsel. I would see "1916" through to the end.

I got as far as June—June the tenth, to be exact. It's obvious to me now that of the five senses, the visual in me takes the far lead. I went past the caption altogether, my habit being to speed-read past whole sections of "society" comings and goings that postured as news, so it took the now-familiar smile, the saucy tilt of the head, to alert my wandering eye. It was a full figure of a still beautiful Reba Luskin posing in front of a brownstone. She stood over some kind of statue, a bottle of what was obviously champagne in one upraised hand. The caption over the photograph read: REBA CHRISTENS "LUSKIN HOUSE." Just "Reba?" The brief description that followed was of a "quaint boarding house for unsettled unmarried women who come to Manhattan to seek their fortune." The address given was identical with the one listed in Judge Costantino's files.

Abandoning the microfilm machine, I went in search of a Manhattan telephone book.

I had dinner two blocks away in a brightly lit cavernous underground restaurant in Grand Central Station known as the Oyster Bar, by turns awed and appalled with the vitality of my surroundings, a hackneyed phrase turning round and round in my brain: the city that never sleeps.

I, myself, slept like a baby in a room (overlooking *the* Park Avenue) at the Martha Washington, a small unpretentious hotel, secure in the knowledge that, down-at-the-heels or not, the place catered exclusively to women. A preview, I remember thinking as I drifted off, of the quaint boarding house for unsettled, unmarried women I would be seeing first thing in the morning.

There was nothing down-at-the-heels about Luskin House. My eyes, on that brisk mid-May morning, couldn't get past the ground-floor entrance. White marble portal gleaming in the sun.

Massive oak door. Two pairs of wood-trimmed etched-glass windows on either side with an intricate tapestry-like design. Marble planters directly underneath, full of juniper bushes and late-blooming roses. A statue . . .

The news clip hadn't done justice to it. Six feet of white marble stood balanced on the rectangular planter to the left of the entrance: young woman, head angled in the direction of the brownstone, flowing tresses decorated with grapes, more grapes in her arms, grapes pressed against a firm bosom, one shapely bare leg parting the diaphanous folds of her gown. Right then something tugged at me, but the truth is, I was much too impatient to let it take form. I rang the bell, thinking that the four sturdy fire escapes that rose all the way up to the fifth story didn't so much mar the facade as cast me back to the charm of a different era.

Inside, the air was thick with it: Old World charm. It was in the dark-paneled reception room—hand-carved craftsmanship from ceiling to floor. It was in a parlor resplendent with silks and brocades, so rich with color and brimming with the comfort of plump sofas that the room might have been transplanted from my mother's cherished *Old Rose and Silver.* The chandelier was awesome—a great gathering of crystal teardrops. I followed the scent of wood smoke to a rose-marble fireplace that dominated the parlor. Polished silver on the mantle, while above it—

Reba's portrait. The same oil that hung in the kitchen at home. I was stunned, too embarrassed to let the woman from reception—a matronly sort with alert gray eyes that matched her close-cropped hair—see through my little subterfuge about renting an available room. Wordlessly, I followed her up one staircase. Up another. I made appropriate responses, seeing little, hearing less. By the time we had returned to the main floor, the woman's replacement had arrived.

"A minute of your time?" I pleaded, leading her back to the parlor before she could elude me. "The lady in this painting—"

"The founder of Luskin House," the woman said with a smile that transformed her plain features, adding a touch of mischief.

Mischief? "Reba Luskin," I said slowly with a knowing look.

"Why, yes! You know about her, then?"

"Not as much as I'd like to," I admitted. "Who was she?"

"Madame of one of the more successful of New York's houses of ill repute, as they used to be called. She retired at age forty-five—much to the chagrin of her tony clientele."

Why wasn't I surprised? "The statue outside . . ." I murmured.

"A dead giveaway, isn't she? The goddess who catered to lusty appetites. Apparently, Reba couldn't bear to part with her even after she'd transformed this place into a boarding house—five years after her retirement, it was. Nineteen sixteen."

"June tenth," I said, frowning at a connection I had missed: Fanny and Joseph's fifteenth wedding anniversary. "So all the years since," I reflected, an image of my youthful grandmother springing, unbidden, to my mind, as she crossed the Atlantic to her new home in America—in New York!—"Luskin House has been a sort of haven for the . . . unattached woman."

"This city can be a frightening experience, at first. Somehow, *she* understood that." The woman's expression, as she glanced at the portrait, was fond. "It's why she devoted her considerable fortune, in trust, to the care and maintenance of Luskin House."

I'd read that much in the public library. I thanked the woman and took a last look around, the sense of a dead end weighting my shoulders. I made a silent apology to my mother.

I got as far as the front door.

"Won't you take this? In case you change your mind."

Ah yes, I thought, the would-be renter. Outside, I paused before Reba's goddess, literally sitting, for a moment, at her feet. Leafing through the colorful brochure I'd been given, I planned my return to the normal and the humdrum: a subway to Penn Station, the noon train back to Mechanicville—

Was she smiling just a little, the goddess, as, eyes wide at a dawning possibility, I looked up at that proud profile?

Stuffing the brochure in my pocket, I hailed a cab like any veteran New Yorker and, for the second time in two days, headed for the New York Public Library. This time, I would start with "1901" and go backward.

* * *

On the train ride home, I mentally laid out all the pieces, still giddy from the glass of wine I'd consumed by way of celebration while waiting for the four-fifteen. Don't misunderstand, I still hadn't tumbled to Fanny's secret. But I was heart-poundingly close.

Fact: Fanny Frank, twenty-one years of age, leaves her native Austria, setting sail for the New World. The year: 1901.

Fact: Fanny arrives in New York City. The month: June. The first week of? It *had* to be.

Fact: Reba Luskin, thirty-five years of age, returns to New York from a European vacation. The date: June the fifth, 1901.

Fact: Reba's Hester Street "house of ill repute" falls victim (for the first and only time, according to the brochure) to a police raid, during which a young woman (from "abroad" and "speaking not a word of English!" according to the microfilm) is mistakenly caught in the net and taken to the station—name withheld to protect the innocent. The date is June the sixth.

Fact: Reba Luskin is maid—madame?—of honor at a civil ceremony in the chambers of Judge Angelo Costantino at which one Fanny Frank and one Joseph Marsicano are joined in holy wedlock. The date is June the tenth.

Speculation: On board ship, had the glamorous, worldly Reba befriended the innocent from abroad? Conversed with her in Yiddish? Issued an invitation to tea?

. . . At the "house" on Hester Street?

Questions, then. What happened between the fifth and the sixth? Where did my future grandfather fit in? What was Fanny doing in New York, anyway, when her only American relatives—

Lived in Providence, Rhode Island. It came back to me in a couple of lightning flashes—bits of conversation with my mother while we did the dishes or caught up on laundry or were elbow deep in a batch of peanut butter cookies. The young Fanny, not liberated from a domineering mother so much as released into the care of a kindly but equally domineering older brother—by now firmly established in some forbidding faraway place. The brother, unable to leave his business, arranging for someone to help shepherd his youthful charge through immigration, then on to the family homestead in Providence. Fanny, disappearing before the day is out. No word for days until the unthinkable— Fanny, married to stranger. To a goy!

Fanny, ostracized. Orthodox style, my mother had explained during one of our nostalgia fests. I thought about what that meant as the train rolled on. As I picked up my car and made the twenty-mile drive to my home. With my young girl's affinity for melodrama, I had always regarded the somewhat vague tale of my grandmother's "punishment" as the stuff of high drama. The relatives in Providence had held a funeral for the errant Fanny! They had suffered no form of communication. They had not relented for ten long years.

Oh, Fanny, I thought now as I let myself in, to have cut yourself off like that. And for a man you barely knew . . .

I had no appetite, too fearful, if you want to know, that I was teetering on the edge of failure. It was no longer a matter of keeping a deathbed promise. I harbored the painful illusion that my mother's melancholy lay like a light blanket on her soul, that it was up to me to shake it off, to set her free. I brewed a favorite tea—hers and mine—and took it to the hope chest, longing for a clue or an insight.

I dug deep. And found confirmation, of sorts. A snapshot. Two figures on the deck of a ship. A smiling, languorous Reba Luskin, lace at her throat, long hair whipping about her face. A sober-eyed Fanny Frank, posture perfect in long, dark skirt and sleeves as full as bellows.

The visual is your long suit, Gloria. An apt reminder. I spread my meager collection on the kitchen table: one shipboard snapshot, the wedding picture I'd made a photocopy of in New York, the Luskin House brochure that featured a four-color reproduction of the "famous portrait." Portrait, singular. No mention anywhere that there were two. *Were* they identical? I stood before the one in the kitchen—a wedding present?—and painstakingly compared it section by section to the one in the brochure. Reba at her most seductively beautiful: same smile, same provocative tilt of the head, same windblown look to the hair. The crimson velvet gown, the slightly deeper shade of the cushions she leaned back against, one bare arm relaxed on the gilded arm of her chair, the other resting on a marble end table, same, same, same, all of it the—

Not all of it! The rose marble end table—in Fanny's portrait, it wasn't bare! On its surface, no more than an inch from Reba's hand, lay a quill pen and, next to it . . . a letter.

Gingerly, I unhooked the painting and lowered it to the floor. My scrutiny shifted from portrait to packaging as my fingers explored every carved notch of wide oak frame. I turned the painting on its back: a clean stretch of canvas. The painting had been stapled to four wooden slats forming a rectangle—from the back, a sort of inner frame. Nothing protruded, nothing caught my eye.

This may sound silly, but what sent me dashing away in search of a thin metal nail file was an inner sound that went off in my chest like a gong—like the chillingly climactic note in a suspense film! I don't mind telling you my hand shook as—slowly, slowly—I slid the file all along the inner wooden frame until I felt something, a slight resistance? Working the file as if it were a precision instrument in the most delicate of operations, ear pressed to the canvas, I inched my way along until I heard . . . rustling. By the time a thin white wedge appeared from under the wood, my blouse was soaked through.

I cried before I even read the undated two-page letter—release of tension, I suppose. When I'd returned Reba's portrait to its place of honor, I sat cross-legged on the floor and devoured her very readable scrawl in a series of great gulps. Then, laughing and crying, I went for the wine and toasted my mother. "Listen to this," I told her afterward, "just listen . . ."

>   *My dear, sweet Fanny,*
>   *By the time you discover this letter, if you ever do, you'll probably understand English good enough to read it! Knowing your good heart, I feel sure you would forgive me your frightful experience down at the station house. After all, look where it led?*
>   *That last day on the ship when I said you should look*

me up if ever you got back to my part of the world, I
could feel how miserable you were. From mother to
brother—like going from one kind of prison to another, is
what you told me. All those questions about Providence,
Rhode Island. What could I say, Fanny dear, except it
was strictly small town compared to New York?

How you'd dreamed of New York! What a bold thing
you were, giving your big brother's man "the slip," as we
say in my part of town. When you told me, later, how all
you had in mind was a few hours to explore, I thought to
myself, now that wasn't so much bold as brave, seeing as
how our Fanny don't speak the native lingo, let alone
know her way about the biggest city in the world. Small
wonder she went and got herself lost!

I'm still busting with pride it was me you reached out
to—still thanking the good Lord I'd had the sense to stick
my telephone number in your skirt pocket. Remember
how wide-eyed scared you was to be staying the night in
the hotel room I got you? Strange men in the downstairs
parlor. Men traipsing down the hallways. All fine and
good in their place, men, but for a girl like you, Fan, I
knew the man had to be special.

That's when it hatched, my little matchmaking scheme.
Because I already knew him. Oh, not in the Biblical way,
Fanny dear, and that's the whole point. My girls had a
pet name for Joe Marsicano—"the perennial bach"—
because dashing as he was, Joe was way too old-fashioned
to fall for their charms. "No offense, ladies," he'd say,
"but I'm saving myself for the girl of my dreams."

Well, of course I couldn't tell you what I had in mind.
How, when I couldn't bring myself to admit how your
"nice Jewish friend, Mrs. Luskin," made her living? Not
that I'm ashamed, mind, but there are lines you don't
cross in this life and one is what I like to call sullying the
innocent. I couldn't even tell Joe. It had to be him finding
you for himself, not his madame friend making the intro,
don't you see?

How excited you were next morning when you got to Hester Street! How you adored my "entertaining" parlor, never dreaming what kind of entertainment we gave our gentlemen callers—not even after the cops barged in, acting tough and making arrests. Me and my girls had a hard time keeping a straight face. I mean, most of those fellows were steady customers!

What I'm trying to say is, I set the whole thing up so that later, down at the precinct, with you in your Gibson Girl outfit bawling your eyes out and jabbering away in Yiddish, the sergeant on duty would just naturally call for Joe Marsicano like they did whenever they needed somebody to translate, seeing as how Joe had grown up with one foot in little Italy, so to speak, and the other in Hester Street, and could swear like a trooper in both languages!

You know the rest. One look and the perennial bach was a goner. And don't think the sergeant on duty didn't know what he was doing when he "released" you into Joe Marsicano's custody. Life without probation, right, Charlie?

Well, now you know. Or maybe you don't. Either way, my conscience is clear. I figure since Joe finally told you about your friend, the madame, and you never did point a finger, you won't be real upset hearing about how she pulled off the matchmaking feat of the century!

Want to know something, Fan? Just getting it all down on paper like this, having it all come back like it was yesterday, makes me wonder if maybe I'm in the wrong business. Have to think about that.

> *Your eternal friend,*
> *Reba.*

Was the christening of Luskin House, fifteen years to the day after Reba's "matchmaking feat," a coincidence? I didn't think so. No strange men traipsing up and down those stairs because

New York could be a frightening experience, at first. Reba understood that. Thanks to Fanny, she understood it.

Had Fanny ever discovered the hidden letter from her "eternal friend?" Impossible to know. Some secrets you take with you to the grave.

. . . Shy, reticent Fanny, who, despite her gentle nature—her utter inexperience—had had the courage to reject the safe and easy way. Bucking tradition, she had reached boldly for the brass ring. Fanny's secret was the birth of something, my mother had insisted.

She was so right.

For Peter, of course, it was the death of something that never should have begun—he saw that, finally (or pretended to).

The house my mother and I had shared was much too big.

She was right about that, too. It was the reason I gave when, next morning, I put it up for sale and arranged to have my furniture put in storage.

A familiar voice took my call at Luskin House. "I've changed my mind," I told the gray-eyed woman who had handed me a magic carpet posing as a brochure.

The woman's good cheer turned to distress. No room available for nearly a month. Nothing until June the tenth.

Fanny's gift to me? Or my mother's?

I booked the room.

EDITOR'S AFTERNOTE

"The House on Hester Street" has special meaning for Erika Holzer, as it is loosely based on the life events of her own grandmother, whose name really was Fanny Frank. As in this short story, Fanny met her future husband, Joe, after getting caught up in a police raid on a mysterious friend's house of ill repute. "The raid in my story is a romantic setup," Holzer says, "whereas, in real life, it was a real raid. The part about Joe Marsicano being called in to translate and coming to Fanny's rescue is true." Despite family objections and religious conflicts, the couple married immediately.

"My own mother, Phyllis Marsicano Tate, really did have a romantic streak of her own and, like the mom in my story, an ineffable touch of melancholy about her as well," Holzer says.

A lawyer, whose most recent novel, *Eye for an Eye*, has been made into a movie starring Sally Field and directed by John Schlesinger, Holzer represented Ayn Rand in the sixties, helping to recover the lost film classic, *Noi Vivi*, a 1941 Italian film adapted from Rand's first novel. Admirers of Holzer's writing can look forward to her upcoming courtroom drama, *Guilty as Charged*.

Unprintable
Joyce Carol Oates

"How hideous!—how pitiful. Who *are* they?"

En route to the awards ceremony at the Ethical Arts Center, as the long sleekly black limousine made its way through congested city streets, she saw them. Not clearly, but in glimpses, her vision blurred by the limousine's dark-tinted glass. Strange human figures at the curbside, or wandering out into traffic—to beg? to coerce money from intimidated drivers? Faces loomed close to the car's rear windows that were pale as bread dough, or red-boiled like lobsters, with running sores and lesions and features that seemed malformed, or incomplete; avid, hungrily glistening eyes like rodents' eyes fixed upon her—an impossibility since, in fact, the limousine's windows were so darkly tinted no one could see inside. And even if they could, what had these pathetic strangers to do with *her*? Even if they were capable of recognizing her, they would have no idea who *Celeste Ward* was, nor could they have cared.

She brooded about them: these casualties of a great American city—unwanted creatures, unwanted probably since birth; unwanted as pregnancies in their hapless mothers' wombs. Innocent victims of the Darwinian horror of unthinking, rampaging reproduction—the infliction of male desire upon female acquiescence. What heartrending tragedy, unwanted babies born into the world, lacking the love and nurturing to make them fully human! This was in fact the Cause to which Celeste Ward had devoted her entire adult life—the complex moral issues of planned parenthood, the technology of contraception, abortion rights. The Cause for which she'd sacrificed her own personal, emotional life and for which, tonight, the night of her sixtieth birthday, she was to be publicly honored. Yet: seeing these strange misshapen creatures that rose up, loomed close, fell away from the car as the driver increased his speed, Celeste was stricken with a sense of foreboding. *Why did I accept? Why, another public honor? Is it mere vanity?* Celeste Ward, vilified at the start of her crusading career in the mid-fifties, had been, these past few years, so often publicly honored as to have become an American "name" even to those who knew nothing of her actual career and, had they known, would have disapproved; she was accumulating enough awards, citations, honorary doctorates, and hefty brass plaques to last her the remainder of her life. Tonight, in a program organized by the Women's Unity Force Foundation, which had funded a number of Celeste Ward's projects, including her most controversial, the promulgation of abortion techniques for the layman, Celeste was to be one of a number of featured feminist speakers and was to be, at the program's culmination, honored for her "selfless contribution to the Cause of promoting women's rights worldwide for nearly four decades." Celeste was flattered of course—yet, wasn't there a posthumous tone to this, suggesting perhaps that her activist years were over? That younger, more energetic women would be taking her place, revising her methods, even her ideas? Her first impulse had been to decline, in a show of modesty that had been in fact a nervous reaction. But the foundation organizers, and others, had protested. Telephone calls were made, letters sent to her. A special plea from Celeste's publisher, who was reissuing in paperback her much-attacked, much-acclaimed *The Trap of Motherhood: A Sociological Study.* And there was Celeste's biographer, an intense young woman who idolized Celeste, arguing that a woman of Celeste Ward's achievement owed it to those many women who admired her and whose lives she'd touched to appear in public on the occasion of her sixtieth birthday—"Only think, Celeste, if you hadn't been born! How different things would be for women in America today!" This was an exaggeration, but uttered with such affection, it was impossible for Celeste to say no.

And so, again, another time: yes. The triumph of vanity.

Tonight was a fated night. Celeste, never a superstitious woman, could not shake off a premonition of dread. Since waking that morning she'd been feeling a quickening of her blood, a pressure inside her skull, not pain but on the verge of pain, as if something wanted to burst loose. Birthday cards— from old friends, acquaintances, associates in the Cause, strangers—telephone calls, flowers, gifts, raining upon Celeste Ward as if this were, not merely her sixtieth birthday, but her last birthday. She, a solitary woman for whom sentiment was an embarrassment, especially when it pertained to her, exacerbating her aloneness, which had been a fact of her life now for many years. *Happy birthday, Celeste! happy birthday! happy birthday!*—it was a dirge. And how ironic, no one except Celeste knew, for, as she'd been told many times as a child, by her mother, neither her mother nor her father had wanted her to be born.

In that era, 1933, abortion wasn't a possibility, still less a legal right, for most women.

Of Celeste Ward's secrets, this was the most precious because it *was* the most ironic. But she had other secrets, too. Which no biographer would ever discover.

As the limousine turned onto the boulevard, Celeste saw up the block a group of about thirty demonstrators milling on the sidewalk and in the street, restrained by police cordons, and knew, with a stab of apprehension and excitement, where the Ethical Arts Center was. Her enemies! Enemies of the Cause! These men and women, Christian Pro-Lifers and fervent foes of abortion, were almost comfortingly familiar. They'd been picketing Celeste Ward's speeches, the Cause, and abortion centers for years; in the South, they could be dangerous, but in this northern city they acquiesced to the law, knowing that local sentiment was strongly against them. Unlike the diseased, deformed street people, who filled Celeste with horror and repugnance, the Pro-Lifers were almost like kin; ideological enemies, reliable in their opposition, they had their role as she had hers. She'd long since memorized their accusatory picket signs, their self-righteous prayerful chants—"PRO CHOICE IS A LIE! NOBODY'S BABY CHOOSES TO DIE!" *They* held no surprises for her.

And where they demonstrated, there was often news coverage—which was helpful to the Cause. Celeste saw television camera crews, reporters in front of the center, awaiting her arrival. Her! Already, Celeste was feeling better about the evening.

The stately limousine drew up in front of the building, the uniformed driver opened the door for his distinguished passenger—"Here we are, ma'am! Careful getting out." Celeste glanced up at him—then stared. (She would have no time to contemplate the surprise of his blackish-maroon skin, pocked cheeks, blood-veined and subtly derisive eyes, for events moved too swiftly; no time to consider how the man's face resembled certain of the faces she'd glimpsed on the street. Unless she was imagining it?) The program organizers greeted Celeste warmly as several cameras flashed. There were many well-wishers, most of them women, and very handsomely dressed women, who had bought tickets for the program; there was a flattering contingent of a half-dozen policemen; the Pro-Life demonstrators, waving their signs and shouting in her direction, kept their prescribed distance. With the organizers were several reporters and television interviewers with questions for Celeste Ward—such familiar questions by now, Celeste could have answered them in her sleep. But she rejoiced in these questions, and in these occasions, because they *were* familiar; even when, like the present time, she wasn't feeling entirely herself, she could answer such questions clearly and forcefully, confident she was in the right. Through her adult life Celeste Ward, like other successful feminist leaders, had appreciated the great value of educating through the media, even when the media meant to deride; the great value of manipulating public opinion—"It isn't enough to *be* right," Celeste would insist, "you must convince others that you are." Only at the start of her career in the tumultuous, disorganized sixties, when civil rights activism, anti-Vietnam War activism, and women's rights activism had frequently clashed, had Celeste betrayed her emotions in public. (And, too many times, in private!) Since then, she'd systematically remade herself as a model of feminist persuasion linked with intelligence, courtesy, and tact. As the last-born in a working-class family of seven brothers and sisters, Celeste had had to scramble for her place in the world—even her place at meals—but, considering her public manner, you would have supposed her of a genteel, well-educated background. Not even her most savage detractors could accuse Celeste Ward of being "shrill" and "unfeminine"—never did she raise her voice, never did she resort to quarreling; never did she allow any camera to catch her attractive features in any sort of grimace. What Celeste Ward might be secretly thinking, what raw emotions coursed through her veins, no one, not even her biographer, would ever know.

Asked, as Celeste was now, by a young woman interviewer for a local television news program, how she felt about being called a "murderess"—as the Pro-Lifers were chanting—Celeste appeared to think carefully, then said, "I've never taken accusations by ideological opponents as anything but ideological—that is, impersonal. I live with the hope that opponents of the Cause will see that the issue is not 'abortion'—for there will always be abortion—but 'abortion rights.'" This was a reply Celeste had given numerous times, yet she felt the truth and the rightness of the sentiment as if she'd uttered it spontaneously.

She knew she looked, and sounded, convincing. That was all that mattered.

Then, this: as the interviewer asked another, final question, Celeste happened to notice a TV monitor on one of the mobile units and saw, to her astonishment, that there was, on the small screen, in addition to the young woman and herself, a mysterious third party—an upright creature, fleshy, of the hue of raw meat, with a flat, vaguely human face, shallow indentations for eyes and nose, a slack mouth. *What could it be? What horror!* Celeste blinked, and stared, and turned back to the interviewer who was smiling respectfully at her, awaiting a reply, but all Celeste could do was stammer something not very coherent, excuse herself abruptly, and turn away. She did not dare look at the TV monitor again. *Because of course no third party could be on the screen.*

Other interviewers would have swooped upon her, but the program organizers, officers of the Women's Unity Force Foundation, politely detached her from them and marched her up the stone steps—such dauntingly steep stone steps!—into the lobby of the Ethical Arts Center. She was badly out of breath by this time, her heart pounding. There was a good deal of excited talk aimed at Celeste, only a fraction of which she could absorb. She gathered that the center's eleven hundred seats had been sold out and the program was to be taped for rebroadcasting over PBS and there were a number of distinguished persons in the audience, including wealthy donors. Someone thrust a bouquet of red roses at her—"Happy birthday, Miss Ward! And many more!" Her hand was vigorously, repeatedly shaken; unfamiliar faces loomed close to hers, their features distorted as if by magnification. Such a crowd! Why didn't the foundation officers see her plight, and protect her! It was all Celeste could do to maintain her composure—as if pulses were not beating, thrumming, in her brain—managing to smile, to exchange greetings—"Yes, thank you, you're very kind, it *is* a happy birthday. The happiest in memory." Many admirers clamored for Celeste's autograph in copies of *The Trap of Motherhood,* which was being sold in the lobby. A fierce-eyed woman with graying-brown hair to her shoulders declared, "This is the book that saved my life, sprang *me* from the trap." She would have squeezed Celeste in a bear hug had not one of the foundation officers intervened.

Celeste was escorted through the crowd, led into a private lounge backstage. Thank God! The roses were taken from her to be put into a vase. She sat relieved on a sofa, passing her hand over her eyes. Someone offered her a glass of Perrier water, which she gratefully accepted. Someone asked if she minded being photographed. (She murmured yes, in fact she did, but in so low

and apologetic a voice, she was misunderstood: cameras flashed.)
Her hand shook, nearly spilling her drink. There was something
disturbing—something terrifying—she needed to contemplate;
something to do with the TV monitor?—but, in the confusion of
the moment, she couldn't remember what it was.

A mistake. Birthday. Should not have accepted. Where?

Another time, the previous week, she'd canceled an appointment to see her doctor. The thrumming in the brain, the sparks of
light in the corners of her eyes—these symptoms, if they were
symptoms, had diminished. *Of course, I'm fine. My enemies
would despair to know how fine.*

More admirers, more almost-familiar faces loomed near.
Members of the foundation, their friends and family members;
other women who were to speak this evening, whom Celeste
knew very well—except, damn it, laughingly she forgot their
names! She'd been hoping for a few minutes to relax and glance
through her speech before the program began at eight o'clock—
it was seven-forty now—but evidently that wasn't to be. She
heard herself speaking gaily, bubbling with her old famous
energy, "Yes, thank you, of course I remember you!—yes it *is* a
happy birthday. The happiest in memory—" Though, at the
moment, Celeste could barely remember any previous birthday.
Is everything being erased? Is that the plan? In the midst of a
conversation with a woman who claimed to have been a student
of Celeste's twenty-five years ago (at Barnard? Vassar?
Radcliffe?—it wasn't clear), Celeste happened to glance down at
her right wrist, which was smarting, and saw to her astonishment
what appeared to be a red bead bracelet—no, it was a thin
scratch, oozing blood. What had happened? Had one of her well-
wishers accidentally scratched her? More startled than alarmed,
Celeste examined both wrists, both hands—there were no more
scratches. She dabbed away the blood with a tissue, quickly, so
that no one could see. Of course: it must have been the rose
thorns.

"Miss Ward? Celeste? You're looking a little pale. Is
something—?"

Celeste was about to slip away to a restroom, to hide for a few precious minutes, but here was her biographer looming above her. A long-limbed coltish girl of about thirty-five with a startled expression, large, intense, glassy-bright eyes, a nervous habit of smiling too often, especially in Celeste's presence, and baring her considerable gums. Celeste had not noticed her in the crowded lounge, but she did recall, with a sinking heart, having been informed that the biographer would be here this evening, and would in fact be introducing Celeste. "No, not at all, I'm perfectly fine," Celeste said quickly. There was no avoiding it, the biographer sat down beside her on the sofa, spreading her unwieldy gear—an immense gold-lamé shoulder bag, a tape recorder, an oversized notebook into which, at inspired moments, she lunged with a ballpoint pen.

"What an evening! What an occasion! Happy birthday!—I have a little something for you later. I'll give it to you at the reception," the biographer said breathlessly, yet with an air of apology, as if this were a matter of great significance. "You *are* well, Miss Ward? I mean—Celeste. You do remember who I am?"

Celeste had insisted that the biographer call her by her first name. Yet, now, to her embarrassment, she could not remember the biographer's name—though she smiled warmly, and said, "Yes, of course!" With awkward formality they shook hands; Celeste shivered at the touch of the young woman's cool, bone-thin fingers. And that damp, gum-bared, toothy rapacious smile. And those eyes—enormous, dark, avid with curiosity. There was a certain species of female admirer—earnest students, fervent disciples—who sorely tried Celeste's patience, though Celeste was the most patient of women. Just her bad luck, her "authorized" biographer was one of them.

"Do you mind?—I don't want to miss a syllable," the biographer said, switching on the tape recorder. "I have just a few quick questions that weren't quite answered, from last time—"

"If you insist," Celeste said, resigned.

It had not been Celeste Ward's wish that there be a biography of her, authorized or otherwise. Her heart sank at the prospect. Yet somehow, like this evening's celebration of her birthday, it had happened. Out of nowhere the eager young biographer had appeared, with ample evidence of her sincerity—published articles on feminist history since eighteenth-century England and France; lavishly admiring reviews of Celeste Ward's work. The Cause had given its blessings to the project; a reputable New York publisher had issued a respectful advance; wheels were busily in motion that could not be stopped. Each of the several strained interviews biographer and reluctant subject had had thus far confirmed Celeste's instinct that the biography was a mistake. Her head had rung with pain, her eyes streamed tears, her very soul cried a strangulated *No! no!*—yet, somehow, the project was to be. *Like a pregnancy, a giant fetus. Taking root. Taking nourishment from any source. Unstoppable.* It was Celeste's belief that the biographer, for all her professed adulation of Celeste Ward, secretly hoped she wouldn't live too much longer. Or, at any rate, wouldn't continue an active career in the Cause. The biographer had already accumulated many cartons of materials, including transcribed interviews with people who'd known Celeste Ward from her Minneapolis girlhood onward, and this made Celeste uneasy. Her public life was, as she'd often said, an open book; her private life, of which she never spoke, was something else entirely. *What shame, if my secrets are exposed! I can't bear it.* At the same time, Celeste resigned herself to the fact that, for better or worse, Celeste Ward had had an historical role in twentieth-century American feminism, and that couldn't be denied. Beyond the merely personal was the impersonal, the political. *But no: I can't bear it!*

Like a dog sniffing out a buried bone, the biographer was asking questions Celeste had managed to elude last time. Childhood memories? relations with her parents, long since deceased? It was hardly the time for such an interrogation, in the midst of others' conversations, and only a few minutes before the program was scheduled to begin. What was wrong with the biographer? Did she lack common sense, ordinary tact? Her girlish-gawky manner suggested naiveté, like the odd way in which she wore her thick, dry, crackling red-brown hair, parted in the center of her head, brushed severely back and fastened with old-fashioned mother-of-pearl clips; yet Celeste sensed, from time to time, a calculating shrewdness beneath. Like that lover of Celeste's of many years ago who seemed to have wished to triumph over her resistance to him, her virginal fearfulness, and not to have wished to love her, at all. *This one wants my blood. Wants to suck me dry.*

"Miss Ward? Celeste? What is it?"

Shakily, swaying, Celeste had pushed herself to her feet. Why was she wearing shoes with so impractical a heel?—and why this silk-and-wool suit with the long narrow skirt, that made sitting and standing and quick escapes so difficult? Celeste excused herself, saying she wanted to use the women's room before the program began. Her biographer leapt up to assist her as if she were an elderly woman and Celeste all but wrenched herself away. "Please, thank you, I'm capable of walking by myself," she said sharply.

The biographer stood, teeth and gums bared in a pained grimace, watching Celeste walk away.

This birthday. A mistake? Though she was not, had never been through her life, what you would call a superstitious woman. Nor even, since her early blunders, a woman prone to surrender to weak, wayward emotions. In secret she might have thought that to be a *woman* was in fact to be weak and wayward and generally at the mercy of others—which is to say, *men*—whose primary lust was to propagate the species by seduction, coercion, or both. But though she was a *woman* she was by no means an average woman and in this she took considerable pride.

In this, my escape! My salvation!

Celeste did not think of herself as a fastidious woman, but in private, increasingly with age, she was becoming so. Involuntarily glancing into sinks in public restrooms—into toilet bowls—steeling herself for the sight of another's filth. Checking out grime on floors, dust in corners. And then her own frowning scrutiny of her appearance in mirrors—not her appearance, which was superficial, but the *self* her appearance suggested. And now that she was so advanced in age, the vanity she'd never guessed at in herself, when younger and reasonably attractive, was emerging.

Others, her admirers at least, saw a carefully groomed, elegant woman of indeterminate age, with silver-streaked fair hair, a high, virtually unlined forehead, eyes that radiated calm, intelligence, discretion. There was an unmistakable fleshiness to the mouth and the underside of the chin, the sign of incipient collapse—yet, still, Celeste *was* attractive, and made it a point never to appear in public without being perfectly groomed. *I've invented my life, why not my public image?*—she leaned close to the mirror, staring at her eyes, which had a sort of bluish shadow beneath. The thin, dry skin of her cheeks, which had borne the brunt of so many years of smiling, was finely creased as a leather glove crumpled in the hand. *What a good, "selfless" woman you are! And nobody to know better!*

Celeste heard a scrambling sound, a clicking as of—what?— tiny claws? teeth? She saw a blurred movement in the mirror, beneath one of the toilet stalls, but when she turned, astonished, there was nothing visible. She went to the stall and pushed the door open and screamed—there was something in the toilet bowl, a hunk of raw, bloody flesh, writhing and squirming. What was it! What horror! Aghast, yet even in her shock reacting practicably, Celeste flushed the toilet, and flushed, and flushed it.

When the program organizers came to seek her out, they found her there, in the stall, her face ashy-pale and her eyes glassily bright, flushing the toilet.

An evening of celebration and applause—"TOWARD THE YEAR 2000." A standing ovation greeted Celeste Ward's appearance on stage and continued for several embarrassing moments before she took her seat, flanked by the executive director of the foundation, a vigorous iron-jawed woman with whom, years ago, Celeste had had a feud, over issues long since forgotten, and a younger woman, a recently elected congresswoman actively associated with the Cause. The stage was blindingly lit; there were several immense floral displays, as at a funeral; Celeste Ward displayed unflagging, alert interest as one by one, in a program that seemed to go on interminably, speakers were introduced, gave their prepared speeches, were warmly applauded. From time to time Celeste heard her name and smiled to acknowledge a flurry of quick applause. How safe she was, here among friends! *That thing in the toilet, it had not been hers. Nor had it been alive. Where was the proof?* Her thoughts drifted like froth on the tide. The blinding lights were a kind of comfort. She was thinking of her first lover, so long ago. His name forgotten. And that love—wiped clean, scoured and scrubbed and gone. Yet she could see the boy's face—a boy, not yet a man—though urgent, even anguished in his masculinity—sexual desire rising in his eyes like liquid changing color. *Yes, no, I hate you, I can't help myself I love you—I will die if you leave me.* But of course she had not died, she'd survived. And so knew to counsel other distraught young women, others girls wanting absurdly to die in the bloom of youth. *You don't, you don't die, you survive. Something else dies, in your place.*

It had been Celeste Ward's life, or—that other's. She'd been the one to make the choice.

After that first, terrible time. So young. After that, the healing amnesia. With each subsequent lover, coolly chosen, to prove, yes, she *was* a woman, she possessed that power. And the "accidents" seemed somehow part of it—three or four times, or was it, impossibly, five?—as if to prove, yes, she could. Each pregnancy terminated out of conscience and necessity *I have my own life, I own my own life, no one can trap me* and the proof flushed cleanly away, gone. The doctors' names—if indeed the men were doctors, in those days—unknown. Payment in cash: a business deal. The wisest course, seeing she had no instinct for motherhood, no wish to be encumbered; in any case, no father for the baby, nor was likely to acquire one. The most practical course, considering her career. The most moral course. *And did I look back?—I did not look back. I do not recommend looking back. What is gone, is gone.*

Except: her secrets would remain secrets.

Except: she *was* safe, among friends. Listen to the applause!

Her biographer was introducing her at last, hunched over the podium like a beaky bird of prey, big teeth and pale gums exposed in twitchy smiles, heaping her with praise—Celeste

Ward rose to a thunderous ovation, felt a moment's touch of panic as she blinked into the void beyond the glare, then smiled, stumbled on her way to the podium but took her place as her biographer stepped aside with a rapturous look, and removed her speech from her bag, and fumbled to put on her reading glasses, and began.

Celeste Ward's much-awaited speech—"Toward the Year 2000." The words were her own yet unfamiliar. The syllables sounded in her ears harsh, sibilant; patently insincere; there was a crackling, derisive undertone—the microphone? someone in the audience? She could not catch her breath—she, Celeste Ward, who had given hundreds of speeches! She stopped, began again. Mouthing prepared words in celebration of the Cause to which (since it was so frequently reiterated, it must be true) she'd given her life. *But I had no other choice, I had no other life.* The audience was strangely silent. Her hands shook holding the speech, her unflattering half-moon glasses slid down her nose. She was perspiring, yet shivering. Through rents in the glare she could see her audience—rows upon rows of them, stretching to a shadowy horizon—and in the balcony—but there were two balconies!—gazing at her with flattering intensity. Yet here and there amid the adulatory crowd of well-dressed women and the occasional man were misshapen, hideous figures, hardly more than upright clots of flesh, balloonlike hairless heads with eyes set deep and glittering in their sockets, spindly shoulders and torsos, bloated bellies—Celeste Ward saw, and looked quickly away. She was terrified of losing her place in her speech which was like no other speech she'd given in her career because it had been cynically spliced together out of previous speeches of hers by a malicious stranger, an enemy who knew her work intimately, thus could sabotage it with devastating skill: sudden jumps in logic, incoherent transitions between paragraphs, repetitive phrases, a number of the words—*eyrrism, troese, dysphisis*—unknown, unpronounceable to her. This, the final speech of Celeste Ward's career—which cruel fact she was somehow allowed to know, a chill breeze blowing toward her out of the future. The audience had begun to grow restless. There were whispers, coughing spells.

Celeste, reading rapidly now, stumbling and skipping parts of sentences, dared not glance up, in terror of what she would see even as she knew *they can't be here, there is no trace of them here, only we who deserve to live.* Then words ceased suddenly. Someone approached her hesitantly asking with hushed solicitude is something wrong? Miss Ward, is something wrong? and now there was absolute silence as if a single great breath had been indrawn as, gripping the podium to keep from falling, her face chalky-white and eyes wild and mouth trembling, Celeste Ward cried hoarsely, "—You don't, you don't die! You survive! Something else dies, in your place!"

She would have slumped to the floor had not someone caught her in thin steely arms.

Then, unexpectedly, this: passing the attack off lightly, backstage. Insisting she was fine, only a momentary dizzy spell caused by those damned lights, she had them occasionally in stressful situations, but there was nothing to worry about her doctor assured her and so she who was no hypochondriac did not worry and thank you but no she *would not* consent to be taken to a hospital, what were they, her friends, thinking of?—on the night of her birthday? Her biographer was holding a glass of water to her lips, tepid city water tasting of rust, but it seemed to help. Of course, Celeste Ward would not miss the reception in her honor and disappoint so many hundreds of well-wishers—"If you think I'd do such a thing," she protested, "you don't know me at all."

So by the genteel forcefulness of her personality managing to convince the organizers against their sounder judgment not to call an ambulance but to show her to a restroom so she could freshen up. This time, a small private lavatory adjacent to a dressing room. Celeste promised to be just a minute, then she'd join them for the reception, infinitely relieved to be alone at last—free of prying eyes, those looks of concern and pity, damned vultures!— and the luxury, thank God, of locking a door. And this lavatory was at least cleaner than the other.

You're safe! nobody knows! it's your secret! don't be weak, ridiculous! Celeste ran cold water into the sink and splashed her

fevered face and rubbed her eyes vigorously to restore their vision
daring only to glance at herself in the mirror. She was unwell, but
safe! safe! The thrumming pulses in her brain had begun to leak
into one another like spies whispering secrets, but she was still on
her feet and she was sixty years old and her enemies had not
triumphed. Glimpsing one of them then in the mirror, a blurred
undersea figure scuttling along the floor behind her, but they
could not overcome her, she was alive, she had triumphed, and
they had not. Was she not superior to them, because of this? That
she had life, and they had not? A vast teeming ocean of them,
waves threshing with their terrible hunger, but it had nothing to
do with her. One of them clutched at her ankle with stubbed,
mangled fingers, in horror she felt its toothless gums gnawing at
her flesh and kicked it away. "No! Leave me alone!" she cried.
Another was clawing at her skirt, wanting to tug her to the floor.
She screamed, slapped, kicked. But grunting it held tight as
another, larger and more robust, with a fully formed hairless head
and torso atop a stunted body, seized her right leg at the thigh
and began to bite—this one, with powerful teeth! Still another,
the size of a spider monkey, leapt to her shoulders, tore open her
jacket and blouse, and began to suck, bite, gnaw at her breasts.
Celeste fought wildly now, blinded, desperate, fighting for her
life. Even in the midst of her terror she was incredulous—for had
she not, unswervingly, been a good woman? a woman of principle
and a woman of character and a woman of exemplary courage
and a woman upon whom countless women had modeled
themselves? Why, to these hideous creatures, these ravenous
mouths, did none of that matter? She, Celeste Ward, was of no
more significance to them, who were now rising out of the room's
dark corners, scuttling rapidly across the floor, than a carcass
being devoured by sharks.

She fought, she screamed until they felled her, they had her, all
words ceased.

Fatally, the door was locked from the inside. The organizers
knocked on it, as minutes passed knocking more urgently,
anxiously, calling her name—to no avail. When at last, after
about fifteen minutes, a custodian was located to unscrew the

door from its hinges, the first person to enter the lavatory was Celeste Ward's biographer—aghast at what she saw. How the corpse lay on the floor with legs twisted beneath her in a posture of struggle, her jacket and blouse torn open as if, suffocating, she'd torn at her clothing, her eyes open and glassily unfocussed and the thin pale lips drawn back from the teeth in an expression of angry incredulity.

These impressions, Celeste Ward's biographer would note. Even in the midst of her shock and horror, like any professional.

⮑⮐

EDITOR'S AFTERNOTE

Currently collaborating with composer John Duffy on an opera version of her book *Black Water*, Joyce Carol Oates is the greatly admired author of more than twenty novels, plus numerous volumes of short stories, poetry, and essays. *Zombie*, her latest novel, appeared in October, 1995, and those who also enjoy this National Book Award winner's anthologies, can look forward to *American Gothic Tales*, due out fall 1996.

Depending on what philosophies the individual reader brings to it, guilt may or may not have a voice in "Unprintable"'s controversial theme. When asked, however, if she thought guilt was inherent to the relationship between a mother and her children, Oates replied, "I think it must be culturally determined, and very possibly class, ethnic, religion determined. Caucasian-American middle-class women are not the universe, after all!"

Mother Tongue

Amy Tan

I am not a scholar of English or literature. I cannot give you much more than personal opinions on the English language and its variations in this country or others.

I am a writer. And by that definition, I am someone who has always loved language. I am fascinated by language in daily life. I spend a great deal of my time thinking about the power of language—the way it can evoke an emotion, a visual image, a complex idea, or a simple truth. Language is the tool of my trade. And I use them all—all the Englishes I grew up with.

Recently, I was made keenly aware of the different Englishes I do use. I was giving a talk to a large group of people, the same talk I had already given to half a dozen other groups. The nature of the talk was about my writing, my life, and my book, *The Joy Luck Club*. The talk was going along well enough, until I remembered one major difference that made the whole talk sound wrong. My mother was in the room. And it was perhaps the first time she had heard me give a lengthy speech—using the kind of English I have never used with her. I was saying things like, "The intersection of memory upon imagination" and "There is an aspect of my fiction that relates to thus-and-thus"—a speech filled with carefully wrought grammatical phrases, burdened, it suddenly seemed to me, with nominalized forms, past perfect tenses, conditional phrases—all the forms of standard English that I had learned in school and through books, the forms of English I did not use at home with my mother.

Just last week, I was walking down the street with my mother, and I again found myself conscious of the English I was using, the English I do use with her. We were talking about the price of new and used furniture and I heard myself saying this: "Not waste money that way." My husband was with us as well, and he didn't notice any switch in my English. And then I realized why. It's because over the twenty years we've been together I've often used that same kind of English with him, and sometimes he even uses it with me. It has become our language of intimacy, a different sort of English that relates to family talk, the language I grew up with.

So you'll have some idea of what this family talk I heard sounds like, I'll quote what my mother said during a recent conversation which I videotaped and then transcribed. During this conversation, my mother was talking about a political gangster in Shanghai who had the same last name as her family's, Du, and how the gangster in his early years wanted to be adopted by her family, which was rich by comparison. Later, the gangster became more powerful, far richer than my mother's family, and one day showed up at my mother's wedding to pay his respects. Here's what she said in part:

"Du Yusong having business like fruit stand. Like off the street kind. He is Du like Du Zong—but not Tsung-ming Island people. The local people call putong, the river east side, he belong to that side local people. That man want to ask Du Zong father take him in like become own family. Du Zong father wasn't look down on him, but didn't take seriously, until that man big like become a mafia. Now important person, very hard to inviting him. Chinese way, came only to show respect, don't stay for dinner. Respect for making big celebration, he shows up. Mean gives lots of respect. Chinese custom. Chinese social life that way. If too important won't have to stay too long. He come to my wedding. I didn't see, I heard it. I gone to boy's side, they have YMCA dinner. Chinese age I was nineteen."

You should know that my mother's expressive command of English belies how much she actually understands. She reads the *Forbes* report, listens to "Wall Street Week," converses daily with her stockbroker, reads all of Shirley MacLaine's books with ease—all kinds of things I can't begin to understand. Yet some of my friends tell me they understand fifty percent of what my mother says. Some say they understand eighty to ninety percent. Some say they understand none of it, as if she were speaking pure Chinese. But to me, my mother's English is perfectly clear, perfectly natural. It's my mother tongue. Her language, as I hear it, is vivid, direct, full of observation and imagery. That was the language that helped shape the way I saw things, expressed things, made sense of the world.

Lately, I've been giving more thought to the kind of English my mother speaks. Like others, I have described it to people as "broken" or "fractured" English. But I wince when I say that. It has always bothered me that I can think of no way to describe it other than "broken," as if it were damaged and needed to be fixed, as if it lacked a certain wholeness and soundness. I've heard other terms used, "limited English," for example. But they seem just as bad, as if everything is limited, including people's perception of the limited English speaker.

I know this for a fact, because when I was growing up, my mother's "limited" English limited *my* perception of her. I was ashamed of her English. I believed that her English reflected the quality of what she had to say. That is, because she expressed them imperfectly her thoughts were imperfect. And I had plenty of empirical evidence to support me: the fact that people in department stores, at banks, and at restaurants did not take her seriously, did not give her good service, pretended not to understand her, or even acted as if they did not hear her.

My mother has long realized the limitations of her English as well. When I was fifteen, she used to have me call people on the phone to pretend I was she. In this guise, I was forced to ask for information or even to complain and yell at people who had been rude to her. One time it was a call to her stockbroker in New

York. She had cashed out her small portfolio and it just so happened we were going to go to New York the next week, our very first trip outside California. I had to get on the phone and say in an adolescent voice that was not very convincing, "This is Mrs. Tan."

And my mother was standing in the back whispering loudly, "Why he don't send me check, already two weeks late. So mad he lie to me, losing me money."

And then I said in perfect English, "Yes, I'm getting rather concerned. You had agreed to send the check two weeks ago, but it hasn't arrived."

Then she began to talk more loudly, "What he want, I come to New York tell him front of his boss, you cheating me?" And I was trying to calm her down, make her be quiet, while telling the stockbroker, "I can't tolerate any more excuses. If I don't receive the check immediately, I am going to have to speak to your manager when I'm in New York next week." And sure enough, the following week there we were in front of this astonished stockbroker, and I was sitting there red-faced and quiet, and my mother, the real Mrs. Tan, was shouting at his boss in her impeccable broken English.

We used a similar routine just five days ago, for a situation that was far less humorous. My mother had gone to the hospital for an appointment, to find out about a benign brain tumor a CAT scan had revealed a month ago. She said she had spoken very good English, her best English, no mistakes. Still, she said, the hospital did not apologize when they said they had lost the CAT scan and she had come for nothing. She said they did not seem to have any sympathy when she told them she was anxious to know the exact diagnosis since her husband and son had both died of brain tumors. She said they would not give her any more information until the next time and she would have to make another appointment for that. So she said she would not leave until the doctor called her daughter. She wouldn't budge. And when the doctor finally called her daughter, me, who spoke in perfect English—lo and behold—we had assurances the CAT scan would be found, promises that a conference call on Monday would be held, and apologies for any suffering my mother had gone through for a most regrettable mistake.

I think my mother's English almost had an effect on limiting my possibilities in life as well. Sociologists and linguists probably will tell you that a person's developing language skills are more influenced by peers. But I do think that the language spoken in the family, especially in immigrant families which are more insular, plays a large role in shaping the language of the child. And I believe that it affected my results on achievement tests, IQ tests, and the SAT. While my English skills were never judged as poor, compared to math, English could not be considered my strong suit. In grade school, I did moderately well, getting perhaps Bs, sometimes B+s in English, and scoring perhaps in the sixtieth or seventieth percentile on achievement tests. But those scores were not good enough to override the opinion that my true abilities lay in math and science, because in those areas I achieved As and scored in the ninetieth percentile or higher.

This was understandable. Math is precise; there is only one correct answer. Whereas, for me at least, the answers on English tests were always a judgment call, a matter of opinion and personal experience. Those tests were constructed around items like fill-in-the-blank sentence completion, such as "Even though Tom was _____, Mary thought he was _____." And the correct answer always seemed to be the most bland combinations of thoughts, for example, "Even though Tom was shy, Mary thought he was charming," with the grammatical structure "even though" limiting the correct answer to some sort of semantic opposites, so you wouldn't get answers like, "Even though Tom was foolish, Mary thought he was ridiculous." Well, according to my mother, there were very few limitations as to what Tom could have been, and what Mary might have thought of him. So I never did well on tests like that.

The same was true with word analogies, pairs of words, in which you were supposed to find some sort of logical, semantic relationship—for example, "sunset" is to "nightfall" as _____ is to _____. And here, you would be presented with a list of four possible pairs, one of which showed the same kind of relationship: "red" is to "stoplight," "bus" is to "arrival," "chills" is to "fever," "yawn" is to "boring." Well, I could never think that way. I knew what the tests were asking, but I could not block out of my mind the images already created by the first pair, "sunset is to nightfall"—and I would see a burst of colors against a darkening sky, the moon rising, the lowering of a curtain of stars. And all the other pairs of words—red, bus, stoplight, boring— just threw up a mass of confusing images, making it impossible for me to sort out something as logical as saying: "A sunset precedes nightfall" is the same as "A chill precedes a fever." The only way I would have gotten that answer right would have been to imagine an associative situation, for example, my being disobedient and staying out past sunset, catching a chill at night, which turns into feverish pneumonia as punishment, which indeed did happen to me.

I have been thinking about all this lately, about my mother's English, about achievement tests. Because lately I've been asked, as a writer, why there are not more Asian-Americans represented in American literature. Why are there few Asian-Americans enrolled in creative writing programs? Why do so many Chinese students go into engineering? Well, these are broad sociological questions I can't begin to answer. But I have noticed in surveys— in fact, just last week—that Asian students, as a whole, always do significantly better on math achievement tests than in English. And this makes me think that there are other Asian-American students whose English spoken in the home might also be described as "broken" or "limited." And perhaps they also have teachers who are steering them away from writing and into math and science, which is what happened to me.

Fortunately, I happen to be rebellious in nature, and enjoy the challenge of disproving assumptions made about me. I became an English major my first year in college after being enrolled as premed. I started writing nonfiction as a freelancer the week after I was told by my former boss that writing was my worst skill and I should hone my talents toward account management.

But it wasn't until 1985 that I finally began to write fiction. And at first I wrote using what I thought to be wittily crafted sentences, sentences that would finally prove I had mastery over the English language. Here's an example from the first draft of a story that later made its way into *The Joy Luck Club,* but without this line: "That was my mental quandary in its nascent state." A terrible line, which I can barely pronounce.

Fortunately, for reasons I won't get into today, I later decided I should envision a reader for the stories I would write. And the reader I decided upon was my mother, because these were stories about mothers. So with this reader in mind—and in fact, she did read my early drafts—I began to write stories using all the Englishes I grew up with: the English I spoke to my mother, which for lack of a better term, might be described as "simple"; the English she used with me, which for lack of a better term might be described as "broken"; my translation of her Chinese, which could certainly be described as "watered down"; and what I imagined to be her translation of her Chinese if she could speak in perfect English, her internal language, and for that I sought to preserve the essence, but not either an English or a Chinese structure. I wanted to capture what language ability tests can never reveal: her intent, her passion, her imagery, the rhythms of her speech and the nature of her thoughts.

Apart from what any critic had to say about my writing, I knew I had succeeded where it counted when my mother finished reading my book, and gave me her verdict: "So easy to read."

EDITOR'S AFTERNOTE

"I was getting my hair done when I saw a young woman with her Russian-Jewish mother sitting in the chair, telling the hairdresser how to fix her mother's hair," Amy Tan was quoted during an interview for the theatrical release of *The Joy Luck Club.* Wayne

Wang had just directed the movie version of her best-selling novel. Said Tan, "I could see this woman's face keep falling and I saw a tear in her eye. I thought: what a horrible scene, how sad.

"Then I thought: This is like every mother and daughter; the mother wants her daughter to be so proud of her, yet the daughter is ashamed. I knew I had to write about it because I was seeing myself."

Author of *The Kitchen God's Wife*, *The Moon Lady*, and *The Chinese Siamese Cat*, this National Book Award finalist is working on her latest novel, *The Year of No Flood*. She lives in San Francisco.

Quality Time
Barbara Kingsolver

Miriam's one and only daughter, Rennie, wants to go to Ice Cream Heaven. This is not some vision of the afterlife but a retail establishment here on earth, right in Barrimore Plaza, where they have to drive past it every day on the way to Rennie's day-care center. In Miriam's opinion, this opportunistic placement is an example of the free-enterprise system at its worst.

"Rennie, honey, we can't today. There just isn't time," Miriam says. She is long past trying to come up with fresh angles on this argument. This is the bland, simple truth, the issue is time, not cavities or nutrition. Rennie doesn't want ice cream. She wants an angel sticker for the Pearly Gates Game, for which one only has to walk through the door, no purchase necessary. When you've collected enough stickers, you get a free banana split. Miriam has told Rennie over and over again that she will buy her a banana split, some Saturday when they have time to make an outing of it, but Rennie acts as if this has nothing to do with the matter at hand, as though she has asked for a Cabbage Patch doll and Miriam is offering to buy her shoes.

"I could just run in and run out," Rennie says after a while. "You could wait for me in the car." But she knows she has lost; the proposition is half-hearted.

"We don't even have time for that, Rennie. We're on a schedule today."

Rennie is quiet. The windshield wipers beat a deliberate, ingratiating rhythm, sounding as if they feel put-upon to be doing this job. All of southern California seems dysfunctional in the rain: cars stall, drivers go vaguely brain-dead. Miriam watches Rennie look out at the drab scenery, and wonders if for her sake they ought to live someplace with ordinary seasons—piles of raked leaves in autumn, winters with frozen streams and carrot-nosed snowmen. Someday Rennie will read about those things in books, and think they're exotic.

They pass by a brand-new auto mall, still under construction, though some of the lots are already open and ready to get down to brass tacks with anyone who'll brave all that yellow machinery and mud. The front of the mall sports a long row of tall palm trees, newly transplanted, looking frankly mortified by their surroundings. The trees depress Miriam. They were probably yanked out of some beautiful South Sea island and set down here in front of all these Plymouths and Subarus. Life is full of bum deals.

Miriam can see that Rennie is not pouting, just thoughtful. She is an extremely obliging child, considering that she's just barely five. She understands what it means when Miriam says they are "on a schedule." Today they really don't have two minutes to spare. Their dance card, so to speak, is filled. When people remark to Miriam about how well-organized she is, she laughs and declares that organization is the religion of the single parent.

It sounds like a joke, but it isn't. Miriam is faithful about the business of getting each thing done in its turn, and could no more abandon her orderly plan than a priest could swig down the transubstantiated wine and toss out wafers like Frisbees over the heads of those waiting to be blessed. Miriam's motto is that life is way too complicated to leave to chance.

But in her heart she knows what a thin veil of comfort it is that she's wrapped around herself and her child to cloak them from chaos. It all hangs on the presumption that everything has been accounted for. Most days, Miriam is a believer. The road ahead will present no serious potholes, no detour signs looming sudden and orange in the headlights, no burning barricades thrown together as reminders that the world's anguish doesn't remain mute—like the tree falling in the forest—just because no one is standing around waiting to hear it.

Miriam is preoccupied along this line of thought as she kisses Rennie good-bye and turns the steering wheel, arm over elbow, guiding her middle-aged Chevy out of the TenderCare parking lot and back onto the slick street. Her faith has been shaken by coincidence.

On Saturday, her sister Janice called to ask if she would be the guardian of Janice and Paul's three children, if the two of them should die. "We're redoing the wills," Janice reported cheerfully over the din, while in the background Miriam could hear plainly the words "Give me that Rainbow Brite right now, dumb face."

"Just give it some thought," Janice had said calmly, but Miriam hadn't needed to think. "Will you help out with my memoirs if I'm someday the President?" her sister might as well have asked, or "What are your plans in the event of a nuclear war?" The question seemed to Miriam more mythical than practical. Janice was a careful person, not given to adventure, and in any case tended to stick to those kids like some kind of maternal adhesive. Any act of God that could pick off Janice without taking the lot would be a work of outstanding marksmanship.

Late on Sunday night, while Miriam was hemming a dress of Rennie's that had fallen into favor, she'd had a phone call from her ex-husband Lute. His first cousin and her boyfriend had just been killed on a San Diego freeway by a Purolator van. Over the phone, Lute seemed obsessed with getting the logistics of the accident right, as though the way the cars all obeyed the laws of physics could make this thing reasonable. The car that had the blowout was a Chrysler; the cousin and boyfriend were in her Saab; the van slammed into them from behind. "They never had a chance," Lute said, and the words chilled Miriam. Long after she went to bed she kept hearing him say "never had a chance," and imagining the pair as children. As if even in infancy their lives were already earmarked: these two will perish together in their thirties, in a Saab, wearing evening clothes, on their way to hear a friend play in the symphony orchestra. All that careful mothering and liberal-arts education gone to waste.

Lute's cousin had been a freelance cellist, often going on the road with the likes of Barry Manilow and Tony Bennett and, once, Madonna. It was probably all much tamer than it sounded. Miriam is surprised to find she has opinions about this woman, and a clear memory of her face. She only met her once, at her own wedding, when all of Lute's family had come crowding around like fog. But now this particular cousin has gained special prominence, her vague features crystallized in death, like a face on a postage stamp. Important. Someone you just can't picture doing the humdrum, silly things that life is made of—clipping her toenails or lying on the bed with her boyfriend watching *Dallas*—if you hold it clearly in your mind that she is gone.

Lute is probably crushed; he idolized her. His goal in life is to be his own boss. Freelance husbanding is just one of the things that hasn't worked out for Lute. Freelance fathering he can manage.

Miriam is thinking of Rennie while she waits through a yellow light she normally might have run. Rennie last week insisting on wearing only dresses to nursery school, and her pale, straight hair just so, with a ribbon; they'd seen *Snow White*. Rennie as a toddler standing in her crib, holding the rails, her mouth open wide with the simplest expectation you could imagine: a cookie, a game, or nothing at all, just that they would both go on being there together. Lute was already out of the picture by that time; he wouldn't have been part of Rennie's hopes. It is only lately, since she's learned to count, that Lute's absence matters to Rennie. On the Disney Channel parents come in even numbers.

The light changes and there is a honking of horns; someone has done something wrong, or too slowly, or in the wrong lane. Miriam missed it altogether, whatever it was. She remembers suddenly a conversation she had with her sister years ago when she was unexpectedly pregnant with Rennie, and Janice was already a wise old mother of two. Miriam was frantic—she'd wanted a baby but didn't feel ready yet. "I haven't really worked out what it is I want to pass on to a child," she'd said to Janice, who laughed. According to Janice, parenting was three percent conscious effort and ninety-seven percent automatic pilot. "It doesn't matter what you think you're going to tell them. What matters is they're right there watching you every minute, while you let the lady with just two items go ahead of you in line, or when you lay on the horn and swear at the guy that cuts you off in traffic. There's no sense kidding yourself, what you see is what you get."

Miriam had argued that people could consciously change themselves if they tried, though in truth she'd been thinking more of Lute than herself. She remembers saying a great many things about choices and value systems and so forth, a lot of first-pregnancy high-mindedness it seems to her now. Now she understands. Parenting is something that happens mostly while you're thinking of something else.

Miriam's job claims her time for very irregular hours at the downtown branch of the public library. She is grateful that the people at Rennie's day care don't seem to have opinions about what kind of mother would work mornings one day, evenings the next. When she was first promoted to this position, Miriam had a spate of irrational fears: she imagined Miss Joyce at TenderCare giving her a lecture on homemade soup and the importance of routine in the formative years. But Miss Joyce, it seems, understands modern arrangements. "The important thing is quality time," she said once to Miriam, in a way that suggested bedtime stories read with a yogic purity of concentration, a mind temporarily wiped clean of things like brake shoes and MasterCharge bills.

Miriam does try especially hard to schedule time for the two of them around Rennie's bedtime, but it often seems pointless. Rennie is likely to be absorbed in her own games, organizing animated campaigns on her bed with her stuffed animals, and finally dropping off in the middle of them, limbs askew, as though felled by a sniper.

Today is one of Miriam's afternoon-shift days. After leaving Rennie she has forty minutes in which she must do several errands before going to work. One of them is eat lunch. This is an item Miriam would actually put on a list: water African violets; dry cleaner's; eat lunch. She turns in at the Burger Boy and looks at her watch, surprised to see that she has just enough time to go in and sit down. Sometimes she takes the drive-through option and wolfs down a fish sandwich in the parking lot, taking large bites, rattling the ice in her Coke, unmindful of appearances. It's efficient, although it puts Miriam in mind of eating disorders.

Once she is settled inside with her lunch, her ears stray for company to other tables, picking up scraps of other people's private talk. "More than four hundred years old," she hears, and "It was a little bit tight over the instep," and "They had to call the police to get him out of there." She thinks of her friend Bob, who is a relentless eavesdropper, though because he's a playwright he calls it having an ear for dialogue.

Gradually she realizes that at the table behind her a woman is explaining to her daughter that she and Daddy are getting a divorce. It comes to Miriam like a slow shock, building up in her nerve endings until her skin hurts. This conversation will only happen once in that little girl's life, and I have to overhear it, Miriam is thinking. It has to be *here.* The surroundings seem banal, so cheery and hygienic, so many wiped-clean plastic surfaces. But then Miriam doesn't know what setting would be better. Certainly not some unclean place, and not an expensive restaurant either—that would be worse. To be expecting a treat, only to be socked with this news.

Miriam wants badly to turn around and look at the little girl. In her mind's eye she sees Rennie in her place: small and pale, sunk back into the puffy pink of her goosedown jacket like a loaf of risen dough that's been punched down.

The little girl keeps saying, "Okay," no matter what her mother tells her.

"Daddy will live in an apartment, and you can visit him. There's a swimming pool."

"Okay."

"Everything else will stay the same. We'll still keep Peppy with us. And you'll still go to your same school."

"Okay."

"Daddy does still love you, you know."

"Okay."

Miriam is thinking that ordinarily this word would work; it has finality. When you say it, it closes the subject.

It's already dark by the time Miriam picks up Rennie at TenderCare after work. The headlights blaze accusingly against the glass doors as if it were very late, midnight even. But it's only six-thirty, and Miriam tries to cheer herself by thinking that if this were summer it would still be light. It's a trick of the seasons, not entirely her fault, that Rennie has been abandoned for the daylight hours.

She always feels more surely on course when her daughter comes back to her. Rennie bounces into the car with a sheaf of papers clutched in one fist. The paper they use at TenderCare is fibrous and slightly brown, and seems wholesome to Miriam. Like turbinado sugar, rather than refined.

"Hi, sweetie. I missed you today." Miriam leans over to kiss Rennie and buckle her in before pulling out of the parking lot. All day she has been shaky about driving, and now she dreads the trip home. All that steel and momentum. It doesn't seem possible that soft human flesh could travel through it and come out intact. Throughout the day Miriam's mind has filled spontaneously with images of vulnerable things—baby mice, sunburned eyelids, sea creatures without their shells.

"What did you draw?" she asks Rennie, trying to anchor herself.

"This one is you and me and Lute," Rennie explains. Miriam is frowning into the river of moving headlights, waiting for a break in the traffic, and feels overcome by sadness. There are so many things to pay attention to at once, and all of them so important.

"You and me and Lute," Miriam repeats.

"Uh-huh. And a dog, Pickles, and Leslie Copley and his mom. We're all going out for a walk."

A sports car slows down, letting Miriam into the street. She waves her thanks. "Would you like to go for a walk with Leslie Copley and his mom sometime?"

"No. It's just a picture."

"What would you like for supper?"

"Pot pies!" Rennie shouts. Frozen dinners are her favorite thing. Miriam rather likes them too, although this isn't something she'd admit to many people. Certainly not her mother, for instance, or to Bob, who associates processed foods with intellectual decline. She wonders, though, if her privacy is an illusion. Rennie may well be revealing all the details of their home life to her nursery-school class, opening new chapters daily. What I had for dinner last night. What Mom does when we run out of socks. They probably play games along these lines at TenderCare, with entirely innocent intentions. And others, too, games with a social-worker bent: What things make you happy, or sad? What things make you feel scared?

Miriam smiles. Rennie is fearless. She does not know how it feels to be hurt, physically or otherwise, by someone she loves. The people at TenderCare probably hear a lot worse than pot pies.

"Mom," Rennie asks, "does God put things on the TV?"

"What do you mean?"

Rennie considers. "The cartoons, and the movies and things. Does God put them there?"

"No. People do that. You know how Grandpa takes movies of you with his movie camera, and then we show them on the screen? Well, it's like that. People at the TV station make the programs, and then they send them out onto your TV screen."

"I thought so," Rennie says. "Do you make them sometimes, at the library?"

Miriam hears a siren, but can't tell where it's coming from. "Well, I organize programs for the library, you're right, but not TV programs. Things like storybook programs. You remember, you've come to some of those." Miriam hopes she doesn't sound irritated. She is trying to slow down and move into the right lane, because of the ambulance, but people keep passing her on both sides, paying no attention. It makes Miriam angry. Sure enough, the ambulance is coming their way. It has to jerk to a full stop in the intersection ahead of them because of all the people who refuse to yield to greater urgency.

"Mom, what happens when you die?"

Miriam is startled because she was thinking of Lute's poor cousin. Thinking of the condition of the body, to be exact. But Rennie doesn't even know about this relative, won't hear her sad story for years to come.

"I'm not sure, Rennie. I think maybe what happens is that you think back over your life, about all the nice things you've done and the people who've been your friends, and then you close your eyes and . . . it's quiet." She was going to say, ". . . and go to sleep," but she's read that sleep and death shouldn't be equated, that it can cause children to fear bedtime. "What do you think?"

"I think you put on your nicest dress, and then you get in this glass box and everybody cries and then the prince comes and kisses you. On the lips."

"That's what happened to Snow White, isn't it?"

"Uh-huh. I didn't like when he kissed her on the lips. Why didn't he kiss her on the cheek?"

"Well, grown-ups kiss on the lips. When they like each other."

"But Snow White wasn't a grown-up. She was a little girl."

This is a new one on Miriam. This whole conversation is like a toboggan ride, threatening at every moment to fly out of control in any direction. She's enjoying it, though, and regrets that they will have to stop soon for some errands. They are low on produce, canned goods, aluminum foil, and paper towels, completely out of vacuum-cleaner bags and milk.

"What I think," says Miriam, after giving it some consideration, "is that Snow White was a little girl at first, but then she grew up. Taking care of the seven dwarfs helped her learn responsibility." Responsibility is something she and Rennie have talks about from time to time. She hears another siren, but this one is definitely behind them, probably going to the same scene as the first. She imagines her sister Janice's three children bundling into her life in a whirlwind of wants and possessions. Miriam doesn't even have time for another house plant. But she realizes that having time is somehow beside the point.

"So when the prince kissed her, did she grow up?" Rennie asks.

"No, before that. She was already grown up when the prince came. And they liked each other, and they kissed, and afterward they went out for a date."

"Like you and Mr. Bob?"

"Like Bob and I do sometimes, right. You don't have to call him Mr. Bob, honey. He's your friend, you can call him just Bob, if you want to."

Instead of making the tricky left turn into the shopping center, Miriam's car has gone right, flowing with the tide of traffic. It happened almost before she knew it, but it wasn't an accident. She just isn't ready to get to the grocery store, where this conversation will be lost among the bright distractions of bubble gum and soda. Looping back around the block will give them another four or five minutes. They could sit and talk in the parking lot, out of the traffic, but Miriam is starting to get her driving nerves back. And besides, Rennie would think that peculiar. Her questions would run onto another track.

"And then what happened to the seven dwarfs?" Rennie wants to know.

"I think Snow White still took care of them, until they were all grown up and could do everything by themselves."

"And did the prince help too?"

"I think he did."

"But what if Snow White died. If she stayed dead, I mean, after the prince kissed her."

Miriam now understands that this is the angle on death that has concerned Rennie all along. She is relieved. For Miriam, practical questions are always the more easily answered.

"I'm sure the dwarfs would still be taken care of," she says. "The point is that Snow White really loved them, so she'd make sure somebody was going to look after them, no matter what, don't you think?"

"Uh-huh. Maybe the prince."

"Maybe." A motorcyclist dodges in front of them, too close, weaving from lane to lane just to get a few yards ahead. At the next red light they will all be stopped together, the fast drivers and the slow, shooting looks at one another as if someone had planned it all this way.

"Rennie, if something happened to me, you'd still have somebody to take care of you. You know that, don't you?"

"Uh-huh. Lute."

"Is that what you'd like? To go and live with Lute?"

"Would I have to?"

"No, you wouldn't have to. You could live with Aunt Janice if you wanted to."

Rennie brightens. "Aunt Janice and Uncle Paul and Michael-and-Donna-and-Perry?" The way she says it makes Miriam think of their Christmas card.

"Right. Is that what you'd want?"

Rennie stares at the windshield wipers. The light through the windshield is spotty, falling with an underwater strangeness on Rennie's serious face. "I'm not sure," she says. "I'll have to think it over."

Miriam feels betrayed. It depresses her that Rennie is even willing to take the question seriously. She wants her to deny the possibility, to give her a tearful hug and say she couldn't live with anyone but Mommy.

"It's not like I'm sending you away, Rennie. I'm not going to die while you're a little girl. We're just talking about what-if. You understand that, right?"

"Right," Rennie says. "It's a game. We play what-if at school." After another minute she says, "I think Aunt Janice."

They are repeating their route now, passing again by the Burger Boy where Miriam had lunch. The tables and chairs inside look neater than it's possible to keep things in real life, and miniature somehow, like doll furniture. It looks bright and safe, not the sort of place that could hold ghosts.

On an impulse Miriam decides to put off the errands until tomorrow. She feels reckless, knowing that tomorrow will already be busy enough without a backlog. But they can easily live another day without vacuum-cleaner bags, and she'll work out something about the milk.

"We could stop here and have a hamburger for dinner," Miriam says. "Or a fish sandwich. And afterward we could stop for a minute at Ice Cream Heaven. Would you like that?"

"No. Pot pies!"

"And no Ice Cream Heaven?"

"I don't need any more angel stickers. Leslie Copley gave me twelve."

"Well, that was nice of him."

"Yep. He hates bananas."

"Okay, we'll go straight home. But do you remember that pot pies take half an hour to cook in the oven? Will you be too hungry to wait, once we get home?"

"No, I'll be able to wait," Rennie says, sounding as if she really will. In the overtones of her voice and the way she pushes her blond hair over her shoulder there is a startling maturity, and Miriam is frozen for a moment with a vision of a much older Rennie. All the different Rennies—the teenager, the adult—are already contained in her hands and her voice, her confidence. From moments like these, parents can find the courage to believe in the resilience of their children's lives. They will barrel forward like engines, armored by their own momentum, more indestructible than love.

"Okay then, pot pies it is," Miriam says. "Okay."

EDITOR'S AFTERNOTE

"Quality Time," Barbara Kingsolver notes, was written, "to explore that awful and wonderful thing that happens to parents when life with our children suddenly opens wide in the narrowest passages."

Author of three award-winning novels, including the best-selling *Pigs in Heaven* and *The Bean Trees,* Kingsolver's current project is the forthcoming collection, *High Tide in Tucson: Essays from Now or Never*. She lives with her husband and daughter in southern Arizona.

Heartburn

(an excerpt from the novel)

Nora Ephron

My mother was an agent in Hollywood, a lady agent, a classic forties career woman: she had short hair and bangs, she wore suits with shoulder pads, and she talked in a gravelly voice. She handled what were known in the business as specialty acts, which is to say mostly midgets. After they stopped making movies like *The Wizard of Oz,* the midget market dried up and she moved into actors with scars. In the meantime, we had a lot of midgets hanging around the house, and as a result my mother often served food that was a little too bite-sized. My sister Eleanor gets very churlish about my mother's cooking, and she always points out that my mother's fling with rumaki lasted considerably longer than it should have; but Eleanor hates to give credit where credit is due, and the fact is that my mother had enormous flair when she was paying attention, and when she didn't feel like paying attention she threw in a lot of butter. She could also Keep Help, which I was raised to believe was no small thing; indeed, I was raised to believe that almost the worst thing that could be said about you after you grew up was that you couldn't.

Every New Year's Day, my parents had a big party, and their friends came over and bet on the Rose Bowl and argued about which of the players on either team were Jewish, and my mother served her famous lox and onions and eggs, which took her the entire first half to make. It took her so long, in fact, that I really don't have time to give you the recipe, because it takes up a lot of space to explain how slowly and painstakingly she did everything, sautéing the onions over a tiny flame so none of them would burn, throwing more and more butter into the pan, cooking the eggs so slowly that my father was always sure they wouldn't be ready until the game was completely over and everyone had gone home. We should have known my mother was crazy years before we did just because of the maniacal passion she brought to her lox and onions and eggs, but we didn't. Another thing my mother was famous for serving was a big ham along with her casserole of lima beans and pears. A couple of years ago, I was in Los Angeles promoting *Uncle Seymour's Beef Borscht* and a woman said to me at a party, "Wasn't your mother Bebe Samstat?" and when I said yes, she said, "I have her recipe for lima beans and pears." I like to think it would have amused my mother to know that there is someone in Hollywood who remembers her only for her lima beans and pears, but it probably wouldn't have. Anyway, here's how you make it: Take 6 cups defrosted lima beans, 6 pears peeled and cut into slices, ½ cup molasses, ½ cup chicken stock, ½ onion chopped, put into a heavy casserole, cover and bake 12 hours at 200°. That's the sort of food she loved to serve, something that looked like plain old baked beans and then turned out to have pears up its sleeve. She also made a bouillabaisse with Swiss chard in it. Later on, she got too serious about food—started making egg rolls from scratch, things like that— and one night she resigned from the kitchen permanently over a lobster Cantonese that didn't work out, and that was the beginning of the end.

Shortly after that, she went into her blue-chip stamp phase. She wasn't alone, of course. It was 1963, and there were a lot of American women who were saving blue-chip stamps and green stamps and plaid stamps and whatever stamps their supermarkets were giving out; still, ladies in suits with shoulder pads were supposed to have more sense. My mother, who had spent years avoiding supermarkets, made at least one trip a day to the local Thriftimart. (The scar-face market had gone pretty dry on her at this point, and she had very little else to do.) She would get into her 1947 Studebaker and set off for a day in the aisles. She developed passionate and brief attachments to new products. One month she fell in love with instant minced onions. Another month it was Pepperidge Farm raspberry turnovers. The next it was frozen chopped chives. She would return home with her bags of groceries, leave them in the kitchen for the housekeeper to empty, and go up to her bedroom, where the card table was equipped with one of those little sponge-and-jar contraptions you use when you have a lot of stamps to stick.

I was living in New York at the time, and I heard about most of this from my sister Eleanor, who was perfecting her sanctimoniousness under the aegis of my mother's progressive insanity, but I saw a little of it firsthand when my mother arrived in Manhattan one day with a ten-speed blender she had purchased for me with twenty-six books of blue-chip stamps. She had carried it onto the plane and held it on her lap all the way to New York. The next day my apartment was burglarized, and they took the blender, complete with warranty. They also took my typewriter, the television set, and my gold bracelet. My mother surveyed the wreckage and then, instead of just going out to buy a new blender for sixteen dollars, went off to the nearby A & P and spent six hundred dollars on groceries, just for the plaid stamps. Then she returned to my apartment and began pasting them into stamp books. That's what she was doing when the police finally arrived—sitting there at the table, laughing her gravelly laugh and licking every so often as the two policemen told us what they thought were a lot of rollicking stories about New Yorkers who'd been burglarized of all the presents under their Christmas trees. We all had a drink, and then we all had another, and four hours later my mother was singing "When that midnight choochoo leaves for Alabam'" and the policeman whose lap she was sitting on was taking little nips at her shoulder. Then she got up and did a tap dance to "Puttin' On the Ritz" and passed out in the middle of it. It was a fabulous pass-out as those things go. She was in midair when it happened—she had both her legs up to one side, and she'd just managed to click her heels together when her eyes clanged shut and she slid on one side of her leg to the floor. I put her to bed.

"Was I very bad?" she said on the way to the airport the next day.

"Not really," I said.

"Please say I was," she said.

My father was a specialty act himself, though not in any formal sense. He was a character actor—he worked under the name of Harry Stratton, the name he still uses—but he played the kind of characters who have no character: he played kindly lawyers and kindly doctors and kindly teachers, and he said kindly things to whatever leading actor was about to lose heart in his fight to discover penicillin or defeat the outlaws or rout the Nazis. He made a lot of money—so did my mother—and they invested it in Tampax stock, and one day they were rich, and a good thing they were, because my mother's medical bills were enormous. She drank and drank and drank and finally one day her stomach swelled up like a Cranshaw melon and they took her to a very fashionable hospital for rich people with cirrhosis and the doctors clucked and said there was nothing that could be done. My parents had moved to New York by this time, and my mother's hospital room had a view of the East River. She lay there slowly dying, with my father impatiently standing by. "Pull the plug," he would say to the doctors, and the doctors would calmly explain that there was no plug, there was just the wasting away of life. A few of her former clients came to see her—the scar faces frightened the nurses and the midgets made whoopee on the electric wheelchairs—and now and then she came into focus and made deals. "I think we can get you a hundred thou on the next one," she would say; she hadn't handled a client in years, but she went rattling on about points and box office and below the line and above the line. The nurse would bring lunch. "I think I'll take it in the commissary," she'd say. One day my father called and said, "You'd better come. I think this is it." Of course, he telephoned every day and said that, but it always sounded like wishful thinking; now, finally, I knew he must be right. I went straight to the hospital, and when I went into her room she was sleeping. Suddenly she opened her eyes and looked at me. "I just screwed Darryl Zanuck on the remake," she said, and gave a little croak, which I didn't know at the moment was a significant thing, the actual croak—I thought it was just her gravelly laugh—and died.

"Mother's gone," said the nurse. Not "Your mother" but "Mother." I stared at the nurse, stunned not so much by my mother's death, which after all had been promised for months and, as far as my father was concerned, was long overdue, but by the nurse's presumption. "You can call your mother Mother," I snapped, "but you can't call my mother Mother." The nurse gave me one of those withering looks that are meant to make you feel as if your thoroughly understandable rage is mere female hysteria. She pulled the sheet over my mother's face. "We're going to take Mother away now," she said in a tone so condescending that I became even more wild with anger. "She's not your mother," I shouted. "On top of which, she's not gone, she's dead. Do you hear me? *Dead*. And what you're going to take away is her body, so call it a body. Call it a corpse, for Christ's sake." The nurse was now looking at me with an expression of complete horror, which I thought at the time was on account of my behavior, but it wasn't really; it was complete horror at what was happening behind me, which was that my mother had chosen that moment to make a full recovery. The sheet began rising like a slow-motion poltergeist, and then, in a burst, my mother whipped off the cloth and shouted: "Ta da!" Then she fainted. "Fainted dead away" is what the nurse said, which just goes to show you another anomaly of hospital life, which is that they only use the word "dead" when it doesn't apply.

"We thought you were dead," I said a few minutes later, when my mother came to.

"I was," she said, "I was." She shook her head slightly, as if trying to remember a fuzzy dream. "I floated away in a white organdy dress and black patent-leather Mary Janes," she said. "I looked like Baby Snooks. I tried to get something to wear that was more dignified, but the dignified clothes were being used on another set." She nodded; it was all coming back now. "I looked down, and there was your father, clicking a clapboard that read: 'Bebe's Death, Take One.' The camera started rolling. I was floating further and further away. I was definitely dead. Your father sold the Tampax stock and bought himself a Borsalino hat. 'Print,' he said. 'It's a wrap.'" She began tapping her breastbone defiantly. "*I* was the one who sat next to Bernard Baruch at a dinner party in 1944 and heard him say, 'Buy something people use once and throw away.' *I* was the one who stuck a Tampax into my twat in 1948 and came out of the bathroom and said, 'See if this is traded over the counter.' *I* was the one who made us rich, and now the bastard is going off and spending my money on bimbos while I'm stuck in goyishe heaven in an inappropriate costume. Fuck this, I said to myself, and at that moment I came back."

The next day, when I went to see her, she was sitting up in bed smoking Kools and doing the Double-Crostic. "I have experienced a miracle," she said. "You know what that means, don't you?"

"No," I said.

"It means there's a God," she said. "If you believe in miracles, you have to believe in God. One follows from the other."

"No it doesn't," I said. "It doesn't follow at all. It doesn't have to be the sort of miracle someone's in charge of. It could just have been an accident of some sort. Or a dream. Or a misdiagnosis on the part of the nurse."

My mother shook her head. "I was dead," she said. "You should have seen it up there. Fluffy white clouds, and little angels with pink cheeks playing tiny harps."

"Lyres," I said.

"Miss Smart and her college education," said my mother.

A week later, she checked out of the hospital, filed for divorce, and went to New Mexico to find God. And she did. She found God and she married him. His name was Mel, he honestly believed he was God, and as my first husband Charlie said at the time, "If there's one thing we know about God, it's that he's not named Mel." Mel took my mother for every penny she had, plus Charlie's old Swedish-modern couch and a set of flatware I was very attached to. Then she died again, this time for good.

I would like to ask her what a person who is seven months pregnant is supposed to do when her husband turns out to be in love with someone else, but the truth is she probably wouldn't have been much help. Even in the old days, my mother was a washout at hard-core mothering; what she was good at were clever remarks that made you feel immensely sophisticated and adult and, if you thought about it at all, foolish for having wanted anything so mundane as some actual nurturing. Had I been able to talk to her at this moment of crisis, she would probably have said something fabulously brittle like "Take notes." Then she would have gone into the kitchen and toasted almonds. You melt some butter in a frying pan, add whole blanched almonds, and sauté until they're golden brown with a few little burned parts. Drain lightly and salt and eat with a nice stiff drink. "Men are little boys," she would have said as she lifted her glass. "Don't stir or you'll bruise the ice cubes."

EDITOR'S AFTERNOTE

Writer-director Nora Ephron grew up the daughter of a working mother. Her parents, Henry and Phoebe Ephron, were the writing team behind such legendary films as *Desk Set, Daddy Long Legs,* and the Academy Award–nominated screenplay adaptation of *Captain Newman, M.D.* Ephron expressed the ambivalence that comes from such a childhood during a talk with the *Daily News* of Los Angeles in 1992.

"On the one hand, everyone wants their mom to be a regular mom, whatever that thing is. They want their moms to make pancakes and be there for them. Even nowadays, when there are almost no 'regular moms' left in America, I think people still have a yearning for this fantasy, Hallmark-card mom."

On the other, Ephron was "fantastically proud" of her mother and her accomplishments.

Like mother like daughter—Ephron has received her own Oscar nominations for the scripts *Silkwood* and *When Harry Met Sally*. She also has two sons, Max and Jacob. Her directorial debut came with *This Is My Life,* a film for which she possessed a strong affinity, particularly the film's lead character, a stand-up comedienne struggling toward stardom who happens to have two daughters.

Said Ephron of the comic's children, "They want her dream to come true and they want it not to cost them—which is, of course, something that can't be."

Ephron is currently coscripting two more movie projects with her sister, Delia Ephron, *Hanging Up* and *Michael*.